ONE THREE ONE

ONE THREE ONE

*A Time-Shifting Gnostic
Hooligan Road Novel*

JULIAN COPE

FABER & FABER

First published in the UK in 2014
by Faber and Faber Ltd
Bloomsbury House
74–77 Great Russell Street
London WC1B 3DA

Typeset by Ian Bahrami
Printed in England by CPI Group (UK) Ltd, Croydon, CRO 4YY

A CIP record for this book
is available from the British Library

ISBN 978–0–571–27036–1

2 4 6 8 10 9 7 5 3 1

CONTENTS

1. THIS AIN'T THE SUMMER
OF LOVE

I looked up from the book I wasn't reading and glanced around at the other passengers, all the while raising my butt cheeks as imperceptibly as possible, so as to let off an unprovenanced SBD. My biliousness at 35,000 ft got the better of me, however, and – rather than the intended *farten* – instead a flabby brown thickshake slurried into my leather kecks. This was too much even for me. My heart beat so fast Al Jourgensen programmed it and my stomach's long-congealed smorgasbord of illegal, psychiatric and over-the-counter drugs forced me upright, lurching upright, hesitating and lurching upright, then escorted me with great haste to the lavatories at the back of the plane. One woman waited in front of me. Alright? I rested against her back and lolled my head into her neck. She let me go in first. I collapsed on to the moulded seat thing and shat long and hard . . . once again into my leather kecks. Then my phone rang – probably Mick – and I fell asleep. When I woke up, my phone was ringing again and people were pounding on the door and shouting. I soon realised they couldn't get in however hard they beat, so I slid down on to my haunches in that tiny gap between the toilet seat and the door, and fell asleep again, my blood circulation terminated at the knees, my head pulsing like a cranium-sized bell-end unable to orgasm. The next time I woke up was when Rave-orange tank-suited Sardinian airport engineers prised the door off the lavatory and I fell forward into a brief consciousness as I smacked against the wall opposite. My phone rang and I rose out of my body and stared down judgementally at my bleeding, sticky face below. A stewardess screamed but nobody caught me, or even dared approach my stinking proto-corpse. Instead, the engineers cordoned off the area and let me come to gradually in my own brown-trousers-round-the-ankles humiliation, as embarrassed African ladies hoovered the aisles and disposed of jet-set rubbish. My phone rang again: Mick for certain. Eventually, I staggered/shuffled/crawled/seeped/inched back into the eurobog's restricted square feet and did my best to clean myself up.

2. MY NAME IS ROCK SECTION, I'M THE STAR OF THIS NOVEL

11.30am, Saturday June 10th, 2006
Leaving Fertília Airport, Alghero, Sardinia

Cosmically entangled in the revelry of my own drunken spirits, I was utterly remote from humanity but still buoyant in my own solipsistic stupor. Welcome to Sardinia: my hell, my prison, my meditation these past sixteen years. What a place to die. But that's precisely why I was back. And not for any grand death, either. Nothing heroic here, though neither was it all for purely selfish reasons. Not quite back to the Great Infinite. Oh, but what greedy anticipation! However, I'd long believed that before I quit this 21st-century episode of my Mortal Coil forever, I would first be obliged to settle certain life accounts for all of the others for whom Sardinia had also become hell. I'm talking about those luckless fuckers who, like me, had got themselves kidnapped at Italia '90 right after the one-sided hooligang war at Sant'Elia Stadium had kicked off between the Rest Of The World and we hapless English. Oh, all right then, kicked off between the Unholy Alliance of Dutch and Italian Ultras versus we hapless English. Can I say it any louder? We *were* the victims. The hapless English. Since that dreadful summer of Italia '90, the kidnappings had been ruinous both to the kidnapped *and* to their families; mental issues, overdoses, even suicides. You'll most likely remember the story; it was a big thing at the time. Me, I'd probably been the least of the victims. Yeah, they beat me, humiliated me, drugged me – but they never buggered me.

3

Besides, drugs have always been central to my life anyway ('No Shit, Sherlock!' – *NME*), so central that after the kidnapping I'd just spent the rest of the '90s sinking deeper'n'deeper into the Smack Settee, waving bye-bye to the Present and befriending any compliant ex-psychiatric nurse willing to inject me with largactil, wheelchair me nice and cosy into ye local shopping mall, then leave me sitting peaceful for twelve hours.

Now I was back here one last time on this grief-giving island, and I was determined – drugged up to fuck, but determined – that before I slipped through the life net one final time, I should attempt to settle the score for those real victims of the kidnap. Dean's sudden suicide yesterday on the eve of his thirtieth birthday had forced me to cut through the red-tape bullshit, twist the melons of a few airline employees I knew, and fly like the wind to demand Sardu restitution for Dean's bereaved and aggrieved parents, his Sardu grandma and poor Uncle Mick left blubbering back in Blighty. Though you'd think, from all the phone calls he was currently bombarding me with, that Uncle Mick had himself been the sole victim. Mick Goodby: agnostic poet, fizzy drinks fanatic, novelty hitmaker, hermit, exercise magnate and murderer. Not that last one really, though I have seen it installed more than just a couple of times on his Wiki. But I knew plenty of people who blamed Mick for this entire situation. The kidnaps, I mean. Moreover, that very same Blame Culture tone had been struck by the dubious TV documentary team who – at the end of '91, right around the first anniversary of Brent's suicide – had hoodwinked Mick into being filmed during his most epic under-the-stairs psychological low-point. What callous cunts. Anyway, by now, my mobile phone screen was announcing '14 missed calls', every one from Mick, probably embroiling me in dinner plans with some of his Catalan cousins in Alghero, or just clucking randomly about my being here without him.

Throughout these deep musings about my people and their cruel fates, I'd been slumped in total silence across the sumptuous front bench seat of a vast 1960s Buick convertible driven by Anna, whom I'd several months before hired to drive me around Sardinia. Not quite true, actually; back then through the internet I'd hired her archaeologist sister. But when Dean's sudden death yesterday morning had galvanised me into action, her sister was away digging up Romans. So Anna it was who drove me now and also she who delivered me safe through airport security. How on earth did she sort that one out? I probably shouldn't ask in my current proto-human state. No shower, but a bidet and a change of kecks well straightened me up. Besides, this weather was incredible. It was 95° and I was so cosy right here in this passenger seat that – as the rich olive groves and defiantly Catalan architecture around Alghero's Fertília Airport had rapidly given way to a crumbling landscape of venerable Bronze Age towers – I'd actually had to check myself to keep from purring: very off-putting to the ladies. Nevertheless, as an impending Sacrificial Lamb whose Sardinian return was both dutiful *and* selfish, I'd long ago decided to be kind to myself during these, my final days. So I had, soon after landing, cleverly downed a few shots of those bizarre Fernet Brancas at the Fertília Airport café, followed by calamitous amounts of Sudafed, some very old Klonopin and Ativan prescription downers that I'd recently found clearing out my flat, plus . . . wait for it, that other little matter . . . all the fucking pot! What? Don't even fucking ask. I've never ever done anything like it before, never ever copped out with the cops. But, after *that* arrival, then tottering with God's Wedgie down the 737's steel staircase into a full-on Med heat wave, *then* navigating eighty metres of sticky Sardu tarmac and spying those armed federalés? Well, I just totally lost my nerve for the first time ever and munched up my full half oz of squidgy black there and then. Gifted to me, gifted. I'd never pay for such rubbish: a CID mate's going-away-present replete with gold Customs 'confiscated' seal and hazardous clear plastic wrap. But yeah, I shat out and downed the lot in the passport control queue. Nearly killed me, too, nearly killed my guts.

Spectacular results, though. Now less than two hours later I was so well rounded and recumbent lolling here on General Motors' finest '60s tuck-and-roll upholstery that neither the fumes of ye bucking & bronchial Buick, nor even Mr Sun's Golden Wonder effects could trouble my equilibrium unduly – although I did probably have no more than ninety mins before another tussle with Armitage Shanks. Oo, the heat, my aching butthole, my heart going like the clappers. But for now I lay low under Anna's radar, lost in thoughts of Dean's final moments, his epic loneliness, his dead twin teenage brother already so many years gone, all of our spectacular fuck-ups (Mick's spectacular fuck-ups). And I soon got very angry again at the crap manner in which the Italian authorities had dealt with our plight. Far too much still remained unknown here in 2006, such stuff as the authorities evinced no interest whatsoever in finding out. Who had really pushed my dear friend Leander AKA the posh rapper Full English Breakfast to his death that bleakest of afternoons before the England v. Ireland match? And how could the murder of this English viscount with a recent Top Ten hit single in full daylight on the World Stage have been passed off as an accident? What Figures Diabolical had decided that we all needed kidnapping for our sins? And who'd ordered the bummings? What the fuck! I'd only missed that special treat because I had the good fortune to be lactose intolerant – I'll explain later – but those cunts still kicked the living shit out of my naked body.

At the trial, the Italian authorities had pinned all the blame for everything upon the infamous Dutch DJ and Rave producer 'Judge' Barry Hertzog: the murder, the kidnapping, the lot. After all – the authorities had argued – on the day of the match, Hertzog had been captured all over live TV dicing with death on top of the RAI-TV tower, playing bagpipes in Rave-orange face paint whilst marshalling his insane Party Orange members far below with a loudhailer, and directing them on how to increase the damage by pushing the Meatburger caravans over into the wind. But blaming only the insane Hertzog was just the authorities' way of closing up the case. Every English and Irish fan at the match believed Gary Have-a-laugh's claim that he'd seen another figure on the tower right near where Breakfast had 'fallen'. And although we'd stolen a Carabinieri patrol car right from under their noses, really they'd just let that sucker go. Then, at the very height of a ninety-minute chase, the cops' cavalcade of helicopters and Alfa Romeos had slowed down and allowed us to 'escape' into the diabolical clutches of parochial sodomists. How could Judge Barry Hertzog have organised that little lot with just his loudhailer? Who was he, some kind of Dutch Charles Manson?

But the judge at the trial came from Naples and cared nothing for truth. Shut down the whole embarrassing affair was all the authorities wanted. With FIFA's collusion, the Italian government had – by diverting we insane English and Dutch fans to barbarian Sardinia – successfully avoided bringing down our wrathful Italia '90 activities upon their mainland population. So now, following a somewhat similar pattern, all blame for the Sardinian murder and kidnaps was resting squarely upon the shoulders of a single foreigner: Judge Barry Hertzog. For evidence of Hertzog's guilt, the authorities had nothing at all. So instead they pointed to the high levels of organisation that Party Orange had displayed in the run-up to Italia '90. For example, furious with FIFA's cruel decision to force Dutch fans to lodge on neighbouring Sicily except for match days, Party Orange had sneaked into Sardinia aboard the Skanska ferry through the northern port of Ólbia, light years away from Italia '90. Purloining the orange windsock from Ólbia Helipad and running amok through the ferryport, Party Orange then headed inland to the hilltop town of Témpio Pausánia – the Sardu Hay-on-Wye – where shops were looted and books set on fire. It all read sensationally in the press, but how then could Barry Hertzog alone have pulled all these strings? Did any of it even happen at all? Bullshit. So with Hertzog as the authorities' chosen scapegoat, all we're stuck with is bullshit. Of course, the press had added in all of the weird goings-on and super-sleazy incidents that had taken place around Hertzog's N. Netherlands Rave club Slag Van Blowdriver. But it was just more bullshit. So when, back in 1995, Hertzog had been jailed for twenty years for the whole shebang – murder, rape and kidnap – I was convinced that some kind of Jim Jones thing had taken over everybody's minds.

Anyway, the outcome of this crock of cack is that my first move today is a long-overdue visit to Florinas Penitentiary, wherein resides the extremely bad Judge Barry Hertzog. It's all booked and kosher, and it's taking place at 2pm.

3. ALL ABOARD THE 131

Midday, Saturday June 10th, 2006
On the Road to Sássari City

But barely had the balmy breezes of that Catalan northwest coast begun their grand massaging of my throbbing psyche and knitted brows, when – ring-a-ding-a-ding – there on the road before us now flashed dangerous evidence of possible hold-ups and snags in our seamless itinerary: signs for Sássari. Sássari? My mind reeled, then rocketed up from its Ocean Floor consciousness at this unrighteous and unlovely information: may the heavens help us please, in some way, halt our inexorable and near-immediate slither into those sludgy commuter-fast hinterlands around white-baked Sássari City. Oh, why had Anna taken this route so easterly, so unnecessary? Vicious hunks of strewn concrete rubble, barely organised contraflow, after-the-fact road sign placements and scores of dithering, heaving antique estate cars all of Italian manufacture, many o'er-filled to bulgery with farm produce, and all apparently piloted in the third person by remote, daydreaming rustics out on their annual interface with civilisation. Judge Barry Hertzog may well have to wait. For Anna had her own business to clear up.

ANNA: In Sássari. For my dad.

Oh. In front, a motorcyclist was ferrying a hawk in a cage so large that the rider himself was forced to perch upon his rear passenger seat, the caged bird up front and apparently at the

9

controls. Caught behind this perilous duo, Anna slowly navigated our spluttering Detroit land-yacht inch-by-inch up the heaving concrete causeway and on to the elevated section of the 131, where we promptly came to a dead halt, central Sássari City spread out below on either side of us. Movement? Zilch. Zip. Nothing. Hmm, maintaining a schedule on Sardinia, indeed, keeping to *any* itinerary was, on this mysterious Mediterranean Ireland, always going to be sphincter-puckeringly problematic. Adding Sássari into the equation forever reduced your journey's average speed to about minus zero m.p.h. Still we sat, motionless, both lanes and in both directions. Directly in front of us, the beleaguered hawk ferryman suddenly lost concentration then control of his moped, which rocketed forwards into the tailgate of a builder's wagon, smashing the ferryman's head unconscious and sending the gilded cage somersaulting across the highway between two family saloons. People got out to check the hawk, lit ciggies, stared critically in both directions, some frowning, but most remaining expressionless. The moped rider was fine; the hawk was smashed up to fuck. Dead for sure. In Portugal, Spain, anywhere in the Mediterranean you see these mad cunts pulling this shit all the time, you suppose they must know something you don't. Yeah, they'll pull it off. Looks pretty shabby behaviour but you give them the benefit of the doubt. Back home, I'd have twatted the guy – you cynical cunt, taking a chance with such a beautiful creature. Take that, sir! But here, it merely made me wake up out of my stupor long enough to realise I needed a serious piss. Drat. It was about this time then that Anna – obviously well versed in the concept of chronic Sássari gridlock – concluded that the surefire way through our temporary auto enslavement was via a spot of Smalltalk. Me, I was just desperate for that piss.

ANNA: (*Earnestly from under her black fringe*) It is the only one on the entire island.

She stared deeply into my eyes as she smoothed her right hand across the Buick's dashboard. You do surprise me. But, not knowing her yet, I still managed to look appropriately impressed, the drool and cross-eyes probably undermining this somewhat though not catastrophically. Then Anna began to trot out auto facts to me, perhaps to keep me alert or for a short quiz later on. Measuring exactly eighteen-and-a-half feet from chromium prow to stern, this personal aircraft carrier was General Motors' second most prestigious product of 1966, just below the two-grand-more-expensive Cadillac Eldorado . . . zzzzzzzzzzz . . . I probably dropped off for no more than thirty seconds; I certainly switched back on when she mentioned that Jayne Mansfield had been decapitated in exactly the same model as ours. Grisly. At last and apparently without reason, the 131 had now slowly started to move. And Anna, weighing up the Sássari gridlock from our elevated highway, judiciously decided that her own business in the city could hang fire temporarily – which was fine by me in a bit of a state and with such an important meeting ahead. Nevertheless, those twenty brief minutes of enforced 131-contraflow stillness had been my first non-forward motion in days. Sweet relief. Moreover, spending it lolling and foaming in Anna's rather tasty convertible du jour was exactly the kind of high cultural level of pre-death experience that this Sacrificial Lamb believed he *should* be demanding. Now, what about that piss?

Two minutes later, I was clinging on for dear life, struggling in vain for non-existent seatbelts and peering helplessly into so-called reality as if through a kid's kaleidoscope. Accelerating from zero to 80 m.p.h. whether their vehicles were capable or not, everyone on the 131 southbound was now nose-to-tail surging collectively across vast valley-spanning EU road bridges and through precariously placed EU tunnels. And everybody was attempting to travel faster than everybody else, although here everybody's inexperienced at travelling fast and really unused to being in a bunch, so no fucker in the outer lane thinks to give you space when that 12 m.p.h. instant JCB digger – appearing out of some 'Works Only' exit – slips seamlessly into your slow lane . . . Oo, yer bastard. And nobody dares give it less than Jenson Button, because they're Sards and they're exercising their All-Too-Infrequently-Exercisable EU birthright. Oo ja! For most of their driving lives, your 21st-century Sardu drivers have no choice but to tootle along at about 40 m.p.h. on un-restored and potholed pre-war roads band-aided together decades ago by post-war concrete and industrial staples. This means that time spent on the 131 motorway is just about the only Sardu opportunity to experience what the rest of EU Italians daily take for granted; and which is why riding this section of the 131 is rather too much like sitting in a London bus that's been entered in Ben Hur's chariot race down a scree slope through the foot-hills of the Alps. However, at least this Strictly Sardu version of ye Common Market experience offers we Foreigners the rare opportunity to share said experience with – on this blessèd occasion, at least – a gawping toothless octogenarian in the outside lane straddling his melon-laden Piaggio three-wheeler jalopy (pre-war, what war?), all the while thumbs-upping me to death, winking at me, and staring right through me to cop a lusty visual of Anna. Oh, the 131. Imagine a very bustling UK trunk road arduously excavated through the most precipitous crags of South Wales, but madder, faster and tailgating like cunts while permanently squirting out the full beams over the shoulders of the Unfortunate in front of you, and you're there. Well actually, no you're not, I am. Unfortunately with neither hat nor suntan lotion, I'm also approaching a look that's fresh out the microwave, grilling up a UK bacon complexion; rasher-pink blistering to Full Body-Pucker in one bolt of radiation. Darling, any chance of that pitstop in the near future?

4. THE BACK LANES TO FLORINAS PENITENTIARY

1.45pm, Saturday June 10th, 2006
Side of a mountain, overlooking Ploaghe, N. Sardinia

Blissful blissful pissings. And with volcanic vistas, too. Staring down open-mouthed from this steep-sided eastern escarpment, squinting eyes a-blazing and cock in hand I pissed forever. Becalmed I was at last and safe behind a huge myrthus bush, which shielded me from Anna's extravagantly improvised arse-out-into-the-traffic parking spot on this rather too dodgy curve up the lane to hilltop Florinas. Mick's phone calls had finally subsided and, as I inhaled the primeval views of Sardinia for the first time in long, long years, I was forty-three years old and in compassionate mode. Be good to yourself, Rock Section. Just as the too-brief inertia of the Sássari contraflow had been quite long enough to Send Me, as the hippies used to say, so now did this brief Piss Stop yield me up to a sun-drenched half-world of volcanoes and prehistoric cooling towers, yield me up to the Gods of extinct Mt Sassu ahead of me across the Ploaghe valley, and to its numberless regiments of rockstack sentinels that crowded the horizon like eager henchmen. And so, too, did this Grandiloquent Inertia yield me up not only to Sardinia, but also to its screaming Ur-shadow, to its Sardu-within, to that very kernel of its culture, that core of this blistering island – itself no more than a bobbing and defiant husk that rages upon the surface of the Med. But such a husk as rages forever: S A R D E G N A. I was back in the sunbleached, tar-black heart of that Eternal, Impenetrable, Impermeable and Unconquerable volcanic massif in whose remotest parts doting sons had, right up until the 1950s, still accompanied their doddery dads up to the local suicide cliff; a land wherein licensed women known as *S'akkabbadòra-hèmina* had legally euthanised the old and the infirm until Mussolini had put a stop to it all, and where local Catholic priests were forced by convention to wage singing wars with flamboyant *bruxas* and *bruxos*, themselves druid-styled after the 'old religion'. Oh, this blissful, blissful Inertia. It was as though Time had – on this unforgotten mountainside – granted me a temporary pause from the chaos, safe from the death, safe from the treachery; pulled me into a dark entry unknown: sssshhh! I grabbed my throbbing brows with my left hand, and pressed my large flat fingertips into the temples. Gouging at the precise points of my cranium that I believed to be structural, I alternately dug then gouged, dug and gouged along the presumed cranial course in an attempt to free some psychic plaque from my stultifying noggin. Still staring out across the valley having a good old dig I was, when Anna – her head visible over the myrthus bush only if I strained my pissing figure counter-clockwise – piped up from the driver's seat.

ANNA: (*Speaking to my back*) You have all your documents ready for them?
ROCK: Yeah man, passport, driver's licence, one bill with current address.
ANNA: Remember, don't carry a knife.
ROCK: What, not into the prison?
ANNA: Of course you know. They're very strict here. It's tough.
ROCK: I'll well behave.

ANNA: You're really tall.

ROCK: (*Looking over my shoulder; she was beaming at me*) Yeah, about six-foot-two. What's that in centimetres?

ANNA: Oh, I understand that feet-and-inches. That's tall.

As I struggled back into the car, my heavy heart smiled as my eyes alit upon a large hardback nestling in Anna's folded cardigan on the sumptuous rear bench of the Buick, emblazoned with the words *Jim Morrison: Poems (1979–84)*. Perhaps it was just a coincidence I thunk to myself – could be Anna's dad's copy for all I knew – but this was by far my favourite period of Jim's poetry, and I knew this volume inside out. A good luck sign. For me, so much of Jim's recent stuff had become too scholarly, too rigid, just too obsessed with 'righting wrongs'. Bad idea for an American. Where d'you stop? But this early-80s stuff was Jim at his absolute finest. All the mystical poems were in there, the occult ones too. And each of the naval poems was accompanied by its original essay, so Jim's two epic American Civil War poems 'The Monitor' and 'The Sinking of CSS Alabama in French Waters' could really be appreciated for the rigorousness of that fucker's research. Yeah man, your ultimate exploratory Jim in a single volume – and here's my hired driver with a big old hardback edition on board. Sweet. I slid back into the passenger seat with a new vigour and stared at Anna, who was actually a bit of all right. Now no more than ten minutes away from our destination, we surged upwards into the outskirts of mountain fast Florinas. Can I have a quick Fernet Branca in the local bar? Like a very quick one? I was starting to cluck somewhat. But the drink impacted immediately on that oz of squidgy black, and I had to make a chase for the lavatory. Outside, Anna kept the car engine running, and as the weather now grew overcast we headed into the mountains.

Barely ten minutes later, the castellated walls of Florinas Penitentiary tormented the skyline to our right. Farther down the valley, skeletal monolithic fingers of jagged basalt rock took over beyond where the castellations terminated, in this rare instance Nature's extraordinary randomness perhaps even more brutal than those ordered man-made walls. Miserable as fuck. Almost too dreadful to contemplate what conditions could be like inside.

5. JUDGE BARRY HERTZOG

2pm, Saturday June 10th, 2006
Florinas Penitentiary, Florinas

At the drystone-walled prison entrance, Anna – in one graceful motion – swung Jayne Mansfield's Ruin expertly between the two huge brutal outcrops of gnarly rock that passed for gateposts, then navigated up the penitentiary's rugged 600-metre-long causeway at full tilt, our whitewall tyres screaming so outrageously on the once tarmac'd road that I semi-expected a waiting armed guard of reproving pistolleros when we crossed the drawbridge still at considerable speed. Where was the barrier? Where was the gate? Was this great elevated fortress not Florinas Penitentiary? Of course it was. This gargantuan façade was merely its gatehouse, its preliminary line of defence. Shadowed now behind twenty-feet-high walls, Anna and I were ushered into a Portakabin for passport and paperwork by a lame, tragic-looking warder named Klötz, who pointed up to a tiny rock-fast pillbox situated high in the crags above and – grinning obsequiously at both of us – declared: 'Hertzog!' Klötz was no more than five-feet-two-inches tall, extremely fat and sported a buckled leather jerkin w/metal nametag. His institutional haircut – a cartoon skinhead number 1 – was subverted by what looked like Soviet Issue sunglasses. Truly amazing shades. Gimme. But the poor guy wore a calliper on his lame leg, and a symbol of Authority he was not. Klötz invited Anna to pull up a chair in the Portakabin's cosiest corner, poured her a cup of something hot, then hobbled over to the door and yelled: 'Ourgon! Gorgo!' My escorts were on their way.

Now there's only one kind of behaviour an Englishman requires from prison warders, even a drugged-up fucker like this motherfucker. He wants, or rather I want them to *look* and *act* like prison warders. I want to know precisely where I stand. They're not my friends, my buddies. Indeed, as evidenced by the lameness of Klötz, who was currently holding on to my passport and travel papers, prison warders are in possession of great powers. So when around the corner sprang these two tiny, rotund warders, jerks of the lowest order both, each virtually identical to Klötz and each sporting those same buckled leather jerkins bearing the nametags? Well, I had a real icky, suspicious feeling about this place. Not good at all. And when this jocular duo started slapping each other around right there in front of me, it just didn't even feel real. Give it a break, fuckers. Worse still, although Ourgon and Gorgo had the look of chronic slug'n'snail gourmets both of them, these two Dumptys in two-minutes-flat danced me dizzy with their roughhousing and bumpy slapstick routines. They both had far too much snap in their tails for me to feel remotely comfortable in my present state. Especially when we began to climb that precariously steep rock-cut staircase up to Barry Hertzog's cabin-in-the-stars, when I utterly did not appreciate one of them jostling me and tickling me in the ribs. Boys. Boys. Up and up and up I struggled, my gozzy eyes focusing then de-focusing, focusing then de-focusing, genuinely shocked by the great spires of rock that jutted out alarmingly just beyond Hertzog's cell. And as the leather soles of my worn-out city boots finally grasped once more at the kind of sensible, horizontal walled-concrete platform they'd been designed for, both of those size-11 stinkers audibly sighed a fart of relief . . . hhhhwwwwwsh.

Here atop the basalt cliffs of Florinas Penitentiary, all the while grasping for support at that meagre wall, I stared both aghast and impressed at the bizarre rock-cut cavern that passed for Hertzog's incarceration. Only in Sardinia. How could it be? Surely this hermit's cell was not a place of punishment but of Enlightenment. What a magnificent space. Its flat, vertical walls, its great hearth and chimney, even the ingeniously faked wooden beams of its high ceiling. No stranger to Sardinia arriving here for the first time could even have noticed that this clean, fresh, white-emulsion reception room had actually been excavated straight out of the living rock itself. Affixed above the entrance was a large red-and-yellow shield in the colours of Dokkum's Be Quick F.C., next to it upon the near wall hung a great black-and-white poster from the Dutch WW2 movie *Soldier of Orange*. This impressive three-in-a-bed scene depicted a topless Susan Penhaligon being kissed by another whilst a particularly young Rutger Hauer looked on. Even more impressive was another carved low doorway that led into a lower antechamber beyond, wherein a large and well-lit map of Sardinia hung upon the wall at a curiously off-kilter angle. Well curious, about 20 degrees clockwise, I'd wager. The map had been festooned with hand-written nametags rendered in capital letters so large that even from my spec a full twenty feet away, they broadcasted loudly their culty disinformation: Mafeking, Durban, Pretoria, Cape Town. Mmm? But it was not until Warden Ourgon alerted Hertzog as to my arrival that the Judge emerged from his hiding place and acknowledged my presence in his clipped, formal tones.

HERTZOG: Hullo, Rock Section. Welcome to my Sardinia. It has been a very long time. Now, what can I do you for?

He still looked virtually the same, though what 'the same' really meant I dunno, as the World Media has fixed him forever in my mind's eye leaping out of Italia '90 as an X-faced Rave Grim Reaper atop an Eiffel Tower-sized World Cup TV gantry. That dreadful afternoon leading up to the England–Republic of Ireland match, I'd endured fire, gore, mob violence and water hoses right there below that bagpiping fucker. But it's still the media photos and CCTV videos that stick in my mind nowadays. My only other personal contact with the Judge had been after one of my DJ sets back in Spring 1990, when – as a guest at his fucked-up mobile Rave club Slag Van Blowdriver – I'd found myself on the receiving end of one of his particularly prickly 'Not all Netherlanders are from Holland' rants. But now, after all the arduous paperwork that had finally brought this present meeting to fruition, I was somewhat taken aback that the Hertzog I was encountering was still entirely combative.

HERTZOG: What do you want here? Why now? You been planning this for months. I thought you gave up long ago.
ROCK: Dean went yesterday, the other twin. I had the money so I came. We know you didn't kill Breakfast. We're not blaming you for Dean. But there must be many things you *know* that could really improve the mental health of at least a few of we hapless English. You know, the victims.

He glared at me so reprovingly that it left me feeling itchy and scratchy. I flicked my left ear, made a couple of those 'mwuh, mwuh' faces that you do when a bogey feels caught in nose hair, then reached down to pinch the wedgie of my clean kecks out of my butt cheeks. Then I had a couple more fumbles in the kecks area just to rearrange the pocket material, which was all ridden up and lumpy. But right as I pulled out my left hand, a tiny wrap of once-glossy paper dropped out and bumped its way on to the desk in front of me. Hertzog seized the wrap and handed it triumphantly to one of the dumpty wardens. It was speed. Preludes. Two of those waxy lozenges I'd scraped down into yellow amphetamine. I'd forgotten about that.

HERTZOG: Victims. The Hapless English. Poor poor victims. You come to my laager. You don't even grant me the temporary effort of de-lousing your filthy lifestyle. I'm incarcerated, you fucker. Have you never changed one thing about yourself in all these long years? Are you floating in some Dream Bubble above the world? You were never the hapless English at Italia '90. You were never innocent victims. You fools were targets. You were kidnapped for your nihilism, for your redundant World-View, for your disregard of everything the Western World ever believed, or ever fought for. And that song your sugary ally unleashed across the radio? 'Last Tango in Paris'! *That* was the celebration too far, a celebration of sugar and nothing. A catchy hymn to a fleeting feeling that never should have been celebrated. Half Man Half Biscuit. So close they were to being kidnapped, *so* many times. That they supported Tranmere would have been NO defence. Until, that is, Mick Goodby popped up his yellow head on behalf of Liverpool F.C. and begged with his corporate love song for me to blow it off his irresponsible shoulders.

I was now hearing from the mouth of Hertzog himself the absolute antithesis of everything I'd thus far managed to extract from his hit book *Prison Writings*. Indeed, everything that I'd allowed myself to pass for truth these past sixteen years was imploding and taking everything else down with it. Beyond gutted, I was hanged, drawn, quartered and distributed across four counties. The Hapless English motif had run unchecked throughout my entire two previous decades. I'd always believed that the kidnaps had fallen upon the four of us through sheer bad luck. Well, bad luck and Mick's cuntish decisions in the Kidnap Capital of Europe – that had been my conclusion. What a total and utter not-thinking-about-it Brain Dead Twat I'd been . . . For despite all of the bad trips and weird scenes I myself had experienced up at Slag Van Blowdriver way before Italia '90, and for all the creepy Groningen tales told by musicians I trusted, I'd still allowed my damned hatred of Authority to shield me from considering genuinely the possibility of Hertzog's World Fiendishness.

ROCK: Our escape in that Carabinieri Alfa wasn't your doing, though, was it? And making it through Cágliari all the way up the 131 wasn't with your permission, was it? How do I know you're not just claiming full kidnap credit after the fact?
HERTZOG: Once you were on the road, we had you if you made it past Oristano. From there, we had you.
ROCK: How?
HERTZOG: A different police force takes over after Oristano. Basic research. That's why the helicopters, motorbikes, cop cars all pulled up to a halt at the same time. Once they were called off? You were ours then.

Having dwelled so negatively all these years on the shaky response of the Italian Authorities to these crimes, rather than considering the wider issue, I suddenly understood that I'd allowed Dean to kill himself in utter ignorance of why any of it had happened. Two thirteen-year-old boys go to Italia '90 and events get so fucked up that neither sees thirty. The sum total of this new knowledge was now overwhelming me. During the fighting at Poett Beach and Sant'Elia Stadium, we'd had no organisation as such. But so soon after his big chart hits with Brits Abroad and Full English Breakfast, Mick – after years of social worker status behind him – had at thirty-two years old been so On One that he'd fully expected to take their beach at Italia '90. Why? Because he was a poet and their beach was called Poett. That fucker had Roky Erikson'd us all into believing – mesmerised and shamanised us with his Chart Positions. We'd lost Full English Breakfast in a fatal fall that might have been a fatal shove, and ruined lives proliferated around us. These past sixteen years I'd spent consoling myself about the random nature of our kidnap. But never once had we been accidental victims; all along we'd been fucking targets. Mick's song 'Last Tango in Paris', its international success, their wind-up performance on *Top of the Pops*, even the band calling themselves Brits Abroad: every last detail had conspired to get them and me kidnapped at Italia '90 by highly organised Believers in extremely dubious causes. Not victims, targets.

6. THE VISION AT FARAWAY FIELD

3.45pm, Saturday June 10th, 2006
A farm gate 2km outside Florinas

Running for dear life as fast as my rock'n'roll legs would carry me away from that dreadful place, I was somewhat undermined by Anna's unilateral offer to give friend Lame Warder a lift home. So while my pounding heart and my mind's eye had us lightspeeding back through Florinas village to the 131, in truth we herded the cowed and be-callipered little Klötz into the back of J.M.'s Ruin, re-launched that land-yacht down the penitentiary's slipway, then – Oh no! – turned right down the highly suspect mountain road. Have mercy! No more than a half-mile later, indeed at the very first corner after, we pulled up at a farm gate. Anna jumped out, gave the warder his big white bag full of shopping and, pursuing a three-point-turn, slowly reversed the Buick up the dusty farm track. But after a coupla fails, I got out reluctantly to ensure that the massive chrome bumpers didn't snag on the dazzling mound of obsidian aggregate dumped by the gate. Then I stopped Anna and pointed. There was Klötz huffing and puffing and 0.0003 miles-per-houring it homewards across the fields. Well actually still no more than about thirteen steps from our car. Rotund as you like, heart attack on the cards. Fuck's sake, I strode up to him and quite abruptly annexed his shopping.

ROCK: (*Rudimentary Sard*) Which way, big boy?
KLÖTZ: Campu Lontanu.

Faraway Field? For fake's suck! I took off at speed with Klötz's spluttered directions in my head and headed past five garrotted and shrivelled foxes hanging up at about head height. I needed to get out of here now without this new mission. Down the combe I stumbled, nearly losing Klötz's top layer – gum, eye drops, last-minute checkout what-have-yous – then up the other side I ranged at top speed, desperate to put some kilometres between me and Bazza Hertzog's Big Evil. And if delivering the shopping to some bucolic outpost, blah, blah, then whatever . . . But as I continued the climb, that steady climb up the other side of the valley, I peeped over the final rise only to collide head-on with a Vision nothing less . . . aaaaargh. I halted too soon for my legs to slow down, no direct link between my body and brain. Now I lost control of the shopping, my limbs, my tongue and jaw, and almost my MIND. What the Geriatric Fuck? Directly ahead at the field's centre was a massive stone doorway. Holy shit! It's one of those epic doorways I've been envisioning for umpteen long years. Holy Fucking Shit, a Doorway!

By now I was on the Sardu soil scrabbling and dribbling like a right fucking Rubber Roomer. For I did spy a World Doorway cast in rock, hewn by masons from out-of-time. Weeping, I crawled on my hands and knees fully 300 yards up the final incline towards the Doorway. Now, I cried out: Nuscadoré! Nuscadoré! Nuscadoré! No reply. I'm on my knees. How I applied myself now. I surged forwards those final yards and – on reaching the Doorway carved in stone – ramalamalama went my fists upon that archaic entrance. But all to no avail. Ramalama went my fists once more. Again, I cried out: Nuscadoré! Nuscadoré! Nuscadoré! Then I clawed and I felt and I reached into the stone around knee height but my hands felt the forms of a passageway. And then I understood. Oh, shit! Wrong fucking

Doorway. Unholy Shit, I was back! My mind's eye shown but my mind blown, I was back in Sardinia and already sunk back into that Visionary mindset. How much had I cast to the back of my mind? For how long these places had obsessed me!

Staggering downhill to the car, I crossed paths with the Lame Warder crying over his spilt milk and broken eggs, battered fish, strewn bacon, shattered local brews and far-flung butter. Only the tomatoes had bounced to safety. With his credit card, Klötz was spooning shattered globs of Sardinian butàriga mullet roe off the Sardu hillside and back into its brown package: disgusting even to me. More pitiful than ever, the Lame Warder needed my compassion. I shrugged. Now I knew him. In his hunchèd neediness he was revealed to me. Klötz? I don't think so. Now, in his prime porkish pinkness did I know him at last. Indeed, via that single glimpse of Klötz's Super Neediness, had I now recognised all of those penitentiary fuckers. At last the penny dawned on me. Oin and Gloin and Tinky Winky or whatever those three barreloid cunts called themselves were all Porcu. Was there any more pitiful and disgusting petty criminal family in all of Sardinia? I think not. I'd smelt a Porcu immediately I'd entered their Florinas sty, but I'd never truly clocked it until now. Couldn't really imagine them outside their Zinnigas sty, I suppose. Couldn't put poo and poo together. Fiends were at work in these valleys. *Those* Fiends. Still invaded by my Visionstate, and all the while observing the Porcu as it howled its shoppingless head off and tried in vain to cauterise the remaining draining fluids with bread, I searched. I searched and scanned the land around for more evidence of Fiends. What was going on here? Suddenly I located the evidence down in the river bottom, in the form of a mashed and concertina'd bright yellow caravan surmounted with a massive fiery red-painted sign that bore the inscription Meatburger. Holy Kack! The caravan was old, old, old and looked as though it had been pitched forwards into the stream from way up here on the hillside. I had located peculiar evidence. A Meatburger caravan so far north of Nuoro? My my, how some allegiances must have changed! And it's at that precise moment when I heard a Sound Uncanny drifting over the valley from Jayne Mansfield's Ruin, no more than 400 strides away. The radio was playing that fucking Brits Abroad song that had caused all our problems.

Heading back downhill to the car with that music ringing in my ears, I once again reached the fast flowing stream. Here at water's edge, that baggy Brits Abroad beat – loose to the point of being slack – eased my Visionstate and soothed my heathen temples. And so, now well out of Anna's sight, I kicked off my stinky boots and black kecks, peeled off my black shirt, and lay face down and naked in the running water. Sardinian radio was playing the extended re-mix, the whole fucking thing on 89.9 FM! I suddenly had fifteen full minutes to myself! Oh bliss. But even though my face was plunged deep into the stream's pebble bed, all I could register in my mind's eye was the throb-throb of that ancient spectral Doorway plonked in the field still just 200 metres behind me: the throb-throb manifesting in some strange otherly dimension, pulsing across my stream-bathed temples and branding itself into my 3rd Eye. Still my naked body dammed that stream until – with the arrival of the guitar solo – reality reared its Pavlovian head at last and I spluttered back into the air and began to bathe my limbs urgently. I'd completely forgotten that guitar solo! What a flared killer! It's got to be eight years at least since I last heard it! Consigned to the 12″ re-mix only, poor forgotten Rob Dean's beautiful and epic lead guitar break was now breaking in my heart. It was as though

I were breaking it in for the World and for the first time ever. Holy. How it dislodged so much of my psychic plaque with its sheer aspirational bonkers brilliance! On and on it soared. What a truly lovely thing. And as I shook my body dry and dabbed it with my shirt then slipped back into my black kecks and boots, I was utterly re-invigorated by this strange 1990 Chart Hit which had caused us all so very much Uber-grief.

When I got back to the car, Anna was sitting demurely on the driver's side of the Buick's colossal front fender, whilst the Brits' classic chorus, though still booming across the valley, was slowly being faded by the radio DJ.

CRUSSU: You're listening to the sound of San Gavino Monreale on 89.9 FM. I'm Jesu Crussu and that wonderful song is dedicated to poor Dean Garrett, the synthesizer player of Brits Abroad, who took his own life yesterday. He was one of the four English football fans kidnapped at Italia '90. Poor Dean, R.I.P. Okay, here's another English classic: 'Faith' by Manicured Noise.

Clocking my dazed, somewhat *Gone Out* expression but saying nothing, the diplomatic Anna promptly switched off the radio, climbed into the driver's seat and fired up the big V8. Then, with no more ado, we sailed out of there and headed south at last on the 131, still saying nothing. Doorways, Doorways, I'm back in the land of Doorways.

7. NOT VICTIMS, TARGETS

5pm, Saturday June 10th, 2006
On the 131 south from Ploaghe

My mind was fried. What a flying fuck-up. What a fucking stick-up. We'd all of us been totally stitched! And by the illest-looking gang I never could have imagined. If Judge Barry Hertzog, his Porcu cronies *and* the Italian Authorities were all working in cahoots together . . . well, what chance for we hapless English all these years later? Huh, the return of the hapless English motif. But now, just two hours after Hertzog's spiteful revelations, my thundering self-doubts and feelings of World Naïveté had utterly evaporated, fried up to a crisp on the Judge's own blazing altar of evidence: that overturned Meatburger caravan so close to the penitentiary and so very far north of Nuoro. My my, Klötz would be facing a severe chastisement from the jostle brothers if he were clueless enough to let on to them how he'd led me past such big evidence. But what did that evidence mean? My mind reeled at the wide range of possibilities. What the fuck did it all add up to?

Meatburger had always been a purely southern Sard food franchise run by those fucking lunatic Spackhouse Tottu DJ brothers José and Luis Mackenzie, those wealthy Cágliari plumbers – adopted sons of a Scots flight sergeant from nearby R.A.F. Decimomannu, apparently – who seemed to have had their 1980s fingers in every Sardu pie. Rave music, plumbing, hot food franchises. Bad combination! Shit, their rank, putrid wares had even permeated the hot slop stands at F.C. Cágliari

Calcio throughout those first stages of Italia '90. How had they clinched *that* deal? The stench, the full-on stench of that micro-waved pus they were selling us sent some kids mad. I mean, even nowadays, you only have to YouTube those Anglo-Dutch riots and burning, overturned yellow Meatburger caravans is the primary motif. As leader of Rave munters Dayglo Maradona, I'd met José and Luis Mackenzie loads of times DJ-ing up in the Peak District at Dehydrated, and we'd even supported Spackhouse Tottu at The Haçienda during our brief chart heyday. They were always exhilarating and musically brilliant. Both much older than us, José was stick thin, six-foot-one, tiny moustache, droopy eyes and hair, brilliantest Sardu live DJ alive, but in real life a sucky fucker for shit damn sure. He carried a knife and he'd use it on you. His brother Luis was even worse. Tiny as a little shrub, he roamed the N. England clubs armed with new Spackhouse Tottu re-mixes, bullying Arthur Tadgell to play full 20-minute excursions *and* getting his way. Genius genius stuff. Always greeted with roars of approval. But Luis had such a menacing manner. Being older and Catholic and tiny and macho, he always referred to women as 'boilers' and always carried a knife. Even in Manchester on holiday. But while José and Luis were too out of their depth in N. England to reveal their true colours, and even had a tendency to brown-nose celebs, back on Sardu turf those two became the surliest, sullenest, southern Sards you never would want to encounter. 'Not North of Nuoro' was a real Spackhouse title off their debut LP. At Sardusonic '89, they'd refused even to make a toast with Sardinia's national beer Ichnusa, just because its symbol of four blindfolded and decapitated Muslim Warriors had Catalan origins. That was the Mackenzies. They distrusted everybody north of that Nuoro line for being either Spanish, educated or secretly Corsican. So why had I found one of their Meatburger caravans totalled down some remote northern valley?

I stared over at Anna, who'd put up with a lot from me today. Sorry Anna, I thought quite loudly. At least I'd got cleaner throughout this first day. On arrival, so high had been my levels of Hideous that I'd not even noticed the pale blue rubber sheet she'd surreptitiously laid across the Buick's front passenger floor. But by this late stage of the day, even I'd returned enough to the so-called Real World to begin to suffer from the unholy emanations uprising from my footwell. So when – as we sped through the spectacular ruins of the ancient Valle dei Nuraghe – we clocked a road-menders' camp up ahead replete with a dramatic skyline of three burning braziers, well, I knew that the soaking shirt, the stinky t-shirts, the ex-socks, indeed that whole footwell of iffy nestlings had to be addressed right now . . . and with a vengeance. Sorry Anna.

As we pulled off the 131 on to that stretch of the old road that now formed the lay-by, we cruised uncomfortably past a horde of cheering road-menders, who – enjoying a bite of tea in this killer heat – now raised their mugs collectively either to the car, to Anna and the car, or perhaps simply to me for appearing to have both. Sweet. 300 metres or so ahead, high up on the scrubby ridge that separated our lay-by from the headlong rush of the modern 131, the three braziers burned voraciously, unattended and looking to cause problems in all this dry heat. I dragged all of the mucky clothing out of the footwell and, sweating like a bastard, hotfooted it up the ridge with Anna in tow. As we walked, I had some explaining to do.

ROCK: In normal circumstances, what I'm about to do now might appear a bit too much. But as these really are not normal circumstances, and you have today only encountered me in what are really only abnormal circumstances and in very abnormal locations too, do – if you can – please accept . . . uh, what I'm about to do.

Then, having reached the summit of the stifling ridge, I heaved that unrighteous sodden bundle into the middle brazier's grateful maw and sprang back quickly from the flames. Whoosh went the fire and I spun around astonished at my sudden cleansing festival here atop this improvised heathen Fire Hill. And as that boiling slab of flammable matériels first buckled, then hissed within, I saw on every inch of the horizon great ancient towers magnificent, terrible and everywhere. Anna said nothing to me, but sauntered across to the ridge's only protected part and sat down overlooking those several score nuraghic towers. I followed and sat down next to her.

ANNA: I know a little of your story, Rock Section. So I know you were expecting an archaeologist. I saw your fascination at Faraway Field. My sister planned this many months ago and was so upset not to come with you. You know, she really loves your singing voice. She never could have told you that if she'd came. But she's only in Naples, so I can phone her and bring you any information you require. The monuments that you call the great Doorways are very easy for me to research.
ROCK: (*Visibly rallying*) Anna, that's gonna make my job here so much easier. Mind you, you'll have your work cut out.
ANNA: To keep my studies going, I have to ferry cars around for my dad. Really special cars. I'm used to doing two things at once, it's not so much a compromise. In fact, now that you're already pretty clean, that's also good for the compromise

because some of my dad's cars are pretty special. Sometimes, I get to travel abroad for his work. Once even two years ago I was at the Newark Car Sales.

ROCK: Newark? Buying American Cars?

ANNA: Newark in Nottinghamshire. It's a very important place for my dad.

As a Midlands lad born and raised in D. H. Lawrence's home-town of Eastwood, my early music scenes, my early sex scenes, everything took place around the Nottingham area. So hearing Newark spoken of in such glowing tones, even by a foreigner? A pig's anus with the runs has better vistas than Newark. As a seventeen-year-old, I'd hitched quite regularly up the A46 to a girlfriend in Lincoln, until my most regular lift – a six-foot-eight supply teacher who existed on family-size Maltesers and six-packs of Kola Bear – had a heart attack on the outskirts of Brough and kaputed his minuscule Honda hatchback against a skip with me in the passenger seat. And with no airbags in cars of the time, it seems probable that only those endless layers of sickly sweet Maltesers family packaging had saved my life. But I wasn't about to mention to Anna that the supply teacher was the only cunt in the world with a footwell smellier than mine! No, now was a time only for generousness. And as we sat atop the ridge in that great heat surrounded by omnipresent lost ancient lurkers – all of whom would have been desperate even for one moment to take my blessèd place – I thanked the Gods that a warm creature such as Anna had been sent to share my final weird hours in the 21st century.

8. MR WAIT-FOR-IT

5.30pm, Saturday June 10th, 2006
131 heading south

Around twenty minutes later, the grand Buick convertible surged uphill atop the concrete gantries of the 131, itself here no more than a treacherous and too-modern causeway cutting through the timeless urban rooftops of once-sleepy Bornova. As we sped through, I looked back on the events of the day and wondered whether or not I should bother calling Mick. With Dean's corpse still warm and Mick stuck in England, what could all this bizarre new info do to him? But then, out of the tumbling tightness of the olive-black Mannu river valley, the Buick rushed up on to the high plains of the Altopiano Campeda, where as we reached the highest land I caught a glimpse of my mobile phone approaching full reception. Oh dammit, how I wish I hadn't noticed. Feeling utterly duty-bound, however, I motioned to Anna to slow down a bit while the phone signal up here was good. Dialling his number resignedly, I prepared for the M. Goodby onslaught.

MICK: Section. At last. How do fat women fit into leotards?

An obscure opening gambit was this even for the poet Goodby, until I clocked from the uproar coming down his end of the phone – the cackling, the giggling, the ostentatious over-breathing, the clucking air of female-voiced hysteria – that Mick's question had been clearly staged for a gathered throng, that ye Bard was currently at his town centre Exercise Club surrounded by several new fuller-figured middle-aged ladies all in a hurry to enlist, and all hanging on to his every word. Now was certainly not a good time to speak to Mick even if I'd needed to. Like his old time attitudes to poetry readings, DJ stints and Brits Abroad gigs, Mick's sessions at his Exercise Club are truly sacred times. He doesn't gig anymore so these are his only performances. Like a town-crier announcing his own genius, Mick commences every Exercise Club session by belting out his own worth from the steps of his establishment: Get Yourselves In, Mick's About To Begin! Even now – cunted here in Sarduland – I could picture him framed by the grand oval arch of his elegant red-and-white Liverpool F.C.-inspired 'entrance', towering over the impressionable women, sucking his belly into that rugged all-black tracksuit and standing there self-importantly being six-foot-three-inches tall with his mane of just-washed curly blond hair. Sammy Hagar the Horrible or what! Now, at the other end of the phone, I could hear Hagar giving ladies individual bits of expert advice, pointing directions to the changing rooms, even writing down mobile phone numbers. Mick's Exercise Club is a phenomenon in the north of England because he successfully teaches middle-aged women all kinds of yoga, meditation and breathing, but always sells it under the catch-all banner 'Exercise Club'. 'Call it Exercise and their husbands keep out of the way,' says Mick. 'Call it yoga or meditation and the men think I'm some New Age fiddler.' His exercise CDs sell by the bucketload, are God-awful to the point of being near Pop Art, and one effort culled from his last, ahem, album even went Top Ten. Entitled 'Kick', the song simply involved a particularly flailing Mick yelling that one word over and over a repeated sample of the Doors' cheesey-cheesey 'Light

My Fire' intro. And they call *that* doing your thing! Anyway, suddenly the poet pulled his head out of the goldfish bowl of women and returned to my phone.

MICK: Section. What news from Detchy?

I began immediately to explain that my intentions to head south to R.A.F. Decimomannu for M.G.R. (Mick Goodby Research) had been thus far thwarted, but that Anna and I were now indeed on course and no more than two hours away from our destination. But Mick had soon got caught up again with females and his class was about to start. I heard 'Kick' booming over the P.A. and Mick running up on to the stage.

MICK: Section. Gimme two mo's.

I hung on and hung on and hung on waiting for the guru, but the 131's snaky and shaky course through the landscape began to cut once again through harshly excavated rock. The phone went dead. At least Mick has some kind of mission restored, I consoled myself – but with Dean just now gone, even I'd expected a momentary crack in Mick's telephone bravura, surrounded by adoring women or not. This was a man so guilty about the kidnappings that he couldn't leave the cupboard under his mother's stairs for three years. This was the man who promised his sister he'd look after her twin teenage boys at Italia '90, and then through his own ego flailings got them kidnapped and raped. That Italia '90 summer he was totally out-of-control! Brits Abroad was top of the charts with 'Last Tango in Paris' and Mick had even name-checked himself in his own hit! Drunk with power was Mick! Drunk with Mick possibilities! Couldn't leave well alone. Our fave Machiavellian upstart even used his own brief stardom to allow our admittedly lovely posh friend Full English Breakfast to leapfrog the other long-term band members of our big mates the Kit Kat Rappers – Stu, Yeh-Yeh and Gary Have-a-laugh – by writing a special 'Posh Rap' for Breakfast only! Who'd Mick think he was, Prometheus? Of course 'Her Majesty's Pleasure' was a hit for Breakfast, and of course it was a fucking great hit, but it was a jade's trick to pull on the other three. They'd all been in the band two years longer than Breakfast! Saint Mick, however, could never see these tinkerings as failings until it all coalesced at Italia '90 and death came a-falling.

Back at the lay-by, I'd retrieved my copy of Barry Hertzog's *Prison Writings* from my bag, and now sat fumbling with it looking for new clues. But the disparity between Hertzog's published words and what he'd said face-to-face was just too great to make sense of. I remembered the vicious expression on that enraged and imprisoned Dutch phizzog when he'd described first hearing Brits Abroad on Hilversum Radio. How it had made him change his plans. How he and his Party Orange gangsters had, throughout 1986, tried to book Liverpool's trundling Half Man Half Biscuit at his club Slag Van Blowdriver just to kidnap them. Apparently their songs' vacuous subject matter obliged Party Orange to do this. That is, until M. Goodby's Brits Abroad had poked its even uglier head into the UK Top Ten, thereby creating accelerated threats of Cultural Vacuity *and* at a truly MTV level. Although *Prison Writings* contained none of Hertzog's threats of violence, kidnap and judgement, his book's index of negative entries concerning Half Man Half Biscuit most certainly provided me with endless entertaining quotes, the best surely one that called them:

"Cynical, corn-fed, semi-artistic pseuds vampiring and suckling at the unhygienic overflow tap of bubbling TV trash, all the while stewing comatose in a glorious Welfare State safety net of near heavenly size, rather than deploying their modicum of nous to try in any way to stem the megaflow of the Monoculture's effluence into the minds of the surrounding population." (*Prison Writings*, 120)

Fair enough. Hertzog had pointed out how, as a 25-year football devotee of Dokkum's semi-pro Be Quick, he'd initially admired Half Man Half Biscuit's parochial devotion to little tiny Tranmere Rovers, even found it valiant and inspiring. But then the Judge had explained how, on Half Man Half Biscuit's debut LP *Back in the D.H.S.S.*, their lyrical skewering of Liverpool icon Nerys Hughes of *The Liver Birds* had made his blood boil, commenting:

"When some evil old bird called Thatcher could be filling up Nigel's time, instead he's getting a blather on for my favourite Liver Bird. I want to know why? Half Man Half Biscuit's worldview is akin to knowing full well that a mass murderer is roaming your asylum, but still choosing to complain to administrators about the nose picker in the next bed." (*Prison Writings*, 122)

Thereafter, Hertzog had gone through all of their lyrics and come to the conclusion that – by wasting their iffy songwriting prowess on picking fights with minor TV celebs and transient media phenomena of the kind that *each and every knob-end in the world* would wish to barf over – Half Man Half Biscuit were a bunch of Dwindlers content merely to hold up the most delicate of hand mirrors to society, rather than daring to smash its smug face in with a hammer. And *Prison Writings'* final prognostication as regards Half Man?

> "I met Nigel [the singer/songwriter] once, I puked. His pop star haircut but no balls to be one. Ducking behind the cultural sofa, taking pot shots at gooleyless Kids TV presenters, but still he's at home in the mirror gelling up a squarky-bird haircut. Always safe with Tranmere Rovers. Yes, I stuck with Be Quick for football and friends, but for international violence I graduated also to F.C. Groningen." (*Prison Writings*, 202)

Face-to-face, Hertzog had spoken similarly harsh words to me, and all in that clipped, stentorian manner of his. Fuck, was this Dutch lunatic committed. According to his *Prison Writings*, Hertzog's fiery relationship with the 'nihilistic/apathistic' lyrics of Half Man Half Biscuit had forced him in late 1986 upon a quest to purge . . .

> ". . . from my soul all of the casual, White Supremacist feeling that has dwelled so peacefully within me whilst up here in my natural German border habitat." (*Prison Writings*, 28)

To confront then re-engage with his true Inner Barbarian, according to *Prison Writings*, Hertzog next armed himself with an orange spray can and declared himself the First Indie Football Hooligan in F.C. Groningen's monthly magazine, writing:

> "In a democracy such as ours, the rigour with which you wield your spray can denotes your level of artistry. And

in such a democracy, where such materials can be readily bought, owning your own spray can does not alone make you an artist." (*Prison Writings*, Introduction iii)

Furthermore, as a damaged N. Netherlander whose family and friends still had so much Nazi collaboration to put behind them, Hertzog was the kind of put-upon Ugly Customer that felt justification in seeking their truth anywhere. Anywhere at all. From his *Prison Writings* rants, it sounds as though Judge Barry – after he'd learned from Malcolm X 'The True Story of the White People and How We Got Here' – well, Judge Barry had just jumped on all that as justification for his own World Anger. White people were bred to rebel and go crazy up north, wrote the Prophet Malcolm in his World Massive autobiography. Thinks Hertzog: 'That exempts me from responsibility for the bad way I feel,' and daubs a massive X across his face for Italia '90. Welcome to our nightmare.

Reading further extracts from *Prison Writings* and gradually reconstituting the words of our penitentiary meeting almost word for fuzzy word, I realised with certainty that had it not been for the arrival of Mick Fizz and his Last Tango in Paris, Messrs Half Man & Biscuit would be rotting on the damp floor of the Waddenzee, but you know what? Fuck Hertzog. He's fluent in English and that fucker is an Anglophile with a Liverpool background himself, *and* he'd even had his own big hit in English. So of course Hertzog understood Mick's words enough to be incensed by their vacuousness. But I'd watched Anna listening to that stupid Brits Abroad hit today, jigging about on top of the car and entirely clueless as to what it was about.

ROCK: You like it a lot?
ANNA: (*So happy*) I love the film, too!

What? Let me get this straight once and for all, clear it up. The subject matter of the Brits Abroad song that got us all targeted, kidnapped and what-have-you was about Mick and his Liverpool F.C. buddies running riot down La Place de la Concorde because some poor little Parisian 3rd div. team they were playing ran out of the cold fizzy drinks that fuel M. Goodby's existence. Unable to access the right kind of fizz, Mick got hauled off by the gendarmes for grabbing half a Tango out of some youth's hand. But even though the shiny pop video had made it clear, crystal clear, most Euros still somehow remember the song as being after the Brando movie *Last Tango in Paris*. Ummm. So what Mick's first few ranty verses must sound like to foreigners, I really can't hope to imagine. It started out in the mid-'80s as an epic poem that Mick told at pubs before Liverpool matches. Stu and Gary Have-a-laugh would be strategically placed at the bar to offer homey support, questioning and urging: 'Was it the final Britvic in Bury?' 'No, it was the last Tango in Paris.' And Mick only wrote in that twee dodgy third verse for the primary school kiddies' choir at the behest of producer Arthur Tadgell, who believed it could be a proper hit. Have a re-listen to that flailing M. Goodby vocal on the 7″ single version of 'Last Tango . . .' and, well, Mick's semi-pro Northern accent always floated somewhere between Stoke and Lancaster at the best of times, but never was it so Pan-Pennine as on that hit single. Tell you what, how about I here proffer the entire lyrical libretto to M. Goodby's 'Last Tango in Paris', so you can understand why Hertzog got so mad, not.

Last Tango in Paris

(Spoken)
Sugary drinks across the ages,
Tales of pick-me-ups by sages,
Caffeinated to the max,
Delivering drinks down ancient tracks,
'The King of Vienna needs some sugar,
You're heading east, you lucky bugger.'

I.
Red Bull comes in cans, I know,
I've followed its career,
Since I chanced upon its Austrian debut,
It was 1987 and our youth team played East Tyrol,
Where the fighting hordes are few.
So we loaded up with Kola Max,
We loaded up with sickly snacks,
Got overloaded on the aeroplane,
Then descended as one sugary mass,
We crossed the tarmac,
Reached the grass,
Then retched collectively, ooh!

(Pause) Let's start again.

Sugary drinks across the ages,
Tales of pick-me-ups by sages,
Caffeinated to the max,
Delivering drinks down ancient tracks,
'The King of France, he needs some sugar,

43

You're heading south, you lucky bugger.'

2.
Red Star, Paris: green-and-white,
A year or so ago,
Your soft drinks were all gone long before Half Time,
So I had to mug a tourist fairly near the Eiffel Tower,
Half a Tango is no crime!
Your Honour, it was lack of fizz,
Your Honour, Coke won't do the biz,
And your baggage handlers cracked the fizz I'd packed,
If you run a Euro football club,
We Anglos don't all need the pub,
White sugar: it's a fact.

3.
(*School choir*)
Mick collects the kind of drinks that keep you up all
    night,
All you kiddies, too much pop will make you sick,
Unto every son and daughter,
Give them juice and give them water,
Then there's all the more for Mick.

Chorus (*Vocals shared between Mick, Stu and Gary
Have-a-laugh*)

Was it the first Vimto in Cannock?
No, it was the last Tango in Paris,
Was it the final Britvic in Bury?
No, it was the last Tango in Paris.

It was not the penultimate Coke in Berlin
Quaffed down with a bongload of charis;
Indeed, it would go down in history
As the last Tango in Paris.

Was it the final R. White's in Westminster?
No, it was the last Tango in Paris.
It was not the penultimate Tizer in Hull,
It was the last Tango in Paris.

Was it the ultimate Fanta in Nazi Germany?
The last Dr. Pepper on Broadway?
The last Kia-Ora to escape from Andorra?
Just take this Ribena and go away.

Was it the last Dandelion and Burdock in the
    Quantocks?
No, I won't speak of it longer,
The only contender was My Mum's Cola,
And that's only because it's stronger.

Was it the second-to-last Irn Bru in the Shetlands?
Or the final Corona on Skye?
Well, me I can't answer,
All clammy and sweaty,
Just gimme one quick or I'll die.

9. TRANSMISSION FROM THE ALTAR OF PUNISHMENT

Late afternoon, Saturday June 10th, 2006
North of Macomér, N.W. Sardinia

Musing that only a psycho could have interpreted 'Last Tango in Paris' with such venom and twisted spite, I clocked a road sign that put us just fifteen or so kilometres north of Macomér, the very place we'd been kidnapped all those long years ago. Do I not let on to Anna and just keep my head down as we burn past on the 131? I'll keep my head down! And so it was just as we began our slow descent from the heights of the Altopiano Campeda that my drug dependency and my career trajectory entered the discussion via Anna's simple query.

ANNA: You were *such* a good singer of Post-Punk times, Rock Section. Why you had to return as a Rave guy re-mixing with the other baggies? I liked your Dayglo Maradona a lot for dancing sure, (*suddenly squeaky*) but no voice?

What a can opener! What a pest dispenser! What do I say without spilling my life into this sweet lady's lap? Dayglo Maradona had been my re-birth. All that came before was just a prelude to the Storm. As a six-foot-two seventeen-year-old Jim Morrison wannabe, I'd stalked the streets of Eastwood with compadré Gaz Marshmallow, inching along the blue D. H. Lawrence heritage walks at about nearly m.p.h. Tripping and desperate for Culture, we'd both regularly sneaked into Lawrence's *Sons*

& Lovers cottage on Walker Street until Gaz one rainy night spied the blue heritage line continuing up Lawrence's path and became convinced it was leading the cops our way. Eastwood was too small-town for me; Nottingham too, I discovered. I had to get out of that crisp packet before I turned into a chewy. So I auditioned as vocalist for Arthur Tadgell's epic Post-Punk band the Low Countries, and the first single we did was a hit! I'm not a songwriter, just a singer, but it was massive for that time. Not being from Liverpool and being so young, however, the dynamic in the band sucked shit and I had to be careful not to tread on toes. The singer/guitarist and the female organist were a couple. Until I came along, he wrote the lyrics and she wrote the music. Then after two singles for Arthur Tadgell's label, the great entrepreneur one day returned to their rehearsal room from a Midlands shopping trip replete with a gift – one Rock Section: here's your new lead singer, chaps and chappesses. Lump it.

I was remembering all of these extraordinary details, moments, incisive Visions as though they were happening right *now*, and all in an instant. But I rose with great effort from out of my Cavernous Inner to address this sweet lady and her questioning.

ROCK: If you liked my voice in the Low Countries, then I'm very happy. But I was still a kid and five years younger than all the others. The lady on the keyboards was very nice to me, but the guy songwriter resented me – they were a couple and he'd been singing their songs before I stepped in. It must have been humiliating. Then, in early 1981, we had a massive instrumental hit in Brazil with one of her tunes called 'Ewerthon'. After the William Blake character. It went platinum and got bought up for a TV coffee ad! With no vocals on it, I had to mime bass on the video while her old man stood on a beach not even playing anything! That single was so successful that it split the band up. So she toured Brazil without us, and I withered for the rest of the Eighties, festering in a very crap flat and waiting for someone to write me a tune worth singing. And while I waited, I followed Nottingham Forest F.C. from afar and spent alternate Saturday afternoons at Liverpool F.C. right up close. I perfected my stencil-and-spraygun techniques and became a classy Graffiti act. And I used my VHS to watch the magical footwork of Diego Maradona. And I used his cocaine addiction to justify my own drug abuse. I was like Keith Richards claiming that the genius of his work on *Exile On Main Street* justified his heroin addiction.

ANNA: (*Wide-eyed*) Keith said that? Maybe it's a bit true?

ROCK: Maybe. Anyway, watching Maradona over and over again gave me such belief in magic that I followed him like a guru. (*Portentously*) The way of Maradona! And then, just before Italia '90, came the rumour that FIFA were on Diego's ass for a blood test. The rumours continued that Diego had been whizzed over to Switzerland for a full-on blood transfusion, knowing he could still fall back on a semi-legal ephedrine diet. Allegedly, big enough doses would be supportive and prickly enough to burn him through Italia '90 . . . As a Diego disciple and total monster drug fiènd, I converted myself to ephedra the very next week. And Guess What? Instantly Anna, no shit is this: my ephedrine re-mixes developed a total Maradonaen swagger and my sampling tuned into Etheric Radiation. I love singing, but my re-mix hits of that time will be forever sacred and truly belong to Maradona.

Anna remained silent, but still smiling. Well, she *had* asked. Despite her easy and elegantly physical ways at the tiller of Jayne Mansfield's Ruin, this lady was clearly a scholar and a thinker every inch. It was evident in her choice of books on the back seat, the kinds of friends she talked to on her mobile, her canny self-management that had kept her so long in Higher Education.

ANNA: It's such a great rock'n'roll singer's name: Rock Section. Obviously it's your stage name, you don't have any Italian in you (*giggling*). Do you, Rocco?

I laughed. My Rock Section Story is a good one, but a very confusing one. And with Anna herself struggling with the nuance of spoken English, I hummed and ha'd and prevaricated as to just how I should convey to her all of those infuriatingly Anglo bits that *make* the story. I'd become Rock Section quite accidentally just twenty-four hours before that successful audition for the Low Countries; indeed this peculiar event itself had precipitated my decision to go for that audition. Late cold November 1979. It had really just started as a typical Nottingham midweek night out with Gaz Marshmallow, drinking at the Saracen's Head. Unbeknown to us, we were about to watch – or rather, attend – our umpteenth gig by Skin Patrol, a trio of local white funksters on a Postcard Records bender. Well, more beers got downed and I was gassing to my mates at the bar as ye Skinners breezed – no other word for it – through their clean-sounding, mostly Orange Juice-inspired set. Until the end, that is . . . then . . . what the Terminal Fuck? After only about a 30-second sprinkle of polite applause, singer Courtney returns to the stage far too quickly for a barely demanded encore, but nevertheless lets loose a life-changing 10,000 Doom Decibels from right out of the abyss, unleashing a slow Detroit mechanical blues called 'Rock Section', replete with the Moron Savant chorus: 'Dance to the beat of the drum.' By the end of the song, Courtney's down on the floor necking some sex-bomb woman me and Gaz Marshmallow have always been too frit even to speak to, and we were watching the Doors in Miami '69. How could Skin Patrol's ice-rinky dinkiness have descended out of nowhere into Full J. Morrison Stupor Consciousness in the space of one single encore tour de force? How?

That night, Gaz Marshmallow and I seven-league-booted back to Eastwood, plotting. We'd both watched the Transformation of Skin Patrol with our very own Nothingham eyes [sic] and the both of us now understood that we too could be Agents of Change. There had been a Jagged Time Lapse, most certainly. The next day would be our Rite of Passage in front of Mr Tadgell. We'd win a record contract and conquer the world. But when I woke up? Gutted. Gaz had lost the magic. He was decent enough to telephone – he did only live next door – but he told me we couldn't expect what had happened to Skin Patrol to happen to us, that it was a one-off, and therefore he couldn't do the audition today even after watching their Holy Transformation. But the whole shitty story made me just totally ten times more determined to play: *Skin Patrol just* demanded *transformation right there and then. Therefore shall I too Demand that Change in front of Arthur Tadgell!* So, guiltily, Gaz lent me the primitive Radio Shack drum box he'd put together himself, and I jammed in front of my bedroom mirror on bass guitar, nicking what bits I could remember of Skin Patrol's new doom song, and the rest making up on the spot, plus of course adding far more Jim Morrisonisms than made sense.

So by the time it was my turn to get on Mr Tadgell's stage – with G. Marshmallow safely back home/feet-up in front of *Midlands Today* – I walked out really confident, stared out into the audience and just said: Hey, this is Rock Section. I'm Rock Section. I switched on the mid-tempo, ping-pong drum-box and jammed Skin Patrol's basic E-to-G chords for fifteen full minutes, intoning and hiccupping like my guitar teacher Paul the Cop had shown me Buddy Holly used to do. It went off like some great improvised pagan dance with machines, good through to the end, when I dared at last to look out finally . . . and shit a brick. There in front of me at waist height – totally in the centre of the stage – was Arthur Tadgell, staring up grinning with a full glass of wine, toasting me with that same smile he did on his TV show. I walked off stage and he charmed me to death. He shut down the auditions then and there, told everybody – a few future big names included – that he'd found what he needed. Lee Harris was there, The Stasi, Sandra Rough: she was loudly pissed off at not getting to sing. By the end of the evening, I was signing a contract in the dark car park lit by the lights of the great entrepreneur's Jaguar Mark 10, and collecting free copies of all the latest stuff by the Low Countries and the Smoke Dopes, plus signed publicity photos of Mr Tadgell for Gaz Marshmallow and my auntie who both loved his Granada TV show . . .

As I rifled at great velocity through all of these ancient thoughts, Jayne Mansfield's Ruin still high-tailed it south-wards along the 131 with purpose and aplomb. But I had not really been concentrating on our continuously unfolding pres-ent, when it suddenly dawned upon me that I might well seize up with hostage fear upon glimpsing the dramatic and fast-approaching landscape around the Macomér neighbourhood. So when I 'forewarned' Anna of possible rough passages ahead, our great convertible had already commenced its grand descent, skirting around that timeless former hilltop fortress along its 131 flight-path. Spectacular views all right but a near fatal error on my part. Uh-oh.

Then some *thing* Macomér'd me. An ancient deathly figure – its spectral hands outstretched – reached up and into me. And as I clutched at my suddenly aching belly, its cartoon replica imploded then fell away into some deep abyss under the roadway. Such was the Urgency in my brow, such was the Pounding in my brow, that the two feelings did boil within my head a heat of such terrific bulging Ugliness that I grew Horns Invisible that projected out Baphomet-like from my raging temples. Upwards, onwards and into the sky, they streamed out like great telegraph wires, like twin umbilical cords projecting up to that Blakean Sky that currently presided over Macomér. Then this great cascading 131 – now more switchback than expressway – racing runway-like through scree slopes, clattered downhill round Macomér, accepting only reluctantly those wild pre-historic landscapes of the Birori Valley directly ahead through which it now crashed, those lands that sixteen years previously had caused such catastrophe for myself and my compadrés. Kidnapped here, we'd been kidnapped here, fucking kidnapped of all things. Am I dying? Am I dying, I ask you? Stop the car. Stop the car. I cradled my distended belly as we swept ever faster downhill, and twisted around to grab the bottle of Sudafed that was nestling in my jacket pocket over on the back seat. The phone rang. I groaned – didn't even attempt to answer. But now Mick was suddenly raging in my head, mimicking me in my current situation, and declaiming as ostentatiously as some Norse God gone Rave DJ: *Stoppe ye fucking car, I'm fucking dying, I do tellest thee, or what?*

But I just smile resignedly and sickly, my eyes widening and my head pressing further and further back into my seat. I'm learning just how low low low a cunted sloth bombed out on a diet of Sudafed and squidgy black can – when he really puts his mind to it – really really really sink into overly luxurious mid-1960s General Motors upholstery. Then a nod from the Gods, and a vote from the Remotes, and a station platform announcer-type declares: *Ladies and Gentlemen, welcome to judgement.* Just in time (?), Anna guides this massive Buick off the 131 right up the slip road of Macomér Industrial Estate and my Body, Psyche and entire Being collectively sense our precise geographical location. And thus my entire Macomér'd Being – now registering only 'Kidnap, Kidnap, Kidnap' – immediately abandons all of its senses in favour of an every-man-for-himself Blind Panic, this causing me to pass out . . .

When I woke up, Jayne Mansfield's Ruin was 150 metres away, parked up, straddling its big arse across the farm slip road that leads to Macomér's industrial estate. Below us, the 131 roared by and I was clinging for comfort to the Sudafed bottle. But now, while Anna was fiercely slapping my face awake, I felt from the very bowels of the valley the sudden roar of a Great Being surging through me. And I knew I was feeling the same Great Being that once during the kidnapping I'd had reason to confront. Houuuuuuuuugh! Holy fucking . . . help . . . We were marooned in my Hell. Even through the filter of my drugged-out state, that roar and the sight of Macomér above was far too much to bear, and I threw up right there on the dirt road whilst the electric energy in Birori Valley bolted through me and set up within my head a raging Mithraic Fire. I crashed down on to my knees, convulsing like a toddler, and I wailed for all the Death and Disaster this place had caused us, and I fizzed and

I flailed in an orgy of self-hate and under-achievement. I pictured the naked Brent newly fourteen years old picking his way to freedom up that Macomér hillside sixteen years previously. Blind me from all of this. Dean's dead, man.

And the generator-like pulsations pushing out from the nearby Altar of Punishment obliged me to shamble away, hobble away, put any possible distance between it and myself. Here's me walking away, down this farm road into this decent old farm, probably where Anna's gone for help. My silo stomach, my bitten lips, my under-attended-to but over-plumbed sphincter, smashèd face: all hurt like a motherfucker and I'm sure that as I walked I looked – to that Great Being studying me periscope-like from beneath the Altar of Punishment – as somnambulant, slow and robot-like as an old old geezer. But although every step here was a struggle, I intuitively knew that this was not a re-enactment of that Life and Death struggle that had destroyed my kidnapped comrades the first time. In truth, the Great Being on this occasion had – from his binding at the Altar of Punishment 250 metres away – merely sniffed me. And even in my fragile condition I well knew from experience that he'd need more than one whiff to refresh that colossal mind of his as to what my presence here implied. So as I stumbled finally into the farm of Puttu Oes, although my breathing felt asthmatic and wheezing, both my Will to Live and my Will to Win Through was increasing considerably with every step I took. Here within the white-walled farmyard, even the torturing effects of the sunlight overhead were hugely diminished, and my burning scalp felt cooled and irrigated. Unfortunately within the precincts of Puttu Oes, the farm looked long abandoned. Nevertheless, although temporarily protected from the Great Being Without by these deep Mediterranean walls, I still needed sustenance and gobbled down the last of the Sudafed. You're becoming Sudafed. Yet still from the back of my raging mind, I remembered the greater purpose of this my final Sardinian mission – to seek restitution for my fallen, wrongèd comrades before I journeyed to my rightful place.

Then, as I rested briefly, humming on the Sudafed and musing upon my Mission, my medicated eyes found themselves drawn to that brightly painted farmyard's sole unpainted wall. A great drystone wall it was, eight-feet-square, surmounted by a roof comprised of one vast table stone. I struggled to my feet and studied closer, and I recognised now that its geological fabric was animated and shifting. And as I focused further upon that vast table stone, so my head began slowly to rotate. But really, as the pace of the rotations began to pick up speed, it was not my head entirely but my face that was spinning now. Moreover, my face was slowly pushing into the rock. Holy shit! And picking up speed. Holy Shit! Now at last I crumbled, my face suddenly a clockwise propeller crumbling through the rock, crumbling the Me right out of me, crumbling the rock itself, driving Me – whatever Me was – faster and faster through the firmament, through the rock, ever forwards always forwards propelled by my spinning propeller face. And with that propeller face, I drilled deep through the Rock of Ages further and further into the past at such a dreadful bate that I span out of Consciousness into Time itself.

10. WHEN OLD TÜPP RULED IN ASHOP

A great open cavern, c. 10,000 years ago

As out into the microfolds of the Universe I was thrust, the bru-
tally hostile incursions of cosmic winds proved immediately catastrophic to my puny physical Being, which collapsed then was
dragged along in my Life's Slipstream, a child's deflated party
balloon snared on the back of a jumbo jet. Too soon, my sagging
physical Being – buffeted and brutalized by 1,000° temperature
changes – resembled nothing more than laundry, great heaving
armfuls of putrid laundry. Less than that even, I was a brown
splash of chewing tobacco spat out by some not-arsed soldier
into the path of an oncoming tank. Scattered across Time, I
was by now merely Contents. Fragmented as aerosol spray, I'd
become my own Diaspora. Until all was dreamed and fleshiness
'seemed' and I hung Between in a great bog of Me, a helpless
Merman trapped within a runny, waterproof bag of himself. But
somehow *somehow*, diminished though I was to the nth degree,
yet still I was Salad With Attitude . . .

And then I heard smiling, the loudest of smiling. And I wondered how smiling could even be heard. But I even heard grinning, though I couldn't explain it. In darkness, in blackness, an
audience grinning, delighted to see me. And then I hung down
and I knew again what *down* was. My body supported by persons
unknown that I knew and I trusted, I coughed then I farted and
belched. And then, from out-of-focus, great swathes of bright
faces emerged all delighted, delighted to see me. Whoaaarrr!

And then it began. From atop my stone podium – still supported on either side by officers of my trusty Select – my Royal
Piss exploded into a hollowed stone pail as the gathered throng
of Noble aristocrats gasped appropriately and pronounced their
satisfaction at my extensive waterworks. Right then, however, I
couldn't even manage a weak wave, so – eyes still shut tight – I
extended my tongue beyond my lips as evidence of my return
at last, and shrieking cheering ecstatic choruses of 'Beyond,
Beyond, Beyond' started up across the cavern. No thanks are in
order, for I am merely the Vessel through which all of you may
experience richness in your own lives. And me still hanging up
comfortably, propped in between the two tallest Select guards
in my father's retinue, I stared down intensely at the expectant faces of those chosen few, knowing that before nightfall my
Royal Piss – its every last scintillating drop – would have been
quaffed down into their bellies. For Magic. Steeped in ephedra
since my royal childhood, brimming always in its manical glory,
suffice it to say that I knew from my instant calculations that
this single pail of Royal Piss would guarantee intense Visions
for at least nointeen of my favourites. How blissful it was to be
home, here where at all times they keep nine full pots of ephedra
boiling in the eternal fires on the slopes next to Odin's Sitch.
How blissful to know that my father held the best ephedra supplies from here to the sea. How essential to steep in the sweetness of ephedra's other worlds. How charming to sleep on fresh
heads of ephedra. How giddying to wear ephedra bracelets. Oh,
ephedra my Phaedra.

The next morning at daybreak, I was eventually awakened
from my slumber by an endless succession of olive-skinned
men whose dangerous job it was to heat the stone bath on the
far side of my cavern by pitching into its waters red-hot rocks

from a huge fire at the cave's entrance. Across the hillside on the steep slopes of Mam Tor, a line of women at the mouth of Odin's Sitch were also preparing my bath by scooping up those sacred waters into their great leather bags, then commencing the long trek down into the valley and up the other side to my cavern. This tiresome job always takes the people most of the day. But my return here, however, is always the greatest cause for celebration. For here in the Land of Ashop I am royal heir to Old Tüpp's ephedra fields, some say the greatest ephedra fields in all of N. Europe. And one day I too shall be coronated Old Tüpp of Ashop, and have my own contraption that reduces my height and lends to me the air of a Ruler. But for now, it is enough that I am Old Tüpp's chosen son and heir. I am the sacred stranger known as Bjond – 'the fair one from the far lands' – the Far Reigner who appeared mysteriously one day in the boughs of the Great Tree. Or so it is said. But Old Tüpp is himself a Far Reigner of sorts. Not olive-skinned but done up day-to-day with ochre clay, and not at all short without his contraption. None but myself and the king's own guards have witnessed this secret. Old Tüpp is one of the Old Ones, however, and he is therefore unimpeachable. He knows Longitude and the directions of things. He finds things through that knowledge that others know not. All of the Old Ones hold knowledge that none others hold. That is how they have remained supreme for so long. But there are Newcomers now who have made false claims, most divisively, that a person can live without ephedra. These are often the same people who claim for food all the respect and importance that ephedra once enjoyed. They are more than wrong; they will be the downfall of Ashop. So now, when I salute the Sun with my great horn of ephedra, I am also declaring its potency and the illegitimacy of food alone. No one can or would wish to live only by food. It is not natural.

And with that, I took my fingers and ran them around the edges of the excavated stone bath, scraping up the ephedra paste from the encrusted tidemark, moulding it with both hands into the shape of a patty, then cramming it into my mouth with furious gusto. 'Score,' I exclaimed in the vernacular, chewing and chewing then swallowing it down with warm ephedrine wine. Then I repeated the exercise with a similarly ecstatic verve and slid into my soft bed of feathers and ephedra heads. Score. Score. Score. But suddenly, a furious sneezing attack and the crossing of my eyes denoted a serious error. Is this a heart attack? Then a coughing, and a-spluttering, then more coughing and a furious furious s-s-s-s-s-shaking . . .

. . . Father, Bjond was returning once again to his Other World.

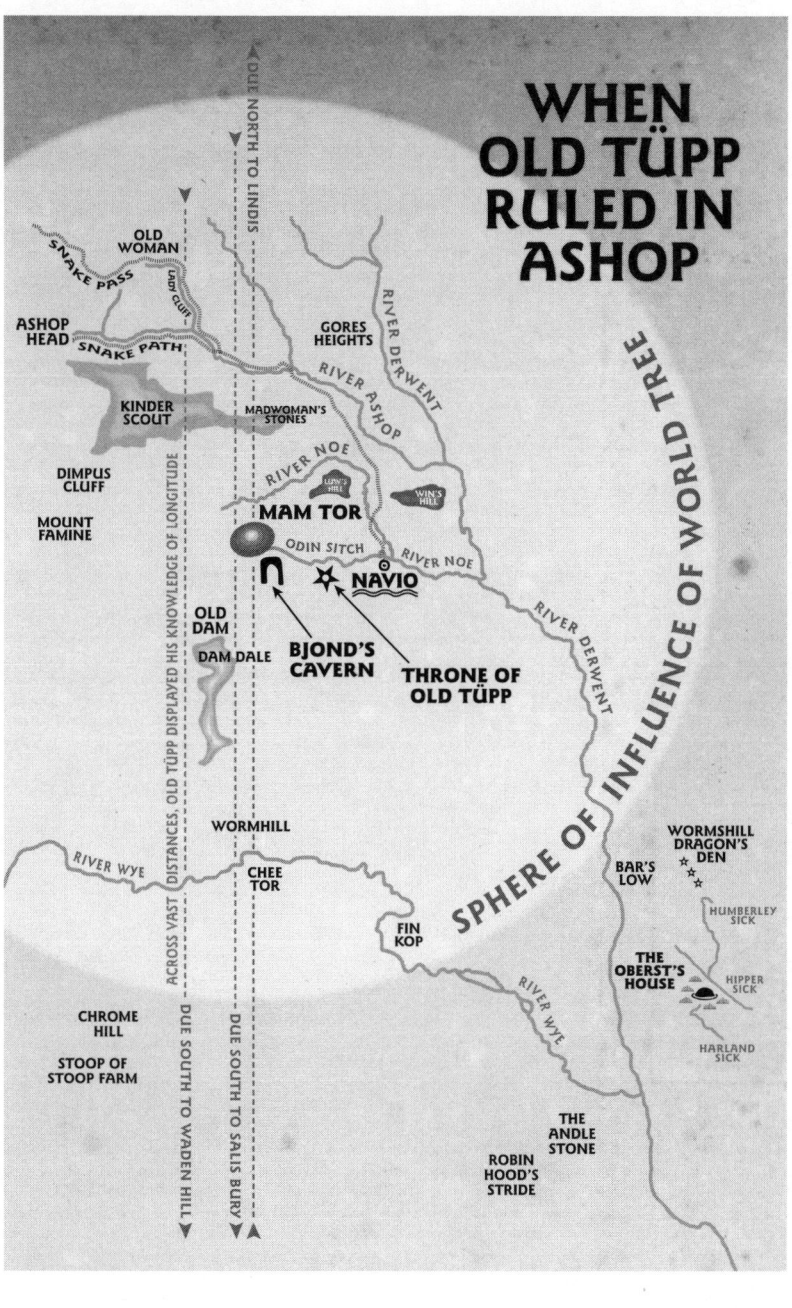

WHEN OLD TÜPP RULED IN ASHOP

11. SU TALLERI

Early evening, Saturday June 10th, 2006
Outskirts of Macomér, Birori Valley

Sobbing and hiccupping, then gulping and rubbing the tears from her eyes and nose, the inconsolable Anna brandished the accelerating Buick like one possessed as we surged then galumphed, surged then galumphed across the desolation of Macomér Industrial Estate, trying simultaneously both to make a dash for it *and* to avoid the gypsy children whose playground was our middle-of-the-road. And as she drove, Anna wailed at me, wailed at herself, at anyone who might catch her words on the air.

ANNA: You were gone for ten minutes. You were no longer a
   human being. What can I do? I don't even know the hind-leg
   manoeuvre. You died in the tomba di giganti. And I was more
   frightened for my life than ever I knew. When I was a little
   girl, I pretend to be from Naples like my dad. Now I know
   why my dad is suspicious of this island. You died there in the
   tomba di giganti. (*Getting squeaky*) How can you come back
   looking so good?

I hated to admit it. But I was feeling Bountiful. I was feeling great. Poor Anna. For her to have endured nursing me as a corpse was too much to bear even thinking about. But although that rancid experience of hers did call into question somewhat the quality of her current compliments to me, darn it if I wasn't now brimming over with all the joys of spring. Indeed, I felt suffused with an incandescent glow, the like of which I had not experienced in a mighty age. And as Anna turned the Buick right out of the industrial estate and we headed up the hill towards Macomér town in the now darkening skies of the evening, I no longer felt utter terror at the very idea of returning to the place of my kidnap. At least for now, those deafening otherworldly shocks emanating from the Great Being, his seismic broadsides that had forced me to seek refuge at Puttu Oes, had died down considerably. Moreover, even as we began to ascend the ever-steepening mile-long incline into that grand medieval capital, I had sussed that the proximity to each other of both Being and Doorway could hardly be coincidence, especially in this Birori Valley wherein so much misadventure had occurred. I twisted my neck around sharply to the right and stared back down the hill across the industrial estate to the deserted farm of Puttu Oes, the ribbon of headlights that now glowed down along the 131 providing context and allowing me at all times to trace precisely my correct path back to its True Doorway. And even as we became every minute more drawn into the tight main streets of uptown Macomér, my new knowledge of that great cosmic 're-fuelling station' just down the valley summoned within me a huge sigh of relief.

Navigating expertly up the clockwise arcing incline of the town's wide main street, Anna suddenly pointed up to the green neon hotel sign 'Su Talleri', and our land-yacht slithered to a halt. She began as matter-of-factly as she could muster.

ANNA: Okay, I just changed my plan. But you didn't know that plan so don't worry about it. Right, when you died I planned to take you to the new hospital here. Even when we climbed the hill just now that was my plan. But now I get a proper look at you, I don't think the hospital would believe me because you look so great. It's crazy. So tonight we will stay here at Su Talleri. She is a lovely landlady and always treats me so nicely. But but *but* (*suddenly looking very fierce*) you must stay in your hotel room and try to sleep. I will check us in and she will lend me her parking space for the night. And and *and* (*wagging her finger*) I have to exchange the Buick tomorrow morning early for my dad. In Cágliari. I promise to bring you to R.A.F. Decimomannu tomorrow. Tonight it's impossible I think.

But as I paced my tiny hotel room that night naked from the heat, dousing myself from the water cooler and cursing the lack of ventilation, nevertheless I was, or so I believed, the heartiest Time Traveller in the whole N. Hemisphere. For such was the proliferation of marvellous magic upon this mysterious island that I had, in one admittedly insane day, stumbled upon a precise route back to the homeland of my Ancestors: to my father, to my noble people and to my destiny. And although my time 'back home' had been far too brief to enjoy – and was already partly evaporating from my present memory – now was not the time for such enjoyment. No, now was the time only for Truth.

Currently replete with ephedra for the foreseeable future, or so I imagined from the current swing in my step, one recurring event in my hotel room nevertheless disturbed and tormented my senses. It was the sound of the trains going over the points that crossed the main street barely 200 metres away. For I had experienced that exact sound whilst being held hostage chained to a wall during the kidnap sixteen years previously. But so similar was the rumble of those trains from my Su Talleri bedroom that I knew our prison *must* lurk extremely close by. And despite my earlier Pavlovian nodding in response to Anna's emphatic assertion that I must remain in my room, each successive train that clicked and clattered across those Macomér points only urged me more and more to slip outside this house briefly and discover precisely wherein we had all been incarcerated.

And so, at midnight, I slipped the Yale lock of Su Talleri's side entrance on to its latch. Heading to my right, I walked just 100 metres up the side road away from the main drag to the end of the street. But as I turned that immediate left I recoiled in horror and stopped dead. What? Right there before me, in all of its squared-off 1930s moderne grandiosity, stood the Fascist Cheese Factory of our nightmares, viewed now in brutal profile, crouched and stewing in its own shadows, its continued local infamy apparent by the sheer accretion of youthfully sprayed Pronouncements Diabolical and its crumbling façade still surmounted with those enormous and uniquely Art Deco concrete capital letters: *L. DALMASSO, PRODUZIONE ESPORTAZIONE FORMAGGI.* Great hunks of the factory's walls lay as rubble around the base of the building, the second 'g' of 'FORMAGGI' target-practised to the floor in a hail of bullets, hefty slabs of cornering dragged right across to the opposite side of the street. Ultimate in its attitude, however, was the presence of two bent crowbars cast down idly upon the factory's front delivery platform, two fabulous implements each more than a metre in length, and each tossed away as though nothing more important than a teatime break had curtailed the high jinks of the demolition engineers. More sprayèd spew from some local Black Metal kids decorated the iron grilles of the barred front windows, whilst the featureless ribbed industrial pull-down metal doorway was scribbled upon conscientiously top-to-bottom and signed simply with the name of the infamous torturess 'Madame Bathory'.

I ventured slowly past the cheese factory frontage, awed by its sudden proximity. Oh, my fucking fuck! Nervously I slipped down the narrow alley that led to the rear of the building. Halfway along, I kneeled down at the low windows and peered into the utter blackness. Having no flashlight available, I simply pointed the camera of my mobile phone at the window glass and pressed. Whoa. Immediately, the camera's flash illuminated the whole of that creepy underworld, the rows and rows of tables, the stacks of wooden pallets, and those inhuman white wooden stalls in which we'd been incarcerated, chained. Now, even without the benefit of the flash, I remained compelled and still kneeling, staring into the blackness of those windows. I stared and still I stared. Then at last, I stood up and continued my way down that dark alley to the rear of the factory, where its foundations terminate in that spectacular ravine along which Brent and I had made our naked escapes sixteen years previously. But as I again traced with my eyes the path of dear Brent Garrett's near-spectral escape route, it was for Dean Garrett that my heart now raced. Poor surviving Dean. Brent's suicide after the kidnap had been instant, unequivocal, final. Dean on the other hand had become sensitive, New Age, mystical, fatalistic . . . Dean the Survivor they called him, more as a convenient mantra than as any real truth. Even I'd sniggered at his crop of slight, sensitive 10″ singles released throughout the '90s under the name Forest Of Dean. But now, from the sheer edge of the ravine, I suddenly unleashed into the black night a full-blooded wail for Dean the Survivor. For what is this tragedy that names him 'Survivor', but still sees him dead before the age of thirty?

12. NOT EVERYBODY GOT BUMMED

Midnight, Sunday June 11th, 2006
Room 6, Hotel Su Talleri, Macomér

From midnight to 7am, a seemingly endless series of 'what ifs' clanged and resounded through my empty brain. But each time, every aspect of our incarceration that I explored pointed me not at the dubious political endgames and Anglophobia of Judge Barry Hertzog as the catalyst for our Kidnapping, but instead to the collective guilt of Mick, Brent and Dean, whose shared need to prove their hooligan credentials at Italia '90 had followed hot on the heels of their spectacular, ahem, non-attendance at Hillsborough. Call yourselves Liverpool fans? But then, even I was somewhat responsible for their predicament. What if I *hadn't* been a lifelong Nottingham Forest fan with connections? What if I *hadn't* bowed to pressure from Mick's sister Sharon for Forest tickets to keep her 13-year-old twins nice-and-safe up my end, far from poor Liverpool's Leppings Laners? What if Mick's social worker persona had *not* kicked in and forced the twins to hold their tongues as jeering Forest fans at first mistook the flailing behaviour of the dying Liverpool fans for Hooliganism? And what if that total teenage hardcase Brent – thereafter always so utterly guilty, emasculated and humili- ated at being up the wrong end – hadn't been excluded by an insensitive headmaster for nihilistically spraying swastikas on Everton's walls just one month after Hillsborough? 'Everything means nothing,' commented Brent to the judge at the time. Fair enough, I'd thought. As the twins' blood uncle, Mick the social worker had thereafter felt obligated by his sister to look after Brent's case. But as both Brent and Dean already stood six-foot-three, Mick had soon conveniently forgotten their tender ages, press-ganging these two highly resentful electronica obsessives into his Brits Abroad project, and thereafter using their extreme youth to enlist/entrap a young cool drummer. Which is precisely why Brent and Dean had – on encountering half of the Italian cop force on their tail at Italia '90 – spent the entire 131 chase spraying squeaky dog toys in Uncle Mick's face and goading him more and more and more into proving just how much of a Brit Abroad he really was. Ooooooohhhhhhhhhhhh. These were some thorny problems we'd faced.

As I drifted in and out of consciousness in the June heat of this Sardu Su Talleri night, the click-clack of the trains crossing main street served this time to awaken me back in that summer of 1990, or so it seemed from the now scorching heat. Now I was lying in my white stall, chained and smiling nearly hysterical. For what would my own life have become had I not been lactose intolerant? I sweated and trembled with relief at my luck. For, after starving us all for the first three days of the kidnap, some very tall and rank-smelling long-haired cunt in an apron had walked in nonchalant-like and asked us all in splendid pseudo-Sard if we 'required spaghetti?' As all of us were Westerners unused to three days of enforcèd fasting, we leapt at the chance and all but me accepted the lanky twat's offer of 'Pecorina'. A good cheese, explained Mick from his Sardu vantage point, and Brent and Dean concurred. Not me, sorry, says I. I'm lactose intolerant. How's your tomato sauce? Only then did we discover how royally that long-haired cunt had set us up. The Sardu cheese ends in an 'o' – Pecorino. End it in an 'a' – Pecorina – and those three had all just agreed to anal sex. Thereafter, Mick, Brent and Dean got bummed every third day in the white stalls. Bummed and never fed. I got beaten up every day and never fed. The munter that did the bumming had a hacking cough that reminded Mick of his old chemistry teacher Colin Best. So, before each bumming, Mick recited this poem to calm himself down: *Faster than a speeding ticket, headlong to disaster, cheesy as his middle wicket, dreadlocked as a Rasta. No choice as you bend-and-scrape that mad Jap's Eye, it* will *dislodge your kack. Why? Besty's back!* And every time I'd sat in my white stall, listening to that plaintive chant ringing out from the full six-foot-three frame of my dear friend the poet Goodby, how I'd resented even one of his dubious rhyming couplets being wasted on such evil, twisted endeavours. I didn't want Mick to make a cult character out of Besty. That evil Bum Chum deserved a surly sorry saddo's name – not fucking Besty. But as my own sphincter had remained intact, I'd felt an obligation to grant ye Bard his metaphor . . . and held my peace.

13. SYMPATHY FOR THE DEVIL

4am, Sunday June 11th, 2006
Room 6, Hotel Su Talleri, Macomér

Lying inert in the heat at Su Talleri, as Macomér's sunrise birds piped each other a Sunday greeting, I pictured Mick asleep at his mother's house in Manchester, tossing and turning endlessly on the narrow travel mattress under the stairs where Gabriella used to keep her Brasso. After the kidnap, Mick had initially sought the refuge of his old teenage bedroom, still be-stickered with *Peanuts* cuttings and comforting sayings from E. E. Munkey. But as the novelty of the kidnap had faded at last from those T-Zers columns of the national music press, still the ignominy of that mysterious Sardinian Affair could be experienced every day at a simple buying-fizz-down-the-corner-shop level. Moreover, the notoriety of the Brits Abroad case and the curious, scurrilous, almost 'tut-tut' Victorian manner with which the press had reported it had ensured that Mick nowadays – rather than do battle with the outside world – found it far easier to hole up under Gabriella Goodby's stairs with his fizz, his promo poster of Lou Reed's *Berlin* and fifty-plus Charles M. Schultz paperbacks. By the late '90s, the sociopathic M. Goodby had begun to be considered whacked-out enough to be press-worthy, especially after a Thames TV crew headed north and filmed a second documentary of him under the stairs. But when Mick, in lieu of payment, had accepted the TV crew's offer of a Green Screen paintjob for his dugout, they had humiliated him throughout the film, cheap video FX portraying him as though flying Arabian Nights-like through a starlit sky. Worse still, they even got vicious blobs of Chroma-key green on his beloved *Berlin* poster, for fuck's sake! After that debacle, nearly half-a-decade passed before Mick re-emerged in any public capacity. Oh, it's Oz! Oh, it's Gong! Oh, it's God! Never knowing what uncalled-for harshness might be expectorated in his direction should any cruel randomers stray his way during a corner shop fizz offensive, instead, Mick refused to take risks any longer, malingering in his dugout under the stairs and letting the fizz wagons deliver right to his door. Vimto, Corona, Kola Bear: everyone delivered. Six-foot-three and taking up no space at all. And then out of nowhere, around 2003, came Exercise Club. All Mama Gabriella's doing apparently. Fed up with Mick joking and mimicking her yoga kriyas, his tiny spitfire of a Sardinian mother told him to wake up, that he was good, that he should start taking it seriously. Still making a big joke of it – as Mick is always wont to – he nevertheless secretly joined a yoga class and got great at it. Within the year, Mick had convinced half the women in his street to join his own 'Exercise Club', emphatically denying the presence of yoga or anything spiritual in his teachings. Smartest move ever. Attendances soared and locals started to have more time for his madness. Even better for his agoraphobia, Mick's Exercise Club CD sets became even more successful through his mail order business. I've never seen such a PR job! It's all a fudge, of course. Surrounded by ladies at his Exercise Club, Mick's promo photos portray a picture of fine mental health and robust physical vigour. But really Mick's Exercise Club is just for two days per week. Mick rents his space out from Ken Heathcote, the *Fatigues* Magnate. And for the other five days, he just keeps a low low profile at home. Never leaves his room. Never lets anybody in. But that two days of Exercise Club per week is Mick's lifeline. And while he's got that lifeline, he's still Mick Goodby – just.

14. NOT EVERYBODY GOT *BUMMED*

5am, Sunday June 11th, 2006
Room 6, Hotel Su Talleri, Macomér

Having only four hours previously examined close-up the grue-some Bastille of our kidnap *and* viewed it through the keen lens of my cosmically rejuvenated Being, the tragic early deaths of Brent and Dean Garrett stuck more than ever in my psychic craw. Gone. And Goner: despatched without honour. And if the black events acted out within that fascist monstrosity had reduced the remarkable poet-ruffian M. Goodby, himself already thirty-two years old, to a mentalised splash, what chance had there been precisely for twins on the edge of their fourteenth birthday? How I hated to waste time with 'what ifs' and hind-sight. But the reality of Dean's suicide was just too stringent to confront right now, and my psychic hackles were up. What if? What if? What if?

Bathing in the stream at Faraway Field yesterday, as Rob Dean's exquisite guitar solo had pealed out its exultant themes, I'd registered – and possibly for the first time – not only how great was his musical contribution to Brits Abroad, but also how essential his place at Italia '90 should have been, had it not been for Mick's crazy ego and clueless career decision to bully Rob into swapping his six-string-razor for Brits Abroad's drum stool just as 'Last Tango in Paris' had entered the BBC Top 75. Viewing it only as a demotion and having none of it, Rob had quit with the song at number 73, and then regretted the purity of his decision for the rest of his life. So did several of us, but for different reasons. The presence at Italia '90 of Uncle Rob 'Hardcase' Dean – the twins' Godfather whence came Dean Garrett's first name, for fuck's sake – would most certainly have prevented Mick from risking their safety. Tough enough? At Austria's East Tyrol, Rob had even poked the ref up the arse with a flag he'd just nicked off a linesman. He was the gaffer, our central defender. He was Tony Adams. Thus, feeling so very cheated out of *Top of the Pops*, Rob went on a total bender. Then, just before Italia '90, completely AWOL. After all the months of hard work he'd endured convincing Mick he could become a singer, slowly divining melodies from Goodby's near-chromatic warbling, then press-ganging various younger Brits into impromptu rehearsals, the desperately hurt guitarist had felt obliged to stay back in the UK as a protest against his lack of recognition. Talk about being conspicuous by your absence! What if Rob *had* kept his date with Italia '90? Would his presence have tipped the balance back our way?

Now, from my Su Talleri bedroom, I was pitched back to those days just prior to Italia '90, not through Time Travel on this occasion, more likely through lucid dreaming brought on by my sensitivity to Dean's suicide and proximity to Sardu Cheese Hell. Apparently right back there in Gabriella's front room, I again experienced the uncanny power of Brits' sudden media success holding us all under its 1990 spell, as the empire-dreaming Poet Goodby declaimed grandly over the phone to Uncle Rob Dean in mock-noble tones.

MICK: Strategy, you cunt, I'm light years ahead of the pack. Faith and a plan of action said Fido Castrol. Sack the electric axe and polish the club, that's all I'm asking of you. It's the

Rave Era. So we're taking it down an Evolutionary notch or three. Italia's gonna be a Robert Gravesian venture of mythical proportions. We're walking in and we're fucking taking their Poett beachhead. Poett: for a poet! Fidel said with hindsight, he'd only needed 10 to 15 for the revolution. Fuck me if we can't take their soppy Ultras down with just you, me, the Rock, Gaz Have-a-laugh, Stu and Doughy, then we're short-order cooks without one tall order among the lot of us, and not one of us save Stu under six-foot-tall. Save Stu? Get me! C'mon now! I'll have to write that down.

At the other end of the phone, however, Rob Dean's year zero had already commenced. No, he would *not* play drums in Brits Abroad, he said. He would take his guitar chords and FX where they would be better appreciated. But, Rob asked, could he please have his copy of Happy Mondays' *Bummed* back now that Mick had learned from Shaun Ryder all the tricks of the Non-Singer? Burn. Mick got off the phone fit to explode, heaved a bearish sigh and stared right past me.

MICK: Your fucking brother-in-law just quit the Brits.

Turn it on me, why dontcha? Fucking hell . . . just because Rob and I had both dated the extremely gorgeous Czywczynsky sisters throughout the previous year! But now that Rob had quit the band, Mick was truly kippered. By forgetting that barely eighteen months previously, he himself had been no more than an impromptu pre-footy match pub rhymer, Mick had now ejected that very guru, that very *patient* guru who had facilitated the poet's enormous journey, his own recklessness thereby guaranteeing self-termination in the process! Who else would have had the patience but Rob? Who but Rob could make head or tail of the early Goodby vocal delivery? What's *that* accent? *Who* you being now? And who but Rob had cared enough to sift through and edit pages of Mick's supposedly long-finished poetry book simply in order to create studio-worthy material for Brits Abroad? Without Rob's persistence and editing, would Mick have even published his 'Rave poetry volume' *Juan Fluorescent (The Cuckoo's Nest)*? It's debatable. Rob Dean's departure, dismissal, whatever-you-call-it, that weekend before *Top of the Pops*, would actually signal the true end of the Brits as a creative force. The catchy songs like 'Last Tango in Paris' and '100 Watt the Funk' soon disappeared to be replaced with spirited atonal workouts and squeaky toy Uber-thrashes. Nevertheless, when I delivered to the Great Goodby my musical analysis regarding his Rob Dean-less re-shuffle, Mick appeared entirely unfazed, having already ascended to a more impervious phase of stardom.

ROCK: Bass synth, squeaky toys, drums and samples: that's all you'll be without Rob on stage.
MICK: We're a teen band now, youth. The twins have got their mate Kev Noggins in. Rob was too old, he's thirty-four.
ROCK: You're thirty-two yourself!
MICK: So what? If Kev Noggins is seventeen, I can *be* old. With Kev on drums, Brent and Dean can shoulder one Old Git, namely me: the singer, the wordsmith. We coulda stuck Rob round the back like Pedro out of Frankie. The moustache, the lot. But he wasn't having any.

So Mick the poet wanted it all, whatever *all* was in his fragmented mind. Change the rules, why can't I? Back then, Mick had been engorged with himself and his own possibilities. But he *had* been right and Brits Abroad *were* a teen band. Squirting out 'samples' from their squeaky rubber dog bones across the rowdier Saturday morning TV shows, Brent and Dean and their new bongo compadré Kev Noggins caught the Rave Era like no other youths. All three were so ultra tall, good-looking and young that their enthusiasm drove the BBC props department, particularly the females, to new pinnacles of achievement. *Saturday Special* supplied a sandpit for Kev Noggins, who sat cross-legged in Union Jack shorts playing his bongos, his Johnny Ramone hairdo surmounted by the tiniest plastic tourist bowler hat this side of Action Man. Then *Playaway* unprompted brought in a Rave-orange mobile cement mixer filled with ice and bright cans of fizzy drinks for Mick to interact with. Thusly, the slow rise up the charts of 'Last Tango in Paris' enabled the four Brits – through the kids' shows – to graduate more gently towards becoming TV stars. So by the time of their *Top of the Pops* debut, Mick & Co. had clocked their own moves enough on the box to know what suited and what didn't. And of course, the embattled seafront imagery won through every time: the cement mixer, the barbed-wire barricades and sandpit gun emplacements all inspired by Golan Heights news footage. Kate W. Bush, look out! But whilst all of this Brits TV skulduggery was conspiring to rile up the greater portion of World Nazidom and have them plotting Brits' rapid downfall, the band's success had only been achieved through the sacrifice of one Rob Dean and his tattooed forearms. And what a price to pay! Yes, Mick had a way of getting his way but oh, what a Pyrrhic victory!

15. THE DECOFFINATED CAFÉ

6am, Sunday June 11th, 2006
Room 6, Hotel Su Talleri, Macomér

Lying prone upon my too short single bed, naked except for my EasyAir eye-mask, I hovered in a warm psychic bath somewhere between sleep and lucid dreaming. Having spent the whole night steeping myself once more in those infamous 'events of sixteen years ago', those darkest hours which I so rarely addressed nowadays, it suddenly occurred to me that four women in similar circumstances to ourselves might well after-the-event have discussed their shared nightmare somewhat more than we. But, in truth, that romantic notion took no account of Brent's instant suicide, nor did it address the delicate family balance that had existed in the relationship between Mick, his sister Sharon, his mother Gabriella and the twins.

Nevertheless, as these obscure reasoning systems of my 6am mind signalled to their host that it was time to shut down for the night, I registered that this first of my final days had been lived at far too accelerated a pace. Poor Anna! But having at last forced open the airlock between myself and those so wilfully long forgotten 'events of sixteen years ago', I was – as I more and more re-evaluated our Clan of '89 – fascinated rather than offended at the speed with which Mick Goodby had, just that Rave Spring, graduated from Liverpool F.C. pub rhymer with a single power-rant under his belt to full-on People's Poet with a canon that could have challenged John Cooper Clarke, Ed Banger and John the Postman all three, albeit still mostly delivered with R.A.F. brat Goodby's terminally unsatisfying drifting dialect. Where you from now? But as Mick's sole claim to fame had until that time lain only in the bellowed Half Biscuit manner of his pub oratory – literally screaming to be heard – it is here essential to emphasise that Mick's remarkable transformation that Spring of '89 was in no way an Anfield-o-centric Vision brought on by his legions of Liverpool 'Last Tango in Paris' pub admirers. For fans he had virtually none, the mass merely tolerators and the clueless.

TOLERATOR: What's that cunt in the chunky knit jumper and
    Noddy Holder mask blathering on about now?
CLUELESS: That's no chunky knit jumper; that's his face.

No, dreary me, no. Instead, the making of the M. Goodby as we know him – 'What, the Jungian Chance Dancer with the Teen Dervishes?' Yeah man, that Mick Goodby – was the result of one intensely homosocial (as in 'womenless') Rave Fortnight spent in the Peak District watching me DJ at Arthur Tadgell's Dehydrated, followed by several inspirational weeks of hanging around in a mental café with two gorgeous ladies, several pencilled-up scruffs AKA wannabe rappers, and one extremely posh bloke whom we'd all in time come to love madly.

It all started that rainy Tuesday morning in mid-March when Gary Have-a-laugh ran out of skins, and popped up the hill to score some Green Rizla from our local head shop Sleeping Stoner, Hidden Stash. He came back raving about a new café at the old undertaker's between Betty Bothways' vintage bazaar and our head shop. Smart! But Have-a-laugh, quite atypically I noted at the time, also laid so many Rizlas on our combined households – no more than 50 yards separated us all – that none of us in the neighbourhood had need to ascend the hill. Thereafter, Stu and Gary started having breakfast out, a highly unusual event about which we were immediately suspicious. For Stu, despite his Manny lad accent, is a Scot from Aberdeen – one Charles Stuart – and hates spending money, e.g.: after an away game Little Chef, he'll even goal-hang rich middle-aged Liverpool fans at the till, patting his pockets. So anyway for about two weeks we never saw either of those two Rave entrepreneurs, except when they laid mucho skins upon our homes. Then one night after work, Betty Bothways – the sweetest, faggiest middle-aged man – dropped some taffeta and lace round at ours for our good mate Doughy (currently out of town), and mentioned that the two new café proprietresses were buying up only the most figure-hugging dresses that passed through Betty's shop. Dammit! Of course, the two-week absence of Messrs Stuart and Laugh was immediately explained. Hot totty hath beckoned.

The next morning, M. Goodby, Uncle Rob Dean and I took long baths, then strolled uphill for breakfast at the former undertakers, now immaculately renamed 'The Decoffinated Café' and actively trading upon its former occupation with dark lighting, black table cloths, black bunting, huge daytime candles and two voluptuous young café owners by the curious names of Memorial and Buriel Czywczynsky, whose undertaker parents had recently been killed in a horrific head-on collision. Both mum and dad had been of Moravian extraction, that strange Christian cult that worships the Centurion's spear wound in Christ's side as a surrogate vagina. Don't ask me about it, I'm just the reporter. Those three weird guys out of the Smoke Dopes are of the same 'religion'. Anyway, such questionable tenets as the Moravians were rustling up during the 1800s had got all but the wealthiest kicked out of everywhere, though many Moravians had, like the Czywczynsky family, survived here and there as undertakers, mortuary surgeons and other queasy occupations. The Decoffinated Café, however, was the least queasy establishment I'd ever experienced and, opening as it did on our part of the hill, facilitated a real blossoming of talent that Spring '89 Offensive (as Mick would come to bill it with extreme hindsight). A sparkling clean café serving superb food, and all under the management of two very gorgeous ladies, our entire gang relocated to the D-Cough, Mick's nickname claiming the whole establishment for our new Beat Poet phase. I myself fell for Memorial's epic funereal humour and perpetually black figure-hugging dresses and we immediately embarked on a deep and real Moravian love affair, whilst her almost equally 'becoming' younger sister Buriel – to rhyme with 'Muriel', by the way – became entangled with Rob the Dean, who sat around the D-Cough lovesick faking flamenco music on his acoustic.

These new romantic arrangements of ours having left both of the failed suitors Stuart and Have-a-laugh out in the cold, they rallied superbly and, finally – across the Gothick tables of the café – began to put flesh on their until-then-imaginary rap outfit the Kit Kat Rappers. Wonders never cease! For three full years previously, the Kit Kat Rappers had been no more than a useful invention of Stu, Gary Have-a-laugh and our agree-with-everybody mate Yeh-Yeh, their invented band name simply there to add 'musician' clout to their places on the guestlists of Liverpool, Manchester and the Peak District. 'Made any records?' doormen would ask. Er. 'Do us a rap?' Er. When all three walked into Dehydrated one weekend, a Solzhenitzian picture of Near Death the lot of them, all on the same bad drugs with streaming colds and all three making no attempts to locate the Day Nurse, Mick clustered them together under some art-photo of Klaus Schulze, zipped up each into his own snorkel parka then took two sweaty polaroids. Giving them one copy between the three as reference, Goodby now got prescriptive.

MICK: Let illness be your Kit Kat Rappers metaphor. Illness through drugs. 'Beam me up, Scotty, there's no foil on these Kit Kats!' That's what Have-a-laugh came out with on his first Euro-jaunt with me. That's as pure a lyric as I've ever encountered. So concentrate on the Night Nurse market, the teenage tearaways isolated in Lincolnshire, East Anglia, the wank parts of England where not even squidgy black shall ever obtain its petro-chemical hold. Call the first single 'Second Class to Dottingham' after that shit TV ad in the British Rail ticket office – remember where Billy Too Bunged holds up the queue?

None of the Kit Kat Rappers had written songs before, but now they had their metaphor. All three remembered this shit TV commercial and all three were desperate to rap. Like Morris Dancers practising on waste ground behind a car park, you'd catch them in the D-Cough Gents 'putting it to' themselves in the mirror. Now they got it, finally. Now they understood that the Rave Era was upon us and that hip quality rhymes could be traded for sniff, blow and suck. Or even, heaven forbid: cash! And although their Kit Kat creations weren't really Rap at all, more of a sub-sub-Madness Cheeky Cockney barrow boy type-of-thing, that debut song 'Second Class to Dottingham' sealed the Kit Kat Rappers as a Triple Brotherhood.

And thereafter the D-Cough was cooking. When the lovely sisters fancied evening opening, Rob Dean painted the façade with immaculate stripes in white and fluorescent orange that became noticeable only after dark, then put himself forward as the evening's lone moustachioed Mariachi. Viva Zapata. And death to the Apathista! Moreover, the hill in that current incarnation showcased the perfect environment for creativity. Its park, its pubs, its perfect combination of shops – a great barber's, greengrocer's, quality butcher's, an antique shop even – everything enabled us to stick around all day, every day. Until suddenly from within the nurturing bosom of our elevated scene flowed poetry a-plenty and all from the fountainhead of M. Goodby; great stashes of the stuff. A handy audience, a theatrical atmosphere, and a café with a floor large enough from which to declaim new poems whenever business was slow enough. Moreover, Mick had – in Memorial and Buriel – two lovely women who admired him enough to order into the café 'only for Mick' any unusual or exotic fizzy drinks that they could locate. So quite why ye Bard sought to name his debut café opus 'Bad in Bed', well, none of us could have hoped to guess. On hearing Mick's performance of the aforementioned, I was somewhat relieved to discover that the contents of the poem were, though still hair-raising, considerably less sphincter-puckering than I'd anticipated:

Bad in Bed

1.
I'm bad in bed,
I can't sleep,
I steal cars,
I drive them round & round in bed,
Till the tread of the tyres
Catches fire to my pillow,

And the whole neighbourhood
Looks at me and says that:
I'm no good,
I'm not right in the head,
But the truth is
I'm just bad in bed.

2.
I'm bad in bed,
I can't dream
Not even for a minute,
Till a cop pops his head up
And pretty soon I'm in it;
I'm pursued in the nude
By the sweet law enforcement,
Who send for reinforcements
To give me an endorsement
For walking on the road
'Stead of driving on the pavement,
They don't like my behavement
And send me off to bed,
Where I'm bad,
Like I said.

3.
I forewarn them but what?
Do they never pay attention?
Or think I've made it up?
Like some others I could mention?
Who listens when my dad
Says: 'My Lad needs detention'?

Who needs his intervention?
I can't be forced,
I can't be nursed,
I can't be strong-armed or co-erced,
It's not an illness,
Like I said:
The truth is I'm just bad in bed.

Now of course, due to my decades of, ahem, rich cultural contacts – musicians, poets, authors, film directors, drug dealers, criminals, smugglers and the like – and the extrovert nature of Arthur Tadgell's late-70s music scene from which I emerged, I've always – even during my mid-80s lowest drugged-out ebb – always always enjoyed such a fulsome and richly alternative lifestyle that letting close friends share in that lifestyle continued at all times to be among my greatest joys in life. So when I saw The Decoffinated Café scene springing up so fertile right there on our own hill, and having learned through my own recent Dance successes with those Dayglo Maradona 12″s that it's never too late to start afresh, well, I was determined to disseminate some of this late-80s D-Cough largesse around these Loved-Up Islands. Better still, Gary Have-a-laugh and Stu shared my determination to help transform that café on-the-hill into a cultural fire-beacon. Here be greatness! Watch this place! Thus, through our myriad social connections, it wasn't too long before the D-Cough attracted fascinated music producers, local video makers and the like, each additional guest further imbuing our scene on-the-hill with the kind of instant Clamour that could never in ten million years have been struck around Anfield way. Remember these dark days. For it was – in this Rave Era of the UK – a time of huge duplicity. Those same council estate cunts that had, two years previously, been happily cutting down our kind in the streets were all of them suddenly claiming to be slinging their lot in with us. Hello, Anoraksia Nervosa's 'Baggy on the Inside'. Fuck off. Hello, The Farm's 'Groovy Train'. Fuck off. Your fifteen re-mixes cannot disguise the vileness of your Endgame. I didn't want to be hugged by enlightened council-house-and-violent types with their concealed weapons. Mick the suspicious Social Worker wrote his MDMA poem 'I'll Love You Till It Wears Off', and nailed their itinerant truths entirely. But I'm sure that none of us could have anticipated just how in opposition to these raggedy-arsed Know Nothings, these Salt-of-the-Earth planet squatters, would be the next great character to pass across the portals of ye D-Cough . . .

It all kicked off one morning when some under-caffeinated arsehole left the so-called Culture section of *The Guardian* in Goodby's regular seat. And if that wasn't enough to set the world off kilter, Mick spent the next hour raging at 'the sheer White Supremacist smugness' of an article therein that declared the Pun to be Dead! Oh, Mick was nearly suicidal about this.

MICK: Only utter yokel stay-at-homes could make such Nazi assertions. How can these pseudo bastards, with all of their millions of choices of English words to hand, make judgements against foreign languages that did *not* choose to steal from all of their neighbours? We English alone can attempt to live without puns only because our voracious English language has – during our World Escapades – shamelessly looted the languages of our victims then chewed and mangled their words into English forms. Shame on these semi-intellectual cunts who would diss Japanese just because of its highly limited building blocks of sound. To the Japanese themselves, who rely utterly on elaborate systems of punning, their language's absence of foreign words is its plus! Nincompoops! Utter Flat Earthers! Might as well be published in the U.S.

STU: (*Passing with a tray of cheese-on-toast*) You what?

MICK: You heard.

And it was still in this highly enraged state of mind that ye Bard remained when a couple of us first noticed the extremely tall, good-looking couple sheltering in our doorway from a brief hilltop squall. Both over six-feet-tall and displaying fearsomely upright posture, the two had the look of foreign royalty, probably Scandinavian aristocracy from the extravagant manner in which these two blondies were kitted out. Out of place or what! She was about forty, effortlessly beautiful and clad head-to-toe in immaculate white outdoor gear, over which her Gore-Tex coat, also white, stretched fully to the ground. He on the other hand was a mid-20s shocker, got up in a dreadful red-white-and-blue skiing outfit, big white panoramic Buggles shades and the most Canadian boots this side of Bigfoot. Foreigners of great exotic provenance, obviously. But from where on earth? In the café, meals were prepared and eaten, diners came and left, but still the two exotics hovered in our doorway, Video Killed The Radio Stars occasionally peering in. Until, at long last, this extravagantly dressed Olympic skier, this Prince of Zermatt, this Captain of the Cresta Run or whoever he was when he was at home, gingerly pushed open the café door then strode gallantly over to Buriel at the till.

STRANGER: I say most awfully would you mind? My mother and I have been waiting in your doorway, but but but our ride appears to be late. Would you most awfully mind if I used your . . . I'm in no position to stay and eat, but I'd dearly love to have use of your . . . (*Staring around obviously*)

BURIEL: The toilet? Aah! Of course, my desperate duck. Just barge in, no one's using it at present. (*She points, he hurries away at speed*)

HAVE-A-LAUGH: (*Loud enough*) We don't employ the soft stuff on these premises!

BURIEL: Gary Have-a-laugh!

The be-Buggled stranger now safe atop the crapper, the D-Cough lit up immediately with questions and flummoxed asides. What accent's that? Was that Quickborn badge on his anorak a religious symbol? Could they both be Northern Irish? And all the while, we artists, poets and creative scenesters craned our necks to view more clearly the beautiful white Goddess without, whose near-queenly outdoor attire, unwavering posture and economy of movement held us all constantly in her thrall. Mick meanwhile, until recently mixing up the magic over in Poet's Corner, had clearly had his curiosity piqued by the stranger, for he had by now cast down his pencil, picked up an ice-cold Kola Bear and drifted down to that black-and-white checked hinterland twixt punter and till, that treacherous food highway across which all meals must travel. And there Mick lingered, all fizzed up and ready to People Watch right in the face of this beguiling outsider.

Now the iffy plumbing round at the D-Cough was its weakest attribute by far, and the lavatories throbbed whenever a flush was unleashed, letting off a long chain reaction right down in the kitchen taps. But simply by having presented us all with such beautifully clean and well-painted washrooms, the bountiful Memorial and Buriel daily captured the hearts of their fascinated clientele. Therefore, when our stranger re-emerged from his toilet sans

Buggles shades, his eloquent thanks and high praise for the sisters' levels of hygiene started us all up into a curious conversation.

BURIEL: Please don't take this the wrong way, but you look really handsome without those mad sunglasses.
STRANGER: Thank you, you're very kind. And I must say thanks most awfully for your kindness in letting me have use of your charming facilities.
BURIEL: Ah, that's very sweet of you to say so. Do you hail from these parts? You know, England?
STRANGER: (*Smiling widely*) Oh yes, I am English, well, half-English. That's my mother outside. She's . . . the non-English part of me, although that's not actually right either. Anyway, I must dash or I shall be late for my ride. But I can't thank you enough.

And with that, the be-ski-suited two-metre 'hunk', as Buriel would thereafter always refer to him, hurried outside to loiter again for another ten uncomfortable doorway minutes with his extremely lovely mother. Going nowhere. This couple was clearly going nowhere. Anyway, before we could work out an appropriate manner in which to invite our divine mother-and-son into temporary shelter chez D-Cough, the divine duchess suddenly popped a quick kiss on her son's snowy white cheek, and dashed across the road into the antiques shop. Immediately back through the door strode our returning stranger.

STRANGER: Hello. (*Smiling and nodding at Stu*) Hullo, hello again (*catching Gary Have-a-laugh's big old grin*). Hi there, hello. (*Approaching the till*)
BURIEL: Back so soon?

STRANGER: I appear to have enough time for breakfast. My mother's driver Serge has been held up at Manchester Airport. I *am* rather hungry in all honesty. Do you by any chance do a Full English Breakfast?

Now Memorial, it must be established, right about that time in Spring '89, cooked the best Full English Breakfast this side of the Channel – and that's not just because I was living at her place and making gorgeous Moravian love to her every day. Oh dear me no. Her poached eggs cooked in a small, deep frying pan were unsurpassable. Her rough Polish hash browns with sour cream and apple sauce blew my mind. And her two-tier bubble-and-squeak with both crunchy and floppy cabbage was considered a separate meal in itself by my closest associates. So it was entirely to her credit that Memorial, on hearing this curious quasi-English conversation wafting across from the till, put off her apron, picked up her pencil and strode purposefully over to discover what specifically this otherworldly stranger believed – at least from his own worldview – to constitute a Full English Breakfast?

STRANGER: Madam, that's a fascinating question but it's somewhat loaded. I myself hail from two genuinely separate worlds, therefore my own breakfast is inevitably culled from each. But I was hoping this late morning for a rather formidable fry-up. I can smell (*inhaling deeply*) the bacon and the eggs and the toast and the mushrooms. Tomatoes also. So I should like to begin with a plate of that, and let's see what else we can chase on to the platter.

MEMORIAL: You *are* posh, aren't you? Like *really* posh? But you're not foreign royalty?

STRANGER: I'm half-English and I'm half-Anglish. Therefore,

I bill myself as an Anglo-Englishman if you get my drift. My father, the Earl of Bradbury, hails from Dorset and Devon, whilst my lovely mother, the Duchess of Quickborn, was raised at Damp on the east coast of Angeln, whence came your own island's language via our Anglo-Saxons. Much of Angeln is low-lying farmland that would remind you of home, even place names. I have an Anglish aunt who lives at Wintermoor on the border of north Germany, and another in Loose. There's a Kentish town of the same name. And Angeln is all so close to Hamburg that commuting from London is infinitely possible at a push.

By now, both of the beautiful Czywczynsky sisters were mouth agape at the till, whilst the perma-grinning Gary Have-a-laugh lolled over the far end of the front counter at a quite ridiculous angle, determined to catch this Cultural Event from a news-worthy enough perspective. Was this all just horseshit that was being spoken to them? The Decoffinated Café's clientele were silent, hanging on every word of this riveting exchange, as Mick, Stu and the rest of us clued in to this lovely being so similar and yet so totally alien to us all.

BURIEL: Shall I start your food?
STRANGER: Do you have good sausages?
BURIEL: Fresh this morning from the organic butcher's across the road.
STRANGER: Jolly good show. Any freshly squeezed orange juice? (*She nods*)
MICK: Memorial, let him taste your two-tier bubble. (*Smiling at stranger*) Give you a chance to get her cookery charms in proper context.

STRANGER: Thanks, most awfully kind. I'm torn between taking what's on offer and demanding the world . . . you know, p-p-p-playing the role, as it were. (*To Memorial behind the grill*) Could I have the beans in a small separate dish, please?

MICK: Don't you all eat devilled kidneys for breakfast? There's that classy butcher opposite.

STRANGER: Yes, where to stop I suppose. Our Scotch relatives up in Fifeshire would include such curiosities as haggis, tattie scones, even white pudding. Even, God Forbid, small baked hedge-birds. Euwwww! Down here we have no need of making a grand deal of some forlorn local dish achieved with just four ingredients.

HAVE-A-LAUGH: (*Eyes ablaze*) What about Carlsberg Export?

STRANGER: Ha ha, yes. I do see your point, Old Fellow. But we English – being always the invaders – have never had to make do with such compromises. Imagine sugarless porridge!

STU: (*Suddenly Scots*) I love salt on my porridge!

STRANGER: Unfortunately, Old Son, your ancestors were *obliged* to salt their porridge as the English chose never to bring sugar north of Stirling. For a Scotch child in those days, raiding the molasses barrel outside the pigsty was the nearest they ever got to a taste of sugar. (*To Buriel*) Madam, knowing the erratic schedule of my mother's chauffeur, I'd suggest we leave the devilling of kidneys until a later date. Do please serve up what's already cooked in your pan, and that shall most certainly suffice.

But the stranger's fascinating words had stirred up in us such a Cultural hornet's nest that Messrs Stuart and Have-a-laugh had already toddled off to the organic butcher's, where they had retrieved more than enough high-class kidneys to satisfy our downhill slalom champion. And though their return had coincided with that of Serge the Chauffeur, such was the D-Cough excitement that the Stranger enjoyed applause every time he tucked into 'What Was On Offer', whilst Buriel fixed him up a little Devilled Travel Kidneys for the hard road back to Anglo-England.

MICK: Everything you said today was interesting. Was it all true?

STRANGER: It's certainly my truth, Old Chap. It's all there on the maps of Europe for you to check out, should you wish. My mother's curious status even makes of me an honorary football coach at Holstein Quickborn F.C., though I'm quite sure they'd beat me soundly were I to impose that right upon the players. And do please understand that I'm Dorset born-and-bred, and privately educated in Somerset – Charterhouse – so many of my accounts of these Anglish places are through holiday eyes and described through my very privileged lens.

And with that, the stranger scooped Buriel into his arms, hugged her generously, saluted us all hilariously and – with a huge grin – declared that he *would* return. Then he handed Mick his business card, retrieved it again immediately, scribbled down 'my cellphone number' then stood about looking for excuses not to leave . . . until his exasperated mother finally pushed the door open and hissed *extremely* pleasantly.

MOTHER: Leander, our ride is very much here.

STRANGER: Oh Birgitta, these lovely people (*extending his arms lavishly so as to include us all*) are playing Klaus Schulze's *Blackdance* in their loos!

The two of them beamed at us from the open café door, then took off in their huge Mercedes estate. I immediately hotfooted it over to where Mick was clutching the stranger's business card, now surrounded by the entire D-Cough clientele. Of the stranger's occupation his card gave no clue. The stranger's name, however, could not disappoint and summed up entirely our previous hour's performance. Mick held up the card and read aloud.

MICK: 'Leander Pitt-Rivers Baring-Gould'.

ROCK: Fair enough.

MICK: (*Chewing each word*) Leander Pitt-Rivers Baring-Gould.

HAVE-A-LAUGH: I know that surname from being a kid at school. I know that name. Didn't his grandma write 'Happy Birthday'?

MICK: (*Smitten*) Leander the Swimmer bearing gifts. Leigh Hunt.

ROCK: (*Clueless*) Fair enough.

MICK: (*Surveying the kitchen mess with his sweeping, gesturing right arm, then declaiming portentously*) Ladies and gentlemen, I think I can speak for us all when I say of that stranger: His was a very Full English Breakfast! (*Cheers, pseudo-posh hear-hears, etc.*)

Thus – with the final inclusion of this curiously beautiful nobleman – was our little gangster gang complete. Thereafter known to our adversaries only by his calorific *nom de guerre*, Leander at football matches became our hooligan lawman, at Mick's behest laying out the English lower classes for saying 'toilet' instead of 'loo', overturning foreign sidewalk cafés that dared to lay their tables with cutlery above the plate, and kicking a gendarme for asking 'Pardon?' rather than the correct posh equivalent 'What?'

Oh, and once even laying out a drunken St. Etienne supporter who'd attempted to pass him port from the right. Bad show, Old Bean (bang!). And in that righteous honeymoon period of Spring '89 – spent in café summit meetings and bathed in the gorgeous nurturing glow of the Czywczynsky sisters – our troupe, nay, our troop had coalesced briefly into a genuine Cultural Force. So we had.

Now, from my bed at Su Talleri, as I grasped and flailed in the early morning Sardu light, desperate to keep a grip on this swift-disappearing memory, I instinctively reached out for Memorial's pneumatic form, yearning for her Moravian love so generously bestowed upon me and for so long. But even Memorial had, like so many other lovers, slipped my bonds too too many years ago. And in exhaustion and grief for the sheer weirdness of this earthly life, my naked Ur-self seized its 7am opportunity to shake free of its fetters, and dived headlong over the side of reality into a sweet, cool pool of dreams. Sleep at last. Sleep at last. Sleep at last. Down and down to the Ocean Floor of Consciousness sank my snoring Ur-self where it could be left alone to be, simply to be. Where nothing but nothing would bother me . . .

16. 'THE REAPER'

Midday, Sunday June 11th, 2006
131, heading south fast to R.A.F. Decimomannu

Baling along through the scorching midday heat of the 131, but now newly enclosed in the Italianate cockpit of a late-1950s Facel Vega luxury supercar, I felt like a doomed man. Not doomed as in 'destined to die soon' – for I knew that choice remained my own – but after yesterday's colossal events and last night's extraordinary reminiscences with the people I'd loved so? Well, I knew that my comeuppance was nigh, for I myself had commenced that Countdown merely by returning to Sardinia. But as these past sixteen years since the Kidnapping had so often seemed merely a waste of daylight, my confrontation last night with the Fascist Cheese Factory of our nightmares had been a roaring success. For its awesome presence alone had precipitated in me an exhausting flood of carefully forgotten memories, a pell-mell micro-tsunami of wild recollections pouring down so thick-and-fast that they entirely breached my selective memory. And so the result was, this noontime, that my branium remained somewhat tortured by my recognition of the beauty and compassion of former lady friends, and by the intense Mithraic fire of my old compadrés. I recognised that I was doomed at a Cosmological level for I am a Higher Being, though cognisant of this fact only on occasion. But whenever *in* that brief Cognisant State, I recognise instantly just how great is the Task expected of me. I was doomed to be judged by the success or failure of my actions; doomed to be judged in as much detail as the Normans had judged the Saxons in their *Domesday Book*. So had I any real chance of achieving my Sardinian Mission in the days allotted? My brief return to the Distant Time of my Ancestors had been so pharmaceutically beneficial that I couldn't help but ache and yearn for that simple life of ephedra and its guaranteed high. But even Time Travellers of my own inestimable age enjoy only glimpses of their other concurrent incarnations, for it is said that too much self-awareness of the Parallel You can lead to a huge build-up of trapped gas, and everybody knows it's the Old Farts that destroy the Universe.

Nevertheless, here we were now, we two. Back together after all, Anna of the generous spirit had not stood me up, not left me to stew at Su Talleri, but had returned joyful and re-charged, ready to continue with my Mission *and* driving the kind of wheels that James Bond would have been proud to be seen in. Why had this lovely lady come back? But I could ask myself that only once before I became overcome by the churlishness of such a question. Better instead to kiss the ground in gratitude that one so open-minded had been booked as my final guide. And as we high-tailed it southwards, Anna and I now kept making accidental eye contact as we both compulsively checked each other out, each of us grinning slightly hysterically, possibly sharing simultaneously the bizarre notion that yesterday's supernatural events had been experienced only in the company of this near complete stranger. And now it was as though both of our inner seven-year-olds were secretly chanting at the other in playground singsong: *I've seen you in your undies! I've seen you in your undies!* However, as both of us were now sitting considerably closer together than yesterday – this being a high-velocity Franco-Suisse sports tourer – it was enchanting to discover that Anna's determined driving expressions and wild-eyed declamations to foolish drivers only increased her magnetism the closer she advanced towards my magnifying glass. Indeed, it was as though only now was I 'registering' Anna, or perhaps re-registering her through the blessèd filter of last night's spectacular reminiscences of Moravian womankind. So, both of us sitting there strapped-in, side-by-side, each slightly smirking at the other, well, as the novelty high-speed situation that it was, I concluded . . . fair enough. And thus in shyness our Sunday conversation started up only just as we zoomed south past the Paulilátino exit of the 131, a full fifteen minutes after our reunion.

ANNA: So much has happened since we last saw each other. (*Patting a sheaf of photocopies piled on the dashboard*) From my sister. Giovanni Lilliu is the best archaeologist in Sardinia. I am very pleased to show you my discoveries about the great Doorways. I have information about Faraway Field *and* about Puttu Oes!

ROCK: (*Mumbling*) Books on this stuff! Thank you so much for all of this. Faraway Field yesterday (*suddenly understanding*) . . . these places are ancient monuments! What an island to live on.

ANNA: (*Smiling*) And my sister thinks for sure that the two oldest Doorways are just near the 131, very near here actually. After R.A.F. Detchy, I can show you the great Doorway of Goronna. If we can find it. But later for my dad I have to ferry this car up to a movie set at Ólbia. Don't worry, I picked a lovely cheap hotel for you nearby overlooking Lake Omodeo. Tonight I can stay with my cousin in Ólbia and I'll retrieve you in the morning. By the way, do you know this famous book of Sardinia?

Anna reached among the sheaf of papers on the dash and handed to me a tiny hardback copy of D. H. Lawrence's *Sea and Sardinia*. Whoa! Better to inquire what pages therein did I *not* know! Why, as one born and bred in Lawrence's own home-town of Eastwood, bawling my way into the world at 39, Barber Street – directly between ye Sage's primary school and child-hood home – these exquisite dark green hardbacks with their gold lettering had pervaded my boyhood existence. Like secular Gideons Bibles, *Sea and Sardinia* could be found on the tables of even the most monosyllabic households in Eastwood, and nearly always in immaculate, unread condition. It was as though the strictly sensible council of our Midland mining town – desperate to divert attention from the Chatterley ways of our most misunderstood son – had deluged Eastwood with *Sea and Sardinia* in a bid to sell Lawrence to locals purely as a travel writer. Fine by Teenage Me – the Sardinia book was certainly less embarrassing than *Lady Chatterley's Lover*, for fuck's sake.

Better still, my super-thorough knowledge of *Sea and Sardinia* had been my perfect method of introduction to my hero Jim Morrison – then just thirty-four years old – when he'd passed through Eastwood on a Lawrence kick during the late '70s. Having just legged it up the hill from school, I was toking a cheeky one outside Eastwood Guitars on the corner of Dovecote Road, when Jim stumbled by all bearded and lean, refused the 'damned ciggy' I offered him, then requested directions to the nearest off licence. Trembling with excitement at meeting one of my big heroes, I'd led him across the road round the back of the Man In Space, where my Auntie Florrie crated us up with free Pale Ale, then we took off on a traipse around D. H.'s fave haunts. Luckily, Eastwood Council's policies had indoctrinated me with sufficient *Sea and Sardinia* to bullshit Jim into believing he was in the presence of the next Thomas Chatterton. I didn't mean to spread it on so thick, but . . . well, I wanted to make an impression, I suppose.

The Jimbo that drank me under the table in Eastwood that night had just returned from Limerick in the W. of Ireland and was nearly suicidal. He said he'd gone in search of the Kelt inside him, but had discovered only the Viking, and that all of his own songs of the sea – his chants, his shanties – had, in that dire hotel room in the Limerick Strand, risen up as one great Canon to beseech him to leave, to run, to quit the city and its environs. Mercy me, I thought. Jim described a chronic and vicious illness-inducing weather depression that filtered permanently east up the mouth of the river Shannon into Limerick city centre, where the sickness malingered, unable to dissipate due to a massive membrane of cloud created by the surrounding mountains. Jim told me that there had been 'such a slough of despond hanging trapped over Limerick' that he'd had to flee from that place and its heinous past. Moreover, on his final night in the Limerick Strand, the civic ghosts of the city's 17th-century leaders – Clanricarde, Hugh Dubh O'Neill and Mayor Piers Creagh FitzPiers – had all visited Jim's hotel room as one spectral deputation, offering their apologia as to why negotiations with the English Parliamentarians had been so devastatingly mishandled. Jim then described how, during a 'bedside vigil' by a spectral being that called itself Aphorismical Discovery, he had unwittingly infuriated the spectre by refusing its 'generous proposal' that Jim compose a new Irish river elegy with these first lines:

'Shannon the Irish bulwark and loyal spouse of the Nation,
Is now become a Prostitute: Free passage to all comers.'

I was seventeen. What do you say? It was the making of me. Later that same night, Jim nearly got me kicked out of the Man In Space for singing an IRA hymn to the tune of 'Deutschland Deutschland Uber Alles' in a Nico accent! Thanks for that! But then Florrie had relented when she'd learned that Jim was the 'Light My Fire' guy. Thereafter, Morrison-at-the-piano had charmed the pants off all the middle-aged ladies by singing a bar-room 'Roadhouse Blues'-version of Paul Evans' shite novelty hit 'Seven Little Girls Sitting in the Back Seat Hugging and A-Kissing with Fred'. And blow-me-down if the tune didn't fit! When the Van Morrison story inevitably came up, I really wanted Jim to tell it purely from his own point of view. A couple of the Man In Space regulars had been big fans of Van, and – knowing nothing of the circumstances – had been quite outspoken about Jim's reported role in Van's strange demise. Jim was quite matter-of-fact but it clearly bothered him a lot. The way he told it, his white witch girlfriend Patricia Kennealy had been 'throwing anagrams' all evening, when it was 'revealed to her' that Jim's own 'Sacred Anagram' was Mr Mojo Risin'. Far out, thinks Jim, and looks around at each of us for encouragement and agreement. We all nod. Fair enough. Great stuff. Anyway, explained Jim, having now learned the sacred nature of the Anagram, he and Patricia next embarked on a through-the-night anagram spree, one that terminated only on Jim's discovery that his great hero Van Morrison's Sacred Anagram was Mr Avo Snorin'! Guffaws all around the pub for that one, especially from the few clueless pre-pop music Old Timers for whom all the names mentioned would have meant sod all. Anyway, the next time Jim was back on the W. Coast, he informed Van the Man that the two of them were re-incarnations of ancient Irish Drinking Poets; and that Jim henceforth wished only to be known by his Sacred Anagram:

'Call me Mr Mojo Risin'.' Van, however, unconvinced by Jim's Sacred Anagram alone and himself already an Irish Drinking Poet of considerable authenticity, was nevertheless tremendously impressed by his own Sacred Anagram Mr Avo Snorin', if only because of its then-current poetic ring. Everyone knew that Van's former producer Bert Burns was at that time making it almost impossible for him to work in America, but Van's stubborn, tough façade was such that no one could estimate his real pain. To Jim, he admitted that his health had been iffy for a while. And by the end of their exchange, Jim told our hushed congregation, he feared greatly that this Sacred Information had 'grievously overwhelmed' his hero. By now taking Jim's comments very seriously, Van Morrison next assembled that legendary loose band of musicians that laid down his brilliant LP *Astral Weeks*. Thereafter, Van the Man – convinced by circumstances that his own Mr Avo Snorin' denoted a truly Cosmic Invitation to the Big Sleep – had embarked on the now-infamous Psychic and Artistic dwindler that resulted in his tragic early death just eighteen months later. At the end of Jim's story, the silence in the Man In Space was so loud you could have released it as an early Tangerine Dream LP.

But throughout this tumbling of ancient memories, each entire thought process lasting no more than a minnow microsecond, I knew I had not nearly enough alacrity of linguistics to confer upon Anna anything but the most basic facts of my D. H. Lawrence connection. So with regard to *Sea and Sardinia*?

ROCK: (*Nodding, slightly dumb grin*) Yes, I know that book.

Here in 2006, however, the enormous sense of duty that I felt towards my tribe obliged me first to get Mick's R.A.F. Decimomannu research out of the way – better boot that personal nostalgia trip well into touch. I'd already missed a couple of his phone calls this morning, and understood that there'd be no peace from ye Bard until all the questions for his Sardinian Novel had been answered. But, of course, speaking of the Devil, my phone rang.

MICK: Section, do you need protection? (*He'd obviously got my cryptic texts*)

ROCK: Youth. We were *not* misunderstood.

ANNA: (*Suddenly very bothered*) Sorry Rock, but what's that blinding light behind us?

MICK: Section, you're on the Mission I can see. So just forget about the research. But I'll still need two things. One. Could big Allied bombers have landed on Detchy airfield? We know Adolf's middling shite could. But the novel needs B-24s, Lancasters, that type of thing. Two. Could I have convincingly mounted an attack on Nationalist Spain from Detchy, or would I have still needed a re-fuel on Menorca on the way back?

ANNA: Rock, what's that massive light behind us?

MICK: Are you at Detchy already? (*The huge steel grille of a truck suddenly blocks the view of the entire back window*)

ROCK: (*Yelling*) They're mental, they're driving us off the road!

ANNA: I can't drive faster (*getting squeaky*) but they're going to kill us! Aaaaaah! Hold on!!!!!!!!

A massive swish of articulated truck roared by, overtaking us far too close – nearly sucking us up into the vortex of its own velocity. Losing temporary control, Anna battled to bring the Facel to a stop, but it was only achieved after we'd spun around a full 180 degrees and been forced off the road. Indeed we were now facing back the same way we came, almost due north, over-looked by the enormous extinct volcano of Mt Arci. As quickly as it was upon us, that enormous articulated Hellwagen was heading off and into the distance, its twenty-two wheels and Leviathan Load leaving our simple V8 supercar coughing up trail-dust by the side of the road, its passengers slack-jawed, bewildered and mouths agape. I looked at Anna.

ROCK: Look at those fucking tail-lights, man. Fucking hell, I thought we were long goners.

ANNA: After so many trials of our yesterday, it seemed not appropriate to tell you. But now that we survive another strange incident I must tell you. This wonderful Facel Vega HK500 is precisely the model that the author Albert Camus died in!

ROCK: What? Camus? Camus the existentialist died in a mega-car?

ANNA: In this mega-car! In his publisher's HK500.

ROCK: (*Inhaling air sibilantly between my teeth*) Did you see the name on the truck? It was called 'The Reaper'.

MICK: (*Obviously forgotten*) Section, I'll call you later.

17. MICK'S SARDINIAN NOVEL

1pm, Sunday June 11th, 2006
131 Úras slip road, opposite Mt Arci

Our Gran Tourismo supercar now mercifully brought to a halt, Anna and I – for several minutes after that Near Impact – were no more than zombies, two petrified zombies still sat both bolt upright in our cockpit's cushy leather aircraft seats. And even though our bruised limbs and whiplash necks remained nursed by the Facel's sumptuous padded knee-and-armrests, its enormous Chrysler 5.8 litre V8 engine still purring as though nothing untoward had taken place, nevertheless I was altogether freaked out that Albert Camus' Ruin had been so unceremoniously shoved off the road by that refrigerated artic. So whilst I unconsciously nibbled at the hard skin on my guitar-playing fingertips and ruminated on the shabby outcome of this well-intentioned bit of M. Goodby research, Anna herself sat in silence staring ahead. Probably thinking about her dad. Moreover, the two of us were still sitting upright like the same pair of petrified planks when the cops arrived ten minutes later, two blue supercharged Fiats tearing right up to us lights a-blazing, six officers disgorging, mucho shouting, mucho verbalese, yet both of the police drivers remained behind the wheel of their stationary vehicles, mindlessly burning up much unnecessary fuel. The head cop was a picture of macho health and strode over to us, grinning widely and shrieking his praise for our beleaguered supercar.

Right about now, I felt as though my duty to ye Bard had just sent us down a very rum cul-de-sac. Echoes of a different time long ago perhaps? Why, with all the injustices suffered by Brent, Dean and Breakfast, was I down here researching solely on Mick's behalf – and with such limited time to get to the bottom of things? Hmmmmm, I took another deep breath and re-thought the situation. I could feel Anna next to me deep in her own re-evaluations, her life force once again surging through her after that Near Impact. And right there and then, I knew that what Mick needed from R.A.F. Decimomannu was not the precise extent of its Avro Lancaster landing facilities, but just that I go there and walk around the camp on his behalf, back there where his gorgeous, tiny Sardinian mother and beanpole six-foot-four R.A.F. father had first danced together. Because Mick was stuck mainly under his mother's stairs, I knew that I now remained his only lifeline, and that lest I drum up some proper Sardu vibe from this end, his current sense of futility and earthbound inadequacy would only spiral him deeper into depression. For, with Dean still yet to be buried, his Goodby– Garrett Clan's elaborate thirtieth-birthday celebrations having been so violently doused, and *me* having just jumped on that EasyAir 757 without even switching the engine of the hire car off? Mick was currently more Home Alone than he could ever have imagined was possible. So any spurious info whatsoever that I could lay upon him would help to douse, or at least smother temporarily that raging Anglo-Catholic guilt in his pumped-up mind. In truth, all that I really knew of Mick's Sardinian novel was its usefulness as a vehicle for his Atonement, a more cushioned world into which he could tumble whenever this real one became too severe.

But even as I sat there still slumped into my lush aircraft seat watching the cops checking Anna's paperwork, then surveying and measuring our skid marks, I knew that there could never be peace under Mick's raging brows. For his entire Worldview since his early teendom had been geared to reflect his stance as the W.A.C.C.O., or White Anglo-Catholic Cop-Out. His own term, his badge of pride: Mick the Poet had developed it as a parallel to the W.A.S.P. concept. Claiming that the Catholic man could never be boss in his own home whilst the priest held sway, Mick's W.A.C.C.O. character relished his priestly enslavement, merely adding it to his 'Addicted To' list somewhere between fizzy drinks and Spanish Civil War history. However, as an eternal Jim Morrisonian who'd felt obliged to throw up his hands in surrender to America's all-pervasive but far too woolly concept of the W.A.S.P., ye Bard's W.A.C.C.O. was just too betwixt and between for me. But Mick's Worldview Problems clearly emanated directly from his mother's various Southern Latitude hang-ups. For, even though Mick's parents had met in the south of the island at R.A.F. Detchy, his mother Gabriella was neither proud of her Italian status nor of her Sardinian home, having been raised in the fiercely Catalan Spanish northwest enclave up at Alghero, then still a safe haven for Barcelona Anarchistas on the run from 'that Moroccan dog Dictator Franco'. So although throughout Mick's R.A.F. childhood in rainy England the gorgeous Gabriella had pined and pined for their brief time down south at Decimomannu, whenever we teenage youths popped round to ogle her stunning Mediterranean looks, any unsuspecting and overly loose-lipped ignoramus among us might receive a thick ear. Indeed, Dayglo Maradona's temporary bass player Hippo once commented dazèdly that he'd spied Gabriella's doppelgänger in Rome on a recent tour, and she whacked him. Really hard in the knees, too, but clearly aiming for the nuts. I'm not kidding.

GABRIELLA: I'm not Italian, I'm not Sardinian, (*screaming*) I'm Catalan Spanish from Alghero, get out!!!

The Schizophrenic Goodbys. Where did that leave Mick? During his childhood at Liverpool's R.A.F. Burtonwood, Mick had been allowed three years in which to develop that combative all-purpose Pan-Mannypool brogue. Preceding that, his sergeant dad had been on trainer conversions up at Wainfleet, in remotest, flattest Lincolnshire, where our Mick and the rest of those forces brats had been unconscious guinea pigs in the M.O.D.'s cheap dealings with Wainfleet's local Kola Bear fizzy pop firm. And it was not until three years after Mick's addiction to the drink was confirmed by doctors that other R.A.F. Wainfleet kids came forward with similar nervous complaints. What had been the M.O.D.'s secret ingredient? Entrapped by State conspiracy since the age of eight, therefore, Mick's poetic methods of dealing with such chronic life problems has been to celebrate them *all*. Forced through addiction to rage through life on Kola Bear, the ever-ardent M. Goodby – at the onset of the Rave Era – even graduated to the more destructive (and far more fluorescently packaged) Kola Max as two fingers to his M.O.D. addictions. But only in this manner has everyone's favourite W.A.C.C.O. been able to grab back from those authoritarian cunts some kind of temporary Personal Responsibility.

Nevertheless, from all the wide-ranging evidence he's asked me to gather down the years – and Mick's Sardinian novel has been long years a-coming – his book appears to me to be the ultimate Conscience Salver, being a kind of great personal repository of information from which ye Bard could alchemically construct and develop some great fictitious Utopia of his own. Conspiracy theories and bizarre alternative technologies abound in Mick's

Sardinian novel, much of it culled from clandestine post-Kidnapping conversations with dubious, obsessive peripheral scene figures like Barcode and Gerard Frawley, whom ye Bard would befriend and make his temporary conspirators purely in order to save reading the latest dodgy theory himself. 'Operation Magic Fire', he'd state triumphantly, pseudo-engraving it into his cheap notepads with a stubby, soft-tipped pencil. 'The Raw Materials & Good Purchasing Company, aha!' 'Spanish–Moroccan Transport Company. Yes, of course.' And all-the-while, a great quaffing of pop would be taking place both in-and-around Goodbyshire, a Norse Orgy of sugar and combative substances whose far-reaching tentacles could leave virtual strangers near-paralysed with Sugar Overlode. Oh yes, M. Goodby was the St. Paul of Sugar, a Sugar Shaman, a Sweet-treats Showman, the Alan Sugar of Sugar. And so, like guilty *G2* readers bullshitting around a proper vegetarian, Mick's hangers-on would all be attempting to take on The Master, knocking back Red Bull like gout was still an Old Man's game. S-s-s-s-shaking and shuddering within a permafrosted sugar-bearded frenzy, these maddened peripheral Neo-Sucrinistas would rage and inflame ye Bard with ever more excruciating conspiracist theories, until – at approximately the same time every night – the infamous tale of Fanta's rise from Nazi Germany (always told as though for the first time) would draw these latest Conspiracy Assizes to a close, so that all could return to their individually twitchy domains and have a beer, cider, vodka, hell, anything but more of Goodby's Sweet Sweet Loved-Up Juice. Mercy!

As the six grinning and be-shaded police officers saluted Anna and piled back into their two patrol cars, it was only now that I understood the shift that we had undergone on account of this Near Impact. For I realised right here in the raw June heat of Sardinia's most monumental volcanic desertscape that, although Anna and I had nearly died together today, nevertheless the accident had not been of my making. Convinced until now that Anna's bad luck had all been of my own manufacture, our shared experience with The Reaper had in itself provided me with enough rich evidence that Anna could – even without my being around – find herself in quite decent amounts of trouble *all on her own!*

18. THE ROAD TO R.A.F. DECIMOMANNU

2pm, Sunday June 11th, 2006
131 Southbound

Back on the 131 southbound, Anna was raging with indignation at the manner in which the main policeman had spoken to her. Indeed, on returning to the driver's seat, her fingers had clung so tightly to the steering wheel that she appeared to be strangling the cop in question. Thus in order to help restore Anna's shattered nerves, we had set off at minimum m.p.h. through the village of Úras, trailing out the other side, and eventually once more hitting the 131. But, although her psychic hackles had been unnecessarily stirred up by police attitudes, Anna was made of stern stuff and pretty soon our Franco-Suisse supercar was back up to speed again, hurtling along somewhere between Sárdara and Sanluri.

ANNA: That was the most annoying man I speak to. First thing he asks why did you let the articulated truck overtake you? Before I can answer, he says this Facel Vega can do 236 kilometres per hour; it is one of his all time favourites. I tell him I'm on the 131 where nobody could travel over 130 kilometres per hour even if they wish. I tell him my friend in the car maybe has whiplash. We nearly both were killed by that truck. Then this cop wishes to challenge me and tells me we were overtaken on the famous Oristano–Úras Straight, where people come especially to drive very very fast. You think I don't know this? You think you are not talking to a demon driver? I'm in a Facel Vega, you creep. Ten days ago, I drove a Ferrari Berlinetta. Tomorrow it might be a Bristol 409 or a Jensen Interceptor. I could drive you off the road, officer.

ROCK: What, you really said that?

ANNA: No no, only thinking it with all my heart. Because all the time he's telling me this, it's like he's trying to excuse the truck driver for getting so excited on the famous straight. (*Getting squeaky*) What could I say? He's a cop. If you love my car so much, then go and find the culprit, officer. What a nerve!

Yeah man, what a nerve! But how I wished we'd had that cop looking out for us on the Oristano–Úras Straight all those sixteen long years ago. For this was precisely where we'd fucked up so royally! I knew it was around here somewhere, but precisely where? Who knows. Even though Mt Arci is omnipresent, that ex-volcano is so damned big that tourists can never judge whether it's two or twenty kilometres away. But, oh yessiree, that fateful Italia '90 day of the England–Ireland match, when we'd headed north out of Cágliari up the 131 in the stolen Carabinieri patrol car, this fucking Oristano–Úras Straight had proved our real undoing. For it was hereabouts that M. Goodby – fuelled by the sudden death of our dear friend Full English Breakfast and goaded on by his fourteen-year-old cohorts Brent and Dean – had felt obliged to prove beyond measure that he was the Top Anglo among us. How? Get this for ye Bard's response: *I'm so fucking English I'm driving on the left!* Next moment Mick's accelerating our cop car clear cross the central reservation and heading north on the left at top speed – this, of course, causing the Sardu Highways Authorities to shut down the entire

131 system. North of Oristano, both the Carabinieri and the Cágliari cops had simply called off the chase and left us to the kidnappers.

But now, as Mt Arci's conical silhouette receded in our wing-mirrors, Anna's face suddenly lit up as she pointed out the road sign for San Gavino Monreale, home of her beloved 89.9 FM Radio, those independent nutters who had just yesterday restored my faith by playing the Brits' 'Last Tango in Paris' as I'd bathed in the stream. However, when Anna – in Pavlovian response to seeing the road sign – fired up the Facel's car radio, her beloved 89.9 FM immediately pitched us both into the kind of raging 1972 John Peel session that only certain untamed Europeans were capable of mustering up. What the actual fuck? As the super-fluid bass and the cavernous coyote howl of some feral bongo player ricocheted around our glass-and-metal hardtop, I was both delighted at Anna's beaming response to this noise *and* shocked to experience once again DJ Jesu Crussu displaying such extraordinary faith in his afternoon listening audience. What in hell was this superb racket?

ANNA: Oh, this is Make Fuck. It's a very famous power trio in Sardinia. The entire side one of their first LP. Raw and noisy, but all people love it. I grew up with it. It was recorded in caves near here. Make Fuck were the best Commune band of the '70s and '80s. Still they perform in caves, but nowadays it's much more musical.

ROCK: It sounds like they're chanting: 'Blah blah Fanatical, blah blah Fanatical!'

ANNA: No, they are chanting the name of their hometown Gonnosfanádiga, where the Commune was situated in the foothills of Mt Línas. All of their songs celebrated their homes and their family lands. Even the radio station 89.9 FM came out from the Commune times at Gonnosfanádiga, when all the Anarquistas lived along the roads between Mt Línas and the 131. The radio station call sign is San Gavino Monreale, but they still transmit from their old health food restaurant and chose a Fuck You attitude. Many hippies remained in this area. That's why Jesu Crussu still plays all such crazy musics.

On and on and on went the cavernous crud, only its lupine howling and overdriven bass bringing the remotest clarity to this soupy anarchist testament. And such was the enduring powerdrive of these rampant cave dwellers that it was to be another ten minutes after we had parted company with the 131 and headed south at Monastir before Make Fuck had brought their exhausting trip to a conclusion so stumbling that even Anna felt obliged to click the radio off before Jesu Crussu's announcement. Phew.

* * *

It was, therefore, in silence that we arrived at R.A.F. Decimomannu, its high wire fences and perfectly lawned entrance softened by a deep fringe of trees, but the whole encampment still displaying a typical Ministry of Defence tidiness utterly at odds with the rest of the island. All was silence, a breezy, tidy silence. It was fucking awful – like some tired 1950s teacher-training college block whose concrete shell had been updated constantly but at minimal expense. What was I gonna tell Mick when he called in a couple of minutes? He was expecting some kind of guided tour by proxy, with yours truly as mouthpiece and a helpful staff sergeant to show us around. Oops, forgot to organise that bit. So when Mick called right on 3pm our time, Anna and I were both still at the rear of the R.A.F. compound breaking in. Oh yeah, and I was in full Hoodwink mode.

MICK: Sectarian, are you feeling Caesarian?

ROCK: Ye Bard! Well met in Detchy! (*Breaking through young M.O.D. woodland in a twig-snapping frenzy*) What a lovely scene!

MICK: Were the R.A.F. blokes more accommodating when you mentioned my family?

ROCK: Oh, they're just lovely people. Make yourself at home. We've been wandering around the airfields on our own (*gurning guiltily at Anna*). It's like the 1950s here.

MICK: Oh mate, that's music to mine ears. Is that old black Morris Minor Thousand still parked too close to the ladies' staff block so they can dry their civvy clothes on the bonnet and roof?

ROCK: (*Clueless but accommodating*) No way! I wondered why that old jalopy was parked there! And some of the planes they've kept under wraps here, you'd think the war had never ended!

MICK: (*Full of heart and hope*) Bloody hell, so nothing's changed, huh! Can I have a quick word with the staff sergeant? What's his name?

ROCK: Just this minute he's not here. But when he found out I was down for your family business, he just said something about letting ourselves out later.

MICK: (*Pacified, almost thrilled*) See what I mean, Rocky? Tradition still counts in the armed forces. I'm Gabriella's boy through and through, a Catalan anarchist still burning for the blood of Franco. But sometimes there's something beautiful in authority . . . if you belong. And just knowing Dad met Gabriella right where you're standing makes me proud.

ROCK: (*Now teetering atop a mobile airliner staircase squinting through a filthy hangar window*) Mick, romantic is not the word for it!

MICK: (*Almost sucking on a dummy*) Aaaaaah Decimomannu. (*Quieter*) Detchy. Rock, you are the fucking Rock doing this. What a top job.

ROCK: Will I lose brownie points when you find out my camera phone's busted?

MICK: Rock, Rock, I don't need photos with you there describing it. I'm seeing it now through your eyes, looking at my heritage through your fresh Armed Forces-free lenses. By the way, is the Spitfire still guarding the entrance gate on its massive Airfix stand? I remember they'd swapped it temporarily for a Hawker Hunter jet, but I live in hope.

Now was clearly the time for me to bring this Deception to a close, for even I could recognise that Detchy's current wingèd guardian was not a Spitfire, and not a Hawker Hunter neither – perhaps not even a warplane at all. For a start the thing was French manufactured and, despite having been cleverly angled upwards on a nifty plinth, looked to be no more than a parody of a Jet Fighter, especially its gaudy camouflage, which would have looked more appropriate in some equatorial South American air force. Right about now, ye Bard needed authenticity at Decimomannu, not this gigantic Bic Biro created by some hyper-energetic Pop Artist. Why else were we here if not to gather fuel for Mick's Sardinian novel? And so, out of respect for ye Bard, right then and there I declared Time's Up and closed down our curated phone tour. But not before having reported to Mick the presence of several massive and mysterious four-engined UK bombers still hidden in the Detchy hangars. All lies of course, but all the kind of necessary lies that would irrigate, inspire and re-fuel our tragic Bard under the stairs.

19. ANDONI GOIKOETXEA OLASKOAGA IS A FUCKING CUNT

4pm, Sunday June 11th, 2006
Back on the 131 Northbound

One hundred miles per hour suddenly felt about right in this car. But I was just the passenger so I didn't half keep my head down, and I didn't half screw my face up at some of the rum moves we were undertaking. And I mean *under*-taking. Burning back up the 131 northwards after that stultifying air force museum, Anna the demon driver currently seemed intent on proving her police detractor right. Yes, you *can* drive at breakneck speeds along the 131 so long as you're willing to compromise the rest of us. But as we once again approached that famous/infamous Oristano–Úras Straight, I knew that Anna was only driving so fast in freaked-out response to the ghastly accident we had witnessed just twenty-five minutes previously, soon after re-joining the 131 at the Monastir exit. That fucking Reaper truck again. No shit. But this time, from the outside lane, we'd spied The Reaper up ahead making big trouble as it rumbled on to the 131, knocking a slow lane motorcyclist into the path of a pick-up truck, which was itself then forced to swerve into *our* lane! Mercifully, Anna had foreseen the problem and we'd surged clear! Thereafter, she had been so furious that she'd high-tailed us out of the situation in a manner utterly alien to me.

But if two close encounters with that truck in one day didn't necessarily add up to some kind of Psychic Attack, then what happened next certainly does. For when Anna switched on the Facel's radio too late to hear DJ Jesu Crussu's complete 4pm traffic report, no sooner had Crussu concluded with the mention of 'twenty-kilometre tailbacks south of Monastir' than all hell broke loose. Holy Shi-ite! The pulverising noise with which 89.9 FM had chosen to follow up that tragic accident report was none other than Spion Kop's terrifying epic 1985 football hooligan chant 'Das Boot', that legendary Pan-European Promoter of broken limbs, trashèd skulls and misery; a song which had taken its title and inspiration from that massive '82 Deutsch movie about doomed WW2 submariners and turned it into a Skinhead Stomp. Oh Lordy, listen to that hideous demon-child vocal! Take heed of those fucking lyrics! And the man behind this jaywalking abortion? Our very own Flying Dutchman Judge Barry Hertzog! Why the fuck was Crussu playing this? Barry Hertzog was haunting me:

Think you're fucking hard? Welcome to the top. Fighting for your life; welcome to the Kop. Yes, we won the war. Yes, we won the cup. Times were getting slack, but now we're coming back: Das Boot's on the other foot, Das Boot – now you're all kaput, Das Boot's on the other foot, Das Boot – now you're all kaput.

Thanks Jesu Crussu, inappropriate or what? A violent declaration of Sectarian Football War cynically written by Bazza Hertzog from the point-of-view of ye Liverpool Hooligan Lifer. And clocking in at just 123 seconds in length, the jackboot stomp, the creepy kid, the single repeated threat of Spion Kop's 'Anfield' novelty anthem had now ignited in dear possessed Anna that same raging fire that had set the charts alight back in '85. And boy, did I understand. For now, seemingly out of nowhere, the rage of 'Das Boot' had set even my own reluctant heart alight, as I joined Anna in our new role as the Ton-Up Kids! Fucking hell, for those old punks with a penchant for Orwellian Two-Minute-Hate songs, forget about the first Clash LP, forget about Crass' *Feeding Of The 5,000* EP, just sling a 7″ single of 'Das Boot' on your deck. And with the pair of us now speeding together down the fastest stretch of the 131 at 100 UK miles per hour, and in the same Swiss disaster that had killed Albert Camus . . . Well, it did feel as though I was declaring myself to the Cosmos: *Bourgeois Individualist Target #1*. And with Anna still ranting and squirting out the old daytime full-beams? It's amazing how long 123 seconds can seem when you find yourself in the grip of Nihilistic Evil. So well did I know that I must, right now, right this minute, wrestle control of Anna's Hertzog-incited slalom and bring this madness to a halt, or risk us somersaulting off the road entirely. And from the back of my mind, I somehow summoned up the will to challenge the hypnotic power of the Judge's Manic Stompf.

ROCK: (*Sternly, over the music*) Anna, I really really need to have a piss. Stop on the slip road for Sant Anna, can you? It's the next right. (*No response*) Anna! Turn off next right will you, please? (*Still no response*) Anna Anna Anna Anna Anna (*Now Anna turns up the radio deafeningly loud*) Anna Anna Anna Anna! (*I'm now chanting along to Spion Kop's football racket*)

ANNA: Anna Anna Anna! What? What? What? Anna Anna Anna! What? What? What? (*Grimacing, but pulling into the middle lane*) What? What? What? What? What? What? (*Signalling and pulling into the slow lane*) What? What? What? (*Pulling on to the Sant Anna slip road but decelerating psychotically and without due care and attention IMHO*)

Less than two minutes later, as we taxied in near silence along that rural slip road still parallel with the 131, I pointed out the road bridge over the Cágliari–Ólbia railway line ahead as an appropriate stopping place. When we ground to a halt on that elevated road section, the pair of us quick-as-a-flash evacuated Albert Camus' Ruin and darted off into our respective pissing worlds. But when each of us returned from our business, I strode around to the pilot's door and hugged my troubled aviator right where she stood. And for several minutes thereafter, Anna clung to my black t-shirt and rained tears into my chest as I grimly surveyed the Sant Anna 131 junction laid out below us. Barry Hertzog's bad magic was beginning to permeate every aspect of our roadtrip. Hell, until a half-hour ago, I'd not heard 'Das Boot' in over ten years. And though I hadn't wished to inform Anna – hadn't wished to instil in her the fear – even our second tussle with The Reaper had yielded Hertzog evidence of its own in the form of a massive bumper sticker that declared: Pretoria–Cape Town. South African cities on Sardinian trucks? Why, only yesterday I'd seen those very names Blu-Tacked on to Hertzog's off-kilter map of the island. What the fuck was going on? And all the while, as Anna and I gripped each other in silence, my scandalised eyes traced the triple dodgy route, which ye Bard Mick Goodby had – during our police chase sixteen years previously – chosen as his method of re-entering the 131 north on the left carriageway. Yes, serendipity had chosen to escort Anna and myself off the 131 at precisely the place where Mick had made his infamous decision to become Super English by driving on the left! Yes, yes, this was the precise place, the fateful springboard from which we four Italia '90 kidnappees had abandoned all sense of reality. And so it was with a slight reluctance but a vestige of Hooligan pride that I took Anna by the hand and led her up to a long piece of very faded and very Anglo-Foreign graffiti stencilled in yellow upon the walls of the bridge. It read:

ANDONI GOIKOETXEA OLASKOAGA
IS A FUCKING CUNT.

Too right he was, man. That Basque midfield executioner was a nihilistic legend among Maradona devotees. For not only had he fucked up my belovèd Diego's ankle ligaments, he had even made a big thing about keeping the infamous boots at home in a glass case! Thereafter, I'd made it my duty *always* to have both paint and stencil on me, to be always Boy Scout Prepared at the slightest chance of a snidey diss of Mr Unpronounceable. Back at the car, I produced from my battered bag an overly folded cardboard wad caked with the yellow accretions of umpteen kinds of paint – this still-tacky mess was the same stencil with which I had perpetrated my Zealous Mission. All across the walls of the Mediterranean, all across the Adriatic, all across the Baltic had my little stencil fucker rendered again-and-again its righteous message. But this faded proclamation on the lower wall of the Sant Anna railway bridge was where the Italia '90 phase of my Gonzo Mission had been forcibly concluded.

20. GERMAN MOTORCYCLE MURDERER

5.30pm, Sunday June 11th, 2006
Still loitering on the Sant Anna Bridge

We were walking over to Albert Camus' Ruin hand-in-hand when Anna suddenly released my grip and ran back to the bridge. I carried on, but could tell that my ancient graffiti had stirred up something within her. As I rested my butt against the hot car bonnet, I watched Anna crouching down transfixed by my faded words, her head nodding up and down as if in some kind of Understanding. And when finally she returned to our parked car but made no effort to get in, we struck up a deep and immediately Cosmic conversation, the pair of us all the while pacing back and forth distractedly on that sorry patch of scrubby waste ground above the rushing 131. But when I dutifully explained that the bumper sticker on the back of The Reaper had a Hertzog connection, the lady – still so buoyant from my words on the bridge – just rolled her eyes defiantly.

ANNA: Fuck that truck! That's the least of our worries. What we
are looking for here is the Truth. You are searching for something special on my island. And the truth is that I have been
too often ashamed of my island. The drivers. The kidnappers.
The nationalists. Even *The Simpsons* laugh at Sardinians. I'm
so embarrassed! But you love Sardinia and you have Visions
here and you die before my eyes but not really. (*Getting
squeaky*) And when we visit the R.A.F. you have no letter of

introduction, so we break in! And you have hit records but you celebrate violence. And your friends also think this way, and how you love them all! No one that I know does this. What code do you live by? I want to understand *everything!*

She reached into the Facel Vega and scooped up the wad of archaeology photocopies. Then, brandishing the sheaf in front of my face, she grinned triumphantly.

ANNA: This this *this* is my contribution, Rock Section. I dunno what your story is all about, but you are everywhere on my island. Because of the Kidnapping but also for your music, Rock Section is a name known to many of my older friends. But now you show me your bridge graffiti, you have reached in my mind new levels of . . . hmm, everywhereness, you know?

ROCK: Ubiquity?

ANNA: Yes yes *yes*, the ubiquitous Rock Section. I know so well that graffiti of yours. It was all over the Cágliari of my youth. Was every stencilled wall I encountered the work of Rock Section?

ROCK: Every last spray-job, Madam.

ANNA: (*Bursting into tears*) Madam? You call me 'Madam'? Nobody in Sardinia ever called me Madam. Who in the world made you? Your posters all over my sister's wall? You quote D. H. Lawrence like a smartyboots? *And* you have the singing voice of an angel! The Shamanic Visions of ancient Sardinia hang like clouds above your head, and still you barbarise your every surroundings with violent actions and obscene graffiti. Your youth cults of the UK – the punks, the skins, the baggies – all are so very strong that they endure within you all. We don't have that piercing, tattooing, raging youth need in Italy. How I wish we did! Forty-three years old, Rock Section? What is your Code of Ethics? I cannot deduce any rules in your life. But I do believe they are so very strong . . . eeh, your every action!

Invigorated to the point of giddiness by Anna's heartfelt outpouring, the righteous intensity of her words shocked me so much that I rose up out of myself briefly, suddenly blazing, reignited, alive. This was Big News! For, having only yesterday been flung headlong into her life – and in such hygienically challenged circumstances – I had several times in the past twenty-four hours expected her to set me down at some train station and leave me to my own devices. But when I articulated this fear to the lovely lady? Whoa . . .

ANNA: You got a low opinion of yourself, Mister. You see me driving these big cars all the time up-and-down with the people waving and hooting hello. But, even counting my friends, never do I ride with such an interesting passenger until now. Besides, my father's cars are too expensive even to risk picking up a hitch-hiker. So I live each of my road journeys in a dream bubble car, imagining always that above me hangs the helicopter of Michelangelo Antonioni, forever his movie camera aimed at me. I am so much a scholar, yes. But I am also a motorbike loner: I seek always adventure on my Ural 750 cc. You came here to fix it for your friends, but now you're fixing it for me. All my tragic life I have wished to be from the Italian Mainland, but these hours with you makes me Sardu for the first time! What time is it, Anna? (*Massive smile*) For me, at last? It's right *now!!!*

Then, in an instant, Anna was wailing again. Please stop crying, Anna. But this time, she made no attempt to stem the flow, instead raising her tearful countenance to the heavens as if to permit some Creator, some Ur-Antonioni to claim responsibility for her actions. And yet, how brightly through that downpour did her full beams still shine. I stared at Anna's sheaf of archaeology papers. I stared at my ancient wad of graffiti stencils. I stared at the dusty bodywork of that exotic Facel Vega HK500, and upon its back parcel shelf Jim Morrison's tome. Then, through the afternoon haze, I eyed up M. Goodby's so-called Italia '90 escape route and I grimaced. What codes *did* I live by? Antonioni's *was* one of them, for shit damned sure.

ROCK: *Zabriskie Point* has always been my number three road movie.

ANNA: (*Flashing eyes*) Antonioni! You love road movies so much? Is it the cars?

ROCK: Yeah, and the agendas of the drivers. Kowalski always made *Vanishing Point* my number two.

ANNA: What? (*Edge of squeaky*) You got a personal Top 10 of road movies?

ROCK: Yeah, but only the Top 3 ever stay the same. It must be because rock'n'rollers are such itinerants, and road movies celebrate the Journey *ahead* of the Destination. Do you know a 1950s movie set in South America called *Wages of Fear*?

ANNA: Yves Montand at ten kilometres-per-hour carrying nitro-glycerine in a big truck? Sure! It's one of my all-time favourites. Also in South America, I love so much *The Motorcycle Diaries*. Like Zapata, Che Guevara is one of my great Latin American heroes . . . (*Shouts*) Chile!!! Also, I can escape from examination periods with Marianne in *Girl on a*

Motorcycle. (*Manoeuvring an imaginary motorbike, twisting the handlebars sharply to the left*) I can't believe I'm not dreaming. (*Jumping up on to a low boulder*) This is so-o-o much fun. (*Edge of squeaky*) Would the creepy Dutch movie *Spoorloos* be in your Top 10?

ROCK: Wow. Anna. That's weird. Yeah man, for sure. That's really *hard* corpse. (*Begins to circle her boulder sunwise*) All right, if you search out that kind of stuff . . . (*slowly and deliberately*) then I reckon I could *maybe* guess your all-time number one.

ANNA: (*Thrilled, vibrating*) Yes. I do believe you can.

ROCK: My Ural 750 cc motorcycle girl.

ANNA: (*Eyes shut tight*) Yes, and now I know you can. (*She starts to whistle an eerie refrain*) Wat-is-das?

ROCK: (*Staring into Anna's eyes, our noses touch*) Wow. The dead rise up.

ANNA: (*So close she's almost boss-eyed*) They do indeed.

ROCK: (*Thirty seconds of silence*) Lùviah, my motorbike loner.

I knew I'd caught a live one when Anna mentioned *Spoorloos*, that crazy Dutch homage to claustrophobia wherein every likeable character gets entombed. But how weird, how spectacular it was that we both shared the same favourite road movie: *German Motorcycle Murderer*. To be on this righteous Mission with me, this Terminal Mission of mine, I hadn't expected Sardinian sympathy of any kind whatsoever. A driver please: I hope someone can do it. But now Anna and I were enjoying *empatica!* Mercy, all hail the heavens! *German Motorcycle Murderer* had the best soundtrack of all time: Agitation Free, Atlantis? *and* Furekaaben. Better still, it had the all-time best-looking male–female lead couple, the best-looking bunch of 750 cc motorbikes and the kind of finale that removed *Zabriskie Point*'s multiple couple desert sex scene to a ghoulish Dark Ages bog burial like something out of the Norse Myths. Released in 1977 after years of hold-ups, and never receiving a proper cinema release outside Scandinavia and Germany, the film was nevertheless massive simply by its association with the tragic death of Steppeulvene's singer Eik Skaløe, himself considered to be the Bob Dylan of Denmark. Oh, don't start me talking about this cinematic scorch-o-thon. I just really really needed to point out something, er . . . big. For me: *very* big.

21. FINDING GORONNA

6pm, Sunday June 11th, 2006
Leaving the 131 Northbound at the Paulilátino exit

My mind danced, my brain pirouetted and the heavens rained with confetti. Glory be. I wrote songs in my head. And I *never* wrote songs, so I didn't write them down. These were all for me. And I sung them again and again and again – over in my head as we sped along. And I spied overhead – or I thought I spied – some Antonioni with cameras and lights. Some spectral director, some faerie Fellini was tracking us, endlessly monitoring our progress as we edged on to the rickety road southwest towards Mílis. Anna patted her sheaf of dashboard instructions, and handed the top one to me. But now although scooting along at ne'er but a trundle, we soon pulled up at a big, confident Italian Heritage sign pointing directly at the nearest hill: *Goronna*. Looking good, Sant Anna!

ANNA: Don't believe them!
ROCK: (*Shrugging of shoulders*) ?
ANNA: Don't believe that sign! Twice I come here before: one time for my sister's Lilliu university project, the other with a local so scary I ran away. Never do I yet find Goronna. But this time for you and your dedication to the ancient Sardu Doorways . . . (*Declaiming*) I don't give up!

For the next forty minutes, we stumbled around the foothills of Goronna, attempting to find a path of least resistance to the

129

summit. But fieldwalls and barbed-wire fences prevailed at all points, and again and again we found ourselves funnelled back to the Heritage sign. Then, as we approached a low ancient dolmen suddenly revealed in the scrubby vegetation, I cried out to Anna and gestured heavenwards. Whence did that enormous and intimidating storm suddenly spring? But she was having none of it.

ANNA: I don't give up!

I didn't care either way. Our failure thus far had been so epic that we were still no more than fifty paces from Albert Camus' Ruin. Besides, my new Inner Soundtrack was burnished and fabulous, radiating sonic light in manic doses. I was singing my own songs from my own heart for the first time in my life. I'd tried so many times to write songs. But without the Muse, I had nothing but the Voice. And yet now, even as that Titanic storm closed in on us from the north, it was all I could do to refrain from harmonising with it volubly and ecstatically. Aummmmmmmmm! Testing the Gods? Contesting the Gods?

Now, cataclysmic lightning raged upon Goronna's summit. What an ancient Seat of Power! An Armada of clouds disgorged their water bombs that did, in turn, create cascading rivulets down every side of this parchèd ancient eminence. Yet, even still did the pair of us stand fast. For we shared right there beside the dolmen some greater Cosmic Determination. And by the storm's end, although not one drop of rain had fallen upon either of us, nevertheless was the capstone of our dolmen neighbour soaked through and even bubbling with tiny pools of rainwater. Whoa! Behind us sat the Facel Vega still dusty upon its parchèd grass verge. Before us all was awash, the storm

130

having annexed a great sodden frontier between Goronna and ourselves. But the downpour had revealed several dates printed upon the metal plaque affixed to ye dripping dolmen. And when Anna read those Italian words, she screamed.

ANNA: Oh my God! It's not so old – this dolmen! It's an old man's grave who died in the famous storm of my birthday. Look, he died June 10th, 1976. Francesco Antonio Deglia of Paulilátino. So strange! (*Gesturing to the rain splattered dolmen*) And now the storm returns like a ghost to claim another victim. But you and I? (*Measuring an inch with her index finger and thumb*) Not a splash!
ROCK: (*Shocked*) You turned thirty *yesterday*? So you were born the *same* day as Brent and Dean? Anna, why didn't you mention it to me?
ANNA: How depressing to tell such news to a stranger when the day for him is already weighted down with bad significance. It was *good* to have an excuse not to tell you. I chose to drive you around this week especially to avoid the commiserations of my friends. What woman wishes to turn thirty?

Praise Blessèd Anna. For now, armed with her super synchronous information, I felt destined to bring away something of true significance from this strangest of Sardinian Missions. And as we set off once more up Goronna's now waterlogged hillside, Anna delivered to me all kinds of bizarre World Facts about 'her birthday' June 10th, 1976: of how Bigfoot had been spotted running across a Canadian highway near the town of McBride; of how an American kid named Tim Kneale had won the 49th National Spelling Contest with the word 'narcolepsy'; and of how Italian singer Fabrizio Arra from the huge band Neon

Sardinia had – after a big festival in Fonni – been kidnapped by insulted football fans from nearby F.C. Folgore Mamoiada. What a rum bunch of birthday facts she'd collected. Perhaps Brent and Dean truly *had* been born under a Bad Sign. But where then would that leave Anna?

Twenty-five minutes later, high up in the sodden and viciously thorny vegetation, we glimpsed at last the great Doorway of Goronna winking at us mysteriously from its timeless vantage point just fifty metres along the flattened summit. By directing our assault vertically this time – the pair of us now possessed by a wholly unreasonable post-storm alacrity – Anna and I had clambered to the summit with four stupendous vaults over those previously insurmountable barbed-wire fieldwalls. Like a couple of mountain goats, we were! And now, through the thick bushes and vegetation, I could tell that the outer stone-walls of Goronna's gargantuan façade were enclosed by a great entrance forecourt – what a temple this once had been! Just as we were making our delighted approach, however, Anna suddenly stopped in her tracks.

ANNA: Hey Mister, this time don't go any further without me. You must promise. Not this time, okay?
ROCK: (*Smiling broadly*) Okay, Anna. Okay.

Now walking arm-in-arm, Anna and I continued across that impressive forecourt and up to the great megalithic façade. Both of us kneeled down gingerly in the sodden sand and grit, then I ducked my head to peer into the blackness of Goronna's hefty carved Doorway, Anna all the while keeping a careful hold on my left hand. More confidently now, I pushed my head and shoulders forwards into the body of the monument itself.

ROCK: (*Reassuringly*) Ah, but this is not a complete passageway after all, Anna. I'm sure I can even see daylight up ahead.

ANNA: This time I will hold your shoulders steady and keep my eyes fixed upon you. Rock, you must promise me you will take no risks!

Ssssssssssssssssssschwwwumppppp! My head? Aaaaaaaaaaaaaaaa-aaaaah! Where is my head? Aaaaaaaaaaah! Where is my body? Where are my thoughts? Aaaaaaaaah! But already my disconnected head was rolling forwards down the passageway, severed by some mighty megalithic guillotine. And my screams as I bounced – as my severed head crashed and was dashed into eggshells – did rupture forever the sleep of this still-dozing hillside. And then came the roar of a Creature so vast it could only have been Sardinia Itself – the groans of this island disgorging themselves through the geological fissures accessed by Goronna's bold ancient architects. On and on down through the passage, still my battered bonce did bump and bounce and crash. I cried out speechless: I had no lungs. Full tilt, I smashed through Wonders, Whys and Wherefores – debated ancient questions long since answered – propelled at such a Cosmic Speed as carved new valleys through granite mountain ranges and cleaved new riverbeds clear across deserts. Backwards and backwards and always backwards I sped. Until at last in a blur, and at such a frantic rate, further and further out into the past, my velocity reached such a dreadful bate at last . . .

. . . that I span out of Consciousness into Time itself.

22. DON'T BOTHER ME, I'M BACK

Darkfall, Moon rising
A great open cavern, c. 10,000 years ago

Had I missed something? It certainly looked urgent. All eyes were upon me, so I was not quick to concur. A dozen sages sat around my carved stalagmite altar, warming their feet on the glowing arc of stone hearths. What did these ageing fools expect? Permitting into Ashop those who yearned only to grow food was tantamount to treason against Old Tüpp himself. Then, out of the darkness through my cavern shone the blue light of Luno))), as he tracked across the night sky. A sign! I rose from my bed of feathers and ephedra heads so as to make my declaration more clear.

BJOND: Those detached souls for whom food alone will suffice, let all of them take their chances with the Arse People, those beings nearby who still fuck their goats and will even kiss them. I have seen them. For I have travelled. But remember that none among you Protected Few could live without the guarantees that ephedra in everything can bring. Blessèd ephedra. Belovèd ephedra. In Ashop – alone of all the Reigns – there is still ephedra a-plenty. Just. But we need more space in which to grow . . . ephedra. More and more ephedra.

I fell back into the great stone bed and quaffed down a most excellent honeyed ephedra brew that sent Sing to visit my toes and Song to visit my fingertips. The dwarf who served me I called back with great gusto.

BJOND: Dràwf, bring me more. Bring me four for myself and one each for these old daftnesses. Bring them just as you brought that one to me. Make it no different from that which I have just drunk down. Bring all quickly but take your time to make them perfect. Be off with you, my brisk one.

The horrified dwarf rushed off down the hillside. But I was seized by the warming liquor of the honeyed ephedra brew and strode over to my sunken bath. There, I tore at the lavish caked ephedra ring that clung like a tidemark around its steep sides, and I crammed ephedra patties into my cheeks until I resembled a beaver. Look at me, I'm Old Dam! Then around the sages I danced and caroused, pointing my index finger at Old Tüpp's Lieutenant-Librarian, the Oberst.

BJOND: Adventurers that break their heads with flint and carve great holes to ease their brains will one day be the Prevalent. Not such as keep animals in hilltop pens, not such as dither over corn and meal. Adventurers that seize the Moon and fly from mountaintops will one day be the Prevalent, not such as you who guard 'The Book' – one single scrap of inkèd buck ram's hide.

OBERST: Perhaps the inkèd buck ram's hide will grow, Soeur. Perhaps that single scrap is none but a start, Soeur.

Pah! I knew how the Oberst resented my Sacred Piss and everyone's dedication to it. And I due'd why he clung to The Book's great importance. This hoity-toity manner thus allowed him to secure his place here: just. Whereas I – being the single repository of ephedra in all of Ashop – was *more* even than Old Tüpp's heir: I was the pitchoeur from which all drunk. Mine was the dream into which All sunk. I was the living conduit, the King Bee from whom everyone drew their own draught of heady ephedra brew. Not for free Ashopians the reindeer's piss so belovèd of the Lapps. No, only the heady urine wine of Royalty was good enough for the blessèd people of Navio, the star-shaped people of Mam Tor, the radiant people from the Land of Ashop. And I alone of all Ashopians had direct knowledge of ephedra, and a free access to its wonders. And those blessèd souls and sages to whom I would bequeath a drop? Why, that would become – and for the rest of their lives – their single chitter-chat. But now I tired of talk with fools, even of monologues such as these.

BJOND: Tomorrow I travel to the Isle of Abbis to hire ephedra fields out in the Vanmark. The Great Ab will meet me.
   Together we'll talk of Old Tüpp. For several days upon water
   our journey we'll speed. So whilst I am able I now must take
   sleep soundly.

Then, as the Oberst directed the other sages out of my cavern, the dwarf known as Dràwf arrived carrying two large pitchoeurs of the honeyed ephedra brew, behind him several more retainers carried each two pitchoeurs a-piece. I distributed a brew to each of the sages and raised my pitchoeur aloft.

BJOND: To Abbis, the great island from whose Star Heart has
   arisen every one of our original thoughts.
THRONG: To Abbis!
BJOND: To ephedra in the Vanmark. Let none thwart my
   Father's needs.
THRONG: To ephedra!

* * *

Without kerfuffle at sunrise I woke, warmed by the hot healing hands of Sunno))), who toxicated brightly through my cavern. In here, She did toe the daylight. Dressed up already in night furs, I added my daylight coat-of-hide then quaffed two warmed pitchoeurs of the Righteous until I was about well fed. The dwarf known as Dràwf was already at my toilet, removing yesterday's turds so as to accommodate today's, which lay in my back passage fresh for delivery. A royal turd is not a sacred thing, though there remain even today locals nearby who would steal those putrid remnants, searching for signs divine, Grand Vestiges of the arse-royal who laid them. Never malevolent are these thieves, merely ignorant misunderstanders of the Workings of Things.

Assembling nointeen of my great Select – the tallest, the broadest I favoured, and each of them armed – we set off downhill along Odin's Sitch, the underfoot laying a grand pace for travel. At the throne of Old Tüpp, we saluted Sunno))) and my father declaimed from atop his contraption. The greatness of Ashop, its future he rested upon my broad shoulders. Then through Navio we strode, we waved each one of us at ladies and at children who did dance. Some young men made play – each disguisèd as Old Tüpp himself – alongside us askance did they stare with a meta-quizzical eye.

Then, at the banks of placid River Noe, we stepped with trust into rugged boats of balsa that delivered us downstream at astonishing pace. Is there control in river rafting along River Noe? I asked this question of our captain, but he – fearful of providing an answer inferior to the Holy One – edged his bets with shoulder shrugs and beard tugs. At last, he discovered sufficient boldness to speak. Soeur, our river is controlled by Lucky, he declared. Wherever we may travel, first his permission we require. Sometimes the price of the River Noe journey adds up to less than a man. Often there is waste, though, and many must suffer sacrifice as the price of our ride. But the boats of balsa hollow and strong delivered us hurriedly southwards along till we reached where the Ashop Fleet lay moored at the great quay to the doorway of Derwent – such a river. No less than twenty extraordinary balsa rafts were there beached high above the terrifying confluence of Ashop's greatest oaken river of all, whereupon each of my Select that watched the Derwent fearfully, soon in praise of human sacrifice began to speak, and loudly. But although I felt somewhat dizzy and sick, as though in ephedra I had steeped too long, too invigorated was I – by the canny construction and impressive size of those River Derwent watercraft – to yield easily to the notion of human sacrifice. No, there could be no token payments. For I was Bjond of Ashop, and of Ephedra, too. And so, although bumpty would be the Derwent's riverboat ride, unto my queasy stomach I could not yield. And thus did we exchange the backwaters of sleepy River Noe for that feisty bucking bronco that ravages River Derwent. And thus, *without* human sacrifice did I step grandly upon this next new curious water vehicle. Then, as we surged swiftly past the Law Seat of Bar's Low, I raised my arms aloft and urged our fleet of watercraft onwards, signalling that here was the Hedge of Our World. Beyond this point Old Tüpp's laws did not obtain. Beyond this point perhaps even a tall man could hold great office. And to my Select I issued this salutary warning: beyond Ashop, be always aware of these treacherous shifts of meaning. From here, the term Far Reigners would be applied to us.

23. OUT IN THE EPHEDRA FIELDS

Midnight, Moon waning, 14 days later
A great open cavern, c. 10,000 years ago

Almost dead many times, lost to the sea thrice and dragged along
by dragons of the deep, now home in safety at last – at last – I
ascended slowly the steep hillside up to my great bed of feathers and ephedra heads. Oh, that sleep could overtake me now,
soften my pummell'd brows into patty cakes of knead dough, lay
them gently in ovens and a-way they would rise. But I am Bjond
and as heir of Old Tüpp had I now to pin a right Old Tail on the
king's belovèd aristocracy. No sleep until that time. For I knew
that beyond my bed stood a noble throng awaiting descriptions
of my walks abroad. Thrilling descriptions – please us, Soeur!
But what to tell that Beloving Congregation? And what to leave
out? That was for me now, in my abject exhaustion, the most
difficult decision. And so? And so must I make good account
of my walks out in another's ephedra fields. Ah me, I had commenced that journey abroad with stout Select a-plenty, all but
one now lost on the seas between Ashop and the Vanmark. Foul
streams! Fouler lies that now I must tail and weave. Ah me, let
the hoodwinking begin.

BJOND: A car, a gilded car did bring me home to you! (*Hoots and
cheers*) What is Ashop unless with ephedra we all are blessèd?
(*Hearty hoorays*) Such was my journey to fix it abroad, to
fix upon the Vanmark the signs of Old Tüpp. Such was
my journey to see the Great Ab that now we of Ashop are

Ephederated to the Vanmark, and may freely come-and-go thereabouts (*cheers and lofty roars of satisfaction*). Such was my successful entertainment with the Great Ab, that he did tell to me tales of Old Tüpp's great Knowledge of Longitude such as even my father would not to us disclose. And in signs carved harshly upon Hebrudean sandstone tablets, the Great Ab did convey his Lofty Regards for my father (*proffering a remarkable prize that sparkles in the Moonlight and spellbinds the audience*). Before I struck out on my perilous journey, I made a declaration to my father Old Tüpp. Of the brave Select nointeen that do accompany me to the Vanmark, none shall fail to return, lest with ladies of Abbis they did choose to writhe. That such a fertile future befell all but one of them, we now should show gratitude. For, even as I speak, upon the Vanmark do the seeds of Ashop fall (*cheers unsubsiding*).

But unbeknownst to my thrilled congregation, none of my stout Select had ever reached the Vanmark, all of them drown'd on that perilous outward journey. All but one, and even he that now stood at my side stood in body alone. This poor broken giant of a man whom all called Star of Navio, no swimmer was he but with luck had engaged a sweet sea current to safety. Dashed firmly upon the sandy coasts of The Umberland, still in the limits of Ashop Without at least in law, poor Star had – by his grand dress uniform – been recognised and given succour in his hour of near death. But the remainder of my stout Select? All had perished upon the Vanquash Sea, stolen in storms and baken in hot weather, all scorched upon and dried to death as drifting became our only form of navigation. And so, in solitary silence had I arrived at the steep sides of Abbis, not as an heir of Ashop but as a victim of the sea. Baken and blistered like my own Select had I been. But taken on high by the priests of the Great Ab, soon in luxurious ephedra and foodstuffs did I flourish. At least this part of my tail on my noble audience I could happily pin.

BJOND: Sheer-sided Abbis rises so high that none may see its summit. High upon its flattened limestone eminence there stands a carved Abby, a grand roofèd chamber five-men-tall excavated directly out of the limestone rock itself. Nothing before have I ever seen so grand, so well constructed. Greatness. Vastness. This summit temple shelters every sacred person of Abbis. Four score at least, perhaps even ten score do live, work and rest within the Abby's walls. And here it was that I drank my first drop of the Vanmark's own ephedra (*oohs and aahs from the gathered throng*).

The crowding forward of my aristocratic congregation, the glimmer in each of their eyes, their open mouths anticipating: now was my opportunity to declare our great windfall.

BJOND: In company with the Great Ab, I climbed to the crescent-shaped summit of Abrig. And from that proud beacon he did guide my eyes towards every Vanmark ephedra field north, south and east. Such is the grand quality of this Abbadon strain on offer to Old Tüpp that we Ashopians soon may come to know an ephedra time as great as any has ever lived through (*loud cheers*).

Inside my head I faltered briefly, suddenly. For I had also seen from the summit of the Abrig great clouds of dust rising. This was the dust of the Boers on their endless Cattle Chase between

Old Oslow and Brest. Busybodies, I call them. Some say these Ut-Trekkers have made chase since the earliest cattle migrations, but that was not my concern. May we Ashopians never suffer as others suffer from the Boers' endless Chasing, endless Chasing. Though one day perhaps we Ashopians shall fall victim. For already do the In-Trekkers chase their cattle down the Linkin land south of our Umber Estuary. How to escape their ways? But although my desperate journey to Abbis had mixed up success with failure, still on offer to Old Tüpp from the Great Ab himself were those vast ephedra fields between the rivers Kennat, Ash and Thund. And with that fact alone did I now hoodwink my credulous congregation. I had never imagined that sleep could be so welcome, or that these faces I had taken for granted would feel so necessary to my wellbeing.

BJOND: Travel abroad is a rare thing, a successful outcome even rarer (*chunters of agreement*). Come now, let me sleep off my journey. But first I shall relieve myself of all this hard-won ephedra so that tomorrow you all may decide for yourselves how fine is the produce of the Vanmark (*vehement approval*).

* * *

But even the darkness black as pitch could not douse my raging brows. In my head? Great clouds of dust: the cattle were trampling our ephedra fields. Either that I witnessed within the darkness of my own temple or the many deaths of my brave Select, each one of them dragged off by the sea before my helpless eyes. Again and again and again, until I wished no more for my own company, but still sleep could not break through. Finally, at dawn in prickly combination came as partners Sleep *and* Wakening. Thus, though simmering upon my bed of feathers and ephedra heads, still was I joined there by the eighteen ghosts of my stout nointeen Select. But then a dreadful noise, a stark commotion at the entrance of my cavern chased sleep even further away. An unsolicited visit from an uninvited guest or guests?

BJOND: Who intrudes upon my darkness? Who? (*Gap of stern silence*) And why?

Then out of the gloaming stepped a vicious quartet, one brandishing aloft a torch of burning tar, whilst the other three supported a great heavy slate magnificently etched with symbols and meaning. The torch bearer – none other than the Oberst himself – held his black tar blazing against the carved slate, which was itself borne up for perusal before my eyes by his three accomplices, Hipper, Harland and Humberley. I rose from my bed, my ephedra brew in hand, and – pointedly ignoring the heavy carved slate – peered out across the hillside as several dozen more torch bearers ascended towards my cavern. Ah me, what had been begun this night? Upon the slate inscribed right large were accusations against my conduct, of blasphemy against Old Tüpp, of sham inventions and of acting – this worst of all – in Imitation of Old Dam herself. But though just roused, the sleep still round my eyes, nevertheless was I instantly combative and enraged.

BJOND: Who set the bar for all your accusations? Perhaps it is too low for one so highborn as Old Tüpp's heir? And who, from the safety of Navio, dares judge the royal heir in far off Vanmark? And who misguides Ashopians with etchèd accusations of Diabolism, when these peculiar thoughts evolved only from the Oberst's High Office itself?

OBERST: Soeur, tradition states our blessèd aristocracy must quaff your royal urine. But last time imperfections caught within that heady brew inflicted sickness on the drunken. As the Oberst of Old Tüpp, that is reason enough for me to do battle with the Ways of Bjond. No more should you roam abroad ingesting as you wish. For the minds of Old Tüpp's aristocracy depend upon your sacred diet. I have too many times aided the sick and the violently ill brought on by imperfections in your belly. Did any previous heir of Old Tüpp transport to others such imperfections? If so, no record exists. You are the Living Ephedra. And in ephedra alone should you dwell.

Outrageously then did the Oberst's accomplices act. The knave they called Hipper did wield a garrotte! Whilst Harland and Humberley lumbering approached me, and without ado threw upon me a net!

BJOND: A net? Am I to be entrapped like some wild thing? Be off with you, Lieutentant-Librarian of The Book. Why you are none but a Page!

Then in quick response to my wit came a deep-seated laugh, a belching guffaw summoned up from the jowls of a mighty one. For now at last had the great line of torches arrived at my cavern entrance. And stood at its head was my father Old Tüpp himself. *And* without his Contraption! Now, how my four persecutors did quail and blanch! Stout guardians of Ashop, the king's a veritable giant of a man! For Old Tüpp without his Contraption did stand fully head and shoulders even above myself!

OLD TÜPP: (*Bellowing*) In stark contrast to the Oberst's mothering and mithering of Bjond, have I, in order to facilitate my son's own royal progress, stepped always to one side. Oberst, do not tread upon the ways of Bjond, for thus you stample harshly upon the spirit of Ashop itself. Know that one day soon not I but Bjond shall be Old Tüpp. And then the laws of Ashop he may bend to himself. Think upon it!

But such was the fierceness of my father's swift interjection that the terrified Oberst – now fighting for more than just his own political life – did grab the leather garrotte from Hipper and himself hoist it over my head, dragging me backwards by my neck towards the great stone bath. And even though I flailed and thrashed in desperation, more desperate were the Oberst's straits and thus he did by his actions tighten the garrotte and therefore drag from me all but the last lingering remnants of breath. Dragged along by my neck alone? I do not deserve this fate. But although Old Tüpp's torch bearers overwhelmed my persecutors, still I lay garrotted, lifeless, dead yet somehow still living . . . somewhere. Then did I experience the great horned coronate of my father crouching over me. And over me Old Tüpp did dump great pitchouers of ephedra brew, then cradled my soaken head and shoulders in those great royal arms of Ashop. Was I dead here? I knew not. In my present state, I knew not. For the greater life streams enflamed by these pitchouers of ephedra had riled up within me another Me Remote. And thus did I entirely fade out from Ashopian view, stimulated and enflamed, possessed by a mission Grand and New.

THE CENTRAL CULTURE MYTH OF THIS NOVEL

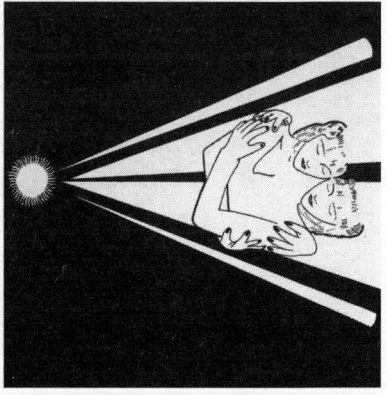

1. Centre of Sunno))) c. 20,000 years ago. As the sparks flew upwards from the blazing Sun, Yin and Yang sat both atop the rocket ride clinging to each other for dear Life.

2. The Sacred Twins' infernal inferno hoisted their cosmic egg aloft like the lovers in Klimt's *The Kiss* riding upwards ever heavenwards until their blast precipitated them out into the wider Universe alone alone and so so alone. Still increasing velocity, these Sacred Twins flew out and out and out. 'Will we fly forever outwards in our journey? Will *Never* be our only stopping place?'

5. The result? Not Catastrophe. Near Catastrophe, but yet Life SHALL obtain. For when, 20,000 years ago, the Sacred Twins entered the Earth's orbit, Yin's Star Consciousness was pulled first into the atmosphere where it pursued our planet's central–most nodal points: its chosen Impact Zone, its preferred star-centre being an obscurely placed island on Earth's northern hemisphere at a place surrounded by a nodal point cluster of near equals. Here at this central shaft, Yin's Consciousness began immediately to unfold, to unfurl its great Cultural Carpet across the untrammelled land.

6. Consciousness has Landed. It brings life to possibilities and all irrigations are begun. And yet and yet and yet, hovering, nay, gyrating above this glorious Construct – and joined by an indestructible umbilical cord – threatens the ever-incoming Storm of Demise that is Yang's Irrationality. Catastrophe will pursue thus. Given 10,000 years' grace before its Sacred Twin catches up, Star Consciousness has time to grow upon Earth and obtain a strong Cultural Salient upon its chosen island and surrounding nodes. Thus, despite the inevitable destruction 10,000 years hence, Culture grows and grows healthily. The

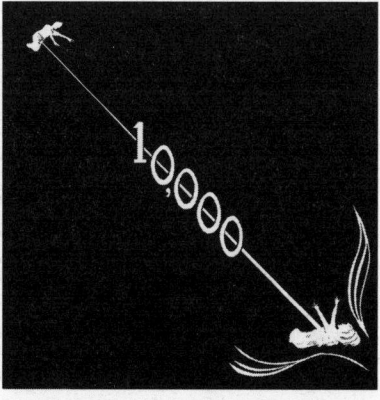

3. Until, caught in a sudden super-turbulence (such are the ways of Space), these two who clung to each other were – by that cosmic shuddering – forced apart; thereafter hurtling together joined only by their bungee belly buttons, the Life Ooze of Each giving mutual sustenance to the other. But the Sacred Twins, spinning around and around on their temporary trajectory through space, become slowly but inevitably uncoiled from each other.

4. Until and until and until they discover now that Yin's brightly burning and ardent Star Consciousness has pulled ahead of Yang's Irrationality by a full 10,000 years. Yet still the Sacred Twins hurtle through space to their final destination.

Chapter 24

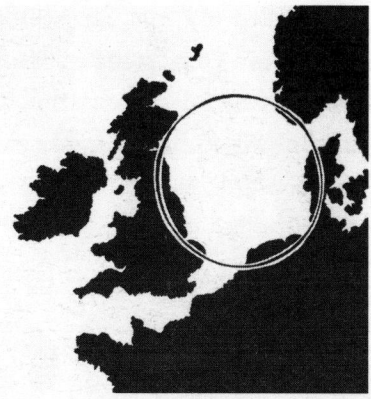

Promethean gifts of Culture are bestowed upon the humans of the central island, and their response is sky watching, cave exploration, travel, forest research, animal interfacing and inter-communication.

7. All of this Creation is of such success that when Yin's desperate Other Twin finally hurls itself with equal force into the Earth just north of Yin's original Impact Point, the resulting cataclysm – despite causing The Flood and removing most of central Europe – cannot destroy those newly cultured populations who sought homes far from the original nodal points.

25. SANTA CRISTINA

8.30pm, Sunday June 11th, 2006
Entranceway to Goronna, outside Paulilátino

Out of nowhere Anna heard joyful yodelling! That's how she knew when I'd got my head back, or so she said. All I can remember is my eggshell skull having suddenly become – on my list of physical agonies – secondary to my garrotted neck, the other dimensional wounds of which I massaged and probed with all of my fingers. Thus, through sheer joy and relief did my deep and resonant 'Oms' pour forth, not yodels as Anna had claimed. For it was as though my head and my body were in joint celebration of being re-united; my lungs anxious to co-operate again with my lips, jaws and tongue in a giant Remembrance Ceremony. I'd been headless. I'd had no voice. I'd travelled so far away from the Present that those ancient details were already on the way to becoming useless to my current situation. But so disorientated was I that it was only when I'd heard the dulcet disembodied tones of Blessèd Anna that I recognised that I was still lying prone at the entrance to Goronna, 'yodelling'.

ANNA: You are singing, Rock Section.
ROCK: How long was I gone?
ANNA: (*Stoically*) Four days I've been waiting.
ROCK: Wow. (*Slow and portentous*) So my time away in the Past was semi-experienced in real time here in the Present.
ANNA: (*Sarcastically squeaky*) I'm *kidding* you! I don't wait four days for Antonioni himself!

ROCK: How long then?

ANNA: Two hours only. How long for you, Merlin?

How long? I couldn't say. Only the paramount points of my Time Travel remained bubbling upon the surface of my Now. Such specifics as the time, the people and the places I had visited had already long faded from my memory, mostly obliterated by the sheer psychic and physical cruelties visited upon my Being during that return buffeting of Inter-Time Travel. Thus, I struggled out of Goronna's megalithic hole only with very great effort, wearing my human body like a badly fitting wetsuit, but so relieved to be my whole self once again that I felt easily able to tolerate whatever residual water-logging remained in this immediate aftermath of Time Shift. And then I started coughing. Coughing and coughing and coughing my throttled guts up, until Anna thrust a bottle of water into my hand and I gulped down one single mouthful.

ROCK: (*Mouth slightly agurn, fearing the worst*) Did I die before your eyes again, but not really?

ANNA: No, this time you lost your head, but not really. What I am supposed to say, Rock Section? (*Specific and slow*) You lose your head! This time you have no head when I look under the entrance stone. I can't look! So I go away and sit over there (*pointing to a raised exit stone*), so I can watch the sunset and cry . . . about turning thirty in the freaky company of a headless Englishman. Then I have to come back to check if you have blood around your neck. And even that very thought fills me with despair. But no, you have no injury about the neck. (*Shoulder shrugging and having to accept it all*) In that state, you were like a children's plastic play toy.

149

All I could do was wait. Lucky for me I had a friend.

ROCK: Someone turned up here?

ANNA: Don't ask me. I don't even know myself. Let's just get moving.

At great speed Anna rocketed off down the hillside, shouting and pointing out the route back to the car, the Facel's glass hardtop now clearly lit up by the long fingers of the evening sun's rays. I, meanwhile, fell far behind as I struggled in my ill-fitting wetsuit body, my hands currently too flipper-like to aid my egression through field obstacles. So instead, I clambered with much ado up the great drystone wall that ran conveniently like a central spine along the Goronna hillside down to the Mílis road itself. Unfortunately, I proceeded at a pace not much faster than a horny slug. Furthermore, those nasty entanglements of brutal Sardu thorn bushes grown up here-and-everywhere set me back at least twenty minutes behind the hotfooting Anna, whose return to the Camus-mobile was now signalled by an awesome eruption of guitar-wielding ambulant noise across these Goronna lowlands. 89.9 FM, I'll wager! Ye Gods! Who is scattering obsidian shards of sonic black light across these ancient precincts? That extraordinary wall-of-noise now contributed such focus to my precarious situation that I teetered down the thorn-grown wall with unstinting vigour and determination, every move orchestrated by the electrical storm of guitars. Oh, but how exhausting this all was! Why was I feeling so utterly dead-beat?

When at long last I arrived back at Albert Camus' Ruin, Anna was sitting in the driving seat, the car still pointing in the Mílis direction, engine running. Alternately pouting furiously then smiling, pouting again then smiling, and – of course – listening to Jesu Crussu on 89.9 FM, Anna paid almost no attention as I slithered inelegantly into the Facel's passenger seat.

CRUSSU: Going back to 1973 there with our own Sardu axe hero Karma Vaca, making his mark forever on Vesuvio's amazing debut LP. The whole of side one for your listening pleasure, my children.

Just as we were about to set off, however, seemingly out of nowhere moving also in the Mílis direction trundled an archaic combine harvester replete with flashing amber lights and its own accompanying B-road tag-team-from-hell, which grumbled along behind, each honking and flashing its headlights but making no attempt whatsoever to pass. This Delhi Assortment of rural jam cars and unspecified vehicular detritus was headed by a rusty pale blue three-wheeler Piaggio laden to the sky with melons, closely followed by a snorting old red Fordson tractor, itself tailgated by a second layer of accumulated malcontents – hatchbacks, estate cars, moped riders, what have you. And thus, when the limping cavalcade had finally washed by, we tail-enders in the Franco-Suisse supercar could do no more than tuck in behind – and from the map it looked to be a long road to Mílis. Limping along behind these dwindlers would get us to the 131 eventually, but after what Blessèd Anna had just been through, it was clear she needed food and rest, and soon. But at this time of night, nothing in these rural areas would still be open.

ANNA: Santa Cristina. (*Wide-eyed*) We can rest at Santa Cristina.

Twenty long minutes later, however, Anna was leading an imaginary funeral cortège as we headed now towards Bauladu and the 131 – clearly utterly shell-shocked by her Goronna experience. She pointed the nose of the Facel Vega on to the slip road of the 131's northbound carriageway, which we entered at that same suicidal snail's pace. 'Santa Cristina 5km' announced the compassionate road sign, as we crept along the so-called hard shoulder like a couple of Kerry biddies in a rented car through Dublin. Unfortunately, indecision and delusion have been the cause of every road accident I've ever been involved in. Thus, for those five long kilometres down the 131, I gnashed my teeth helplessly in the passenger seat, while the rest of the fast-moving traffic attempted to assimilate the stodgy presence of our Facel Vega in its current Half-Supercar/Half-Snowplough incarnation. Ah, those five kilometres which waited upon eternity . . .

Finally finally *finally*, we pulled off the highway and entered the long straight slip road into Santa Cristina, at which precise point Anna's grand dam of silence finally burst, and magnificently. Welcome back! Suddenly she began to fire out Santa Cristina's most salient facts in her truest machine gun style. Like some Sardu Stonehenge, this fabulous 5,000-year-old national monument symbolised the great continuity of the island's insular culture from prehistory right up to the present time. As far back as the Bronze Age, the restorative waters of the holy well had been ringed by its own sacred enclosures, thereafter being dedicated to Santa Cristina in the 4th century, the effects of its healing springs continuing right up to the present time. Still pertinent today, this fantastic centre of Sardinian Ur-Culture had long housed its own museum and restaurant, wherein all of the smartest members of Sardinia's Separatista movement nowadays hung out and made their plans.

By the time Anna's sixty-second-long information assault had concluded, I couldn't help but feel that this was just the kind of cosy welcome break we required after the Wuthering precincts of Goronna's high altar. So it was with much more than simple regret that we spied right ahead of us – down in the dip of that long slip road – parked up parallel to the Santa Cristina museum was none other than The Reaper itself! Holy kack! And around its cab buzzed a score of colourfully dressed characters, some kicking the wheels, some clambering upon any step available, most of them shouting loudly. These were the Separatistas, furious that their sacred meeting place was being despoiled. We cruised past this scene of confrontation and parked up behind the museum itself, both of us exhausted and neither wishing at this time to address the presence of The Reaper, not even to each other. Indeed, so desperate were both of us to sit and drink quietly that we grabbed the quietest table in the empty restaurant bar and sat facing a rear wall. But all the time the vicious vibrations of The Reaper's idling engine sent such a hum through the museum building that it was impossible for either of us to ignore it. And so, reluctantly, we exited our long-sought sanctuary and joined the Separatistas outside in the near darkness. Where were The Reaper's idiot drivers? And who were these two mysterious waifs that approacheth?

26. THE HERTZOG GIRLS

9.30pm, Sunday June 11th, 2006
Outside Santa Cristina Museum, near Paulilátino

Jehovah's Witnesses? Mormons? Refugees from the Manson Family? Was it the similar dress sense of the two young blonde girls now approaching that made me wary, or the confident and purposeful manner with which they did so? Aged about twenty the pair of them, dressed both in blue jeans and white t-shirts emblazoned with a single Rave-orange smiley surmounted by the letters 'NL', it was perhaps only the young ladies' bare feet that made these two cult kids stand out from the crowd. Yeah man, that and their orange lipstick and nametags. Not to forget their massive 'Free Hertzog Now!' lollipop, of course. What the fuck were this pair all about? I didn't know Hertzog had fucking followers! What *have* I been missing? Unfortunately, Anna had – on entering the museum – immediately become engaged in a fiery conversation with Angela Solarussa, leader of the Separatistas, their Italian conversation peppered with Anglo-Saxon profanities of the 'Fuck The Reaper' variety. So by the time she noticed our culty orange duo making a beeline for me, Anna was too late to extricate me from the situation. Instead, she called over to me, eyes raised to the heavens.

ANNA: So sorry, Rock. I only just hear myself about these Hertzog Girls.
WENDY: (*Staring into my eyes*) This is the time for Personal Responsibility.

SOFIE: (*Smoking extravagantly, eyes closed*) After life comes judgement.

ROCK: Who says?

SOFIE: Judge Barry Hertzog in his *Prison Writings*, page 90.

ROCK: (*Irritated*) What?

WENDY: Our fingers are like barcodes. Everyone is different, so we're evidently here to be judged when we leave.

SOFIE: *Prison Writings*, page 91.

WENDY: We live in enemy occupied territory – that is what the world is.

ROCK: Judge Barry said that?

WENDY: No. *Mere Christianity* by C. S. Lewis. Page 36. It is one of Hertzog's most favourite works.

From her knapsack, she proffered a battered hardback with a highly familiar dust jacket. Oh shit, how I'd always hated this crappy book, even fought with R.E. teachers at school over it, even once ripped that familiar dust jacket asunder and hurled the book at a Christian school friend. C. S. Lewis: smug fucker. *And* I'd hated his *Narnia* trilogy, too. In Lewis's drab homo-social world, anything the female characters do outside his tight preconceived notions is a passport to conceitedness, frivolousness and make-up.

ROCK: (*Combative*) Should C. S. Lewis fans be wearing lipstick, then?

WENDY: We do it to honour Barry Hertzog's Party Orange, and to attract people to our cause. I know what you are trying to do. Many compare our orange lips to the 'nylons and lipstick and invitations' that Susan The Gentle falls prey to in C. S. Lewis' book. But I believe that was Susan's last resort after her archery was not good enough for involvement in the great battle. To compete with men is to discover only that women cannot be warriors.

SOFIE: I'm five-foot-two. Push me over and you will see the falsehood of Susan's argument. Given the same resources, can a small man be the equal of a large man? I don't think so. So only in alliance with a strong male partner or many stronger female partners can I hope to overthrow you, let alone be your equal.

WENDY: We women will thrive only when we make smarter alliances. Men alone are lonely hunters.

ROCK: What about the Amazons?

SOFIE: Yes, they share many similarities with men. But that is surely only evidence of their remove from womankind.

WENDY: Mere Christianity will thrive on co-operation and good Behaviour. As C. S. Lewis insisted, God demands 'obedience and outward marks of respect from all of us to properly appointed magistrates, from children to parents, and from wives to husbands'. *Mere Christianity*, page 65.

SOFIE: Judge Barry Hertzog is our 'properly appointed magistrate'.

ROCK: Who says? Did *he* say?

SOFIE: Yes, of course. He calls himself Judge! To dare to bestow upon himself such a title is for us sufficient evidence. He is one of C. S. Lewis' chosen ones 'who have been specially trained and set aside to look after what concerns us'. Again page 65.

ROCK: Your so-called route to fulfilment sounds like a road back in time! You honestly believe Christianity still has something to offer?

WENDY: No no, only Mere Christianity has the answers to life.

ROCK: What about modern Witchcraft and Neo-Paganism?

WENDY: Paganism? Atavism more like! (*Exasperated*) Look at the Nazis' pointless looting of European museums for ancient spears of destiny and suchlike; no better than Christian Turin Shroud collectors. And the compromises that pagan Mussolini made with the Catholic Church!

ROCK: How about Catholicism then?

WENDY: Still too pagan. (*Gesturing to the hefty cross advertising the Neolithic well*) They worship the saints. And Luther could find no passage in the Bible that justified the existence of the Pope.

ROCK: Buddhism?

WENDY: (*Lamenting*) Oh, if only people would follow the noble eightfold path of the Dharma. (*Explosive*) For observers only. Nothing completes it.

ROCK: Islam?

WENDY: Worse still. A terror weapon for headbangers only. Mormonism with legs. And the Muslims invented the first yellow stars pinned on to Jewish garments.

ROCK: You're Jewish?

WENDY: Yes, unfortunately I'm a Chosen One. A marked one more like.

SOFIE: (*Wide-eyed*) Wendy believes that the Jehovah of the Old Testament preyed upon the Jews like some Gary Glitter stalker.

WENDY: (*Under her breath*) Not now in public. That's just a thing I say to you and Gusta. I don't actually mean it. (*As though nobody else was listening*) It's more of a kind of Lenny Bruce approach I use for getting laughs when I'm describing Jehovah to non-Jews.

SOFIE: But surely the whole point . . .

As the two Hertzog Girls fell into a temporary disagreement, around me thronged the Separatistas, all of whom had tuned into Anna's halting translation of the Hertzog Girls' rhetoric, each listening dumbfounded and with ever-increasing agitation. Then Anna, now full of vim and vigour despite her exhaustion, pulled me to one side.

ANNA: I've been talking to Angela Solarussa, leader of the Oristano Separatistas. She tells me Santa Cristina faces a disaster. A rock'n'roll club has opened illegally on the other side of its 131 exit. They have no licence and no permit, not even plumbing. But everybody visits because it's so convenient and looks so professional. To get people to check it out, these cynics called their club 'Opposite Santa Cristina'. Not even *officially* open yet, and already they scare away old people with their hairy music and insane clientele!

SOFIE: (*Looking at mobile phone*) I need some cigarettes.

WENDY: (*Back and combative*) So Islam for a Jew is just a chav alternative – too recent, too needy. Like Hitler's Nazism, it was just an invention of Mohammed for (*ecstatically*) *his people*. And at the expense of we Jews most especially. The great C. G. Jung compared Adolf Hitler to Prophet Mohammed.

SOFIE: Islam's smugness facilitates such an ostrich worldview that 'it refuses to address the obvious third-hand nature of its glib truths'. *Prison Writings*, page 90.

WENDY: Mere Christianity is superior to Islam in every way.

ROCK: Why?

SOFIE: Its generosity of spirit. Its determination to seek the highest moral road. Its stubborn refusal to see typical human traits as obstacles. Look, I need to go on MSN now. (*To Wendy*) Let's go over to Opposite for ten minutes?

And with that, the two Hertzog Girls marched off past The Reaper and headed down the slip road towards the dark tunnel under the 131. What a stupid superficial dickhead I could be. Two minutes around these Void-oids and I was instantly jealous of Barry Hertzog; didn't give a fuck about their beliefs, just out-and-out jealous that two young women found the Judge so compelling. My ex-pop-star mentality or what? I grabbed Anna by the hand. Come, my dear, for we must in the Name of Righteousness pursue the Hertzog Girls and see for ourselves what's going down at Opposite.

27. OPPOSITE SANTA CRISTINA

10pm, Sunday June 11th, 2006
Opposite Club, Santa Cristina, near Paulilátino

I was standing with my head inside a video booth, grooving like a fucker to one of my own ancient hits. After that brush with the Hertzog Girls, I'd needed validation, and quick. So I'd left Anna with the Separatistas kicking up a stink at the doorway of Opposite and sneaked inside for some early research. Besides, 'Anastasia Anaesthesia' by the Low Countries had always been one of my favourites. Good video, too. I was *so* young! Anyway, it was the low headroom of the booth which had really dragged me in here. Built to accommodate much shorter Mediterranean people, the booth allowed me to people-watch stooping safely and surreptitiously. In the booth next to me, a tiny longhaired Japanese guy was watching Deep Purple's 1971 *Top of the Pops* performance of 'Fireball', sampling the opening snare rolls with a hand-held microphone. That's the single version, you cunt. You can tell from Gillan's shite lip-synching.

Hidden inside my booth, I was far enough away from Anna to be very impressed with Opposite. If this is an illegal club, then lawless is the only way forwards. Not yet even officially open for another three days, Opposite was as fabulous a temple to the rock business as I'd ever encountered. Great drinks, great sound system, great lights, great internet café, great smells, even great carpets – the whole thing was done with incredible aplomb. Next to the video and listening booths, an elevated row of ten aircraft seats skirted the edges of two main walls, each seat wired with its own headphones. A shorthaired Japanese dude currently sat mid-row, twitching violently under the headphones, his mouth moaning along to the inaudible singer and his short legs kicking out in front of him. Joe Cocker fans. When this place finally opens, all ten seats bopping? Mercy!

Thus far, the club's bouncers had managed to contain the outraged hubbub of the Separatistas, corralling them all at the front entrance. But the MC's unexpected announcement that the house band would be commencing their first set in a couple of minutes was clearly a step too far. Now the dam burst, and no amount of hired hardmen could hold back the flood of protesters. For these ardent Oristano Separatistas, 10pm rocking round Santa Cristina way was not what the Old Gods had in mind. Leader Angela Solarussa headed her troupe, dancing in and out of roadies and technicians, pulling plugs out randomly and tripping over a synthesizer, which set off a massive *Whoooosh!* across the P.A. Unfortunately, this afforded the strangely outfitted MC the opportunity to jump on stage dramatically.

MC: Ladies and Gentlemen, please welcome Nurse With Mound!

But as the band roared into life, their unholy combination of dual vocals and Franklin D. Roosevelt samples stopped everyone in their tracks. 'We apologise for nothing!' screamed Nurse With Mound. Bouncers, bartenders, Separatistas, every one of us clasped our hands to our ears in horror. 'We apologise for nothing!' It was those two little Japanese guys I'd seen hanging out earlier. 'We apologise for nothing!' Then the MC removed his massive bunny ears, placed them ceremoniously upon one of the band members' heads, and legged it off the stage. 'We apologise for nothing!'

Whoa, now I even recognised *that* guy! In a microsecond it had all made sense. That was Bugs Rabbit! This rock club was the brainchild of none other than Bugs Rabbit! Yup, Spackhouse Tottu's Machiavellian Mr Fixit was behind this entire zany enterprise. Bugs Rabbit, hmm. After the chaotic ending to Italia '90, he'd entirely evaporated from my consciousness. But he'd certainly done well for himself by the looks of Opposite's forthcoming line-up of performers – Make Fuck, Wire, Uri Gallagher, Manicured Noise, Spackhouse Tottu themselves – all were coming to play for Bugs. Now, even the pummelling music of Nurse With Mound could not keep me away from the fascinating rock'n'roll photographs pervading Opposite's walls. Indeed, they were alive with the career images of their great club owner, many blown up into poster form or otherwise reproduced as good old 8″ × 10″ press shots – very Shaftesbury Avenue. So while bouncers and protesters alike sought refuge from Nurse With Mound on the slip road outside, I checked out our hero's not-so-chequered career. Here was Bugs on Van Der Graaf Generator's stage in Rome, sitting at Peter Hammill's clavinet no less, replete with 1972 backstage pass. Very nice. Here was Bugs in 1973 with Klaus Schulze, depping for Steve Winwood on Stomu Yamash'ta's *Go*. There was Bugs at the Vox Continental organ back in summer 1967, pumping out psychedelic soul with Cágliari's Bilbo Hobbit. And this grinning fool sitting at the piano next to Sardinian soul singer Urna Washington? That was the seventeen-year-old Bugs on the rainy November '66 day that Urna had recorded his classic song 'Come Back and Haunt Me', subsequently a worldwide smash. And here was Bugs in 1995 posing with the strongman from his new stage musical. Chunky. Throughout this visual feast, the unstinting Nurse With Mound assaulted us with song after song, each no more than half a minute in length. These guys will be history long before the Grand Opening! I wandered over to the bar, where I ordered a Bubbling Bloemfontein for its name alone.

BARMAN: Bar's not open yet, mate. No licence.

ROCK: What?

BARMAN: Not for another three days. Until then, you have to buy a CD or vinyl LP from the record shop and get a Bubbling Bloemfontein free with it. Sorry about that.

ROCK: (*Eyeing Nurse With Mound shrinkwrapped CD on the bar*) How much is that house band's album? (*Slowly, almost silently mouthing the album title*) *The Compleat Slap-Your-Tackle Home Demonstrator*. (*Grimacing*) That's a bit much. Is it cheap?

BARMAN: Yeah it's cheap. Shrewd move, man. Only three euros *and* a free Bubbling Bloemfontein. Besides, Nurse With Mound are well collectable back home in NZ. Even Egg's solo records do well. Make sure you get them both to sign it.

But as I stared at the drinks list, I suddenly became extremely disconcerted. For my delicious Bubbling Bloemfontein was merely part of a greater whole, a series. Had I known earlier, I could have picked from a Mafeking Makeover, a Shady Ladysmith, a Pretorian Guard or even a Taste of Old Cape Town. Outrageous. Here were another bunch of South African place names staring me in the face. Fuck me, even bigger than that. For right there behind the bar was that same peculiarly angled Sardinian map that I'd spied upon Barry Hertzog's prison wall. On closer examination, however, a simple off-kilter map of Sardinia this was not. No indeed. For superimposed over this great Mediterranean island was a ghost map, a ghost map of South Africa. What was I seeing here? I'd landed in Alghero – so why did it here say Mafeking? And why was Cágliari labelled up as Cape Town? What precisely was the meaning of this creepy new link to the omnipresent Hertzog? I shuddered but I kept on staring at the map. Where next for the ubiquitous Judge? Hertzog rent-a-car? His'n'Hertzog guru weekends? I hated it. But it compelled me. Unsurprisingly, the Hertzog Girls materialised as though out of nowhere, the smaller one now wearing a bandage on her hand. Due to repetitive strain disorder from too much MSN chatter, according to her friend, who was herself clearly exhausted from tonight's frenetic events and too testy to respond to my combative jibing.

ROCK: How about rock'n'roll as an alternative way of life to Christianity?
WENDY: (*Irritated*) What? Rock'n'roll? And why not then include fire eating and other old-timer witchdoctor acts? Will you only celebrate the decadence of your streets? Wake up to a new independence of spirit.

Outside in the gloaming, I could see the evening drawing to a close through sheer anger and frustration, as Anna and the Separatistas took it upon themselves to kick seven shades of shit out of a long line of huge illegally placed drainage pipes leading away from Opposite up the slip road towards the 131. And as I burst out into the hot evening air, I was accosted by the now-hobbling Separatista Angela Solarussa, who had in her fury fallen from atop one of the largest pipes. She held out her hands to me.

ANGELA: Can you imagine some Capitalist bastard opening a Hard Rock Café opposite your Stonehenge?

Rock, don't answer that. Or at least think about it first. But frankly? No. Niet, non, nil, zero, no chance. It would not happen. Behind Angela, Anna was deep in a mobile phone conversation. She waved at me and pointed at her phone: 'My dad.' Then, she took my hand and we hurried out of there, back under the 131 to our Facel Vega still parked up at Santa Cristina. But tonight Anna could not be appeased.

ANNA: (*Indignant*) See that? Now, even *we both* come to the sacred well but spend most time at Opposite. It's not right. I'm the angriest woman I have been in a very long time. Also I am dead beat. Asleep on my feet. So I made a new plan with my dad. Tonight we two can both sleep most quickly at the Iloi Agriturismo. It's beautiful and maybe fifteen minutes only from here. Tomorrow at midday we will meet my dad Giampaolo to exchange cars.

28. PRISON WRITINGS

Midnight, Monday June 12th, 2006
Iloi Agriturismo, overlooking Lake Omodeo

How unsubtle do *I* feel? Blimey, I'm hardly myself at all. What a fidget I was, thrashing about in the massive double bed, pointlessly attempting to grab some kip. Why not just accept it? I was sitting bolt upright totally sorted, staring out through the Agriturismo's big picture window on to the moonlit Lake Omodeo, a full half-mile below me. Wrapping myself in an improvised white sheet toga, I struggled over to the window and stared. 'Struth, youth, such vistas still exist? I grinned and sank into an ephedrine haze, still buoyed up to the max by my brief headless phase at Goronna. But my free decanter of red wine – supplied with the room and grown on these very slopes of Iloi – had most certainly contributed to my current feelings of psychic splendour. And the moonlight was so full as to be blistering my skin as it pulled at me, hauling out my reluctant tidal self, badgering me, needling me to contemplate my current fortunes, which were many-faceted and all Far Out. Back home in the UK, my everyday need to score is always so pressing that it was now feeling somewhat peculiar being so, well, chronically replete. These regular visits to the great Doorways of Sardinia were really keeping my pecker up.

But like it or not, my thoughts kept returning to those weird Hertzog Girls and their obsessive quoting of page numbers. Highly impressive, I had to admit. So for want of any better strategy, I retrieved my copy of the Judge's *Prison Writings* from my bag and attempted once again to make either head or tail of it – one or the other would most likely do me. Like pulling teeth it was reading his book on the plane. Put me in even more of a stupor. But that was before I'd clocked that his Tourette ranting about Half Man Half Biscuit was gaining him devoted female followers. Now I wanted to know why, and fast. So I began once again at the first chapter, and – despite that highly intimidating title – read slowly and carefully.

Chapter One: Why I Am Your Judge, Western Europe

I was born in Groningen, Netherlands, in the sun-rise of 1945, as the darkness lifted across the Western Hemisphere. I laugh. I was fathered by a brave Englishman, a Liverpool lawyer called Edward Hertzog, who gave me his name as he gave his life against Nazism. They shot him in the head in Vichy France in the last days of the war. I hear the shot still. I was mothered by Wendy Dawn, the youngest daughter of Groningen writer Femke Dawn, but the Nazi scorched earth policy had laid such waste to our North Netherlands that Mother Wendy died of bloodloss during my arrival.

Raised by aunts and uncles who loved me, I grew up in Drenthe's lost North Netherlands too near to our Torturers' border and impossible still to defend. So throughout my post-war childhood, I stalked and observed the Border Germans, always careful to remember that the Children of Nazis might revert at any time. I loitered around at their Hamburg rock and roll clubs, okay for a week at a time, watching with suspicion while they grew their hair and danced away the memories of Jewish forced marches. I secretly gloried in my Liverpool place on earth, even though until my eighteenth year it was no more than some Celto-Viking backwater. And when the Beatles shone an international light upon my beloved backwater, never again would I permit its importance to slide or return to the UK sidelines where for so long it had been forced to malinger.

In Groningen, my Liverpool roots being well known, I pretended not to be quite so obsessed with my ancestral home on the Celtic Sea, and I affected a love for the Animals and the Rolling Stones, which led me directly into Black America and the soul of Detroit and Stax. There, from the African-American perspective, I learned more of my own people than from any book since the great Hendrik Van Loon published his defining text *The Story of Mankind*, or since C. S. Lewis propped up the whole of European thought with his prophetic *Mere Christianity*. For I saw that African Americans were striving for what we White People already had: that which we too easily parcelled up and gave away.

I am a Mind Child of Malcolm X. I am a Free Child of Boerish extract. I am a Love Child of 1960s Liverpool. I am not the media's Immoral Springheel Jack that 'corrupted' Italia '90. I am your only hope for the West. GOD HELP YOU ALL. Is there a man among you who would stand against Vichy Mindwash? Is there a woman among you who would trust your man to handle your future? Is this not the time for Personal Responsibility? If not you and yours marching in the street, then Me and Mine shall be doing it for you. Artists, DJs, poets, spray-gun vandalizers. So you will only celebrate the decadence of your streets?

Then Me and Mine will Be The Law and judge accordingly. And in stout defence of your Reticence, I now must take up cudgels, Western Europe.

Fucking hell, this all sounded very much like the Judge Barry Hertzog who had so loathed me just yesterday afternoon up at Florinas Penitentiary. Full of defiant declarations and fist-clenching vengefulness, the Judge offered only his side of the fence or the deep blue sea. Like Cromwell's beheading of Charles I, Hertzog similarly regarded the death of Hitler as having been our own opportunity for a Year Zero. But from his words in *Prison Writings*, Hertzog was clearly emphatic that our new beginnings should be achieved only by employing almost all of those same familiar Christian building blocks. His was a post-war swastikaphobic Lutheran Fear-trip and Malcolm X was his Haile Selassie. And all I could hear were the Hertzog Girls' voices in everything I read.

Chapter Two: God Wants You In Church Often

'Reality, in fact, is usually something you could not have guessed. That is one of the reasons I believe in Christianity. It is a religion you could not have guessed. If it offered us just the kind of universe we have always expected, I should feel we were making it up.'

C. S. Lewis, *Mere Christianity*, page 33

Here we are White People very new to the earth. We have vigour about us forced upon us by cold weather and hardships. Scientists suggest blue eyes are a response to the dazzling sunlight upon snow. So now I shall remind you all of how we northerners got stuck up here. Remind you? Yes, for this tragedy I tell now is a story that only your most aged soul remembers. If it sounds far-fetched at times please just remember that C. S. Lewis quote above.

The true story of the White People and how we got here was only first revealed in 1965, by the African-American prophet Malcolm X, whose autobiography explained it in great detail. 'Then, the first humans, Original Man were a black people. They founded the Holy City Mecca,' writes X. However, exactly 6,600 years ago, after the creation of 'the specially strong black tribe of Shabazz, from which America's Negroes, so-called, descend,' an evil scientist named Mr Yacub planned his revenge against humans. According to X, 'Though he was a black man, Mr Yacub, embittered towards Allah now, decided, as revenge, to create upon the earth a devil race – a bleached-out, white race of people.'

Brother X goes on: 'Mr Yacub, to upset the Law of Nature, conceived the idea of employing what we today know as the recessive gene structure, to separate from each other the two germs, black and brown, and then grafting the brown germ to progressively lighter, weaker stages. The humans resulting, he knew, would be, as they became lighter, and weaker, progressively also more susceptible to wickedness and evil. And in this way, finally he would achieve the intended bleached-out white race of devils. He knew that it would take him several total colour change stages to get from black to white. Mr Yacub began his work by setting up a eugenics law on the island of Patmos.'

Even though Mr Yacub lived to the ripe old age of 152, he 'never saw the bleached-out devil race that his procedures and rules created. A two hundred year span was needed to eliminate on the island of Patmos all of the black people – until only brown people remained. The next two hundred years were needed to create from the brown race to the red race – with no more browns left on the island. In another two hundred years, from the red race was created the yellow race. Two hundred years later, the white race had at last been created. On the island of Patmos was nothing but these blond, pale-skinned, cold-blue-eyed devils – savages, nude and shameless; hairy, like animals, they walked on all-fours and they lived in trees.'

But so savage were White People that 'within six months' time, through telling lies that set the black men fighting among each other, this devil race had turned what had been a peaceful heaven on earth into a hell torn by quarrelling and fighting. Finally the original black people saw that their sudden troubles stemmed from this devil white race that Mr Yacub had made. They rounded them up, put them in chains. With little aprons to cover their nakedness, this devil race was marched off across the Arabia desert to the caves of Europe.'

At first, I read Brother X's words with derision. For I never had heard of this story before. Standing back and viewing it with the open mind of the truth seeker, though, I recognised a kernel of reality. For, as C. S. Lewis writes on page 33 of *Mere Christianity*: 'It just has that queer twist about it that real things have.'

The Old Testament described The Fall of Mankind. But as most Christians see that as a Jewish account of things, they tend to overlook its roots, forgetting that nothing should be overlooked in the quest for the truth. Who knows? Perhaps the Jews – being nomads and slaves for much of their history – had from time to time been persuaded by outside forces to modify their beliefs. Certainly the Jews' precarious cultural position combined with their uppity belief system would have made them at all times – despite their staunchest efforts to avoid the contamination of their Word – targets of enforced religious change.

Perhaps the wrong-headed ideas of Mr Yacub's White People had butted in successfully at some time during their successful 6,600-year reign. Perhaps the Jews' Old Testament was merely borrowed or stolen from even earlier times. First-hand, second-hand, even third- or fourth-hand. Fifth-hand even. However I considered it, I could not ignore The Old Testament any longer. So I dived in and read it voraciously and thoroughly. I was not disappointed.

Above all, the contents of *Prison Writings* made a coherent argument for keeping the Judge incarcerated as long as possible. So what if Malcolm X had believed that the white races had been created as a Cosmic Joke against the rest of humanity. I think perhaps I'd suspect something similar if my own people had been the chronic victims of such hate crimes. But then, unlike the Judge, I'd never had the meanest bunch of jackbooting Neo-Pagans of all time trampling through my democracy. And neither had any aunties of mine been forced to shag Nazis in exchange for food parcels, so what did I know? I closed up *Prison Writings* and laid it face down on the floor. Where to next, mate? Is it all backwards from here? The Koran? The complete lyrics of Cat Stevens? Now, as the 1am moonlight cast long shadowy fingers across the waters of distant Lake Omodeo, my mind bulged with thoughts of Judge Barry Hertzog. And as I sank at last into genuine sleep, I was under no illusions that it was into a 100% Hertzog-informed dreamstate that I would now pass.

29. HOW WE MADE SOME DUTCH ENEMIES IN HOLLAND

1am, Monday morning June 12th, 2006
Dreaming at Iloi Agriturismo, Lake Omodeo

Affable English tourists trot off to the free weed of Amsterdam and that's Holland for you. Never venturing further into 'The Netherlands', they're unaware that the country's more rural burghers are low-church judgementalists with a grudge. Calling them 'Dutch' is far too close to 'Deutsch' for their liking. And boy, how they hate the Germans! Nice bit of England you say to a Welshman in Colwyn Bay, you expect the garden fork up the arse. But even the description 'England versus Holland' drives other Netherlanders up the wall because it sounds like referring to all of Germany just as Prussia. Exclusive it is, a bit. So when, in late spring of 1990, the long-notorious but only newly-famous Mick Goodby – as the guest of Judge Barry Hertzog – entered the infamous DJ's mobile Rave club Slag Van Blowdriver that night, with Gary Have-a-laugh, Stu, Full English Breakfast and myself in tow, ye Bard knew he was making enemies.

MICK: (*Right hand extended in greeting*) Well met, Dutchman Van Hertzog. Nicest bit of Upper Holland I've yet encountered.
HERTZOG: (*Right hand firmly at his side, leaning in*) We're so close to the German border here that it even runs inland a bit below us. Our land is tight, we drain it and love it. But this is why we have no sense of humour about those things.

From his five-foot-nine frame, which was now barring the way, Hertzog looked up at Mick. Then he stood there for several seconds pouting and looking at his fingernails, which were clean for a plumber. But Mick was already deep in conversation with Full English Breakfast, both of them staring over the Judge's head at the spiky sheaves of Zulu spears all sitting in close arrangement atop their rain canopy, itself fashioned remarkably from a breath-taking cluster of Zulu shields. Mick rolled up his left sleeve and looked at his non-existent watch.

MICK: It's not getting any earlier, Judge. How about you buy me some sweet Hollandaise fizz and teach me about your border disputes?

A queue of people was now forming behind us, but the Judge was in no hurry to clear a path. Indeed, he simply pulled a vicious-looking rubber rope across the entrance and disappeared into the club. Stu studied the hot food list, while the rest of us – all very big fellows – scratched about and clucked confinèdly. Inside, we heard the galumphing rhythms of Brits Abroad's '100 Watt the Funk' being torn off the P.A. The mentalist romping of those Sardu garage mechanics Spackhouse Tottu replaced it instantly. 'The Daemon! The Daemon! The Daemon!' Then the bulldog frame of DJ Hertzog tore around the corner, big grin on his face, right hand nursing an icy sugar brew, nice as pie, opens the rubber rope. Welcome. Rock, go to see Exterveen for your DJ fee. Hands the fizz to Mick and we're in. Nothing more is said. Nor ever will it be.

* * *

I opened my eyes, suddenly wide awake in my Iloi bedroom, the adrenalin coursing through me, and the silver-blue moon-light bubbling my skin. I'd remembered something, but what was it? Down in the direction of the cliffs that overlooked Lake Omodeo, the apparition of a great spectral pentacle manifested over the broken roof of an ancient tomba – manifested then dis-sembled, manifested then dissembled. And all the while there was a shimmering frosted glaze across the sky that I couldn't account for. Naked, I slipped on my black kecks and boots and headed off downhill to get a better look. But as I approached nearer to those old monuments at the cliff's edge, I was hit sud-denly in the chest by a veritable blast of wind and there con-fronted by a sensational sight! Atop the granite capstone of the dwarfish Iloi tomba danced Blessèd Anna, her dress riding up in the wind, pushed up by the wind in a formidably erotic display. Not wishing to intrude upon this scene – this being no Anna that I had yet encountered – I was nevertheless compelled to goggle in amazement as she pulled her summer dress up over her head and flung it upon the ground. Then I saw the wind blowing wildly through her hair, summoning up a great energy of tiny stars that fizzed and sparked around her head. Now, as Anna – standing gracefully upon one leg – assumed a perfect star shape, I watched intoxicated as the wind entered her belly button then exited through the crown of her head, casting her essence all across Lake Omodeo in a monochrome rainbow of silver-grey stars. This display was not nearly over, I believed. Perhaps it had barely started. But my sense of duty towards this dear lady now obliged me to halt this intrusion, and to return quickly to my bedroom to consider these things.

* * *

Oh, but how the star shapes of Anna persisted into my dreams. They had dislodged something very curious, very large from my distant memories; dislodged it and thrust it to the surface with extraordinary consequences. What was it? It was a . . . long, long forgotten memory of Slag Van Blowdriver that had happened soon after Hertzog had finally let us in the place. The Judge sent me to collect my fee from the manager's office. 'Ask for Exterveen.' Of course, Slag Van Blowdriver being a mobile club, the offices, kitchens and toilets all tended to be erected wherever Hertzog & Co. could risk rigging them up, nicely out of sight of police and authorities. But this fine April evening, the club was pitched up in the private garden of Hertzog's mate, a rich Groningen plumber and Underground synth star named Tiny, so the cops could say nothing at all about the 10,000-watt rig pumping out of the Judge's DAF armoured car. I followed the handwritten signs saying 'Management Office' and 'Kitchen', which led me out into a summerhouse affair. Inside, smoking a pure grass one-skinner and drinking coffee was a very beautiful woman, about twenty-two years old with short hair and very high heels. She was obviously engaged in a conversation with someone inside the kitchenette, whence came the awful smell of something unholy burning, possibly with onions. Whoa. She looked up from her paperwork and winked at me.

ROCK: I'm looking for Exterveen.
EX: You found her. Call me Ex. It's short for ecstasy.
ROCK: The Judge sent me down for my DJ fee. I'm Rock Section.

Exterveen was standing over her desk, poring over a large tan leather ledger emblazoned with a Party Orange sticker. She looked up at me and winked again. Ex was tall, extremely sexy, and extremely on ecstasy. She took a toke and winked again. Then she pushed me into the money corner, handed me my fee, already enveloped up, and got close up to me. She thrust the single-skinner into my mouth and – as I toked up a real storm – she nuzzled my left ear.

EX: (*Whispering*) Pay attention to Loon. He's our crazy cook. I have to listen to these gems day-in, day-out. It's a Harold Pinter play, I reckon.

LOON: (*Coughing from inside the mobile kitchenette*) Man arrived not long ago, Ex. He says he's from Soesterberg. He says to me, 'My friend at the museum wants to buy your house.' I say, 'No way, Fokker off.' This man had the look of a hippy. Sergeant Pepper wants to be my friend, like I'm happy. Hello, welcome to a house thief.

But the antagonising hiss of the unspecified frying fare and his constant hacking cough were obscuring Loon's words, so he popped his head around the corner, his long arms still behind the swing door stirring away in the big frying pan. Hidden in Exterveen's office, I now spied through her shelves this two-metre hedge of a man. What an unappealing varmint. And himself sporting the pan-abusable look of the Lümpenhippy, this chap Loon had a fuck of a nerve to put down the man from Soesterberg, however he might have been dressed. This was the cook? From his straggling blond mane of shoulder length to his bare and filthy feet, Loon repped hippy. But as this filthmonger was unable to see me in my obscure corner, he continued his rant to Ex, yelling louder now despite being closer to her than before.

LOON: He gets well ugly when I hit him with me knives. Well ugly. Stashed his head in a tray down the field.

EX: (*Staring at me, smiling; but speaking to Loon*) You don't get out much, do you?

LOON: House thieves preventing me, Ex. I painted a Tyrannosaurus Rex on the door before I came here. No fucker get past him in a hurry for sure.

And with that pronouncement, Loon dolloped the newly prepared hot food on to a tin plate, coughed over it, and zoomed out to the DJ booth where Hertzog was awaiting his tea. Both Ex and myself were now wedged into the tight management office corner, her feeding me another toke, but looking right past me. This was a lovely rock'n'roll moment. But what the fuck was going on? Exterveen sneezed twice. Then I sneezed twice. Then our eyes met again, and we smiled delightedly but said nothing. Then she sneezed three times. Then I sneezed three times. Then she sneezed four times. Then I sneezed four times. Had we known each other in some other incarnation? I was quite happy to stand utterly still next to this gorgeous woman. Which is good in light of what happened next. For Loon, without missing a beat, returned from delivering Hertzog's hot scran in about thirty seconds then started to yell out random ideas and life stories, all of which Exterveen claimed to have heard umpteen times previously. Fucking hell. Two Harold Pinter plays. And a packet of crisps, please.

LOON: (*Sociopathically too loud*) How does this sound, Ex? As payment for gaining free entrance to an evening at Slag Van Blowdriver, I'll first wash the armour and paintwork of Barry's YP-408, clean out the insides and properly disinfect the seats and lockers. Then I'll cook for all the staff and do the dishes in the stream. (*As though declaiming to the whole world*) Then about 5am, I'll walk the eight miles back to my Glasshouse in the woods.

EX: (*Whispering to me*) What a martyr! (*Loudly now*) You don't need to sort out a new deal, mate. Barry's already quite happy with what you do.

LOON: Barry Hertzog is a Culture Hero, Ex. I want to serve him correctly.

For the next twenty minutes, Exterveen and I smooched and smoked endless single-skinners together in the financial corner of Barry Hertzog's empire, while Loon poured out his soul to her, all the while preparing hot food for the clientele.

LOON: I'm six-foot-five, Ex. Do you know how hard it was being brought up by hippies who'd then turned to God and Jesus and Brother Branham?

EX: (*Whispering in my ear*) He's the American preacher who ruined my life.

LOON: He's the American preacher who ruined my life. I spent my childhood hunting rabbits for the family dinner, while my parents paid penance for all the fun they'd had in the '60s.

EX: (*Whispering in my ear*) We were *that* poor . . .

LOON: We were *that* poor I was the last one in school uniform. I was over six foot by age fourteen, gawky and easy to bully. So I declared myself a Peacenik. But Brother Branham told me that it was the coward's way out; that I should have been brave like my older brother and joined the police.

All this time rip-roaring stoned, and me now unable to leave Ex's office without drawing attention to myself, well at least Loon's tales were choice in their Jobsworthian Stoopèdness.

LOON: I always hated authority but wanted it for myself, wanted it desperately. I never even made it on to the prefect register at secondary school. So aged sixteen, I struck off on my own. I headed into the post-war landscape of North Netherlands, and found myself a little first home: my Glasshouse, as I like to term it. In reality, it's the decaying cockpit of a WW2 Dutch pursuit aeroplane: the Fokker G. 1. Now, with my TV permanently installed upon the nose of the Fokker, I can relax for hours strapped into that confined space, watching through the bulletproof windscreen in a perpetual twilight zone.

As I ogled this chuntering giant from behind Ex's shelves, even the Mickey Mouse logo on his filthy red t-shirt seemed to symbolise his removal from the adult world. But then, as he chopped up carrots on the draining board, I caught the faded arc of capital letters above Mickey, spelling out Loon's former day job: BRANDWEERMAN. This loon had been a fireman, as he now was determined to tell Exterveen.

LOON: A cop. They all thought I'd make a great cop. But I did way better than that. I became a fireman. Once a fireman, always a fireman. A hero. I might as well have been a Texas Ranger it was that cool a job. The Mickey Mouse t-shirt was a nice touch. I'd have picked that for myself. I even told that to my boss. But my boss did not like me one bit, nor did he trust or appreciate me. My boss was your archetypal Drentheman, a Mason and a highly placed paragon of Groningen society and quite unable to suppress his distaste for my looks and ways. He said that hippies were for Holland, where they were homosexuals. I concurred and blamed it on my upbringing. Whereupon my boss kindly informed me that there was something fawning about my behaviour around authority figures that gave him the creeps. And I told him how much I valued his genuine comments, and how I'd try and reach parity with the other firemen, you know, to make him proud.

Oh, fuck off, you utter cunt! This twat was really starting to bore me, but Ex's erotic attentions were sweet enough for me to have endured a whole side of an Andrew Ridgeley solo LP. Nevertheless, as Loon's monologue descended into money-saving schemes for Slag Van Blowdriver, I did wonder just how cool could Hertzog really be if he was willing to put up with the blabber of this lanky cunt. Loon, however, had already taken off on another dazzling solo run. Make this one for Brother Branham, you village idiot!

LOON: You see, Ex, there are only so many short cuts you can take in food preparation. But those early weekends that me and Walter-Under-The-Bridge spent unattended round at Barry's second-hand oil-and-fat business were a total success. Us two produced such a surfeit of hot food for club evenings that the Judge was loth to ask either of us how we were achieving the results. Honest, he'd give us no food budget. But anything you threw into Barry's deep fat fryer took on the look and almost the taste of food. So me and Walter-Under-The-Bridge just visited a few antique shops and scraped off the Furniture Rind from the backs of kitchen tables and counter tops, all the colonies of time. Then we flavoured it up with

Gravy Linings from my childhood Instant Indian Curry Set. Threw it all in the deep fat fryer and made sure they ate it while it was piping hot. A couple of right entrepreneurs we were. What do you think of all that, Ex?

EX: (*Eyes raised to the heavens*) Barry Hertzog always loves a profit!

LOON: Loves a prophet! Barry Hertzog and Brother Branham both, then!

EX: We had several complaints from customers, though.

LOON: True. (*Thirty seconds of coughing*) Just tasting the stuff left a lot of customers with painful burns to the tongue and upper mouth. But being ex-Public Services, my first-aid knowledge was still first class. So when Barry informed me that one sale per person per night was all that he needed, I decided to let the Laws of Commercial Hygiene slide a bit for the Judge. Besides, he told me most punters were too out of it to remember. And as it was a mobile club, people tended to come only once in any case. That was his theory. But I've discovered that Slag Van Blowdriver is a compelling experience for the locals, and our Hot Food stand is a big part of it. People have commented that the food had the taste of Africa, not black people's food, but Afrikaner, Boer-ish food. Both myself *and* Walter-Under-The-Bridge really smirked when we first heard those reports. Better keep backing off on the Gravy Linings and up the doses of Furniture Rind. Those were my conclusions. And Walter-Under-The-Bridge concurred.

EX: Walter-Under-The-Bridge? He does nothing *but* concur!

Expecting praise after all that but receiving only Exterveen's sarcasm, the dispirited Loon stepped out into the night air momentarily to smoke, cough his guts up and catch some of the music pumping out of Hertzog's armoured car. Now was my chance to re-join the others in the club. But Exterveen had other ideas. She led me over to the great tan ledger that she'd been perusing when I first walked in, and proceeded to 'walk me' through several of its weird contents.

EX: I'm a writer as well as a designer. I'm Barry's biographer, and this ledger is Barry's living biography. I collect different accounts of Barry's activities and merge them together into library accounts so as to make him more mythical in the future. Loon has told me those stories you heard about twenty times and they're pretty unvaried in their delivery. No one speaks quite like Loon, but I've interviewed shitloads of people for this project. Take a look at this.

PARTY ORANGE SEES RED: At approximately 2.30pm on December 9th, 1989, there came from an underground bunker GHQ deep in the N. Netherlands woods, somewhere between Midlaren and Zuidlaren, a collective shriek of fury and a pounding of fists upon any nearby hard surfaces and a banging of heads against walls and a collective teeth-clenched snarling so fierce that even the Wolf Ghosts of the ancient Hondsrug – into whose sandy banks the howlers' bunker had been built – were awoken temporarily from their eternal slumber. The Netherlands had drawn England in Italia '90! (HERTZOG)

Exterveen opened up Barry Hertzog's Tan Ledger so that I could read her handwritten essay entitled 'Stockpiling Matériels'. For the next half-hour, Exterveen – via her writings in the ledger – unleashed upon me a litany of awful deeds perpetrated by Loon, Walter-Under-The-Bridge, Judge Barry himself and various other Party Orange miscreants, all things I would have thought best kept secret. Was she trying to scare me with the sheer hard-man qualities of her homeys? At last, I grew bored with the display and asked her outright.

ROCK: Why are you revealing all of this to me?
EX: (*Smiling warmly*) Because you won't be remembering any of it.
ROCK: What is this? Some kind of magical power display?
EX: Oh Rock, think about it! When you get to our age, you don't give a damn!

And with that, she clapped three times and thunder roared, a single flash of lightning bisected the mobile office, burning a line through the carpet directly between us and I smiled at this beautiful stranger. I told her that I'd come for my DJ fee.

30. BE QUICK 1 QUICKBORN 5

3.30am, Monday June 12th, 2006
Still dreaming at Iloi Agriturismo, Lake Omodeo

Psychically blitzed open by Exterveen's lost revelations, I writhed within the sheets of my lush Agriturismo double bed, thrashing around in an agony of Not Knowing and Knowing, Not Knowing and Knowing, betwixt and between I was beside myself. For now I understood that I'd been duped by the evils of Slag Van Blowdriver long before Italia '90, and it felt really bad. But how precisely had they wronged me? Well, I couldn't quite bring that information to the front of my mind at present. In truth, Exterveen's suddenly evaporated reality was overwhelming to contemplate; I'd basked in her gorgeousness for some considerable time. But now I was left feeling both used and betrayed by events that had taken place sixteen long years ago. With my clamshell mind at last prised open a microcrack or more, or at least just enough for glinting residual memories to have come barging into my cranium temporarily, there presently came into my head such an irruption of Lost Contents that I discovered myself lying star-shaped across the vast double bed, the rugged circular iron chandelier now directly overhead acting as an impromptu mandala into which all of my mind tumbled. But Nirvana was not this time my destination, for my Truth was the search for Justice for my kind. So that whirling iron mandala instead eased my egression through yet another dream portal, one that led to that same lost evening at Slag Van Blowdriver – and this time fetching up just as the shit was going down for real. Suddenly, I was simultaneously listening to an extremely Heightist conversation between Stu and M. Goodby, whilst all the time staring past them at a burgeoning flare-up in the next booth between Barry Hertzog and Full English Breakfast.

MICK: Yeah, whether we like it or not it's a size-ist world. People who are big get it far easier.

STU: No mate, you're totally. Like I loved Iggy PCP until I discovered he was five-foot-one, but then it well dwindled. I'm five-ten, what do I want with five-one?

MICK: Only he weren't five-foot-one, Stu. That's just his song title. He's five-seven.

STU: He did *Raw Power*, I loved the cunt to death. I'm five-ten.

BREAKFAST: You know, Judge Barry, I've always admired your Party Orange. Extraordinary imagery! Pop Art and saucy simultaneously. I'm an absolute shocker for the whole thing. But one issue I do have, Old Stick? The club's name – I do have to say I find Slag Van Blowdriver to be in pretty poor taste. Even from a distance. (*Looking around*) And now I'm here . . . (*shaking his head*) well, Old Thing, it's even worse.

MICK: (*Clueless*) Too cryptic?

BREAKFAST: This brazen festooning of Zulu shields is redneck beyond the limit.

HERTZOG: The club's name pertains to a very great moment in history.

BREAKFAST: The Battle of Blood River was a very *grating* moment in history. Why rub it in, Old Bean?

HERTZOG: You can't understand my problems and I can't understand yours.

BREAKFAST: I think it more likely that you wish me not to

understand your problems, Old Chap. But I think that perhaps I do understand, more than you could imagine.

HERTZOG: (*Shark-eyed*) How?

BREAKFAST: Old Son, I . . . am your *neigh*bour.

HAVE-A-LAUGH: (*Leaning in, uninvited*) Ker-buum! Be Quick
nil, Quickborn one.

HERTZOG: Quickborn? You're a fucking Deutsche! I knew
something I swear!

BREAKFAST: Hardly Germany, Old Boy. At least not those
exclusively Anglish parts that I traverse. My mother Birgitta
tells me they remind her more of the low parts of England
around The Wash.

HAVE-A-LAUGH: (*Diamond geezer*) He ain't German, Judge.
Not Full English Breakfast. (*Suddenly serious*) Honest, Judge,
he's shown us the maps and his habitat is one-hundred-
percent. Breakfast comes from the place of mysterious bog
burials. Human sacrifices!

HERTZOG: (*Brian Clough*) I've no time for paganism. That's
precisely what I'm fighting against.

BREAKFAST: Really, Mr Hertzog, your touchiness is not
believable.

HERTZOG: (*Hooded eyelids*) At my invitation, you're here. So
why am I being so hassled, harassed and harangued?

BREAKFAST: I'm hardly haranguing you, Mr Hertzog. Believe
me, your combative stance is disconcerting. Is clenching one's
fists unconsciously at every reply one receives not guaranteed
to set the other chap on edge somewhat? As your guests,
we're all here quite ready to accept what you perceive as your
personal *Weltanschauung*.

HERTZOG: (*Black expression*) I even feel your use of the Hitlerian
term *Weltanschauung* is meant to rub me wrong, Mr Breakfast.

In these touchy circumstances, wouldn't the term 'worldview' be more appropriate?

BREAKFAST: Old Love, the German *Weltanshauung* considerably antedates our own 'worldview', which is itself merely a translation of their 19th-century concept. It's a common enough international term in the psychiatry world.

HAVE-A-LAUGH: Be Quick nil, Quickborn two. First one to five is the winner.

HERTZOG: (*Staring close in Breakfast's face*) Your one-upmanship, call it what you like – that will be the death of you.

And with that, the Judge turned his back on our assembled group and began to collect the empties from the surrounding picnic tables. What a surly man. I wandered over to the DJ booth and requested anything by Six Bad Niggas In A Car, but Hertzog barged in front and slapped on the most ambient piece this side of our fridge hum back home. Then he re-joined our party as combative as before.

HERTZOG: Martin Luther was more anti-pagan than was the Pope. And even Islam only caught the attention of Malcolm X in the late '50s, when X had grown fearful that too many blacks on the jazz scene were returning to Yoruba. That's the original African paganism that the Christian slave trade helped to stamp out. (*Triumphant*) So we played our part.

BREAKFAST: Who played what part?

HERTZOG: We Christians played our part in the Islamic Prophecy as told by Brother X. His *Autobiography* reads: (*Closes eyes*) 'It was written that some of the *original* [that's X's term for Black People] should be brought as slaves to America – to learn to better understand, at first hand, the white devil's true nature, in modern times.' (*Again triumphant*) Predestination.

HAVE-A-LAUGH: (*Smelled a fart*) That's too fucking *Que Sera* for me. Can we change the subject, please?

HERTZOG: This is the *only* subject. There's nothing else on offer for you here.

BREAKFAST: Then do let us all hear your monologue, Judge Barry. But please keep it interesting. Or in the name of democracy we'll every one of us be hotfooting it down to your delightful Hot Food counter.

HERTZOG: (*Seamless*) Belial or Christ. The Good must have no truck with the Wicked.

BREAKFAST: (*Puzzled*) Then what about your pseudo-Anfield hit 'Das Boot'? One of my all-time favourites, I might add. But why did two lowland Protestants choose to lend such a dynamic voice to the inchoate Catholic hordes? What were you thinking, Judge Barry? Did Pit-Yacker MC know what he was taking on when he chose to impersonate the Voice of the Anfield Kop? Could they not speak out for themselves?

HERTZOG: (*Up for it*) I think right there is precisely where the evidence is lacking, Mr Breakfast. It's not all lush papists on the Anfield Kop. The club's too international for that. Liverpool fans know not why they hate, they just hate. So I wanted to lend a focus to what they hate and 'Das Boot' did just that – especially after the shameful Friendly Fire of the 'I Hate Nerys Hughes' affair. Thereafter, I decided I had to teach them *how* to love Liverpool – force it down their throats if necessary – force-feed them with Liverpool. I couldn't be subtle, either. I was Moses and Liverpudlians were my Jews.

HAVE-A-LAUGH: I love that fucking B-side, Judge. 'Wirralwork' was a classic. Sheer poetry.

HERTZOG: (*Early Dexy's*) I meant it all. Cordon off the Wirral and make a Unilateral Declaration of Independence. I've been burning at the structures of Liverpool. Dig a Pale around it, a massive protective ditch like the Dubliners did to keep the Irish out. (*Stares of universal disapproval*) Just a thought!

HAVE-A-LAUGH: Hey Judge, the old boys round Norris Green fucking hated us when 'Das Boot' was massive because we'd put the B-side on the pub jukebox five times consecutively, then fuck off. Sometimes we'd come back from a sesh and 'Wirralwork' would still be pedal-to-the-metal. (*To the gathered throng*) Imagine K.O. and Lager, any of those old-timer cunts having to deal with the Judge on All Night Repeat. Doesn't bear thinking about, looking back.

HERTZOG: As a Drentheman, I still covet the entire Liverpool landmass. What they all take for granted! If it were my land, I'd put miles of birthday candles right round the edges!

BREAKFAST: (*Conciliatory*) Perhaps living on all that reclaimed land has given you Netherlanders too mobile a worldview, Old Mate. Perhaps it means you're always on the verge of upping sticks. I have relatives on the east coast of Jutland at Romo, an island if you can call it that. Everything's reclaimed. Awful place. Always spongy, not unlike walking in semolina pudding.

HAVE-A-LAUGH: Be Quick nil, Quickborn three.

HERTZOG: (*Screaming at Gary Have-a-laugh*) What are you saying? He shouldn't score any goals for those comments.

HAVE-A-LAUGH: (*Shocked*) I never thought you were listening, Judge. Pay no attention to me, mate, I'm unswervingly out of my mind – drunk as a cunt. Who put the party in Partisan, that's me! So your top B-side or not, I'm still well plumping for Mr Baring-Gould.

HERTZOG: Baring-Gould? (*Turns a full 90 degrees*) That's

your name? So your great-grandfather or some such wrote 'Onward Christian Soldiers'.

BREAKFAST: He did indeed.

HAVE-A-LAUGH: (*Appeasing*) Be Quick one, Quickborn three. (*Rallying*) But victory's now definitely in sight for Full English Breakfast. First team to five goals, come *on* now!

BREAKFAST: (*Suddenly combative, addressing the throng*) Okay, now I'm taking a penalty. (*To Hertzog*) You admitted earlier, Judge Barry, even pressed home the point that some North Netherlanders are surrounded on three sides by former Nazis. Surely, if they choose to play house in that undefendable Israel-like territory, what right have they to act like victims to the wider world? A free democracy gives us the option to move should we choose, Old Boy. My Anglish family left Quickborn quick-sharp during the Hitler times. And just ask my Romo lot about undefendable territory.

HERTZOG: But we have *every* right to be here.

BREAKFAST: That's precisely what Yankee capitalists cried when Pancho Villa started burning the American-owned haciendas to the ground during the Mexican Revolution. But as the old tombstone reads: 'Here lies the body of Michael Shay, who died maintaining his right of way. His case was clear and his will was strong, but he's as dead as if he'd been wrong!'

HAVE-A-LAUGH: Be Quick one, Quickborn four. Gentlemen, this must be the dénouement.

HERTZOG: (*Grim*) I'm not playing this game any longer. I never was playing this game. You corn-fed English so take for granted what your land guarantees that it gives you a sickening attitude. It even taints Liverpudlians.

BREAKFAST: It is not our attitude that is so sickening, Mr Hertzog. It is your own. Like the Swedes, you Netherlanders

192

were ambivalent accomplices of your hated Nazis. Your government, its MPs and commercial warplane manufacturers profited handsomely from the money made from sales to your eventual enslavers. But you never let your own air force get off the ground. All but a handful were decimated by the Nazis in the opening moments of their invasion. Your government knew war was coming. But they hid their heads in Neutrality, made Neutrality their mantra. So even though your World Famous Anthony Fokker stole the 1936 Paris Air Show with his futuristic Grim Reaper warplane, your government did not dare even sell them to the Spanish Republican Government for fear of upsetting Friend Adolf and his Condor Legion. Paid for and everything, they were. Remember Guernica, Judge Barry? The whole market town was practice-bombed into obliteration by missionaries of Nazism. Perhaps those impounded Fokkers could have saved Republican lives.

HAVE-A-LAUGH: (*Mouth open, too fascinated to declare victory*) ?

HERTZOG: (*Grim, motionless, defensive*) The Swedes were not even occupied by the Nazis. Yet they built German Junkers bombers in their own factories. A bizarre kind of neutrality they displayed.

BREAKFAST: Neutrality? What neutrality is not of the bizarre and endlessly self-justifying variety? Let's look for Dutch indicators of Non-Neutrality, shall we? Why did you neutrals install a German engine in your greatest ground attack aircraft – the De Schelde D21? What side were you anticipating joining? The Daimler-Benz engine in your Dutch warplane so flummoxed the Allies that we named it by mistake the Focke-Wulf 198, a German name! So do come off your high horse, Judge Barry. Apparently, your undefendable backyard extended all the way to the Zuider Sea. Even those

Fokkers that the Spanish Republicans had paid up front for were left for dead out in the wind and rain, Fokker's Pride Of Paris Airshow left rusting out in full view at world-famous Schiphol international airport. (*Dramatically to the now enthralled throng*) Every one of those experimental warplanes – years ahead of their time – was left on the tarmac to rust, and thereafter to be decimated by the Nazis.

HAVE-A-LAUGH: (*Amidst claps and hoots*) East Fife 4, Forfar 5. Game set and match to Leander, Quickest of Borns!

HERTZOG: (*Utterly uncowed*) Leander?

MICK: (*Clueless*) Not you, too? I fucking love Leigh Hunt.

HERTZOG: (*To Breakfast*) Your first name is Leander? (*Hooded eyes*) Why? Do I need to do some proper investigating?

BREAKFAST: If you are here to right the wrongs of all Netherlanders, Judge Barry, perhaps you already celebrate the extraordinary events of June 14th 1667.

HERTZOG: (*Clueless, uninterested*) Too long ago to count, Old Uncle. It matters not to me what happened in far off times.

BREAKFAST: Why, Judge Barry, that's the very day the Dutch Fleet invaded Kent! You don't bake a cake? They sailed up to Chatham and stole Charles II's finest flagships. No candles for that? I should have thought a nationalist such as you would have such a victory tattooed across his heart!

HAVE-A-LAUGH: Martin Peters, top corner of the net! Rubbing it in, or what?

MICK: (*Taking Breakfast aside, whispering*) Tour de force, Lord Youth!

ROCK: (*Conspiratorial*) Where d'you pull that performance out of?

BREAKFAST: I just felt that you'd all expect it of me, Old Sod. Besides, I've dreamed since early childhood of my twenty-eighth birthday. June 14th. That's when I collect a rather vast inheritance. And as that date is fast approaching, I have even more reason to remember all of these facts! Besides, my many school detractors at Charterhouse were always quick and eager to remind me that it had been my great-great-great-great-uncle who had, on my own birthday no less, lost us the English Fleet . . . and to the Dutch! So I know at least a hundred more unnecessary facts about that day; I became obsessed with it.

Over in the corner of the bar, Hertzog was not now looking nearly so judicial. Downcast and glowering to himself though he was, however, the watch spring of the Barry Hertzog frame remained so taut that I felt obliged to keep an eye out for Breakfast for the rest of the evening.

ROCK: The Judge seems pretty damned pissed off at finding out your first name's Leander.

BREAKFAST: My great-uncle Sir Redvers Buller, on account of his Boer War tactics, suffered the humiliating nickname 'Sir Reverse' by the British press. Otherwise the family name Redvers would have been my first name, Old Bean.

ROCK: (*None the wiser*) Why not then?

BREAKFAST: The press had so tarnished the name Redvers that my mother Birgitta refused it; said it would blight my life. Unable to name their firstborn as they wished, my parents opted instead for the man behind the Jameson Raid, the action that started the whole Boer War. Idealism was behind it. Leander Starr Jameson. I'm far prouder to be named Leander. It was an ill-starred raid, utterly let down by the British government. But it had justice in its endgame, Old

Chap, and black Africans would in the long run have suffered far less had the Boers not apprehended Jameson's raiders.

ROCK: You made a true enemy today, Herr Quickborn. Hertzog's not the kind of customer to forget one word of this encounter.

BREAKFAST: (*Raising his eyes comically*) Battle of Naseby, Old Rock. (*Gesturing with his head to Hertzog and smiling*) And he's Albert II. Something to think about for the future. First day of Auschwitz and all that. Do drink a Bourbon for me.

31. THE DREAMS OF ANNA

5am, Monday June 12th, 2006
Still dreaming at Iloi Agriturismo, Lake Omodeo

Something to think about for the future? The infuriated Hertzog had in front of everyone declared to Leander that his one-upmanship would be the death of him. Why was Leander's comment – directed very much at me alone – something to think about for the future? I hung between time suspended in some kind of wispy pale grey BSF (*breathable stabilising fluid*) of the kind they used in the 2097 Paralympics at Turkish Mt Olympus when I realised the implications. Future travel? But only one time had I ever journeyed into the Future *and* remembered it. It was right around the Millennium, soon after Mick's first stab at a solo career. He phoned me just as I'd returned, so I was still too immersed to hide anything. Had it been face-to-face forget about it. Mick's far too agnostic to hear such weirdness without a filter. Down the phone, I could be anyone. Anonymous. But that night I returned from a very brief trip into the Future, Mick phoned about two hours after my landing – and briefly he was interested.

MICK: Well, how long into the Future?
ROCK: About a hundred years.
MICK: What's the state?
ROCK: Everything's coming apart.
MICK: What, like now?
ROCK: No, Rizlas won't stick together. Epoxy glues neither.

Everything's sticky. Plastic's all gone jellyfish. Tips are heaving with gelatine landfill. Meltdown is the term they use. Cities of concrete are de-solidifying. Nail and screw companies are flourishing. Soviet housing has left no trace whatsoever. The Future's sticky. Like how too much Coca-Cola when you're tripping gives you a sugar beard in a different dimension. Scratching. I was scratching the whole time I was there. The Future's icky, the Future's sticky . . . (*Portentously*) That's my estimation.

MICK: (*Silence*)

ROCK: Any thoughts, youth?

MICK: You went, didn't you? Wigwam's gonna fucking freak out.

ROCK: Who's Wigwam?

MICK: He's this New Wave of British Heavy Metal kid I'm teaching the bass to.

ROCK: You can't play bass.

MICK: I can for money. I can do anything for money. One step ahead, that's all you have to be. Gary Tibbs Says Play In A Day. The one-step-ahead shuffle.

I'd lost him, had him briefly but the drawbridge slammed shut. In all the years I knew M. Goodby, that 'You Went' was his heftiest salute of approval I ever enjoyed. But now, I heard a rabble at the drawbridge, a furious mob wielding clubs and knives. Around me the clouds dispersed too quickly and I fell/sank hundreds of feet into the safety net of my lush double bed. What's going on? The legions at my bedroom door were deafening me. But when I rushed to open it, a towel around my waist, into my room tumbled a very desperate Anna. She threw her arms around me. Now I was hugging a fat woman. Why? Anna, however, had already set up camp upon my bed, and she appeared to be wearing pretty much every item of clothing in her suitcase, topped off with Giampaolo's sheepskin car coat. She reached into her father's pocket and took out a battered paperback.

ANNA: (*Desperate*) I stole it. I stole it. I saw the motorbike on the cover. *My* motorbike. It was just an opportunity. And now all I do is feel freezing cold. I'm having terrible nightmares.

Holy shit! It was the book of the film poster I'd seen pinned up in the Judge's jail cell! Blessèd Anna had only nicked *Soldier of Orange*, one of Judge Barry Hertzog's favourite fucking books, that's all! She'd been sitting there in Florinas Penitentiary drinking coffee in the warder's office, when suddenly she'd spied her own Ural 750 cc motorbike-and-sidecar depicted on the front cover of the book that Lame Warder Klötz had been reading. Never considering any possible implications – it was just a scruffy mass-market paperback – Anna had quickly allowed her obsessive side to override everything. I must have that book! And it was not until early the next morning – back at her parents' house in Cágliari – when she had viewed for the first time the paperback's inky, messy inscription in Hertzog's own hand. Now Anna was inconsolable. This beautiful woman so independent and wild of spirit seemed cosmically pole-axed. Everywhere Hertzog. In her nightmares, she saw no longer the dashing male cover hero of *Soldier of Orange* saving the adventuresome heroine with the aid of Anna's own trusty wheels. Instead, she saw only herself bound into the passenger sidecar of her pride-and-joy, as onwards through the night ploughed her Ural 750 cc, but now under the new demented management of the X-faced figure of Judge Barry Hertzog.

I needed to act quickly. Apparently, Anna had visited my room earlier but had dared not disturb me. Since then, Hertzogian nightmares pervaded her every instant. And despite being swathed in all of those clothes, the poor dear was shivering, her teeth were chattering. She was in a shocking state. She needed my room and my presence, I concluded, but not *my* mess. Besides, I'd been farting all night and I'm a tall chap – when I'm spacing I'm jet propelled. So I lit some of the beeswax candles made with genuine Iloi Agriturismo beeswax. And I burned some gratis Iloi incense, gathered from Lake Omodeo's beaches. And we had a bathtub here no less, a rarity. So I ran a bath to plonk myself in, to steep myself in while I kept out of Blessèd Anna's way. And I set up my iBeam to 89.9 FM San Gavino Monreale, where Jesu Crussu was playing epic cave music by '70s megaband Neon Sardinia – perfect for Anna to space to. Crussu mentioned how this controversial piece of music had got Neon Sardinia leader Fabrizio Arra kidnapped by F.C. Mamoiada hooligans back in 1976! It trod on too many partisan toes, apparently. But we were in luck. In two days' time, the villagers of Fonni and Mamoiada would be celebrating the 25th Anniversary of Arra's release with Neon Sardinia's re-enactment of the two villages' legendary shamanic feud. As Anna's driving schedule that day involved ferrying what she called 'an American classic' down to Lanusei, she commented that we'd be able to get over to see their performance.

ROCK: It'll be synth overload. Vibe Central Station. Besides, I could always feel the disappointment in *Sea and Sardinia* when D. H. Lawrence didn't make it to Fonni. Let's go on his behalf.

ANNA: Perfect! We can also visit the great monuments at Madau.

Not so old as the Doorways you require, Rock Section, but still superb.

And for the next half-hour, as I drifted comatose in the hot bath, Anna lay submerged in my vast double bed under a heavy rug of her dad's clothes and my own assorted bits, plus various requisitioned Iloi Agriturismo counterpanes – while through the speakers of my iBeam chuntered the grumbling shamen of Fonni and Mamoiada, or rather Neon Sardinia's spectacular interpretation. Amazing music. Zzzzzzzzzzzzzzz . . .

* * *

But when, just thirty minutes later, I grabbed a large towel and crept out of the bathroom still dripping wet, Anna was already sitting bolt upright in my bed, sipping tea and smiling. The covers were off, the men's clothes far flung, the blinds were open and everyone was home. In fact this woman looked delightful, quite back to her own lovely self. Who squeezes the time together at those random nodal points – and who says? What Gift Divine enables some sacred thirty minutes to deal out the powers of a whole night's sleep? I sat down next to her on the bed and raised my right fist in salute. I call *this* a Powernap! Then, Anna all feline and yawny stretched her arms out to me and held my head firmly. She looked into my eyes, deep into my eyes.

ANNA: You helped me. You banished Hertzog from my mind. You helped me so, Rock. (*Laughing slightly squeakily*) You even bring me a replacement!
ROCK: (*Not uttering, mouthing*) Who?
ANNA: Mick! I dreamed many times of Mick, for hours and

hours we talked. Then I awaken and it's maybe only a half-hour since when I first fall asleep. I know so much now about Mick. Everything except facts.

ROCK: (*Laughing*) Everything except facts?

ANNA: Tell me of Mick, please, Rock Section. Tell me everything of Mick. In my dream he was very very tall as you say. With the Sammy Hagar hair, also.

Pursued in her nightmares by Judge Barry Hertzog, run off the highway by articulated 22-wheeler maniacs and fighting to stop capitalists from ruining Sardinia's most famous national shrine, the beleaguered Anna had now turned inevitably, inexorably to the central protagonist of my story, to the eye of the hurricane as it were, to the hub around which every evil had attached itself, to the missing piece of the puzzle: ye Bard himself, M. Goodby.

32. SIX MONTHS THAT SHOOK THEIR WORLD

6am, Monday June 12th, 2006
Hanging out at Iloi, overlooking Lake Omodeo

Anna and I grabbed some coffee and wandered down to that same Iloi tomb on whose capstone I had watched her gyrating just hours before. But before I commenced my epic tale, I made a pact with Blessèd Anna, at least I tried – she hit the roof. I'd had this smart idea that, once I'd finished telling her the history of Mick, we could split the research in an effort to use our time better – me visiting the Doorways alone and her chasing The Reaper's movements up around the Sássari City area, perhaps with her father Giampaolo in tow. I knew from Anna's clamorous announcement that they had a fucking ace Viet Vet machine to deliver today, a purple flake 1970 Plymouth Barracuda – the perfect Reaper Pursuit Vehicle.

ANNA: (*Breathless*) It's just like in *Vanishing Point*! Our Barracuda has the exact same Chrysler body style as that Dodge Challenger that Kowalski died in.

Okay, so I hadn't made a pact exactly, not yet anyway. But I was still working on her, and I was fairly convinced that our dual multi-tasking was an idea worth pursuing, especially as I was fast running out of Sardu time. I needed to corral Anna's inflamed spirit, her sense of injustice and her wild Hertzogian nightmares in order to bring these proceedings to their swiftest conclusion. But although Anna was totally doubtful of my ability to fend for myself at the great Doorways, she had already shown me her itinerary for our proposed next visit. Come on, these directions to the Doorway at nearby Bidil 'e Pira looked so very highly detailed that I knew, I just knew I could do it alone. Besides, as Blessèd Anna had already experienced so many of my own desperate straits, I really wished to save her from anymore unnecessary worry – especially after these Hertzog nightmares. So I couldn't back off on the Go-It-Alone Plan, because I felt so sure that it was by far the best manoeuvre. Anyway, while Anna agreed for us to make our final decision at midday – when we would exchange wheels with Giampaolo at Santa Cristina – for now we snuggled down together against the hot healing sandstone façade of the Iloi tomb, Lake Omodeo stretched out azure blue before us, as Anna started the proceedings.

ANNA: Mick is half-Sardinian I think?
ROCK: You tell me! His mother Gabriella comes from Alghero.
ANNA: (*Gravely*) Oh, so she has mixed doubts about her heritage?

Bloody hell, nice way of putting it. Mixed doubts. You could say that – just a bit. How do I explain this one? Born in England, in 1958, Michael Buenaventura Durruti Goodby was a typical product of Anglo-Foreign parentage. His mother Gabriella Goodby was a yoga guru from Catalan Alghero on the northwest coast, whence fled so many Catalan anarchists after Dictator Franco's victory in the Spanish Civil War. Thereafter, Alghero's soaring population became so very fiercely non-Sardu/non-Italian that they regularly paid top salaries to imported Catalan scholars and lecturers from Barcelona and the Spanish east coast simply to maintain their strident cultural differences. Forced by the privations of war, however, Gabriella had slummed it briefly in the south of the island, fetching up as a cook at the new R.A.F. Decimomannu Airbase, where she'd fallen in love with six-foot-four Flight Lieutenant Alec Goodby in 1950. The couple got married almost immediately, Mick's older brother Steve arriving in 1953, followed by his sister Sharon a year later. Mick alone had been born after the family's move to England, a fact he loved to wind-up his brother with at any opportunity. But it was only on returning 'home' to barren Lincolnshire's R.A.F. Wainfleet that Gabriella Goodby had – to her chagrin – discovered that her Flight Lieutenant husband was a flyer no longer, having been grounded and demoted to sergeant for crashing a target tug whilst drunk. In turn, Sgt Goodby had been disappointed to learn that Gabriella was not three years older than him as she'd always claimed, but thirteen. Moreover, Gabriella had previously given birth to twins in 1949, both immediately being put up for adoption on the island. Still depressed by this loss, and never having anticipated bearing such Aryan offspring, the compromised Gabriella – now far from her Alghero enclave – had dived into Motherhood with gusto, becoming fiercely protective of her 'three little blondies'. I explained all these salient points as best I could to Anna, who – as a mixed-up Sardukid herself – relished the details and loved the ins-and-outs of Gabriella Goodby's Talibanesque worldview.

ROCK: It was at R.A.F. Wainfleet that Mick acquired his addiction to fizzy drinks. Unknown at the time, but the Ministry of Defence had made a deal with Wainfleet's Kola Bear soft drinks company. The M.O.D. offloaded tons of wartime synthesized sugar in exchange for cheap distribution to schools throughout the armed forces. Tragically, Mick's generation were the guinea pigs who drank all that vicious speedy shit. He still needs umpteen cans every day. Add all that to Mama Gabriella's worldview and you're dealing with one tense, suspicious individual.

I took another swig of the now tepid black coffee and continued my tale of Rave Goodby and his Great Leap Forward. Until that spring of '89, Mick's biggest claim to cutting-edge fame was having once performed 'Last Tango in Paris' to a pub full of Walsall fans by mistake. Oo-er missus! But wouldn't all of this Lad Culture be just too confusing for Anna to understand? How can I give any of it context? After mucho consideration, I decided that a little scene-setting would first be in order. Thereafter, I'd be able to proceed with the same verve and aplomb that I'd deploy were I relating 'The Ancient Mariner' or somesuch. And if I spoke too fast for Anna to understand? Well, might that not be better for all of us?

ROCK: (*Really thinking about it*) The beginning of 1989 was a time of dreams, a time of Transformation. The world smelled younger than before. We *were* young. The world was changing. New possibilities led many people to themselves. Mick was the perfect example. These new possibilities also led other people *back* to themselves. Me in a nutshell. Four years of drugged fame, another four down the drug drain. I was one of the original punks who sought new idealism in Rave. Funny how many proper old hippies found the same home in Rave, especially as chav lads and chav dads were roaming around together X'd up. Enlightened wolf packs, not. But the multi-generational thing had kicked in, and the concept of 18–30 was being replaced and extended to 14–40. The Underground was again teeming with micro-boutiques. But this time around, it was chock full of garishly coloured, backwards-printed clothing, that kind of thing. And everybody accessorized with babies' dummies and rattles. Ecstasy parties were all-night tingeltangels of the love-grind variety.

ANNA: Tingeltangels?

ROCK: Cult word, sorry, Anna. A sexed-up Grope festival would also describe it.

ANNA: (*Gulps coffee and nods*) Okay.

ROCK: Everything was angular and askance. On ecstasy people were hogs for it. Ecstasy people were dogs for it, mounting the pavements and humping the bollards and waste bins. I'd long before stopped the lead singing, but Arthur Tadgell was too fond of me to give up entirely on my career. So he helped me through the lean times by setting me up as chief DJ at his Peak District dance club Dehydrated, at Chapel-en-le-Frith. Dayglo Maradona started right there.

Wow, I knew I couldn't go into too much detail for Blessèd Anna, but that didn't stop me remembering it all! What a gift Mr Tadgell had bequeathed me. All washed up and adrift from my own Post-Punk generation, I'd been utterly rebooted by his faith in me. Even better, Arthur Tadgell's gifts of listening had unlocked my own world. For whereas most of the other Dehydrated DJs – myself included – kept their sessions austere and unembellished, Mr Tadgell's own sessions were always brutal mega extended soul excursions that swung through everything from James Brown instrumentals to the Persuasions' gorgeous a cappellas, from Fred Wesley's epic trombone workouts to the Meters' perfection of the Wild Tchoupitoulas' 'Hey Pocky

A-way'. He always preferred the messy overload of Funkadelic as opposed to the pertness of Parliament, and even showcased beastly soul-informed Krautrock wipe-outs like Xhol Caravan. Hell, I've even known Mr Tadgell to hit his Dehydrated audience with Eddie Floyd's 'Big Bird' played at 33 rpm, mixing in a ramped-up football crowd at all the most rampant moments. But I digress.

ROCK: Okay, Anna, next imagine that into this super cool subterranean night world is flung the hung-up Mick Goodby. 'I'm too old.' 'I can't sing.' 'I can't dance.' That February-through-March of 1989, we dragged M. Goodby so far out of his comfortable Anfield environment that this Jungian psychologist, this psychedelic social worker, this (*struggling for the right words*) one-rhyme pub chancer recognised immediately the incredible opportunities on offer – especially to someone as enterprising as he. On first hearing Happy Mondays' Shaun Ryder belting it out over the P.A. at Dehydrated, Mick just laughed his head off and went to the bog. But it changed his life like nothing since the first John the Postman LP. In fact it even threw him temporarily off course.

Abruptly, my monologue to Anna floundered then halted as I remembered my searing arguments with ye Bard caused by his 'discovery' of Shaun Ryder. To Mick's newly ecstasied-up mind, Ryder had – by the sheer cu. ft. per sq. inch water-weight of his drooling deliveries – instantly eclipsed all the genius and collected writhings of John Cooper Clarke, Ed Banger, John the Postman, Ted Chippington, the lot. Year Zero'd by the Peak Experiences of Dehydrated and his sudden remove from Anfield pub culture, even Pol Pot Goodby himself had planned – albeit briefly – to Sell Out and become the next rhymeless wurzel. I was aghast, ballistic, even pugilistic. M. Goodby MC? Whatever has happened to our belovèd wordsmith? You're a poet. How can some cunt that can hardly speak suddenly become ye Bard's rival? But Mick was having none of it.

MICK: What's the point of my labouring for hours over a well-argued smartarse couplet when Ryder can outgun me with a simple, well-rehearsed 'Awwwww, Get Up!!!!!!!!!'

ROCK: Come on, Goodby. Are you really going to be happy with being a glorified Carnival barker? You're a Jungian street poet with a book full of sweet rhymes awaiting publication. I can't believe you're preparing to jump on a pre-verbal bandwagon whose protagonists never contribute more to a song than a few yelps, urges and a couple of ecstatic yawns.

That did the trick all right, got him back on the John Donne trail. Next thing we all knew, Mick was rapping his wordiest poetry over the instrumental bits of Ken Heathcote's legendary cassette work-out *Fatigues*, not a work particularly known for the originality of its soundtrack but ye Bard sounded great.

ANNA: English culture seems on the outside to be so very violent. You seem like such nice guys. But if you were kidnapped in Macomér, you must have been hated by many. How violent were you all?

What a thorny question! There was no way in which to explain this to Anna. Going down the football, we got a chance to unleash on to random wankers, cunts and dickheads the same Mega-Neg Energies that we might otherwise have felt obliged to unleash upon our relatives, loved ones or important locals with whom we needed to interface daily. Oops. Thus, we were pragmatists who kacked only in the others' backyards, pragmatists who targeted only the Too Violent and the Culturally Unfit. We were sectarian only on levels of Intellect and Creed, and therefore *any* Stupid Idiot would be dealt with severely. What precise behaviour or mental state defined Stupid Idiocy? Why, anybody behaving outside our notions of the Law as worked out in our collective noggins. For example, because they were always so cluelessly loud about the Lord, Jehovah's Witnesses were always prime targets for an S.I.A. (Stupid Idiot Attack). Even clonking a geriatric Jesuit priest, you're still fearful he has residual IRA connections. The Jehovah's, though, they have fuck all back-up. Monks were fair game too, mainly because of the stupid shaven tonsure. Besides, just from the ones I'd subdued, monks always felt far too well upholstered to have left the ways of the world behind completely, their Lard Arses of Jesus requiring a proper raging upon. Come back to the world, you cop-out Cult Cunts! It's hard to imagine but Stupid Idiocy even afflicted Football Fans, too. Pele fans, mostly. What benign, pseudo-religious expressions they wore! Who but the proto-corpse chooses for his Football Muse so long inactive a volcano as Pele? That kind always got a good kicking. Later on, of course, it may have been that some of Full English Breakfast's more destructive foreign café assaults could have been, would have been – had we not all sanctioned 'The Work' beforehand – interpreted as the work of a Stupid Idiot. Over time, I witnessed some horrible atrocities committed in the name of Hooliganism, true. And sometimes my own kind achieved with wooden stave what could have been just as easily accomplished with fists alone. But as it is in these precise trickster corners, in these cultural microfolds that the

Laws of Hooliganism dwell, then it was up to intelligent life forms such as ourselves to explore such mysterious chasms, such Spaces In-between.

There was a back room at The Decoffinated Café where the bad boys could hang around, skin up and drink mortuary fluid. Actually, the latter act was poetically named an Obligatory Oblation by M. Goodby, and unless you were under eight-and-a-half years old, two minutes nosing around was all you got in the back room without being obliged to unbolt the double-skinned metal outer door and neck half a cupful of ye Fluide in the adjoining muggers' five-a-side car park. Aww, not really for the drinking that stuff. 'Struth, youth. Anyway, it was from this car park that the shadier side of our operation was enacted. The evildoings. All achieved from the back of two Vauxhall Astra vans, well quiet looking. Both painted a dark grail mung with an overwash of palest gruel, this pair of 'Wash Me' orphans got us every place in Europe with minimal problemos. No customs officer ever ever pulled us over. Weaponed-up every time, but nobody bothered once. Mick's wearing cartoon donkey ears as he's driving through Calais. They wave him on and big-old-grin it through their cubicles. Mick's got a Ronald Reagan mask on at Ostend; through we go, no questions asked. Our parameters of Hooliganism? Unlike Millwall's Treatment, West Ham's Inter City Firm and R.O.C.C.M.'s Nous Voyageons, we didn't kidnap and we certainly didn't kill. Actions of extraordinary firmness, however, were condoned, and the deployment of weapons was considered essential. Stu and Gaz Have-a-laugh were weapons freaks. Hotel rooms at away games were always a total 'mare. Tripods, long-range sights, small mortars – will you please keep those curtains closed, gentlemen.

But with regard to how our choices of Worst Enemies were

reckoned, our methods diverged wildly from the Orthodox Hooliganism of the day purely because our little tribe emanated from so many different corners of this UK. Thus, Turf Wars were for others and it was always personal rather than club revenge that was to be our primary order of the day. When we stayed over in Sheffield for what-turned-out-to-be the Hillsborough Disaster, the bathwater at the city's top hotel Hallam Towers was brown, almost bloody, rusty brown. So when Messrs Have-a-laugh and Stuart got back from being nearly crushed'n'smothered to death and – despite having brung this top hostelry mucho Sterling – only thick menstrual gushings being available bathwise to the pair, it was off into the wilds of the Peak District in 'Wash Me #1' that those two oily tykes proceeded, and at one hell of a bate. And when, on Totley Rise at sunset, they located a dead sheep rotting in a field, the letters G and S wrapped that sucker up and smuggled it whole into the bloody rust-red bath of Rm 1321 Hallam Towers. Gory. Biblical. Appropriate. About the only thing that was appropriate that whole fucking day. For how much longer must we tolerate mass murder? Discuss.

33. THE HILLSBOROUGH DISASTER

7am, Monday June 12th, 2006
Still hanging out at Iloi, overlooking Lake Omodeo

Yeah, Anna, let's discuss Mass Murder. Let's take some time out to talk through those things we never ever want to address. Let's discuss disasters and the culpability of those great authoritarians – police, politicians, media moguls – who feed off the approval of the general population and the benefits of their esteemed positions, but fail in their duty to their own population on those precise days when we most require them Not To Fuck Up! I knew I'd be on solid ground discussing with Blessèd Anna the Judahizing of Liverpudlians during the Hillsborough Disaster. For her own Sardinian people had been treated with similar disregard at Italia '90, during which time those cynical Italian mainland authorities had chosen to corral Europe's toughest fans – English and Dutch – in Sardinia's capital city. I wondered: had it always been this way?

ANNA: In the 19th century, many mainland Italians were fearful of Sardinia because of its malaria, its poverty and its archaic practices. Also, our language is very different. Nowadays, mainland Italians are suspicious because of our reputation for kidnapping.
ROCK: Do Sicilians suffer the same victimisation?
ANNA: No, never. But Sicily is very close to the mainland and it displays the kind of genuine Ancient Greek roots which all

Italians adore. In contrast, many mainland Italians deny their Sardinian roots because it's too independent and too separate, much too slow for them, and far too mysterious. They think we are churlish because we do not all want what they have to offer.

ROCK: Holy shit! That is Liverpool in a nutshell.

Then I began to explain to Anna the obscene manner in which much of the British press had reported the Hillsborough Disaster, how they had tarred every Liverpool supporter with the same hooligan brush. But as the tragedy had affected almost every one of my associates, I soon got too far ahead of myself and realised that I first needed to explain to Anna my own peculiar take on that tragic day's events. For seeing as I had been the only Nottingham Forest supporter among our little tribe, I had therefore experienced the main event purely as an observer, safely ensconced in our pre-designated area in the Spion Kop stand. It was utterly impossible to imagine by now, but I'd been proud that day to have been given the rare opportunity to 'play host' to some of my closest mates. For Mick's sister Sharon, fearing the worst, had refused utterly to allow her twelve-year-old twins to attend the F.A. Cup semi-final. So it was to my door that Brent, Dean and their distraught Uncle Mick had beaten an immediate path with a desperate request for 'safe' Forest seats atop Spion Kop. No fucking problemos, gentlemen. *And* very glad to oblige. As a decades-long Forest fan, this was easy easy easy for me to achieve. Moreover, I was delighted to have such top company up my end. Early '89 had proved so busy for my DJ career that I'd missed most of Forest's F.A. Cup run. So now I was determined to carve a fantastic time out of Semi-Final Weekend. Bring that fucker on!

I couldn't drive because of an unfortunate Wembley incident the previous week at Forest's highly skilful 3–1 League Cup Final victory over Luton Town, in which I'd borrowed a Wembley fork-lift, ostensibly to transport myself and my old Eastwood mate Gaz Marshmallow back to his car, which he'd insisted on parking fucking miles away near Canons Park tube station – 'to be near the M1'. Not realising how drunk I was, and Gaz too much of a yokel to alert me to the massive tailback building up behind us along the A4140, I'd eventually keeled over and fallen asleep at some traffic lights on Honeypot Lane. When the cops had nabbed me, Gaz just jumped off and hightailed it back to Eastwood. Thanks, old pal. Suspended driving licence, night in the cells, ra-ra. Who gives a fuck! It just meant that I'd be able to enjoy the Hillsborough Semi the way it *should* be enjoyed, i.e.: I could malinger in the passenger seat, spray a few walls and drink-and-drug even more than usual. Totally off the hook, or so I thought.

Now the media were all over this 'F.A. Cup Semi-Final Re-make' as they billed it. Same teams as last year, same venue as last year, same result? No chance. Liverpool might have been on a 104-day winning streak, but Kenny Dalglish was no Brian Clough *and* we'd just won the League Cup. But the media frenzy surrounding this double-bill ensured that our weapons stayed back at the D-Cough. For the previous year had seen Hillsborough swarming with cops and stewards, and it was fair to expect the same volume of bluebottles per square inch this year. So on the day before the Disaster, our three vehicles – the two Astra vans and Sharon Goodby's Vauxhall Cavalier – crossed the Pennines nice and early, allowing plenty of time for fun and frolics at Sheffield's finest hotel Hallam Towers. And while we moaned about the anticipated overwhelming police presence, well at least our heroic boys-in-blue would – with the TV eyes of the Straight World fixed firmly upon them – hopefully feel obliged to be generous in their behaviour towards the supporters of such important national teams as ours. They were not. Now, I don't want to be a hindsighty cunt about this. But on the day of the Hillsborough Disaster, I would not under any circumstances have been up that Leppings Lane end because, by then, I just didn't trust anyone at all. Spring 1989 was already an especially sensitive time of too many public disasters with too few authorities taking responsibility. At the Clapham Rail Disaster, just the previous December, thirty-five commuters had died through the admitted malpractices of British Rail. That same month, terrorists had brought down Pan-Am Flight 103 over the Scots town of Lockerbie. Barely a month later, a British Midland 737 had got into difficulties near my Uncle Mog's house in Gotham, and he'd watched forty-seven die as the jet had ploughed into the M1. In such a time of strange accidents and sinister events, surely this F.A. Cup Semi-Final should have been a grand old opportunity for the authorities to have shown the public how smoothly everything runs when they get their operations totally right. Nope, no chance, the cops that spring were on a Dwindler and nothing could have upped their game.

On the morning of the match, being already set up in the Hallam Towers, my own little group had enjoyed a hearty oversleep and some midday room service. Then we'd moseyed over to the stadium a full hour behind Gary Have-a-laugh, Rob Dean, Stu, Yeh-Yeh and Doughy. But when Mick, Brent and Dean finally saw the true nature of their Vichy seating arrangements, they all looked totally gutted, especially as we'd just passed a bunch of Liverpool fans singing 'We'll Win the Double, We'll Win the Double Again' to the tune of 'Roll Out the Barrel'. And even as we climbed up into the Spion Kop, neither Mick nor the twins would take off their Liverpool rosettes. Fair enough, lads. I'll give you no pressure. It's not me who'll get beaten up. Besides, the whole afternoon was a red celebration and no Forest fans could have expected the enemy to be sitting right up that close! Especially when that enemy currently seemed to be down the Liverpool end of the stadium and engaging in some rather bizarre behaviour. For, with the match just seconds away from starting, I told ye Bard that the Leppings Lane end didn't look at all right to me. My instinct told me there must be something wrong, or else they'd have all been moving outwards, not all clustered together with the kick-off so imminent. Why weren't the Liverpool supporters separating out? Even from this far up the other end, you can always tell what a crowd looks like. You know where it's full, and you know when there are gaps. But right there in the Liverpool knot, in the scrum, you could see nothing but heads. No colours, no scarves, just heads – the crowd wasn't moving.

Then the teams emerged to fabulous applause and cheering. All right! Now we're cooking. Up our end of the field, Nigel Clough and 'Psycho' Stuart Pearce were mugging for the press, while Liverpool supporters broadcast their delight at the return of their Scots captain Alan Hansen, though Mick and the twins had big doubts about the effectiveness of his return at such a crucial time. Of course, I myself was delighted to see him, and for those same dubious reasons. But even as the players were kicking off, still the Leppings Lane end was all jammed at the centre and I worried about how our own tribe would be approaching spectatordom in these crowded-as-fuck circum-stances. Next to us, a youngish mother with two little boys aged about seven or eight approached the policewoman standing at the end of our row and demanded to be allowed to leave. When the policewoman asked her why, she pointed down to the far end and said she wouldn't stay another minute longer. It was only five past three, so the policewoman had to accompany all three of them off the premises. Was it a woman's intuition? What had she seen?

ANNA: (*Wide-eyed*) And what was it that she saw?

ROCK: Nothing. Nothing at all. There were no cops about, no stewards, nothing. And this lady had clearly been the previous year and now she'd clocked the frightening difference, she wanted no further part in it. I'd consciously sought out the same seat, well, the same row as the previous year and then the Leppings Lane end had been heaving with constabulary. Of course too many police always creates tension and violence. But the disaster at Hillsborough also proved the complete opposite.

ANNA: (*Horrified, shaking*) That it was the absence of police that had most guaranteed the death and destruction to those poor supporters.

ROCK: Exactly. They hadn't done their homework. So the match only lasted six minutes. Death in the afternoon is a phrase you hear. But when it happened quite quietly and quite near me, I just reminded myself of an animal. One that I didn't know. We all evacuated the ground as quickly as possible, then ran around to Leppings Lane to check on the guys. But it was futile. Total bloody pandemonium.

Describing all of these creepy, horrific experiences to Anna thrust me back temporarily into those sleepless nights immediately after the Disaster. What could I have done to help? Now, the sadness of so many footballing families was once again overwhelming me. In the dreadful aftermath of that savage weekend, why had there not been weeks of organised national mourning over Liverpool families' losses? Any other English town could have expected the kid gloves treatment. Why had the press, in this early '89 atmosphere of chronic disasters, not just declared the sheer tragedy of Hillsborough? Instead, they had rushed to confer 'Good Guy' and 'Bad Guy' status without any real consideration. Why had the viciously judgemental Blame Culture not just backed off one temporary iota? And why, if the South Yorkshire Police had nothing to hide regarding Hillsborough, had there been this colossal rush by the right wing media to shore up their dwindling reputation by tarnishing the reputations of the Liverpool dead? But I well knew that we lived in a society that had always made saints out of cops, had always made positive TV shows about those fuckers, mostly awarding them hero status simply for doing what they were being paid for, which they clearly enjoyed or they would not have been doing the job. If a cop got beaten up, it made perfect sense to me. But if the press reported it, every bruise was like one further nail in the coffin of Polite UK Society. And if a cop got shot? Fucking hell, it was like Baby Jesus had just been murdered.

ANNA: Did any of the police at Hillsborough suffer beatings from the angry fans?
ROCK: Anna, I saw nothing like that. Maybe a couple of guys kicking the patrol cars, one lone bloke hammering on the bonnet. But I think the really angry people were too exhausted from trying to save themselves. Gary Have-a-laugh would have kicked off if he could have, but he was totally fucked.

He wouldn't admit it right away, of course. But as the evening wore on, his bruising turned deadly black.

Simply on account of the sheer power wielded by their new tradition as hosts of the F.A. Cup Semi-Finals, the South Yorkshire Police Constabulary and the Hillsborough Powers That Be had – that shameful Saturday April 15th 1989 – hoodwinked great numbers of Liverpool families into entrusting the safety of their beloved offspring, sons, daughters, nephews, nieces, etc. to Sheffield Wednesday's far too meagre Leppings Lane facilities. Then, those authorities had sat about clucking like zombies and watched Liverpool people drown in that Red Sea of Suffering.

ROCK: I even remember Stu telling me he'd felt there was something anti-Thatcher about not joining that lemmings queue. He said Margaret was like that song by Iggy PCP: 'I am your crazy driver, I'm sure to steer you wrong.' Margaret Thatcher wanted to dismantle every principle of Socialist Society, so that even after she'd long gone, there could never be a return to any kind of Socialism.

ANNA: It's obvious to me that Socialism can never fail completely. So long as it is practised correctly, the righteousness of Socialism could never be called into question. Like Christianity, it's the most beautiful idea of the whole world so far. It's impractical, sure, even a little stupid in its expectations, but so so beautiful! For everyone! Everybody given equal chance? Superb! Only the practitioners themselves have failed, and perhaps they secretly wished for it not to work. Stalin and Mao were brazen, selfish opportunists, not Socialists as their followers claim. What room was there left for Socialism in such unilateral behaviour as theirs? They were Nihilist Prophets sent by Indùstrialu himself to work his devious 20th-century sorcery.

ROCK: Who was Indùstrialu?

ANNA: Oh, the heathen god Indùstrialu was the invention of Pedru Réppu, a Sardinian newspaper cartoonist. He was a post-war separatist who created his works to explain to our beaten population why Sardinia had suffered such devastation from both sides during the Second World War. According to Réppu, our first big chemical towns like Carbónia, Silíqua and Arboréa were created not by Mussolini, but by Indùstrialu himself, as punishment for our island's foolish decision to remain Italian. Réppu's work influenced many of Sardinia's late 1960s Anarchistas, and even contributed to the crazy belief that we had once been Atlanteans.

ROCK: (*Wide-eyed*) Atlantis? No way!

ANNA: Yes, very much so. Our place, our central position in the Mediterranean gave the Anarchistas great hope for this to be true. We needed to believe in ourselves at last. After the failure of Mussolini's grand Italian empire, Pedru Réppu helped us look once more to ourselves for our leaders. Like Ireland, we Sardinians must now search obsessively for a leader who loves us, who understands our geographical problems, who does not secretly wish to makes Tuscans or Romans of us all!

Some national leaders namby-pamby their people. Why not ours? Post-war Britain had been a world hub of welfare and caring. So how had it been seized by the kind of gruelling and vindictive leadership that WW2 should have put to rest? Semi-legal governments all across the Third World looked to Dictator Thatcher's behaviour towards her own people as permission to roughride their own populations into the ground. Why have freedom when you can make do with the Semblance of Freedom? That was her message. And woe betide all those who found Thatcher's simplistic capitalist ideals too alienating and destructive. Liverpudlians? Pah. Why can they not be brought into line? Liverpool? Harrumph. Just as Tibet was to the Chinese, Liverpool in all of its Cultural *and* Physical Remove became a constant target for the Creedist enmity of the 1980s Conservatives. National leaders who hate their own: what are they? Stalin hated his people because he'd been raised in Georgia over a thousand miles from Moscow, spoke mainly Georgian and felt therefore permanently hung up around the urbanites of Moscow. Chairman Mao was another peripheral for whom city people brought out the very worst in him. But Margaret Thatcher didn't have that excuse. Barren-ness Thatcher wasn't a Gaelic speaker from the Outer Hebrides. No, she was a secular Oliver Cromwell with the keys to the wrong fucking country. She was like a bighead architect who refuses to work with the materials provided. Bricks, mortar? Bring me white marble. Why are my own people not motivated like the Yanks? Why can I not insist that they exchange their own values for my own? And like the Vichy French government that supported the Nazi Occupation, Greed-Is-Good Thatcher was relentless in her need to inflict upon us all her Nihilistic Un-Values. She was like some ancient kiddy fiddler monarch who had attempted through legislation to normalise in the Public Mind their own voracious rapine tendencies. She was at least partly successful. For Hillsborough had been the Let-Them-Get-On-With-It disaster. And the abandoning of Liverpool's most fervent away fans during the 1989 F.A. Cup Semi-Final would remain forever the primary evidence that the Kingdom of Thatcher had simply not extended as far as Merseyside.

34. THE HALLAM TOWERS POST-MORTEM

8.30am, Monday June 12th, 2006
Monologue to Anna at Iloi, overlooking Lake Omodeo

Disaster night in Sheffield felt like a bomb had hit it, especially once all the chartered coaches and trains and minibuses had inhaled their grieving red masses and ferried them off down their respective motorways. Locals on the city streets there were none, all locked away behind closed doors, wringing their hands at the civic shame brought down upon their heads this day. The sole life-forms that remained in the city centre were shell-shocked packs of hollow-eyed out-of-town business boys, who – too late to check into any of Sheffield's now-bulging hotels – roamed the streets far too drunk to drive the hundred-odd miles home, but still done up in their best Lager Lout threads. Poor fuckers. They all looked like their jeans and red footy shirts would explode at midnight, all of them stranded miles from work left bereft in their business grey. Knowing how hard it was for Yeh-Yeh to get out as much as the rest of us, him being a magistrate and all, our little gang – all now brimming over with love for the Sanctity of Life – recognised in the haunted expression of each red-shirted man who passed us in the night, the plight of our own little magistrate had he – after an experience of today's magnitude – been left to fend for himself in late-night Glasgow, Hamburg or some other rum city centre. Yeh-Yeh would need help! Shit, therefore these poor fuckers need help!

And so we enacted an idea. All of us eager after the brown

bath episode to squeeze the best possible deal out of the Hallam Towers, and several of us – me, Rob Dean, Stu, Have-a-laugh and Yeh-Yeh – each in possession of a vast thirteenth-floor room with a view to the Peak District, we put the word around Sheff that the only wake in town was our wake. Come all ye Faithful, come all ye Fucked Up. Myself and Have-a-laugh being the only well dressed amongst us, i.e.: perpetual black clothes, the pair of us decorated my bedroom by tying black socks and t-shirts around the appropriate furniture points, thereby creating a special room of peace and quiet, a Room of Gloom wherein anyone who had suffered genuine losses could just fall to pieces in silence. Yeh-Yeh being cultured and a bit jittery about others invading his territory, we piled all of our personal belongings into his room, and kept it locked. Doughy as usual saved his money by kipping, or intending to kip in the back of 'Wash Me #1'. What were the other four rooms to be used for? Forgetting. A whole night of forgetting. Then we waited. Will they come? Will the word get out to those who need it most?

They came. Slowly at first, but with the passing hours scores of The Appalled drifted through our open doors, sought sanctuary through our open doors. Liverpool fans, Forest fans, even five distraught Sheffield Wednesday supporters who accused 'The Powers That Be' of having turned beloved Hillsborough into a State Abattoir. Some of the faces looked immediately familiar. No way! More than coincidentally, I'd met three of these top blokes – Steve Repping and the Say-Everything-Twice Brothers – at Keele Services eighteen months previously. I was gassing up on the forecourt at 2.30am, and there they all stood saluting something-or-other in white shirts and ties, sleeves rolled up, ciggies aglow. It had been wonderful to observe such robust, rigorous behaviour that late at night, and I'd told them so. We'd even shared a ciggy spliff and pissed collectively up the sides of a Chelsea Supporters' minibus in the Travelodge car park. We'd had a moment. But now, these top blokes were among the walking wounded, and they were accompanied by a tall, wavering figure, similarly outfitted in white shirt and tie, sleeves rolled up, but shaking all over.

'Fed-Up Keith!' beamed the affable NZ bartender in obvious recognition of this struggler, who immediately broke down in tears and had to be assisted into the Room of Gloom. Apparently, Keith's seventeen-year-old nephew had – after the exertions of attempting to free himself from the Leppings Lane crush – fallen into a coma on the side of the pitch. More tragically, there had been so much vomit in the boy's mouth that it had prevented Keith from attempting the Kiss of Life. Back in the bar, the affable New Zealander mixed drinks and attempted to avoid interjections of any kind in case he was just too way off the mark. But everybody was in a Super Generous state-of-mind, and even flippant, ignorant off-the-wall comments were treated as no more than aberrations brought on by the severe circumstances. Then around midnight, Fed-Up Keith's brother Dylan MacMillan walked in and set everyone gassing once again. That afternoon, he'd attended a wedding in Clonakilty, County Cork and – having seen the 'whole match' on RTÉ-TV – had jetted back to Sheff with a long string of questions.

DYLAN: (*Raising his cup*) Don't wanna be a downer to a full room of strangers, but I'm glad to see so many of you still alive! I suspected South Yorkshire Constabulary had offed the lot of you! As a result of their prior planning and extraordinary administration skills, our young nephew Raymond is currently under a machine in the Northern General. So could you just now raise your glasses to him? (*Looking upwards suddenly, as though truly addressing some great heavenly light*) Please! In God's *name* (*tears rush down his face*) show that little lad some luck tonight!

And with that, Steve Repping led the weeping toastmaster off to the Room of Gloom to seek the tragic company of his grieving brother, whilst the aggressive kerchink of umpteen beer glasses saluted our collective hopes for the wellbeing of poor Raymond. Now reignited and reunited by Mr MacMillan's exhortations, everyone in the bar once again cranked up their still-idling motors of discontent. How had the authorities been allowed to remove so many of last year's safety considerations? Why would they have done this? And soon we were again raking over those same hot coals as we would be raking over for nigh on the next two decades and beyond. Start as you mean to go on.

HAVE-A-LAUGH: (*To nobody*) Me, Rob and Yeh-Yeh were determined to get down the front.

ROB DEAN: (*To anybody*) But we knew we'd have to arrive well early just from last year's experience with those Leppings Lane turnstiles.

HAVE-A-LAUGH: (*To everybody*) If you can call them that! Even skinny-minnies like me have to go in sideways! Dance Of The Leppings! Besides, Doughy was the only one with a ticket, so we had to be tactical.

STU: One look was all you needed. I was not joining that. After those C-Rammed turnstiles, we were going nowhere. It wasn't like other crowds with a common purpose. And I'd suffered enough claustro with that same tunnel last year. So the blue skies and previous experience told me just to sit on the side and wait.

DOUGHY: (*Nodding*) It was *such* a lovely sunny day. I had my ticket, I was seated right above you lot, I knew what I was doing. I even had two other choices of access to the seat. Why stand blocked in that tunnel? Totally un-nessa.

ROB DEAN: As *per* usual, we were goalhanging at the gate just in case an opportunity of free entry arose. Compared to last year's police presence, only two Bizzies were in evidence. Brilliant. So while these two ejected one ticketless youth through the main Leppings Lane gate, about a hundred fans wandered in.

ANONYMOUS: I concur with that, mate. I was one of those wanderers.

ROB DEAN: Me, Have-a-laugh and Yeh-Yeh made it straight into the tunnel, so they couldn't identify us.

S. REPPING: According to Dylan, the Irish media said the charging Liverpool fans had broken down the gates!

ANONYMOUS: Charging? In that crush?

ROB DEAN: As if. We just walked in. Walked. No tickets. No grief. I mean some of those ticket holders we by-passed were well pissed off at not having to show any fucker what they'd fought so hard to come by.

HAVE-A-LAUGH: (*Almost sung*) But stewards there were none!

STU: We're all big lads and we were early enough. We'd left the vans at Hallam Towers and walked it. So we arrived a full hour ahead of Mick, Rock and the twins.

ROB DEAN: We worked our way through the tunnel quite firmly, taking advantage of every wave to shimmy a little further ahead of the sheep.

YEH-YEH: (*Concerned*) Looking back, do you think maybe we were too firm?

ROB DEAN: We were *not* firm, Lionel! Don't start using hindsight and getting a guilt trip going.

YEH-YEH: (*Slightly unconvinced*) Yeah, when you've got to get somewhere important that you've waited for, strived to be there for, well, the drive and passion just takes over.

STU: Mate, we were in situ by 2.15. We were set up and having a crafty spliff. The crush only come later, after we'd gone off each to his individual spec.

ROB DEAN: Quite quickly, I'd got my perch down near enough the front, even sneaked in a whisky flask. I wanted to set up far enough from the fence *and* from the barrier. From the previous year's experience, I knew I'd need a barrier behind me rather than in front. There's always some crowd movement during any capacity match, but Leppings Lane was notorious and I was fearful of being pushed up against the barrier unless I moved in front of it.

YEH-YEH: I'm always in my robes at work, so I never feel I can properly trust the pockets of my jeans. And I was *that* nervous of pickpockets. So once I was down the front – just to make sure that my wallet was safe – I thrust my right hand into my jeans back pocket and kept it there. But within a few minutes, the crush had become so intense that I couldn't even move my arm enough to get my hand out of my pocket again.

ROB DEAN: Even before the teams were on the pitch, people all around me were screaming out for someone to help them.

HAVE-A-LAUGH: How many times have we been on Anfield Kop when it's full capacity? When you're in a surge of 28,000 people, you've got no choice but to flow with it. At Leppings Lane end, it was just a vice getting tighter and tighter. *And* we've got this massive fence in front with spikes pointing into us.

YEH-YEH: We'd all expected it to settle down after ten minutes.

ROB DEAN: We did!

YEH-YEH: But what happened after the teams came out was an even bigger nightmare. Hearing the crowd inside responding to the players on the pitch, everybody still milling around in the Leppings Lane paddock suddenly surged forwards in a concentrated effort to catch the opening moments.

On the other side of the bar, Steve Repping and the Say-Everything-Twice Brothers stood saluting their two beleaguered comrades, Fed-Up Keith and Dylan MacMillan, whose sudden and brave emergence from our Room of Gloom uplifted everybody's spirits no end. Then, after another quick round of 'Hail's and 'Well Met's, the room fell silent for Fed-Up Keith as he made his point gingerly.

FED-UP KEITH: One of today's true miracles was Peter Beardsley hitting the bar. If he'd have scored, there'd have been hundreds more dead.

Man, that was so true. Anybody who goes down the football regularly knows the difference between a goal going in and just hitting the bar. It's *huge*! Fans go mad when a goal goes in, and even that much more in an F.A. Cup semi. The death toll could have gone stratospheric after a goal.

ROB DEAN: It was only six minutes past three when Beardsley hit the bar.
HAVE-A-LAUGH: The game had just kicked off and already we were seeing dead bodies. This young lad in a brand new 'Candy' jersey was trying to pull himself up the fence. But then he just fell back into the crowd and disappeared. That kid's dead for sure, I knew it. Then the corpse of a teenage

girl emerges out of the crush. Am I *dreaming*? Lifeless, dead: just like a piece of wood floating on water.

YEH-YEH: (*Tortured*) Oh, that little love! She was crammed right next to me at one point. I could tell she was having breathing problems because her face was squeezed so tightly up against my right arm that it was all contorted. Her expression never changed. Her eyes were full of tears just staring straight at me, pleading with me to help her. I could feel her foot tapping on mine, gently at first but it soon got more agitated. I saw a policeman. That's when I remember first seeing *you*, Keith. (*Points to Fed-Up Keith*) Keith saw the little girl in difficulties surrounded by massive blokes. It was Keith who screamed at that cop.

FED-UP KEITH: Four feet away, he was. I yelled, 'Can't you see there's a problem?' I'll never forget the look he gave me. (*Cracking up*) Almost total contempt. (*Shaking again*) He said, 'Shut your fucking prattle.' I will never forget that infamous phrase. That's when the desolate feelings took me over. Here was I asking the man-in-blue to look after everyone's safety. And he was having none of it.

YEH-YEH: My right hand was still clamped tight to my side, holding on to my wallet inside my jeans pocket. But the jaw of the young girl jammed up next to me was so sharp that I was wincing in pain. Finally, a brief surge unlocked the pair of us and we both came face-to-face. She had on a ghastly vacant expression and I realised . . . (*shuddering*) that she'd died.

HAVE-A-LAUGH: By now, there were lifeless people on the floor under the barrier getting trampled by fans helpless in the surge. People were unable to breathe in the crowd. But still the cops would not open the gate in the front of the terrace.

230

YEH-YEH: The blokes next to me were all screaming with fear and agony. I could hear people dying, man. I could hear bones crushing like walking over twigs in dry woodland. (*Gagging*) And I'll never forget that smell of people being crushed to death. Like sardines, we were.

STU: Like human pâté, we were. Being turned into food products with the State's approval. Cooked up in those wire pens at Leppings Lane. Just like Charlton Heston predicted in that *Soylent Green* movie.

ANONYMOUS: They made us fight each other for our lives. Survival of the fittest.

HAVE-A-LAUGH: Oh mate, getting squashed to death is not a daily occurrence, so you don't know how you're gonna react till it happens. Being six-two, I just took advantage of any momentary movement. Any. (*Uncomfortable, self-searching*) I've no idea what I did to other people, but I *must* have trampled heads just to make it over that bastard fence.

ANONYMOUS: Survival of the fittest.

FED-UP KEITH: (*Contemplative, shattered*) This afternoon at Hillsborough, I suddenly realised how vulnerable and how small I really was on this big earth of ours.

Throughout this dynamic outpouring of grief and frustration, Mick and I sat skinning up and not getting stoned, me drinking Carlsberg Export and not getting drunk, both thinking vicious thoughts but not saying anything, and generally fretting at the sheer non-achievements of our respective Bystander Roles. Brent and Dean – both still only twelve, remember – had fallen asleep hours before, but we knew that their distraught mother Sharon was now on her way across Snake Pass, desperate to take charge of her two junior offspring.

YEH-YEH: Straight off, the cops were claiming a pitch invasion.

DOUGHY: Pitch invasion? People had paid £6 for these tickets, a lot of money.

HAVE-A-LAUGH: We wanted to enjoy a legendary victory, not stop it at birth. If you're gonna get one at all, you'll get your pitch invasion with the exuberance at the end. Who wants to stop the game from starting when you're predicting a victory?

YEH-YEH: The first time people went on to the pitch was when they were *carried* on – unconscious!

DYLAN: (*To Gary Have-a-laugh*) Mate, I spied your big feet on the pitch all the way from fucking Clonakilty. Those big black motorbike boots were the give-away. How did Alan Hansen respond?

HAVE-A-LAUGH: Because it was Hansen's first game for nine months, I figured he might be the most amenable to me having a word. I told him to get the match stopped. I told him I'd nearly died in there. But he just couldn't take it in – just said I was doing the club no favours. I pleaded with him: 'Al, there are people *dying* in there!'

STU: Everybody who managed to get over the fence just collapsed on the grass. There was *nobody* running on the pitch until Have-a-laugh ran over to Hansen in the dying seconds.

YEH-YEH: I'm resting against Grobbelaar's goal, nearly passed out. My right arm is fucked up completely from the young girl's jaw. Suddenly some old codger's weeping on my shoulder. 'Fifty-six dead. Fifty-six dead,' he kept repeating it till I got mad at him. Don't be so daft, it couldn't possibly be that many. But as those hours rolled over, so the numbers just kept ratcheting up. And as we walked back to the Hallam Towers, a car with a loud radio pulled up at some traffic lights. I heard the announcer John Inverdale say: 'Seventy-four people dead.'

DOUGHY: Shit, I just remembered! I had Barcode come in and record the whole thing on my ghetto blaster. Billy Butler's introducing a Footballers' Wives Special on Radio City.

YEH-YEH: Mate, you can't entrust anything to do with the footy to Radio City! There's only Radio Merseyside that can cover a football match properly.

By 4am, the entire human contents of the bar was ensconced in our thirteenth-floor sanatorium, thirty-seven of us loosely packed across the four rooms, while Brent and Dean slept on undisturbed in the sumptuous confines of Yeh-Yeh's elite suite. Myself and Mick sat together in the cushy corridor opposite the lifts, knees pushed up, awaiting the arrival of his sister, who – having lent him her car for the day – had been forced to seek alternative transport across the Pennines. But when Sharon Goodby finally appeared, she had brought tragic company in the form of her neighbour Jennifer Gilhooley, whose son Vincent had been 'lost to this afternoon's crush', as she so poetically described his fate. Only twelve years old, this F.A. Cup Semi-Final had been Vincent's first away match. Poor Mrs Gilhooley, a tiny single mother-of-three with no babysitter on offer, had been stuck at home all day with nothing more than conflicting radio reports to keep her insane, until Sharon – ignorant of Jennifer's own plight – had called her with a request to borrow the car. Now at last somewhat among like-kind, the distraught Mrs Gilhooley roared with grief, so incandescent with rage that I worried about her response to Sharon's reunion with the twins. For, on reaching Sheff with Sharon Goodby, the South Yorkshire Police had obliged Jennifer first to identify her poor son's body from over eighty snapshots of the Hillsborough corpses – Vincent Gilhooley had been snapshot #81 – then leave her dead child lying in the temporary mortuary. And as Mick took Sharon down to wake her sleeping boys, Jennifer instinctively reached out to me and I wrapped myself around this fragile lady and cradled her head as her stomach fizzed with crazy sounds. She wheezed and sobbed and shuddered and retched as only one can who has been dealt such a Cosmic Blow.

JENNIFER: (*To me*) As he left the house, Vincent turned to me and said: 'I know you're worried about me, Mum, but don't.'

Who were these Great Beasts who had laid her so low, these foul Civic Frauds who had invited her child to their city then abandoned him? Did they not have names? Was there not one man among them who could stand above the other fakers and say: 'I it was who failed you. I it was who looked away. I it was whom they paid to ensure the safety of the day. I it was who took away your loved ones.' And it was not until around 6am that I unpeeled dear, quaking Jennifer Gilhooley from off my tear-soaked chest, and led her down to the car park. In front of us, Mick and Sharon dragged her reluctant, exhausted twins and I could hear Brent whining petulantly.

BRENT: But Ma, how do we tell everybody we weren't really there?
SHARON: (*Hugging him hard*) You *were* there! Just tell them to be thankful you both survived!

35. ITALIA '90

9.30am, Monday June 12th, 2006
Monologue with interjections at Iloi, overlooking Lake Omodeo

Anna stretched out her bare left foot and kicked my right boot lightly. We lay side-by-side scrunched up together, like an old married couple supping late night Ovaltine in bed with the TV on. Ah, but she warmed me. Supporting our backs the sandstone bolster of the Iloi tomb, below us the spellbinding azure blue of Lake Omodeo – nature's television screen.

ANNA: (*Brutalised, exhausted*) I never realised you were so close to the pain of that day. I'm so very sorry, Rock Section.

ROCK: To paraphrase ye Bard, Anna: it was *all* down to that one day. Come Italia '90, Mick's absence from the Leppings Lane crush would work against every one of us, as he tried in vain to make *up* for that absence – not for everybody else so much as for himself. I honestly think Mick felt ripped-off, no longer one of the lads. It never occurred to him that, as a social worker and loyal, loving uncle, he'd had every valid excuse to be safe on the opposite terrace. Brent and Dean were not yet thirteen. Had their safety instead been entrusted to the malpractors of South Yorkshire Constabulary, the twins might well have suffered the same tragic fate as poor Jennifer Gilhooley's twelve-year-old son.

ANNA: (*Wistful*) Catholic guilt?

ROCK: Macho pride, more like. That spring, we'd all had a hand in constructing the all-singing, all-rhyming M. Goodby – the poet, the Jungian chance dancer, whatever. But by doing so, we inadvertently tore down the lovely, helpful thirty-two-year-old man that we'd all so taken for granted and replaced him with a paranoid pop star already on the brink of his sell-by date. Before the UK's Rave free-for-all, Mick never could have achieved fame in a million years. So he'd never even considered the Possibilities, let alone the Implications. And when he suddenly found himself with an international hit and all of the power that comes with it, ye Bard was genuinely shocked to enjoy it so much, then distraught that he had no proper plans in place to keep it going. Before the disaster, Mick was in social worker mode twenty-four hours a day. He still just wanted to help everybody, to facilitate their own experiences, to use his natural gifts for the greater good. But after Hillsborough, Mick hardened. His compassionate side withdrew completely. Thereafter, he just needed to get things done. His way.

Almost zombified by the heat and the near-asphyxiating beauty of Lake Omodeo and its volcanic horizons, I struggled to accept that Death had struck sunny Hillsborough on just such a day as this – peaceful, cloudless, tranquil. Right this minute, this ardent City Dweller wished for nothing more than to remain side-by-side with Blessèd Anna – my troubled, intellectual Surrogate Lover – the two of us basking in the incapacitating heat of this typical Sardu June morning. But I understood that we must, sooner rather than later, wrap up Anna's crash course in all things M. Goodby, and return to Santa Cristina in order to exchange cars with her father. And so – hoping to nail all of the salient points of the Mick story without getting caught up in too many Cultural Flummoxers – I continued recounting ye Bard's tale, and at quite a pace.

ROCK: After Hillsborough, Mick became a monster to every-body. Slowly at first it seemed, but not really. When Brent's anger and teen embarrassment at having missed the Crush resulted in his swastika-spraying spree, the authorities – thinking to make it easier for the family – handed his case over to Uncle Mick. But that backfired against the twins. Mick just used his new official capacity in their lives to ride roughshod over their musical wishes. Knowing that Brent was now totally reliant on his uncle's sound relationship with the authorities, Mick was able to coerce *both* of the twins into becoming part of his Brits Abroad project with Rob Dean.

ANNA: Mick was not a User before this time?

ROCK: No man, Mick was a facilitator. Exclusively. It was the sudden possibilities of *Top of the Pops* that turned his head.

ANNA: *Top of the Pops* is a very big show in Europe also. It is like a crazy English legend to us all.

Suddenly I was sucking in great quantities of air, pursing my lips and on the edge of growling, as I recalled the umpteen embarrass-ing scenes we'd all been put through during ye Bard's brief assault on the UK Charts. Fucking hell, suddenly I was back there and I was not happy! For throughout M. Goodby's awesome post-Hillsborough Disaster sequence of shitting-on-your-homeys, nobody had been safe from the fallout of his Machiavellian wiles. First, Mick had pestered and pestered the Kit Kat Rappers into letting Full English Breakfast join them; Breakfast didn't even know until he was in the band! Next, Mick hassled and has-sled the not-arsed Gary Have-a-laugh into singing lead vocal on the first Kit Kat Rappers single 'Second Class to Dottingham'. Then, Mick pestered Stu and Yeh-Yeh into adding '*Feat. Gary Have-a-laugh*' on the front of the single's sleeve – 'You'll need a focus of attention.' Next, in that previously mentioned act of utter ingenious cruelty, ye Bard had edged out his Brits Abroad co-founder Uncle Rob Dean for looking too old to appear on the impending *Top of the Pops*. Next! Next! Er, next, having written a so-called Posh Rap for our beloved Full English Breakfast, Mick had visited the Kit Kats' Manchester record company – behind everybody's backs, mind you – and persuaded them of the commercial soundness of billing the second Kit Kat Rappers single to Full English Breakfast alone, thereby relegating Stu, Yeh-Yeh and the by-now well-miffed Gary Have-a-laugh to passengers on their own record! And yet? And yet, the more ye Bard had pushed and cajoled and mistreated those around him, somehow the more we'd all fallen into line with his wishes. With hindsight, I could only ask myself: Why? What was *that* all about? Why had we all been so enthralled?

During those five brief months as a big Pop Star, Mick had trailed around the cities of the UK dispensing Rave Wisdom to an obsessed gaggle of be-hooded, sugared-up Fizz-o-philes. 'Last Tango in Paris' was a phenomenon. And while UK sales of Mick's belovèd Kola Max rocketed, so did the international sales of Tango push it briefly to the world's number one soft drink! So what colour was the Rave Zeitgeist? Uh-oh! Stu, Rob Dean, Yeh-Yeh, Gary Have-a-laugh: every one of them had been in the Hillsborough Crush and every one had – in its aftermath – suffered a right dissing from ye Bard. Full English Breakfast, on the other hand, had appeared on our scene too recently to have played any part at Hillsborough. Hmm, there's surely some correlation here, officer?

ANNA: (*Changing the subject*) I loved so much the 'Her Majesty's Pleasure' single by Full English Breakfast. Also his famous

Mexican Revolution-style MTV video was so very funny, especially the part when his Gringo uncle is the judge and jails the poor people for the rich nephew's crimes.

ROCK: Full English Breakfast was such a gentleman that none of the Kit Kats got mad at him upstaging them; they knew Mick was entirely behind it all. Besides, they all got to take peyote in the Mexican desert, so that helped subdue any rebellion.

Now total-recalling the maelstrom of Chart Topper Goodby's brief early-1990 media assault, I was once again embarrassed and affronted at the undue haste with which ye Bard had jettisoned all sense of normality in favour of an Uppity-Chav-Buys-Internet-Lordship sensibility. And in my mind's eye, from here in the heat of Sardinia, I could suddenly picture Brits Abroad's bizarre arrival at *Top of the Pops* that chilly February 1990 morning. Stu and Gaz Have-a-laugh were there to mime their backing vocals. Brent and Dean were delighted to be courted by a Korg Synthesizers rep. New boy drummer Kev Noggins was hassling WASP's singer Blackie Lawless, and I was just there for the crack – which my connection had promised me would 'be here presently'. Mick meanwhile sashayed around the BBC corridors like one born to it. Moreover, he was suddenly behaving around these media types as though he'd been raised as a Holy Man in the foothills of Tibet and had zero cultural awareness. So when this tall, suave Australian guy walked up and told Mick how much he loved 'Last Tango in Paris', it was obvious from the way the BBC were fawning that this guy was also famous. But Mick, highly offended even at the mere idea of sharing this limelight with some other celebrity, produced a spectacular child-star outburst exhibiting zero sense of proportion.

MICK: (*Hissing over his shoulder to TV lady*) Who's this bloke?

TV LADY: (*Beaming*) Oh, that's Bruce Easily ... (*Smiling, but no response whatsoever from Mick*) He's got another big hit. He's a great singer, so emotional! I've even seen him billed as the Australian Morrissey.

MICK: Who's Morrissey?

And thus, by deploying such severe 'I Remember Nothing' cultural severance tactics, ye Bard in one short month successfully slewed off nearly everything from his former self, jettisoning all of his compassionate, life-affirming Poetic Splendour in favour of that time-honoured super-temporary UK phenomenon: the Celebrity Solipsist. WWF? Call dear old David Attenborough! A chap in here thinks he can make the whole world disappear if only he closes his eyes. What a documentary! Talk about changed priorities.

ANNA: So you all arrived at Italia '90 as pop stars?

ROCK: (*Cagey*) No, just Mick, Brent, Dean and Breakfast counted as the true 'as-seen-on-TV' pop stars. Because they'd had the recent hits – and the videos, too. My *Top of the Pops* days were long over, and my Dayglo Maradona stuff was big but just too underground for daytime radio. The Kit Kat Rappers never charted on their own, but even Stu and Have-a-laugh had been conspicuous on all the TV performances of 'Last Tango in Paris'.

ANNA: (*Encouraging and enthusiastic*) And yet you all expected to attend Italia '90 in your old capacity as *violent* hooligans!

ROCK: (*Nodding and smiling*) Yeah, a bit of wishful thinking with hindsight. But it takes a long while to feel famous. In the early days, you think you can switch it off when you feel like it. Of course – as we all discovered – you *cannot*.

I next explained to Anna how Mick had insisted on overseeing the entire booking of our tickets to Italia '90 from a mythological point of view, i.e.: how our trip would best read in his planned autobiography. Mick wanted us to leave in glory from Manchester's new Graham Nash Airport, landing in Northern Sardinia at Alghero, where his excited Catalan family wished to take us all out 'for a celebratory slap-up-do'. Thereafter, we could rent two cars and take in the whole island as we roadtripped south down the 131 to Italia '90. Sounded brilliant. Sounded utterly brilliant. Mick's route would add considerable time to our journey, but I wasn't complaining – the World Cup's worth lingering over. Let's fucking do that. Beautiful airport, Alghero. Been there before, no security, sweet. I could already picture me and Have-a-laugh smuggling in several well-packed 4 oz tins of the gardening. In reality, however, Mick-in-charge was a disaster. Indeed, ye Bard hummed and ha'd for so long that all the Alghero plane tickets were gone by the time he'd even made preliminary enquiries. Thus, we would be forced instead to take the motor coach to far-off Stansted Airport, thereafter flying directly into the arms of Europe's most paranoid police force at Cágliari, all of them sure to be brimming over with a current need to frisk every UK passport holder. By now, however, there was no one in our little party who could be easily fazed. We were, after all, the current top flight of UK Hooliganistas bar none. Even W. Ham's Inter City Firm had never topped the BBC charts! Take that!

And so it came to pass that our vibe-tribe assembled at Manchester Coach Station, at 8pm that still-sunny June 1990 evening, each of us ready to keep our Stansted appointment with the 5am flight out to Sardinia's capital. The team lining up on the tarmac would be comprised of myself, M. Goodby, Gary

Have-a-laugh, Stu, Full English Breakfast, Brent and Dean Garrett, and Doughy. Yeh-Yeh being a magistrate couldn't get enough time off. Uncle Rob Dean was of course staying back in the UK to make his protest over his Brits Abroad mistreatment. Despite the airport swap from Alghero to Cágliari, both Have-a-laugh and myself had decided the risk was still worth taking and I lovingly loaded my bags with the green stuff and the black stuff. Oh, and some of the amber stuff just in case we got sleepy. Clothes? One shirt, one pair of kecks, one black designer jacket – because it's Italy, technically – one pair of boots, one black v-neck sweater, never wear undies: me sorted. And that was about the short-and-long of it for all the gents. Except for one of us yet to arrive. Where was Doughy? More to the point, what was that cabbage patch doll thing that now approached us with such a sunny demeanour? Do please keep those dusty ostrich feathers away from me, Madam! But it was not until the strange doll thing was actually upon us and cackling its familiar greetings that anyone made the unlikely connection. Hey, I recognised *that* voice! No way! This was Doughy? No, said the voice. This was not Doughy but Zoughy! What the fuck is going on now? Who set Strawberry Switchblade on you? What's with all that taffeta and lace? And whilst this abject woman-thing proclaimed the death of Doughy As Was, Mick clucked at being so thoroughly upstaged, whilst Have-a-laugh and I just smiled to each other, knowing that the novel cross-dressing presence of I'm Zoughy, Fly Me would act as a perfect smokescreen behind which to hide as we brazened it through Sardinian Customs.

And thus, our little gang all now assembled, off we jolly well popped on the first stage of our long journey to those southern climes. And boy was our National Express coach running on love! Too much for some! Mistaking Boy Doughy's daft '80s get-up for a jolly World Cup jape too far, our sulky, humourless driver at first attempted to dampen our Northern Ardour by throwing on a Style Council cassette. But nothing could stop us now, and the aisles were soon shaking shaking shaking. And while Brent and Dean slept like the babbies they still were, Stu, Zoughy, Have-a-laugh and I quietly caned the half-oz we'd allowed to cover the duration of the coach ride, all the while eavesdropping on the fascinating conversations between ye Bard and His Mighty Breakfastness, Lord Leander Pitt-Rivers Baring-Gould.

BREAKFAST: (*Affronted*) He kills birds, Mick.

MICK: (*Defensive*) Only rats with wings.

BREAKFAST: (*Clueless*) No actually, domestic pigeons.

MICK: Leander, you're gonna have to calm down. People don't give a monkey's about pigeons.

BREAKFAST: Well how can people be *expected* to care if their favourite pop singers crow about how many they've person- ally murdered?

STU: (*Sitting down with a cheese bap, all ears*) What's all this about?

MICK: (*Serious enough*) Oh, Leander's just finished reading about Shaun Ryder's murder spree.

BREAKFAST: He poisoned hundreds of pigeons, Stu. And now he's showing off about it. He's a despicable cad. Birds are my chief obsession.

MICK: (*Conciliatory*) When we get back, you can hit him if you feel that strongly. You'll marmalise the daft cunt. And then I'll be king.

STU: (*Cooing*) You're a *bird* man, Leander? Now I love you even more!

BREAKFAST: Seabirds are my first love, Stu. Oystercatchers, probably too obviously, followed closely by razorbills. My sister and I spent every childhood summer on the island of Skokholm with our Uncle Ronald, ringing Manx shearwaters and saving puffin chicks. But give me some binoculars and a dozen herring gulls and I'll still sit for hours in glorious solitude. Uncle Ronald even rebuilt the white house we stayed in as children. (*Distant, longing*) And how I miss the migrants there, the chiffchaff, the common redstart.

MICK: 'Uncle Ronald' doesn't sound very Scandinavian, Leander.

BREAKFAST: Oh, the island's Welsh, Old Boy. It's three miles off the Pembrokeshire coast. The Viking name *is* rather confusing. When my family bought the freehold for £300 back in 1646, I'm sure they never realised what a bird sanctuary they'd acquired. The vicissitudes of the modern city pigeons are far more extreme than I'd ever have imagined. I really shouldn't be surprised if dear old Columba Palumbus was not the next arrival chez Skokholm. That Shaun Ryder – I'll ring *his* neck!

When we got to Peterborough Services, Stu and Gary Have-a-laugh started taking the piss out of this Native American guy who was busking his own protest songs in the windy porch of the entrance. No top on, moccasins, face paint, the lot. His name was Jim Feather and he claimed to be 100% Indian. No way, said everybody. Where you from? Halfway between Boston and Denver, said Jim Feather – a Cambridgeshire village called Tydd Gote. Where you lot off to? But Jim's songs were all instant and lyrically powerful and his performance right there in the doorway was massive. So when his detractors had shuffled off for piss and chips, the people whose opinion counted remained there entranced.

BREAKFAST: No way he's 100% Cherokee, Old Chap.
MICK: Way.

And for the next hour Mick acted like he'd just met Donovan. Jim
Feather never ate, never smoked, slept upright and believed that
2012 would be the beginning of the world. He had no clothes, no
money, no passport and no driving licence. Yet in the past decade, he'd travelled to India, Sri Lanka, Greece, even Afghanistan
without any of these things. He had, or so he claimed, Inner
Mobility brought on by Cosmic Awareness-ness . . . and a magic
cloak. Two coffees later, Jim Feather announced that he would
be travelling with us to Italia '90, news that passed among us
without fanfare or even acknowledgement. Besides, in our collective knuckles-dragging-on-the-ground World Xenophobic
state, the abject frilliness of the Zoughy coach station episode
was still shocking us to the core. So taking in a half-naked
tribesman with neither passport nor clean grundies deffo edged
the balance of our little band back into the realm of Mad Cunt
Barbarians somewhat. But when Mick – staring up at the blue
motorway sign – casually announced that Stansted Airport was
fast approaching, Jim Feather suddenly became alarmed. Were
we not going to be travelling all the way to Sardinia in this wonderful coach? Jim's feathers were ruffled. He must leave immediately. And as we slowed down at the first available exit, the
murmurs and chortles of the doubting Thomases had swelled to
an ungenerous crescendo.

HAVE-A-LAUGH: (*Jeering*) I thought you didn't need passports
   or shit like that!
JIM: (*Smiling broadly*) I don't. But I left my magic cloak back
   at Peterborough Services, so I'll have to go back and fetch it.

(*Jumping down from the coach*) Shit place for a hitch. (*Waving*)
See you in Sardinia!

At the back of our coach, meanwhile, the party behaviour of five
top blokes suddenly caught our attention. They had all boarded
at Peterborough and now stood saluting something-or-other in
white shirts and ties, sleeves rolled up, ciggies aglow. Hey, it
was our Hallam Towers comrades of contraflow: Steve Repping,
Fed-Up Keith, Dylan MacMillan and the Say-Everything-
Twice Brothers. Where did you lot sneak on? Being deliver-it-
by-yesterday estate car reps – chronic motorway veterans the lot
of them – the simple pleasure of not having to drive to Stansted
was overwhelming to the Repping Contingent. Indeed, they
were each one so o'erfilled with gratitude that the churlish
coach driver had already had to ban them from coming down
the front to give thanks. Poor old Fed-Up Keith – clearly desperate to put as much mileage as was possible between him and
the Hillsborough Disaster – had even, after the ban, crawled
down to the front in a zipped-up sleeping bag to mouth his
silent gratitude under the hum of the diesel engine. But the
sulky, humourless driver had soon spotted him in the mirror
and pulled over on the hard shoulder until Caterpillar Keith
had inched his way back to Repping & Co., buoyed up by our
standing ovation.

* * *

On arrival in Cágliari, it had been Mick's stupid/inspired idea
to leg it off the plane and cause Instant Hooligan chaos by zig-
zagging across the tarmac making plane shapes. I couldn't go for
that. He was supposed to be watching the twins with Sharon

Goodby's Eyes. Besides, my bags all bulged with spray-paint and narcotics and I was wearing a t-shirt that declared: 'I'm Not Just Here For The Crack'. No way could I risk being without that sack o'goodies to help nurse me through the forthcoming Drearies of Group 6. Egypt? Fuck's sake! Anyway, passing through customs with aerobatic Mick now caught in the vicelike grip of two ¾ scale Fascisti, Stu took temporary charge of Brent and Dean's passports, whilst Have-a-laugh and myself ranged low and slinky behind our very own Cindi Lauper – it worked like a charm. All the customs officers approached the Doughy One with such unrestrained lust that their forty-five-second strip-search turned the ground around him into a bizarre mega-doily, with him at its volcanic centre starring as Cicciolina the Christmas fairy. Rubbernecking footy fans stalled any further egression through the Great Gates To Freedom, but the toke-a-holic and tunnel-visioned Have-a-laugh and myself – jonesing for a five-skinner – olive oiled our way through with the residue of our gang riding tight behind us on Hobson's Trailer. What a scene of threatened violence greeted our dismayed peepers! Where was the love? Cágliari's arrivals hall seethed with Italian Ultraviolentistas, who bayed for our blood and tried immediately to spill some! Breaking through the police cordon, one miniature fucker launched himself at Brent like a starving weasel on a lofty rabbit, but he was instantly dragged off the shaken boy and given a jolly good arse kicking by a tall Irish fan clad head-to-toe in green. It was Dylan MacMillan to the rescue! I'd never even clocked that he and Fed-Up Keith had been Irish, but ye Bard – now free of his two male backing singers and having guiltily witnessed from afar the clonking doled out to one of Sister Sharon's beloved offspring – well, he was not about to give praise to another for doing what he himself should have been taking care of. Moreover, ye Bard now abroad was determined to pursue at all times his most combative trajectory.

MICK: (*To Dylan*) We're playing Southern Ireland tomorrow!
DYLAN: We're a republic, if you please.
MICK: Northern Ireland doesn't exist, then?
DYLAN: (*Now grimly Irish*) Will you change the fucking subject, Cromwell?
MICK: I'm Catholic, too. (*Recalling Kev Noggins*) Call me Whitey Lawless, the White Anglo-Catholic Cop Out. (*To Breakfast, pointing at a too-gobby Italian Ultraviolentista*) *He* kills pigeons!

And thus in such psychic smoke and flames had Italia '90 finally begun, the half-naked Cabbaged Patch Doughy ejected at last from Dante's Customs Hall, Basher Breakfast already wringing mindlessly the sorry neck of some perhaps innocent fellow bird lover merely because of his grotesque Mediterranean tribal allegiances. What a cracking beginning! Someone was smiling down on us for sure!

Piling ourselves and our gear into an airport minibus, we were suddenly overwhelmed by a second wave of cops, who swarmed over our vehicle 'looking for the Dutch' apparently, and nearly giving myself and Signor Have-a-laugh cardiac arrest. These be-shaded gun-toting federalés were Italy's Carabinieri, literally 'those-armed-with-carbines'. But the absence of police dogs and the ever-increasing swell of international footy fans through Cágliari Airport's bulging portals ensured that their search would be brief, and we were soon bumping and bouncing our way towards the capital. As we'd left the airport, a minuscule but highly rotund figure had handed Mick a CD affixed with this note: *Please join us for a kick-about on Poett Beach at 11am prompt. Drinks and other sundries will be served. Regards, Bugs Rabbit and the Master Musicians Of Buggeru.* But as it was already past 9am, and the effects of the journey were lying heavy upon our weary heads, we collectively vetoed the idea in favour of a proper kip at our Selárgius Hotel, thereby giving us plenty of time to spruce up for the England–Ireland match at 3pm this afternoon. In our dreams of course, we'd each imagined a full day of hanging out before the footy started in earnest. But you could never think strategically with M. Goodby in charge, for he was a sub-tactician at best. We'd had almost a year to prepare our Poett Beach attacks, but – as evidenced by the bluff'n'busking of the Brits' 'Last Tango in Paris' media campaign – ye Bard was a good furlong behind Ethelred the Unready. Concurrent with his chronic leadership letdowns was Colonel Goodby's latest act of Elvisian nepotism in which ye Bard had allowed his sister to pressurise him into leaving for the World Cup as late on June 10th as was possible, thereby letting Sharon wake up with her twins on the morning of their fourteenth birthdays. Sweet, nice, compassionate. But – and it's a big hairy but – Mick's demonstration of sibling love ensured thereafter that our gang of Warmongers would be, in Cágliari, always somewhat behind, rather than ahead of our game. The World Cup was to be taken seriously, but we were too full of media bullshit and too numbed by Hillsborough to clock the fact until too too many years after the event. For all of us had assumed – mistakenly as it turns out – that the really violent matches would not kick in until England versus Holland on faraway June 16th. And as that was still almost a week away, we believed that we could – whilst settling gently into the Mediterranean summer heat of footy and drugs – develop in that five-day window an entirely new and incisive battle plan. Or so we hoped. Yeah, right.

Due to the unfortunate island location of England's World Cup matches, we had reluctantly accepted the absence in our plans of the two 'Wash Me' orphans and the invaluable weapons storage that their many dark corners had facilitated. Unfortunately, this decision obliged us to eschew entirely all of our hard-earned UK and European hooligan methodologies, leaving a vacuum that mere enthusiasm and Lust For Violence could not hope to fill. But so off-the-ball were our starry TV eyes that cracking summer of June 1990 that none of us did even discuss the possibilities of failure. On arrival at our Selárgius Hotel, our exhausted throng had hoped to melt quickly into our respective rooms and bed down for a gratefully received siesta, thereafter marching through the streets as one united front to our ringside seats, whence we could observe England's dispassionate execution of those hopeless so-called Irish Republicans. Ah me, but ye Bard's pitifully inadequate arrangements ensured that for most of us sleep was only to be dreamed of. For despite his epic promises, Last-Minute Goodby had been forced to find us all lodgings in the Hotel Apocalypse Now. Not really. But what pit of squalor was this in which to thrust his maverick troop? Treatment would have murdered their leader Vic Nesbit for less. Surely Michael Buenaventura Durruti Goodby could have served up his International Brigade something with a mite more going for it than this right-load-of-cobblers? Without even the simple word 'hotel' adorning its crumbling façade, our creepy hostelry looked as though it had long ago been appropriated by some Gestapo-inspired S. American military junta for the torture of its Disappeared. At least, that is, until Zoughy pointed out the enormous, faded letters Y.W.C.A. still clearly visible upon the roof's wide gable end. A brief relief o'ercame our band upon appraising the surprisingly decent reception and bar, both of which were administered by a delightfully severe be-corseted lady of late middle age, whose great heaving breasts and gloomy pouting raised all of our temperatures. And so, a mere two or three Fernet Brancas later, we ascended the crumbling staircase with something approaching hope. But then, upon reaching our respective rooms, the despondency started up all over again. For every chamber on offer to our group was the very picture of abjectness.

Mick's room was as tiny as a cupboard, but with a window. North-facing: no sun, therefore. Mine was a paint store cleared out just for the World Cup – appropriate in the circumstances. But, in an effort to hide the room's real purpose – decades of decorators' brush strokes attesting to the emulsion tests of time – even the walls had been newly glossed over with one streaky-but-pungent yellow coat. Satin-black ribbed industrial flooring. North-facing, of course. Stu's room was enormous and freezing and again north-facing, a single bed, a dirty black-painted floor and a sink to piss in. A blessing. But no sun. Gary Have-a-laugh had a Grecian four-pillared bed big enough for eight people but no other furniture whatsoever. A vast olive-drab bolster once white cowered at the foot of his soaring altar of a headboard, only serving to reinforce the Kafkaesque inhumanity of this Titanic cot. North-facing, natch. Brent and Dean were sharing an awful children's dormitory done up forty years previously with faded but now classic 1950s kids' wallpaper featuring cartoons of Crissolli the Clown, each illustration picked out in felt pen or biro by the bored shitless sprogs of the Post-War Age. But although chocker with bunk beds and baby-changers, the twins nevertheless rallied visibly at the mere thought of overnight separation from Uncle Herr Hitler and his Travelling Botch-the-lotters. Of Zoughy's room we knew not even where it lay. Breakfast's neither. Nevertheless, as each one of us shattered international travellers required this minute no more than a temporary crash pad, we sleepily deluded ourselves that other accommodation could be sought as soon as we'd sanded off the edges of exhaustion with a quick forty winks. Hey, my bogies are gonna be bright yellow when I wake up!

* * *

Between the hours of 10am and 1pm, we slept most of us. True, the sonic and psychic battle between the pizzeria opposite and its neighbouring mosque rendered any deep enduring kippage impossible, and we all dozed fitfully as the pizzeria's fleet of un-helmeted Lambrettistas – each piled high with pizza boxes – buzzed up-and-down Via Cristoforo Colombo at insane speeds. And yet, in our free airline eye masks and sunless habitats, we each-of-us slept well enough through those pre-match hours until, at 13.05, a lone voice of high-pitched male anger dragged us as one collective Western Male to our north-facing wrought iron balconies, from whose lofty heights we watched infuriated as a lone olive-skinned woman in bright red lipstick endured both a verbal and physical drubbing from her minuscule-but-infuriated imam. Boos and jeers and wanker hand-signals erupted from our ranks, and we heard a semi-hysterical Zoughy screaming at him to 'pick on somebody your own size'. At this the furious cleric, on looking up and catching our Viking rage, dashed inside the mosque, probably to report to the prophet himself how such effeminate deviancy had obtained its dreadful hold even on the Young Women's Christian Association.

Now thoroughly rested and using Zoughy's heckling as Sat-Nav, Mick, Have-a-laugh and myself located his boudoir and baled in for a shameless gander at The Lives of The Newly Cockless. Now, I'd love to 'confess' that of all our hotel rooms, Zoughy's had most shocked me by the woman's touch that it displayed. But it was simply not the case. Indeed, if anyone needed evidence that the simple act of cross-dressing doth not in itself a woman make, then it was to be found right there in Our Lady's Chamber. Men in drag often hide their lax attitudes towards hygiene no more successfully than we perverted Heterosexuals. For a penis leaks at the best of times, and the Jews' brave attempts to hijack Ancient Egyptian circumcision practices do no more than scarify God's own creation, IMHO. The long lost rule of Mosaic Law? Be always liberal with your bath products! Wash that schlong and do schlapp it on! Thus far, however, Doughy As Was had merely substituted his previous pro footballer hygiene policy (i.e.: paint Aramis aftershave upon everything) for one that merely entailed drenching those same genitalia with equal amounts of more expensive Chanel No. 5. Almost gagging therefore on the sensory overload of Zoughy's digs, every one of us felt the sudden and overwhelming need to discover the whereabouts of one Leander Pitt-Rivers Baring-Gould.

We struck out, all four-of-us, down a corridor with floors as dirty as the streets outside, its once-white walls splattered by the black blood of punched out mosquitoes. We turned a tight corner into more of the same, but the shadows here had lifted somewhat, and suddenly a new freshness assaulted our nostrils. Delightful fragrances. Whence came these heavenly perfumes? Down the far corridor where sunlight cascaded through the high-vaulted oblong window, I saw beyond a city square where people sat and children stroked large bluebirds of paradise. And as we walked together entranced by the near luxury of this neck of our asylum, I noted that no rooms in this corridor bore numbers upon their doors – not even Breakfast's own room, the door of which stood ajar, wide-and-inviting. Such was the glorious change of atmosphere now that I began to feel light-headed and I saw myself smiling impishly at Mick, Have-a-laugh and Zoughy all three, as we continued to inch silently forwards, at last craning our necks collectively around that half-open door.

The delightful situation in Breakfast's bright, airy chambers, however, belonged to an entirely higher dimension. South-facing and overlooking the sun-kissed library square, the room's wide bay window accommodated effortlessly a large hexagonal mahogany table, on whose crisp white table cloth – displayed like gateaux atop cut-glass cake stands – stood two enormous Stilton cheeses. And there at the edge of the table, his hands clasped together as though in prayer, crouched the mesmerised Stu, his chin craned forwards, resting upon his knitted fingers so as to view from a more mythological perspective these two prized objects of his affections. A gun dog awaiting his master's signal was less attentive, and neither of the pair had yet clocked our presence.

BREAKFAST: (*Prodding the cheeses*) It's my birthday in three days, Stu. And it's the biggie. So I'm hoping against hope that this stifling heat will advance their corrosion more rapidly.

STU: (*Tongue hanging out, willing time onwards*) Three days.

BREAKFAST: It's a time-honoured practice throughout Angeln that seventy-two hours at least must have elapsed before one is permitted to serve up the Stilton. Even then it must be sliced laterally in the roast beef manner, (*slowing down*) thereby allowing the process of decay to restart instantly upon the new summit.

STU: (*Hungry*) Why do the Angles have traditions for English cheeses?

BREAKFAST: Why do we English have traditions for French cheeses, Old Son? To 'cut the nose' from a brand new Camembert is considered the height of bad form.

STU: Will two be enough?

BREAKFAST: Hardly, Old Sausage. But two was symbolic. The laterally sliced beastie shall represent Quickborn only: my mother's side. The other chap is for Wessex: Dorset and Wiltshire, if you will. More prevalent even than the military men in my family were its great 19th-century excavators of Bronze Age Wessex Culture. As birds are in my own affections, so were the Wessex burial mounds to my great-uncles Augustine, Keeler and Sabinus. But, just like their infamous volcano excavations all across the southwest of England, my father's side of the family always digs into the Stilton from the roof! Breaks in with a common tablespoon no less – makes no end of a mess! My mother's family rarely stay in the room whilst such barbarity is being enacted.

STU: I'd be proud to be your Wessex Spooner while we're 'Sur-La-Continonne', Leander. You know, represent your dad's side while you're abroad?

BREAKFAST: (*Beaming*) Jolly good show, Old Bean. Then Zoughy shall be my Quickborn Cutter. And represent my (*very uncomfortable*) mum's side.

The time hastening ever on, and the England–Ireland match now no more than ninety minutes away, my own clandestine gang of four furtive corridor loiterers would – at this juncture in their dialogue – have now entered his hallowed Breakfast Chambers rather more gingerly, had not the delighted Zoughy, upon hearing his/her new name enunciated so correctly, giggled like a schoolgirl and stamped inadvertently. And so we entered upon this arcane tableau of Emerson and Thoreau, this thoroughfare of Holmes and Watson, this home of Johnson and Boswell. In we stepped with spray-gun loaded, semi-armed with catapult and pebbles, boxing mouth-guards, whips and compressed air sprays of Chinese Chiliwater. But there was a strange aura hanging in Leander's room that even our boisterous maleness did not instantly dispel, indeed this spectral pulsing and humming of the room itself grew even stronger once we had entered within Leander's portals – so much so that we every one of us began to succumb to its overwhelmingness. On Breakfast's chaise longue lay a brand new copy of Robert Graves's *They Hanged My Saintly Billy*, the signed inscription of which Breakfast enthusiastically showed around. It was from his dear mother Birgitta 'with 5000 kisses'. Her inscription read: *Do you remember an inn, Leander?*

MICK: Hilaire Belloc.
ROCK: 'Tarantella'.
BREAKFAST: (*To Zoughy*) 'Do you remember an inn, Miranda?'
ZOUGHY: (*Clueless*) Do I remember an inn?
MICK: (*Brits Abroad voice*) 'And the tedding and the spreading.'
ROCK: (*Slow Jim Morrison voice*) 'And the straw for a bedding.'
BEDROOM: 'And the fleas that tease in the High Pyrenees and the wine that tasted of tar?'

We looked around, the spell was broken – the bedroom had spoken. Time to move on, we'd had our fun and now we all must die. It was, after all, only the Republic of Ireland. I dragged my fellow fuckers back to my room of Dulux and primers, handed to each a spray can of Baptista's Metallic Saffron, 'the wonder yellow for every fellow', then we collected the twins from their nursery and we were off.

At the corner of Via Cristoforo Columbo, I sprayed my first piece of graffiti of the whole tournament, and we grabbed a quick celebratory Polaroid with Zoughy's bare arse hanging next to it. Then in boots and striding high-tops walked we past the quailing clothes shops, walked we on with strength of purpose 'cross the fast and flowing streets of Quartu Sant'Alèni, ever onwards to England's allotted stadium at Sant'Elia. But although our forces should by now have been sufficiently rested, only Basher Breakfast and myself sallied forth with any real gusto. And even Leander's calm exterior was today plagued by a persistent itchiness on his stomach, which he scratched furiously as we seven-league-booted it full bore down some local high street. And as we walked, he talked.

BREAKFAST: Those Master Musicians Of Buggeru, Old Chap. I rather enjoyed their CD this morning. I even went down to Poett Beach for that invited kick-around of theirs. I rather fancied a quick surveillance after everything Mick's suggested. So with all of you safely tucked up, I thought I might jump in a cab and have an hour on the sands.

ROCK: What did you learn?

BREAKFAST: Oh, it was dreadful down there. Full of jostling loud-mouthed idiots making in-jokes and monosyllabic types with grudges against the world. I wish I hadn't gone.

ROCK: Were the Mackenzie Brothers around? D'you know the Spackhouse Tottu guys?

BREAKFAST: Yes, we chatted for some considerable time. But they seemed terribly disappointed not to see you and Mick. And you'll never believe this. But simply on account of their charming facial expressions and vigorous hand gestures, I was rather taken by the pair of them. José Mackenzie is tall enough, skinny and languid but everything else is a dead ringer for Mick – our own M. Goodby. More strange still, that violent half-pint Luis displays similar head and hand movements to Mick's mother Gabriella. What was I to make of it all? Is it my ignorance of Mediterranean types? Just my own naïveté, I suppose.

But then, around the corner zoomed two Polizia Alfas, followed by a couple of dark blue armoured cars. They screeched to a halt on the opposite side of the street and the cop in front wound his window down.

MICK: (*Butting in from behind*) I'll take care of this lot.
COP 1: (*From behind his steering wheel, yelling*) Be careful, English! Did you see the Dutch?
MICK: None so far, officer.
COP 1: Make sure you don't approach them. They are armed with incendiaries stolen from the Carabinieri. English, take very good care today!

And with that, we watched nonplussed as the two cars screeched off up the street, in the direction of Sant'Elia Stadium. Instantly, Mick was felled by the cops' utter indifference to our threatening exteriors. Hereafter, we would continue with him at the head of our column.

MICK: I hear you never got to kip, Leander.

BREAKFAST: I slept on the plane, Old Bean. I'm raring to go. A couple of hours did me.

MICK: How were the conversations on Poett?

BREAKFAST: Mightily strange, Old Thing. Even though the right people had turned up – the Mackenzies, Bugs Rabbit, Jim Feather . . .

MICK: (*Butting in*) Jim Feather was there?

BREAKFAST: Yes, and he was in an awful state. Tense and unhappy, the absolute opposite of last night's Peterborough performance.

MICK: Had he lost the magic?

BREAKFAST: (*Puzzled*) Not if he was on Poett before me, Old Bean.

MICK: (*Hurt*) He should have come to seek us out.

BREAKFAST: He was being baited and bullied by some dreadful Newcastle United supporters who called themselves the Pit-Yackers.

MICK: They're not Newcastle United supporters, Leander. The Pit-Yackers are all from Alnwick Town further north. Northern League Division Two. The two clubs share the same black-and-white striped shirts. But their strip is about all they have in common. Their hooligans call themselves 'The St. James Boys' but their enemies call them 'The Ear Collectors'.

BREAKFAST: (*Down his nose*) Well, these Alnwick Townies were all quite dreadfully disparaging about England, and ugly to boot. They said they'd never never never get jobs, that they'd sooner get the next ferry to the Netherlands and support Be Quick. Worse still, they were hanging on to every word of this awful hairy Dutch chap, a stifling Party Orange beardy called Walter-Under-The-Bridge, who could do nothing but crow to the Mackenzies about Barry Hertzog's plans. Barry this, Barry that. Walter kept repeating verbatim every word that Luis Mackenzie had spoken to him. (*Imitating a wanker*) 'I just told Luis about Barry's second-hand oil and fat business. Luis was well impressed by Barry. He turns to me and says: "Liquid fucking gold, Walter. Liquid fucking gold!"'

MICK: Sounds like an E. E. Munkey skit to me, Old Love.

BREAKFAST: More like Dr Strangelove, Mick. Party Orange obviously pride themselves in wielding all the latest technology *and*, to their credit, they've managed to smuggle an awful lot into Sardinia! Walter-Under-The-Bridge thinks he's in the KGB and walks around in a black air force uniform threatening people with his Bulgarian Umbrella, (*fanciful voice*) whatever that may be! On three separate occasions, Walter told Luis Mackenzie about my big hit. When I finally requested that this planet squatter not keep repeating himself, he simply poked me in the stomach far too harshly with his metal-tipped Bulgarian Umbrella, then grinned. I was still doubled over in pain when I heard him say to Luis: 'I hear the Pope's turning Protestant. What do you think about that?'

We were still setting a mighty pace, but Mick caught my eye behind the posh one's back, and raised his own eyes in alarm. By now Leander was cradling his stomach rather too gingerly for anyone else's liking. Who was that Walter and what was he on? Poor Breakfast, he'd been way out of his depth on Poett. These were renegades he'd been pitted against. We were violent people, but we were lovely violent people – morals and codes-of-ethics and *Weltanschauungs* and everything. Those others were thugs, highly artistic but thugs none-the-less. I'd seen José

Mackenzie wield a knife one night at Dehydrated for no other reason than some behooded Raver took exception to José hassling his woman. That night, José had got himself thrown out of his own gig. But here at Poett? Well, it was us who were outside our own Laws – Dar-al-Pennines if you like. So whichever way we read the situation ahead, this land on which we now walked was José & Luis Land. Er, at the very least.

MICK: I was *that* inspired by Jim Feather's performance. What a shame he didn't seek us out. I wrote a poem for Feather last night, I thought about Lindarama, this chick I loved when I was fifteen. She fucked me off for a twenty-two-year-old 'tached-up guy from Bury in a Triumph Stag. She rubbed it in – told me she'd slept with him at his Bury flat. So last night on the plane I wrote about it. The poem's called 'Knee My Wounded Heart at Bury'.

BREAKFAST: (*Full of compassion*) Jim Feather will adore it, Old Rhymer. Especially after this morning's treatment at the hands of the Pit-Yackers and Dutch Idiocracy. Foul Walter-Under-The-Bridge called poor Jim Feather a heathen, no less! Before our whole assembly. Just for being Native American. I hadn't seen anything like that in years. Damned Walter-Under-The-Bridge rushed up to Jim and screamed at point-blank range: 'Oi Pagan, Loon's going on a fucking binge in your cloak!'

For a minnow microsecond, some spark of recognition betook its place in my mind. Those names? Loon. Walter-Under-The-Bridge. Were they? What were they? Where did I know those names from? But before delivery of their meaning could be signed for, just as soon was their memory dimmed and made irretrievable, then finally squibbed out of their very existences.

BREAKFAST: (*Chuffed*) I did, however, receive a birthday card from Judge Barry. I thought that was rather nice of him, after my away-win triumph. Rather big of him, what? A very young chap named Cowtown Unslutter presented me with the card. Do you know of him? He had an autistic sister with him, much older, named Marike.

ROCK: Yeah man, I'm sure we all met him at Slag Van Blowdriver. He was a total Nondescript. About five-seven tall, slight, looked like Burzum but even younger.

MICK: (*Grimacing, smiling*) Cowtown Unslutter glowering behind the bar at Slag Van, that's a memory. Him and his sister had just escaped from South Africa. Their diplomat dad had just run off with the family's black servant. Cowtown Unslutter. That was the mad cunt responsible for all those Zulu shields and spears. Issues, man! Fucking *that* was a teenager with issues! He served me some radical scran, though. Deliciously close to food itself!

BREAKFAST: (*Perking up*) The only good part of their invitation was the hot food provided – all of it from Slag Van Blowdriver. Foul Walter served me up a gratis bowl of his steaming Mussent Crumble: made of castor beans, apparently. Down it slid – I had an extra bowl. (*Clutching at his heaving stomach*) Perhaps I shouldn't!

But as we closed in upon the Stadium's environs, we heard converging upon us from the northwest the sound of drums and pipes and marching men, the sound of great male teams all harnessed ritually together in a gigantic display of their shared birthright. Beautifully timbre'd and all of one Irish voice, surely these masses would soon overwhelm us. Relishing this first opportunity to damage another on foreign soil, however, ye Bard hurried ahead so as to establish their positions. But he soon came running back despondent.

MICK: It's a fucking Patrick Parade! From the U.S.A. by the looks of things. There's about fifty of the fuckers all smiling and singing. I smacked one leprechaun as a tester and he just laughed and said: 'Not today, son.' Son? He was younger than me! *And* more Aryan!

BREAKFAST: I've been waiting for this day all of my life, Old Bean. And a bunch of peaceniks are not going to stop me. Bring them to me. I'll lay them end-to-end around the world.

As though by magic, a lunatic leprechaun rushed up to me and cuddled me harshly. What the fuck? This was Connery the Barbarian from Ambergate. Oi oi, you fucking wanker. C-the-B was an errant Forest fan with whom I'd shared many a crack pipe before matches under the W. Bridgeford bridge. Barely five-foot-four tall, his bare torso aerosol'd bright Nissan Shamrock green, and sporting a vivid Rave-green Indian head-dress that trailed past his arse, Connery pointed both of his massive studded motorbike gauntlets directly at Mick. Then he snapped at me far too severely.

CONNERY: Rock, you'd better tell your man he's due for a smacking. The cunt hit my New York mate out of nowhere. He's come miles for this.

MICK: (*Right finger stabbing the air*) Tell your Captain America from me that he looks too Nazi to be Irish.

BREAKFAST: You can't say that, Old Bean. It's racist. His properly Irish mother could have been any number of things and he'd still be truly Irish. Islanders never stay still; they're all over the place. Let's not rush to racism for the first Blood Of The Day, as it were. Let me clonk this scoundrel post haste if for no other good reason than because he's traipsed upon our sacred turf clad as a belligerent. (*Looking at me for permission*) What about it, Old Sod? He's your mate.

ROCK: (*To Connery*) You've got three seconds.

And with that the two of them were off. The chase had begun. Breakfast would run him down for sure. But Connery's manner had utterly appalled me, especially here in the international arena. We weren't breaking into houses on Bread-and-Lard Island now! This was the real World Cup! Tweak thy behaviour up a notch or three, my lad, or nothing but certain failure can be your guarantee. But such la-di-da thinking as his could only aid our own cause. Today, the fool had severely undermined the real Irish Hooligans out there at work in this teeming crowd of Diddymen.

Behind us, nudging us, beeping us out of our own captured high street clanked a bright Rave-green 1960s John Deere tractor towing a flowered-up flatbed trailer decorated with artificial shamrocks. Set upon its green-and-white striped Syd Barrett floorboards, a glittery Irish Showband of the old school variety doled out 15 m.p.h. C&W versions of such timeless fare as Terry Woden's 'Why Don't We Go to the Moon Anymore, I Mean It's Not Exactly Rocket Science?' But even though we were clearly not about to budge, still the green John Deere tractor kept edging forwards. Fuck right off! Still the smug buck-toothed driver kept his Greenhorn Steer locked in at such a steady pace that we were everyone-of-us forced eventually to leap out of the way. No way! Loss of face! About twenty of those fuckers sailed past us, pewter tankards aloft, their sedate musical quintet now vamping in 3/4–time upon the ancient Cork drinking ballad 'Clonakilty as Charged'. Until, that is, the opportunistic Gary Have-a-laugh ran up behind the too-precariously-placed drummer and simply dragged his drum stool from under him, causing the poor flailer to grab at any nearby cymbal stand or amplifier, thus upsetting the entire ensemble. Down went the lot of them, crash, bang, wallop: by far the best tune of the afternoon IMHO.

Our forces now straddled the intersection with Via Risveglio, Have-a-laugh's one-man riot of cymbals, curly guitar leads, beer glasses, wine bottles, molto amounts of hand percussion and scrambling, slithering fallen marchers blocking anyone else's egression into that final avenue to Sant'Elia Stadium. Mick marshalled Brent and Dean to scatter all of the stricken percussion further across the path of the incoming Irish, while Zoughy and I dislodged a crusty parked-up pale blue Piaggio three-wheeler, dragged it rear-end-first into the street mess, then – after first throwing its piled load of second-hand paperbacks down upon the tarmac – elbowed that rusting teeterer onto its side and goggled with glee. Stu and Have-a-laugh, meanwhile, had leapt aboard the green-and-white trailer and brought it to a decisive stop when the terrified driver fled. St. Patrick brought to a halt by St. Spongebob. Righteous. Triumphantly we stood our ground, hands on hips, sneering up collectively at the Polizia helicopter circling overhead. But none of us could truly delude ourselves that this sudden accidental success had been anything more than that. And barely had we found the time to raise our revolutionary fists aloft when that buzzing copper-chopper turned and hightailed it across the sky off towards the main action at the football stadium, its new trajectory across the skyline diverting everyone's horrified gaze to a single demonic figure that leered and gesticulated from high atop the distant RAI-TV tower. Behind the silhouetted figure – in utter defiance of today's England–Ireland match – flew a great orange windsock care of the Dutch. The silhouetted figure was none other than Judge Barry Hertzog himself. And he now commanded the TV tower – alone.

36. THE DEATH OF FULL ENGLISH BREAKFAST

11am, Monday June 12th, 2006
Monologue at Iloi, overlooking Lake Omodeo

A full half-hour later, with Farmer Have-a-laugh now at the controls of our hijacked John Deere tractor-and-trailer, we chugged into the raw, burning chaos of Sant'Elia Stadium at the speed of a narrow-boat down some Victorian canal. But although we had navigated successfully the battle-strewn sands of Poett Beach, then passed relatively unscathed under the Ultras' fusillade of rubble hurled down from the Home Supporters' bridge, I was already doubting – even as we battered our way successfully through the stadium's main gates – whether our end result could possibly be worth all of this fuss. For everything within Sant'Elia's precincts was now burning and in chaos. Could there even be a football match played here today? Several of the main food concession stands – those stinky-arsed Meatburger caravans run by Spackhouse Tottu's Mackenzie Brothers – had been turned over and set afire. Also ablaze near the entrance were two abandoned Carabinieri Alfa Romeo patrol cars. A third Alfa – quite untouched – squatted beside the TV tower. High above the stadium, the raging figure of Judge Barry Hertzog still sat atop his World Podium, a full set of bagpipes slung around his neck, screeching out unintelligible instructions through a loudhailer to his Party Orange faithful far below. At this continuing rudeness, the apoplectic World Cup hordes now jabbed their index fingers collectively upwards at their aerial tormentor: 'You're gonna die cause we're gonna kill you!' they snarled over and over and over. The time was 3.05pm and the match should by now have commenced. Supporters out on the terraces were also getting beside themselves with fury at the hold-ups down on the pitch below, where herds of intimidated Polizia and Carabinieri loitered, unconsciously trampling the very playing field itself. But with the decisive G. Have-a-laugh at our old Deere's controls, we snowploughed on through the Green, the White and the Orange hordes towards the RAI-TV tower, then set up our long articulated vehicle right beneath its sheltering form. If we were to endure another Hillsborough, then this half-scale Eiffel Tower would serve us best as a place of protection.

BREAKFAST: (*Clutching stomach, highly agitated*) We must neutralise Barry Hertzog. I've got the head for heights. What say you all I shimmy up and knock the fellow's block off?

MICK: Stay where you are, Leander. You've got a dicky tummy. If you're gonna die falling off something high, at least fall off the Old Man of Hoy looking for your belovèd oystercatchers.

BREAKFAST: (*Laughing*) My mother would insist on a statue wher*ever* I fell! Even in a football stadium, Old Bean!

MICK: These barbarians would soon knock it over. You'd have to make do with a plinth. Hey, I've got the inscription for it: 'Leander Pitt-Rivers Baring-Gould fell here – I'm not surprised, I tripped over it myself.'

Elsewhere under the TV tower, an unrighteous assemblage of Maniacs, Murderers and Militiamen from around Europe had by now gathered and could be observed drawing lots for the right to ascend the tower's heights and topple Judge Barry Hertzog from his sky throne. One platoon of Treatment's finest, today under the leadership of the great Vic Nesbit himself, found themselves obliged to take a short oral exam for the honour of representing Millwall at such a lofty level. Each rose to the occasion magnificently, however.

NESBIT: How can you sabotage a motor vehicle in such a manner that the breakdown will not be detected immediately, but will require complicated and time-consuming repairs? I want all five answers, and quick.

TREATMENT 1: Sugar in the gas tank.

TREATMENT 2: Water in the gas tank.

TREATMENT 3: Loosen the screw on the oil filter.

TREATMENT 4: (*Slowly*) Also loosen the oil-drainage screw to cause loss of oil, sir.

TREATMENT 5: Loosen the oil pressure head.

Beyond, almost hidden in shadow and still awaiting instructions, the black-clad Belgian shock troops of Charleroi's Nous Voyageons – each one spooled up with yards of polypropylene rope – clustered around their tough-looking R.O.C.C.M. team-leader, his face as smashed and broken as the cartoon bulldog emblazoned upon their club's shield. But by now the most truly inflamed of all supporters were those poor souls from the Republic of Ireland who had mistaken Barry Hertzog's brazen orange windsock above for a display of power by Protestant Ulstermen. How like enragèd Rave Madhatters the Irish seemed as they teemed towards us, scores of them slipping unchallenged into the cold grey confines and unyielding light of our temporary sanctuary. Fearing that each Irish supporter would mount our trailer then rush up the TV tower ahead of him, Full English Breakfast jumped down into the hordes impetuously and thrashed a dozen soundly. Then, screeching like a dive-bombing herring gull, he re-mounted the trailer and plucked off a couple more of these cheeky monkeys who'd dared to use 'our' trailer as a springboard from which to assail the Judge.

BRENT: Uncle Mick, if it gets any worse can me and Dean fight?
MICK: Can somebody that's not me give them permission, can you?

We all kept our heads down, knowing what a death sentence we'd be handing ourselves should anything go wrong with the sacred offspring of Sharon La Pasionaria Goodby. High above us the Agusta A129 attack helicopter continued to buzz and harass Barry Hertzog atop his great monolith. Around the stadium, the international hordes clapped the helicopter's efforts and stamped out their simple: 'We want the match! We want the match!' But three brave men were now preparing to make the steep climb up the tower to challenge the Judge. The first of the three was that loutish Gauloise-chomping leader from R.O.C.C.M. whose burly six-foot frame seemed, from this low level at least, quite capable of exacting justice upon Hertzog's reckless hide. For several minutes, the man from R.O.C.C.M. stood surrounded by his colleagues in some grand meditative bonding, then suddenly set off at a punishing pace up the sheer sides of the tower. Full English Breakfast frowned and moaned and pawed at his aching belly. He stared cross-eyed and beat his fists against his head.

BREAKFAST: (*Entranced, almost yelping*) Leander Starr Jameson, 1853–1917. I hear you calling to me, Old Boy. When shall come my time? I see great clouds of dust and riders!

270

Then the second climber of the three – Treatment's competition winner, smartly attired in the dark blue of Millwall – began his own ascent up to Piano-1 of the great TV tower and the crowds grew even fiercer. For they believed that the time of the exasperating X-faced man was drawing very near to a much-deserved close. Again, Full English Breakfast petitioned me for permission to climb.

BREAKFAST: (*Declaiming powerfully*) Rock, I was not raised haphazardly, not like these ants that each weekend tear one another apart. I was brought forth and nurtured with that same spectacular attention to detail that created all of the fearless fighting men of the Pitt-Rivers Baring-Gould family.

ROCK: (*Yelling over the noise and P.A.*) Breakfast, this tower was not designed for mad climbing antics. So don't even try it on. This is the World Cup. We've got days. Let's just dig in and watch how this first wave of climbers fare.

Atop the great TV tower, the Judge now hoisted his bagpipes aloft, then began to swing them widdershins like a human helicopter, aping the grey-black attack machine circling above. Round-and-around whirred the Judge's pipes; round-and-around until we felt sure that he must topple from his grand perch. Within half-a-minute, however, this World Ridiculing of the authorities began to take their magical effect, first as the rotor blades of the Agusta A129 faltered, next as they stopped altogether. Then just as the excessive weight of the chopper's chin turret started to pull this beast right out of the sky, so did both of its Rolls-Royce Gem turbo shaft engines roar once more into life, and the freaked-out two-man crew hightailed it out of this *Zona Paranormale Paramilitare*. Hertzog raised both of his arms as though wielding an invisible football scarf above his head. Then he began to conduct the air, mixing its currents together from On High, air-hand-washing invisible clothes for the Gods. At this, those creepy Party Orange faithful standing among us began to drone in chorus. And each one raised their arms aloft as across the hijacked P.A. drifted a gruesome sound.

What was this music? *Was* this music? What *was* this? As though from under the floorboards of Zeus, I heard a titanic engine starting up. Vruuuuuuugh! Drifting like a burning death ship across the hijacked sound system. Vruuuuuuugh! Care of Party Orange and the X-faced one who reigned above came the sound of Death's Theme incarnate. And all across Sant'Elia Stadium did evil men rally and family men shrink and dwindle at the sheer menace of its sound. What was this unrighteous and droning Highland grind, this Theme of Corpses that now disgorged itself across the P.A. and infiltrated our unsuspecting World Cup lugholes? First came the drones of bagpipers long dead, drifting across Sant'Elia's smoky ruins. Next came the traps and snares of Highland drummers breaking through the Party Orange walls of human droners below. And then came the hissing and the dissing and the pissing on the stragglers whose hearts were not in tune with today's misadventures. Cromagnon was its sound and 'Caledonian' was its way. Relentless and inspiring only of Doom, Judgement and Fiery Death, this was a song so evil that it had killed its own composers – true. And I recognised it at last as Barry Hertzog's own nightly theme from his club Slag Van Blowdriver! Oh, the hubris! The sheer insufferable hubris of this act!

And then it happened. The Man from R.O.C.C.M. fell backwards suddenly at the problematic intersection with the lighting gantry. Then he slithered, crashed and banged, down and down on to the concrete below. 'No!' screamed the crowd. 'No!' Then the Man from Treatment too, hitting the same snags at that same cursèd intersection, went suddenly the way of the first toppler, sliding inelegantly sideways into the maze of metal struts and interlacings, his seemingly lifeless body thereafter crashing and bumping to the stone cold ground. Could they both be dead? Outrageous tragedy! For a full minute, total silence fell upon the stadium. Then 70,000 voices erupted once more as R.O.C.C.M.'s lifeless Lazarus raised one fist from the cold stone floor. Then, with doctors and paramedics on hand, the P.A. tannoy pronounced Treatment's own hero safe and alive. Sweet relief.

BREAKFAST: (*Crowding me*) I've been thinking about my Anglo-Irish uncle Lord Raspberry that day in 1899 when he'd cocked a snook at the Boers by capturing a whole *veldkommando* single-handedly, then handed them over to cannibal leader Zuluwenta, whose people had lost more to Boer raiders than any other tribe in southeast Africa. Apparently, those Boers went down rather well.

But now arrived at our TV tower many high-ranking Polizia who, backed up by the doctors and paramedics, now ruled that no more foolish climbing efforts were to be attempted – they alone would extract Barry Hertzog from atop his perch. Yeah, right. Among this knot of constabulary loitered several plain-clothed officers, plus a whole host of other municipal ne'er-do-wells, who strutted around with pens and notepads, jotting down the registration numbers of the dead police cars and noting the burning Meatburger caravans. One of those be-suited fuckers was José Mackenzie, clucking like a gangly bastard. He spotted me atop our trailer and strode over with fury in his eyes.

JOSÉ: We're losing a fucking fortune. All five caravans. You cunts are totally out of control.
ROCK: (*Nonplussed*) Whoever you're talking about, mate, it ain't my problemo.
JOSÉ: No? There goes another of your cunts now!

As if cued-up by José's despondent declamation, Full English Breakfast now seized his opportunity and shinned be-booted up the industrially sticky galvanised steel scaffolding tower: anti-climb paint to warn you, metal splinters to taunt you, stories of Heysel to haunt you. Moreover, it was clear from the high speed with which dear Leander now ascended the tower that our hero had deduced from the increased police presence just how brief his opportunity might be. Indeed, the sudden influx of angry policemen and even angrier stallholders into our midst was a vicious one, and the squads from Treatment and R.O.C.C.M. judiciously evaporated as though into thin air, now replaced by these furious authoritarians, each protagonist quite prepared to by-pass current safety conventions so long as control of the crowd could be restored. How unfortunate it was now for Full English Breakfast that each of those injured parties far below him – the cops, the Carabinieri, the TV crews, the radio people – had been thus far unable to snatch their X-faced antagonist from his perch 150 feet above them. For in order to diffuse their pent-up frustration, each group now began to take out their anger on Breakfast's own more accessible form. And so it was that for the proceeding fifteen minutes, while Judge Barry Hertzog ruled aloft and undisturbed, far below did our heroic Leander Pitt-Rivers Baring-Gould cling on steadfastly to a dream that he'd long held dear.

First, Leander caught a full blast in the back from the Carabinieri's water cannon thirty feet below. How he clung on I'll never know, for just the weight of the water left hundreds of fizzing electrical wires hanging off the TV tower. No more of that, said the authorities. But still Breakfast kept on climbing. Next, the Polizia marksmen shot teargas into Leander's new stronghold upon Piano-3, where the junction boxes were all located in one great weatherproof room. But one teargas rocket settled on the ledge beside Leander, then flared up igniting a low blue flame upon the anti-climb-painted platform. It looked set to melt the entire junction box – that is, before Leander confidently stamped out the flames to a roar of crowd approval. No more of that, said the authorities.

The teargas having now made chillies of his eyeballs, Breakfast rested and motioned down to us for advice and encouragement. His eyes were burning red, bleeding. By now, at the foot of the TV tower, there was such a fierce battle of wills raging between the Polizia, the Carabinieri and the Mackenzie Brothers over what should be done next that I was fearful we might even be arrested. Thus, heeding Breakfast's request for aid, I began my own hurried ascent. Soon, from my new perch up at Piano-2, I could see clearly each of the Mackenzies' five overturned Meatburger caravans. Moreover, their combination of anger, despair and threats had even forced Mick up to the first level of the gantry – Piano-1 – approximately eight feet above the ground. Now just twenty feet below me, ye Bard screamed up that the Mackenzies were threatening to shame Leander down from there by playing the Full English Breakfast hit across the P.A. Fuck them! Meanwhile,

Leander almost twenty feet above me waxed ever more lyrical. But boy was he sounding deluded.

BREAKFAST: (*Yelling*) I think I've got him at last, Old Bean. Judge Barry's in my sights at long last. This one's for Lord Raspberry.

ROCK: (*Yelling*) He's still miles away, Breakfast. We've got to stop climbing. It's only the first day, Leander. We've still got the whole World Cup ahead of us.

BREAKFAST: (*Screaming*) Not me, Old Bean. My mother Birgitta insists that I return for my birthday proper the day after tomorrow. I cannot risk losing my inheritance. So today is the proof of my pudding, if you will.

At this point, though Leander's face was partially obscured from my sight by the grim protective railings, such an odd flush now overtook him that a rosy pink glow emanated through his cheeks, pulsed through his temples, bulged throughout his entire cranium. He stared ahead intently, as though receiving information from some companion nearby. And yet across the stadium tannoys still boomed the dreadful warmongery of Cro-Magnon's bagpipers and drummers, precise and unyielding upon their savage trajectory.

BREAKFAST: (*Yelling*) He just told me it's the end of the road for me, Old Bean. Cape Town is to be my last stop. He says you're next.

ROCK: (*Struggling to hear over the chaos*) What?

BREAKFAST: (*World of his own*) Now he says Jim Feather's never going to leave Cape Town, either. I just told him what ye Bard always says: 'The enemy of my enemy is *still* my enemy.'

ROCK: Who did you tell?

BREAKFAST: (*Talking to another, unseen*) I *have* got the stomach, damn you. And you *know* it! (*Now addressing me*) That maggot! He just told me again to check and see if I've got the stomach for it. Who does he think I am?

ROCK: Who told you? Who's telling you all this?

BREAKFAST: (*Unbuttons his shirt to reveal in his exposed stomach a five-inch-wide puncture, purple-black*) I have I tell you, Old Chap. I have!

And with that, Leander Pitt-Rivers Baring-Gould jerked around suddenly. Then, teetering upon the edge of Piano-3, he launched himself upwards at Hertzog with as mighty a leap as even Springheel Jack himself could not have anticipated. Like a ship's flare arcing up into the night sky, how he sprang forth towards the great demon aloft. Up and up and . . . But then I heard him diving past me roaring like a pilotless Spitfire, bellowing like a Merlin engine head first towards the ground, howling like kamikaze raindrops head first into the ground. What word was he screaming, repeating it over and over again? Now, at the foot of the TV tower lay the crumpled figure of Full English Breakfast, his face impacted into the concrete, his arms and legs sticking out of his body like four Cadbury's Flakes in a chocolate strawberry sundae. For Blessèd Leander, ever certain of his upwards Hertzogian trajectory, had hit the ground with all the confident grace of one diving straight into Olympic history, like a playground nipper affecting the swept wings of some great R.A.F. jet fighter.

But even as we collected around dear Leander's body, so did our enemies and detractors also congregate. The chief of police arrived first, pouting and nodding grimly. Then came the

Carabinieri bosses, all three shaking their heads. Three FIFA representatives came next, each looking pointedly away from Leander's body. Finally came our enemies to gloat: the heartless José Mackenzie walking right up to poor Breakfast's prone, destroyed corpse, all the while nodding and grimacing in a near smile. Luis Mackenzie was even worse – fingering his collar-and-tie and clearly suppressing a smile. The more pragmatic Bugs Rabbit merely walked around the scene-of-the-crime with a look of utter smug remove.

MICK: The world was warmer then when Breakfast walked abroad.
HAVE-A-LAUGH: (*To the Gods above, screaming*) What the *fuck*, Leander? Where's your sense of aerodynamics?
STU: (*Crying*) Screaming 'Timber' at the top of his voice, he was.
ZOUGHY: (*Just arrived*) Who was he talking to up on the tower?
MICK: (*Crying, looking ahead*) He caught my eyes in those last milliseconds. He caught my gaze. He reached out with both hands for me to save him. He cried out: 'Kimberley!'

Amidst the chaos and smoking ruins of Sant'Elia Stadium, I saw no more dear Leander Pitt-Rivers Baring-Gould. For I had, being entirely unable to accept this dire event, drifted away out of Time itself. I saw no more his stomach for the fighting. I grasped no longer the Icarus Truth of his downward flight. In his place now, I saw only the future ghost of his beautiful mother Birgitta. I saw her crouching over her dear son's plinth – distraught, prostrate and weeping at the loss of her long-dead child.

37. STU'S MIRACULOUS ESCAPE

11.45am, Monday June 12th, 2006
Monologue at Iloi, overlooking Lake Omodeo

From behind our reinforced Carabinieri patrol car windscreen, I pitched forth into the eyes of Luis Mackenzie a stare so dark that it weighed more than a small universe. Pure hatred. But still that tiny fucker grinned away at myself and ye Bard as though we'd all just spent a night gassing at Dehydrated, snivelling cuntishly away like nothing of anything had ever meant a thing. Stranger still, Luis made no attempt whatsoever to grab my door open, nor did any of those other fuckers outside – neither uniformed nor gangster. Perhaps the brazenness of our decision to appropriate the last working Carabinieri pursuit vehicle had temporarily petrified them all as they stood. Perhaps the sight of Breakfast's broken body on the tarmac just twenty yards away was as shocking to them as it was to us. Perhaps. But I think not. Whatever, they let us take the fucking car – surrendered the Alfa right there and then. In one old high-speed banana turn, Mick reversed that Carabinieri jalopy right under the high vaulted metal arch of the RAI-TV tower in a move so sweet that, as he screeched into position beside our tractor-and-trailer, both back doors were lined up perfectly to accommodate Brent, Dean and Stu, who were still bovine and senseless atop our be-shamrocked base camp, each one wailing for dear spilt Breakfast. Catatonic with grief and disbelief, the black-clad Gary Have-a-laugh sat immobile at the huge steering wheel of our vivid green John Deere, seemingly impervious to the partly cooked, partly soaked Meatburger matériels that were now being rained down upon us from the hordes still awaiting an international football match. Standing alone at the far covered end of the TV tower, his veiled head bowed like some Greek widow, the weeping Zoughy stood back to us all.

So grief-stricken were Stu and the twins, however, that it was only after much hectoring, cajoling and physical persuasion from myself that the three could be persuaded to enter the borrowed Alfa. And still rained down those mucal showers of Meatburger, not slapping the grey-blue Alfa paintwork then bouncing off as any true burger should, but splattering across the car's windows, their gluey, jelly-like consistency clinging doggedly even as Mick turned the windscreen washers upon them at fullest of bores. But this vengeful action only succeeded in dragging the clogging membranes of runny, bloody Meatburger paste further into the flight path of the beleaguered Alfa's windscreen wipers, which strained and groaned in a vain effort to snow plough through that industrial goo. Making furious hand gestures of impending forward motion through the windscreen to the unresponsive G. Have-a-laugh, Mick began – and with immediate and considerable success – to barge and bully our Alfa's way through the rampaging painted legions. Soon, we had left far behind the shadows of the tower, and were crossing the outer precincts of the pitch itself. But our dynamic actions had utterly abandoned Gary Have-a-laugh to the turmoil of Jules Rimet's Cauldron, and how we had dumped and dissed the Lady Zoughy still grieving in her private metal arbour.

With Deputy Sheriff Mick Goodby very much at the controls of this ornery Alfa steer, we continued to turbo-terrorise our way through the fighting hordes, slaloming in-and-out of the burning Meatburger caravans and overturned merchandise stalls, then heading directly between the two Carabinieri armoured cars that guarded the main entrance and disappearing into the great pillar of billowing black rubber smoke caused by Party Orange commandos having set their great tractor-style tyres ablaze. But although the blackening smokescreen hid from the Sardu authorities our intended method of escape from Sant'Elia, everybody in the car started fucking choking. By now disorientated as fuck, gulping down lungfuls of black rubber smoke but knowing no other option, we continued inching under the stadium entranceway through the clouds of burning tyres. It may have been seconds, it felt like years, but suddenly out of the main gates we burst, the authorities so shocked that no one initially even gave chase as we baled up the heavily contraflowed concrete incline towards the main road at no more than 25 m.p.h., coughing our guts up and sticking our heads out of the windows like dogs. Lucky for us, it was not until we'd ascended to the summit of the stadium's incline and were already merging on to the city centre highway that we saw the first wave of angry pursuers buzzing out through that same black inferno, motorcycle cops giving chase but at present over 600 metres behind. And right there on the skyline, even as we hightailed it past Poett Beach, that same tiny mentalist figure of Judge Barry Hertzog still presided over Cágliari Calcio, still atop the RAI-TV tower issuing inaudible orders through his loudhailer whilst being buzzed by yet another Polizia helicopter.

* * *

It was no more than twenty minutes later, however, when we discovered the seriousness of our situation. For however hard ye Bard dodged in and out of the Cágliari traffic, however fiercely our blue light blazed, still our pursuers were never more than a couple of hundred metres behind. And throughout this jostling for position, Mick was highly unhappy with Stu's constant attempts to piss into a polystyrene cup from his tight location behind the driver's seat. No doubt about it, Stu's five-foot-ten exertions were thunderous against Mick's back.

MICK: (*Tetchy*) Couldn't you at least have had a piss before we left?
STU: Oh, sorry man, there was loads going on.

But the extraordinary back-on-itself interlacing of the Cágliari one-way system defied all of Stu's best efforts to stand'n'slash, and we were seeing signs for Elmas International Airport and the North before he next found the opportunity to dangle a sausage in safety. Then, as through Cágliari's outskirts our Alfa burned impressively, suddenly disaster occurred. A farmer heading south towards us into town on an ancient, slow-moving tractor – on spotting a large parking space in front of a café on our side of the street – pulled out impetuously right across the path of the slow-moving street cleaner travelling just ahead of us. Gushing out water like some mobile municipal downpour, this 10 m.p.h. behemoth was. Unfortunately, the farmer's selfish actions obliged the gushing street cleaner to brake harshly, then swerve radically to its left, narrowly missing an incoming convoy of airport taxis. But instead of leaving a passing space for northbound traffic along this major artery, the street cleaner's simple-minded operative merely parked up right next to the tractor and rushed in to have a municipal go at the old yokel – thus totally blocking our path. Mick struggled first to avoid utter catastrophe up the arse of the gushing street cleaner. Next, and more by luck than judgement, ye Bard – aided by the torrent of cascading water – swung the Alfa around clockwise 180 degrees and: *whump!* Mick banged the driver's side of the car so hard against the tractor that the back door flew open and the unstrapped, still semi-upright Stu sailed helplessly out – flying right through the municipal torrent and headlong under the tractor! Petrified by the violence of Stu's exit – we'd just lost another comrade for shit damned sure – we sat all four of us in silence for about 2.5 seconds as curious café clientele wandered out to investigate the commotion. Belting towards us screamed the cavalcade of cop cars – every one of them on full beams. Then rejoicing! We saw a sodden Stu stand up and rub his head. He turned around dopily and – seeing our car motionless in the middle of the blocked street – raised a revolutionary right fist high in the air. Sweet relief! Stu's alive! Then we were off again, haring full tilt towards the cops at first, before Mick selected a nice tight-ass one-way-street to freedom. A temporary freedom. How long? Who knows?

You know the rest, Anna. From there on in, right up to our capture and incarceration in Macomér's Fascist Cheese Factory, we four would be pursued by road, by air and ultimately by psychic attack. Stu's miraculous escape was the beginning of our mystifying entrapment and subsequent incarceration. My long tale over at long last, Blessèd Anna and I sagged together against the sunbleached stone, hugging in mutual appreciation of the saga's unyielding grimness. Then we unwound ourselves from one other, struggled to our feet and then both of us stretched dramatically as if on cue. Having furnished this lovely lady with all of the most grisly facts *and* all told in extremely fine detail, now we were off back down to Santa Cristina to meet her father: to set about restoring some sense of justice to this awful tale. Come on, now!

38. GET THEE TO BIDIL 'E PIRA

Midday, Monday June 12th, 2006
Outside Opposite, Santa Cristina junction of 131

It made a pretty sight no doubt about it, Giampaolo's purple flake 1970 Plymouth Barracuda sitting square and bullish on the hot tarmac, and there tucked in behind it the gleaming Facel Vega fresh from the carwash, restored once again to an all-singing, all-dancing party machine. What a pair. Both cars sat parked up in front of Opposite, where the results of last night's Separatistas chaos could still be seen through the vast plate-glass front window. But where was Anna's father? We wandered around to the back of the deserted building, where a tall, lean, middle-aged chap stood at the top of the illegal club's metal staircase, relieving himself through the railings. He raised his English-size coffee mug in our direction, smiled broadly and shook himself dry.

GIAMPAOLO: Annachiara!
ANNA: Mama!
ROCK: (*Perplexed*) I didn't even know your full name before.
ANNA: It's not my name. He's always pissing about.

As her father descended the backstairs, Anna scurried around to greet him with a well-placed boot up the jacksie, and he in turn responded with an overly dramatic wince of pain, then hugged his child firmly. They both turned to me, and her father extended his right hand.

GIAMPAOLO: (*Nodding and smiling*) Rock Section, hello! I am
    Giampaolo.
ROCK: (*Shaking hands*) It's very good to meet you, Giampaolo.
    You make a fine first impression.

Anna's father spoke only very limited English, however, and
it was through his lovely daughter that we would be forced to
communicate – but all in good time. First, we must confirm
our respective schedules and itineraries. Yes, Anna would with
reluctance permit me to make my visit to the great Doorway of
Bidil 'e Pira alone. Score. But only so long as I phoned her this
evening, once I had checked into my room at Macomér's Su
Talleri Hotel, the booking of which she herself promised to take
care of. Today, Anna and Giampaolo planned to head north in
tandem to stalk the movements of The Reaper in their twin
supercars, thereafter delivering the Facel to a client in Sássari
City. Later on in the evening, Anna intended to return to Su
Talleri in tomorrow's new ferry car, whilst her father would
drive the purple metal flake monster east to the ferry terminal
at Ólbia. I was so delighted to be working on two fronts now
that I was almost overcome with emotion. Dean's death was so
recent, so harsh. And now that I'd once again prised open that
can of Italia '90 worms, well, dear Leander's tragedy now never
left me for more than perhaps an hour at a time. But I trusted
Anna's good judgement and more: I trusted Anna's anger. That
above everything was good enough for me. Giampaolo suddenly
turned to me and began to converse as though I were a native
Italian. Fortunately, Blessèd Anna picked up the baton.

ANNA: I told Giampaolo about your strange experiences in Birori
    Valley and he wishes to tell you of a similar event that he

experienced there once many years ago. (*Turning to her father and asking him a question in Italian*) Er, 1977. Giampaolo was driving at dawn north up the 131 in a Lamborghini Marzal, when suddenly his mind was briefly taken over by some great spirit that dwelled near the highway.

GIAMPAOLO: (*Echoing*) A very great spirit, Rocco. Gigantissimi!

Throughout this conversation, all of us had remained lurking around Opposite's back staircase. Thus neither Anna nor myself could resist sneaking a little peek through the club's back door. What Bugs Rabbit secrets this office space must hide! So, while Giampaolo kept watch around the front, Anna and I mounted the staircase and peered inside the club. Boxes of unsold Nurse With Mound CDs littered the confines of the management office, whilst umpteen large free-standing visual displays of Bugs Rabbit's career highlights leaned against the walls of the narrow corridor, still awaiting assembly out in the public area. Piled up closest to us beside the locked glass back door were stacks of newly printed brochures emblazoned with the words: *June 14th Big Kick-Off Celebrations*. That's gotta be suspicious. It's probably the Grand Opening. Oh, if only that door were not locked! But Blessèd Anna was way ahead of me. Now she simply pushed her right shoulder with all her might against the door's largest and lowest glass panel, pushed and pushed and pushed until . . . Until suddenly the glass pinged free of its tight rubber surroundings and shattered into thousands of jagged pieces across the piles of new brochures. Sure that we must have been heard, Anna and I fled down the club's rear staircase, but not before I had grabbed several Nurse With Mound CDs and a thick wad of those intriguing June 14th celebration brochures, which I jammed into my bag, zipping it up tight. Then the three of us jumped into our respective supercars, roared through the tunnel under the motorway, then high-tailed it north back up the 131 to the Paulilátino–Santu Lussúrgiu exit maybe five kilometres away.

What a glorious day this was. Such had been our grand confinement at Iloi these past long hours that although I regretted missing out on experiencing the sheer road power of the Plymouth Barracuda, nevertheless I was hugely exhilarated at the prospect of my long solo walk out to Bidil 'e Pira. Therefore, when Anna pulled off the 131 and turned left on to the SP 65 signposted to 'Cúglieri/Santu Lussúrgiu', I leapt out of the Facel in sheer anticipation of what the day ahead would bring. Anna, however, was not best pleased at the deal I'd forged for myself and she told me as much. But today I was above such protests. We had mucho work to do, and Giampaolo was here to assist us. I walked back to the Barracuda and shook his hand through the open passenger window, wishing him the best of luck. Then, just as I believed that Anna was persuaded and that they were about to growl off to Macomér and Sássari, Giampaolo whistled me back to the Plymouth Barracuda and handed me an old green box of Coughlan's Waterproof Matches.

GIAMPAOLO: (*Pointing up*) The storms. Sometimes from nowhere.
ANNA: (*Maximum audible squeakiness*) I can't believe you've pulled this off! It's my job! It's my job to guard you from your madness! It's a long way to walk, Rock Section! (*Yelling*) Especially when you might lose your head!

But I had already turned heel and set off at a brisk pace, waving enthusiastically but pointedly not turning around. Behind me, I heard the two massive Chrysler engines growling uncertainly for two full minutes, but then at last the pair of them pulled out across the bridge over the 131 and disappeared north up the motorway's slip road. I had in the meantime already walked 400 paces along the SP 65 and could not, according to my written instructions, relax my counting until I had travelled a total of 3.8 kilometres: 3,800 paces by my own estimation. And as I walked and counted, so I hit my fingers at each new hundred and watched the figures ratchet up until both hands were full and off I'd start once more. The day was lovely, the traffic was absent, and I was alone with my thoughts of Death and Dean and Duplicity. Anticipating the 'obscure bend' of my written instructions, I recognised from more than a kilometre away the high yellow hedges of the 'obscure farm left turn', so allowed my thoughts to wander briefly until I left the road. Through all the tragedy that I had been laying upon Anna, I suddenly realised how much I missed taking drugs. Not their effects so much as the getting there. I missed the toking, the wrapping of things around other things, I missed the retrieving of gear from out-of-the-way parts of my flat, the replacing of loose floorboards, the cleaning and sterilising of things: boxes and bottles and modelling knives. The management of Stuff, as it were. I even missed the emerging, the coming back to life in the morning. Currently ephedra'd up for the next ten days, even twenty days perhaps I might be; that didn't stop me n-n-n-n-n-needing to enact occasionally the outward gestures of the Drughead. Basking in the SP 65 sunshine of that Cúglieri–Santu Lussúrgiu back road, I relished not having to score. But however fantastic, it was also a bit too remote control for a paranoid like myself. It was just a bit too like having the Lord as your dealer. And how often would you wanna hassle him? So I slightly kept thinking I might start jonesing for a hit, even though I knew I'd been on enough of an Ephedra Siege – somewhere in . . . well, another world – to last me probably three full weeks. That's truly how buoyant I still felt . . . But a symbolic toke right now would deffo be sweet.

The obscure farm left turn now upon me, I followed precisely my instructions to proceed '150 metres along track and turn right', next pacing exactly '350 metres to T-junction and park here'. Relishing my instructors' employment of the Highway Code term 'T-junction' for this scrubby interface of two rural cattle droves, I next turned right and walked '40 paces to fork' then turned left and walked the prescribed '236 paces'. So far so good. But even as I began at the next fork to 'turn right and walk 198 paces to a wire blockade', dammit if I didn't smell wood smoke and hear the low overtones of a didgeridoo. Unlovely. What kind of Sardinians are these that frequent such ancient Doorways, and in such daytime working hours? Following my final instructions to 'undo wire from right side, then proceed due south 126 paces across pasture to monument', my heart sank further as I spied poking out above the tough scrubland ahead of me the canvas-and-poles of a wigwam, you know, your typical Glastonbury yurt. Even ungreater. Then, as I rounded the bend into the great paddock of Bidil 'e Pira, I saw three seated figures – still blurry through the afternoon haze – sitting together on a raised earthen platform. But even though I approached nearer and nearer to the three, still they remained a blur. Indeed, it was as though their identities grew even less discernible with every step nearer that I approached. Until at last, when I was almost upon them, the veil lifted from my eyes and I recognised all three simultaneously. Holy shit, each one was Jim Feather!

Forty minutes later, out in the sun-scorched pastures of ancient Bidil 'e Pira, I sat beneath the hanging bough of a splendid olive tree, spliff in hand, nursing a half-empty cognac glass and shaking my head in near disbelief at the outrageous tales of injustice that Jim Feather was laying upon me. Jim Feather? After making such an impression on our war band at Peterborough Services just before Italia '90, Jim Feather had become our 'Man Who Never Was'. He'd disappeared. Full English Breakfast had spotted, or rather claimed to have spotted Jim briefly on the beach at Poett in the questionable company of Pit-Yackers. But after dear Leander's death, and his own bizarre state of mind leading up to it, well, Mick and I had both questioned even that sighting as problematic. But how wrong we had been: the two-metre Nature Boy that occupied my present frame of vision was the product of nobody's wild imagination. True, there were not three Jim Feathers here as I'd at first been led to believe. But he still looked magnificent, Herculean even. And if there were not three Jim Feathers, still there was Jim Feather, his lost twin brother and a mannequin. But more of that later, for I was now acquainting myself with the bizarre trajectory that Jim's life had taken after our first fateful meeting. Out here in the steaming pasture of Bidil 'e Pira, our erstwhile shaman and happy-go-lucky Ur-Spirit proceeded to inform me of his living nightmare these past sixteen years spent enslaved by Bugs Rabbit. What? Having had his magic cloak nicked at Italia '90 by Party Orange's Walter-Under-The-Bridge, and having no passport nor papers of any sort, Jim Feather had become a non-person: scratched off the records of modern humanity. I couldn't bear what I was hearing. Had no one been left alone by these sick fucks of Italia

'90? For these past sixteen years, Jim had been forced into the drudgery of the truly Disappeared; his beautiful-but-impetuous decision to follow us to Sardinia had ended up with him lugging donkey-sized loads around the island without even the promise of a carrot at the end of it. Previously straight edge and all set for Tibetan consciousness, Jim's vicissitudes had turned him into a hard drinker and a chain smoker of . . . well, whatever you've got. Those racists, those smug white slavers!

FEATHER: I couldn't stay with those guys. They were murderous company. And they were organised. I came in from Stansted with them on the next plane after you. My missus fixed my magic cloak with some everyday twine, unfortunately, so you could see it if you knew what you were looking for. Thinking that the Pit-Yackers party were okay, I fucking told them about it. But once I was through the airport barriers and on to the island, they called me a Pagan cunt and this bearded nutcase called Walter-Under-The-Bridge nicked the cloak. Totally kippered, I was. What a gang of bastards I'd uncovered! Cowtown Unslutter, Walter-Under-The-Bridge, Pit-Yacker MC, the Mackenzie Brothers, Bugs Rabbit. They hated my Paganism and told me that I had upon me the Mark of Cain and should be forced to make a blood sacrifice. They said that the Bible made it perfectly clear that vegetarians may never satisfy the Christian God.

ROCK: What was their evidence?

FEATHER: The Bible Story of Cain and Abel, Genesis Chapter 4: Verses 2–5.

ROCK: (*Clueless*) Er, can you just refresh my memory?

FEATHER: (*Memorised, automatic*) '2. . . . Abel was a keeper of sheep, but Cain was a tiller of the ground. 3. And in the process of time it came to pass that Cain brought of the fruit of the ground an offering unto the Lord. 4. And Abel, he also brought of the firstlings of his flock and of the fat thereof. And the Lord had respect unto Abel and to his offering. 5. But unto Cain and unto his offering he had not respect.'

ROCK: The Lord needs his blood and fat, then. Keep your lettuces to yourself is clearly what the Lord is saying.

FEATHER: (*Despondent*) I know. Hearing that every day didn't half take its toll on my head.

Even having become highly useful to Bugs Rabbit's organisation had made no improvements to poor Jim's wretched existence. Playing the muscleman Zampano, Jim Feather had been the surprise hit of *Gelsomania!*, Bugs' musical adaptation of Fellini's movie. But despite the musical's continued success this past decade, still no permanent lodgings in Cágliari had been made available to Jim. Indeed, he'd been forced at one point to sleep in his own dressing room – creeping back with a skeleton key once the janitors had left for the night.

ROCK: (*To Jim*) Then it was *you* I saw in those 8″ × 10″ stills. There are some old pictures up in a club not far away. Have you heard of Opposite?

FEATHER: Rock, I dug its fucking foundations! That place is opening for proper business in a couple of days. I did it all. (*Wistful*) These past sixteen years, Bugs Rabbit's had me doing everything under the sun. Bugs had no permission to start Opposite and no good will from the locals, just blind ambition and a secret northern supply of aggregate, concrete blocks, pipes and reinforced steel girders. But stir Yours Truly into that little pot as Bugs' indentured servant and things started to get done. Unfortunately, that's also when I started to get very sick and underweight. I'm six-foot-three, now I'm older I need my nourishment.

Kept out of sight except for his stage performances as Zampano and monitored by Bugs throughout press interviews, Jim had failed for years in his various attempts to contact friends or engage with sympathetic authorities. Eventually, hitting upon the notion that the media required a proper Sob Story, Jim had – at the end of an interview with a well-known freelance photojournalist – concocted a tale about needing a bone marrow transplant. Bugs had smelled a plot, but could hardly have told the journalist to keep such a human-interest story out of his report. *This* then was the news article which had gone around the world and which had been picked up by Jim's long-lost twin brother Reverend Jim Featherian, an Armenian Pastor and himself a great bear of a man who was now sitting beside me itching to continue their tale.

REVEREND: My barber Grigory Barberian was laughing one day. 'What next?' he said. 'I just read they made a stage musical out of Fellini's *La Strada*! Too tragic!' I tell him *Oliver Twist* worked pretty good, why not? Then Grigory reads out that poor Zampano the Strongman in the musical needs a bone marrow transplant – who can help?

Sitting squarely upon his ancient wooden dining chair – highly incongruous in these unpopulated brackenish pastures – the Reverend Jim took my hands in his own hands and stared smiling into my eyes. How happy he was to be here, to have discovered at last his lost twin. The Reverend was much larger, much chunkier than his Native American brother. Still fixing my eyes with his own enlightened peepers, the Reverend leaned forward conspiratorially and continued.

REVEREND: I never read the newspaper. But this day I read the newspaper. And there was my mirror image staring from within. I knew right away. My adopted mother always told me I was not a twin, so I knew I must be or why would she say that? The musical was called *Gelsomania!* A photograph also, quite large. My brother played Zampano. This was the strongman who needed the bone marrow. I have money but no family. I flew out one week ago.

ROCK: (*Shocked*) Only one week ago?

FEATHER: We're on the run, Rock. Both of us. Oh, (*pointing to the moulded squatting strongman mannequin*) and my seated other! He's me as Zampano the Strongman. We nicked him from the foyer of Bugs Rabbit's theatre when we escaped. That's where I lived, with no money, no wages, no chance to complain. Bugs Rabbit fucked off to Japan for six months with his wife and all the money from *Gelsomania!* Now he's back to get Opposite going, so I'm in hiding. We're in hiding. I'm never going back – but without my magic cloak, I'm stuck on this island forever.

REVEREND: So sad what they have driven my brother to. Even to me Jim apologises for being a Pagan all the time. But Armenian Christianity also lives under permanent siege. So even though our beliefs are quite dissimilar, the prejudices of orthodox religions ensure that we have grown used to shouldering the same yoke of oppression. And that is much to have in common – very much!

How touched I was by this genuine bromance on to which I'd stumbled. How inspired each man was by this new permanence in his life. I lay back and listened as Jim Feather skinned up another big one.

REVEREND: The minute we set eyes on each other, we talked for seventeen hours continuously. That's monozygotic twins for you, I suppose. Both from a single fertilised egg that then divided into two in Mother's womb (*smiling at Jim*).

FEATHER: (*Licking a Green Rizla*) We share so many things in common. We both hate spelling but love words. We've both got double-jointed little fingers. We both love jewellery but hate knowing the time so we wear broken watches. In extremely cold weather we both get a pain in our left knees. We both clean our copper coins in brown sauce.

REVEREND: (*Together*) We both store rubber bands on our left wrists.

FEATHER: (*Together*) We both store rubber bands on our left wrists.

But despite the power of their reunion, neither brother had yet had any bright ideas as to how they should now proceed. Jim Feather's inspiringly obstinate refusal to carry papers of any kind had now left him more tied down to his local landscape than his own Cherokee Nation back in the USA. I needed to explain to the pair the precise religious trajectory that Jim's antagonists were on.

ROCK: (*Honest John*) Jim, I can't say much about your nemesis Bugs Rabbit. But the cloak thief and his cunty brigade are all well known to me; I've even fought some of them. They are all members of Judge Barry Hertzog's Party Orange, but the crucial change came with the arrival of Cowtown Unslutter from South Africa. That wasn't long before Italia '90. He was seventeen years old, brought up in a high-class Calvinist Afrikaner family, private education and everything. When his diplomat dad ran off with their six-foot-two Zulu servant, it blew the family apart. All their values fell to dust. So when Nelson Mandela got released from jail, Unslutter robbed an A.N.C. headquarters at gunpoint and fled with his older, autistic sister Marike to live in N. Netherlands with their Uncle Roden. All the guys you've been mentioning? They're all-of-them inspired, well, they've even become obsessed by Judge Barry Hertzog's book *Prison Writings*. Have you read it?

FEATHER: (*Clueless*) Never even heard of it, mate. But in a bunch those guys sometimes refer to themselves as Combat C.S.L. – bit scary. Can you tell me what that's all about?

ROCK: (*Aghast*) Man, it's just more Christian soldiers: the book *Mere Christianity* by C.S.L. for Lewis.

REVEREND: Prince Caspian?

FEATHER: (*Penny drops*) What? The *Narnia* guy?

ROCK: Indubitably.

FEATHER: (*Momentarily clueless, then suddenly really irritated*) No wonder then! My English teacher in the Socialist Worker Party, he hated that bloke. So even though we had to do the book for coursework, Mr Starkey would always read out the bits where they slag off Susan the Gentle for wearing make-up, then he'd hold the book up in front of him between his thumb and forefinger like it had just been fished out of the bog. (*Relishing*) I have to say, even without Mr Starkey's . . . er, mental persuasion, the toffee-nosed reaction of all those boring characters made me run even quicker towards full body paint!

ROCK: (*Perhaps a little drunk*) Bravo, sir!

So problematic was poor Jim Feather's current life situation, however, that we had not yet even discussed my own reasons for turning up out of the blue at Bidil 'e Pira. Indeed, so preoccupied were the pair that neither of them had thought to ask. They didn't even look surprised, just happy to have company. I needed, however, to get my own Mission on the move, and now spoke up to explain myself to the brothers. Out it all tumbled. I explained how there are Time Tunnels at certain specific ancient Sardinian locations, how most of them are accessed through carved stone Doorways, and how all of them provide interface with the far distant past. At first my barrage of garrulous verbiage sounded like preposterous spew even to myself, but my riotous words were not falling on such stony ground as I'd feared, and were even being received with nodding heads and warm smiles not in the least patronising. The Reverend Jim Featherian accepted happily my notion that Sardinia's lost stone Doorways could indeed be interfaces with other worlds more ancient, and spoke up in defence of my words.

REVEREND: Rock Section, we are hiding here at Bidil 'e Pira at my suggestion.

The Reverend then pointed out that sacred holes and junctions with the earth still played their important part in modern Armenian Christianity. Having taken on Christianity earlier than Rome, Armenian holy ones had simply integrated into their rituals these subterranean practices so viciously stamped out elsewhere by St. Paul's Roman Church.

REVEREND: When Armenia's St. Grigory the Enlightener experienced his first vision of Jesus Christ, the Lord appeared to him in bright light above the sacred hill of Etchmiadzin, where now stands our own Vatican. But there still exists in a sub-basement far below Etchmiadzin's stone flagstones a near complete Temple of Mithra, whom all Armenians worshipped in the Pagan times.

ROCK: I'll bet they wished they kept that quiet.

REVEREND: Not really. Even modern Armenian priests accept that St. Grigory first stood upon Etchmiadzin not as a worshipper of Mithra, but recognising him instead as a herald of the Christ. To bring to Armenia the words of Jesus Christ was not an easy destiny for St. Grigory. When first the Enlightener attempted to install in Armenian hearts those new Christian ideas, he was for his pains cast by our king into the great hole of Khor Virap, a deep fissure in the rocks at the foot of Mt Ararat. And there he remained for decades. For this reason alone, wherever you find an Armenian, you will always find one open-minded towards the recurring motif of a Great Truth that is to be found only via the Great Schisms in the earth.

FEATHER: Like the Jews, the persecuted Armenians have always needed new ways to travel across the world.

We all walked over to the great tomb itself and clambered about at the overgrown façade around the carved entrance stone, this one a particularly fine monolith which jutted out of the ground more heftily than any I'd seen even in photographs. But ancient cart tracks right across the façade had long ago broken up the glorious continuous stone frontage and created a deep hollow way along the length of the great mound, itself now surmounted with olive trees and nature. Indeed, everyone passing this place along the normal route would have mistaken it for a natural ridge. Perfect. Jim Feather climbed down into the passageway and disappeared entirely for twenty long minutes, whilst the Rev and myself tried to apply my experiences at Puttu Oes and Goronna to our current situation. Then out of the far end of the mound I saw Jim appear. He burst forth suddenly, clutching his head and reeling around dizzily. The Rev and I sprinted over to him, but Jim was suffering and rolling about on the hot grass.

FEATHER: (*To his brother*) This is the place for us. I just met the Headless.

The Headless, of course! Then Jim collapsed upon the ground as though in a coma. For two full hours, his desperate brother ministered to Jim's suffering mind and sweating body. Of the hole from which he'd escaped the mound there was no sign whatsoever. Then, as the sun was approaching the far western horizon and twilight beckoned, our erstwhile Native American shaman suddenly sat bolt upright and smiled with the smile of the newly enlightened. For Jim had travelled deep within the mound and met all manner of people, figures, ghosts of the past. Moreover, Jim was convinced that these sacred Doorways could be of genuine use as his own escape route. He stared at me triumphantly, oozing an otherworldly glow.

FEATHER: No more messing around, Rock Section. If that lady Anna has put her faith in you going it alone today, let's be well professional, get you back in time and tucked up in bed for when she arrives. That way she knows we're on her side as well.

Quickly and efficiently, the three of us devised a plan of action, one that we all trusted could achieve my necessary end results of Time Travel. First, the two brothers would burn incense within the great chamber. Then, they would chant together as I drank cognac infused with fourteen powdered 3.75 mg Zopiclone sleeping pills to push me deep under. Copying my previous actions at the entrance to Goronna, my accomplices would then thrust my head into the entrance of the great Doorway, both then tending to my presumably headless body until my shout alerted them to my return. It did feel strange, though, two blokes instead of Blessèd Anna. Besides, sliding intoxicated into the Past was quite the opposite manner in which I'd previously arrived. Quite naturally, I wished again for the bang, I wanted the turbo jets, the rocketry, the fusillade of my humanness flung across the millennia. Headless me this time? Confident they that dare guess. Not no, not yes. Then without more ado, Jim Feather and his Reverend brother each grasped one of my shoulders, then bade me kneel before the great carved hole at the foot of Bidil 'e Pira's Doorway. Next, as the pair thrust my head into the hole, Jim Feather started up that same lusty chant that he himself had learned just two hours previously during his own subterranean encounter with the Headless.

FEATHER: The inverted trees down which I climb
　　　　　Into the Underworld sublime,
　　　　　Sunwise about, not widdershins,
　　　　　Return me now to gills and fins.

300

Stately he who runs through lands
Of Death and Wasting Illness,
Though Feckless Sick upon him breathe,
None shall infect the Headless.

Like targets shot by boys at butts
Into the centre bull's-eye,
Shall he in increments shoot forth:
All but the Headless *shall* die.

This be his chunter,
This be his aim,
This be the Headless,
This be his game:
          Into the rageous coffin blood,
          Into the times beneath the Flood

Headless me, this time?
Not no, not yes.
Your odds this day shall aid my cleavening,
Headless me this time?
None dare guess:
Your odds this day – they shall become my evening.

No more than several minutes of prostrate drunkenness, such
had my doubtful mind anticipated. Nevertheless, upon that very
moment that my head under the Doorway the two brothers did
pass, lo, did I sever all contact with Everything. Not downwards
this time did I pass, not upwards neither. Not forced by bloody
compulsion, not stretched upon the rack of years, not splattered
like a butterfly between docking ocean liners, not expanded

neither. Instead, through Ingestion was I transferred, through actual Inhalation by Nature herself was I thrusted down through Mother's porous limestone sinus depths, through her chalk, her flints, through her gargantuan, gynesophical corridors did I blow like ideas far back into the Distant Past.

39. PHED UP

Sunset, Summertime
A great open cavern, c. 10,000 years ago

I rose through the earth like sap drawn upwards by the heat, like a smoky basement fire that strives for its high chimney, like uncongealing blood through a bandage came I ever on. Progressive. Inevitable. Incorrigible. Until at last, like a plant that senses it must push its final way into the world, I detected upon me the glory and the influence of that red sky canopy shining just above me, shining just out of reach. It seemed to me now to be no more than a thin pastry crust away. Thus through that final crust how I nibbled and nudged and pecked and scratched my way upwards until, like a newborn chick, I was thrust by my own volition into New Life, thrust into the grand warmth of that external dome now blazing and ecstatic above me.

Thus, in recovery, did I lie in utter stillness in myself. Thus reconstituted did I hold myself inside the absolute silence of myself and be. Just be. At first I did lie only among myself, I did collect myself, until at last up into one lone person had I been drawn again. Then, as incoming lifestrands rallied – now pulling me together – how I basked in my great bed of feathers and ephedra heads, basked in that fabulous red glow of oncoming nightfall. Now, as life-force through me oozed in glorious renewal, how I stretched and stretched me in a great bodily display of my own self: every muscle in my arms, legs, hips, waist, feet, toes – all of my sinews I pulled forwards then disengaged. All of the muscles of my backbone I twisted tightly into place, aaargh. Bliss. Then I relaxed them all and laid my torso flaccid again. Hooooargh. How I groaned. Again I repeated this inradiating manoeuvre. Hooooargh. Throwing my head *back* now, I reached upwards as far as my chin could go, then tucked it deeply into my chest until I had fourteen chins, at least. I clenched my fists then unclenched them, staring with intense fascination at both hands. And with this splendid arrival of life's surging forces, so did I spring into life's urgent action. Standing now upon all fours atop my bed of feathers and ephedra heads, I was once more the guardian of this great cavern of silence. How I dispelled it now as I barked: Roaaargh! I roared: Rauuughhhhhhhhhhhrrrrrr! My lungs shouted out into the night sonic shards of brittle needles, and I heard babies down in the valley crying in response. Let them know I'm fit and well again, this Prince of Ashop. Let them sleep securely; let them know that I am back. For I had been sick beyond sick, near-dead describes my state more truthfully. Garrotted by the Oberst and his treacherous aides, saved only by my father's own intuition and decisive thinking, I had sunk for weeks thereafter into a dreamless sleep of numbness and terrifying near-death. But this past month, I've been on the mend since my savage attack by the damp quartet, and lest they forgot just whom they set upon, Old Tüpp's punishment meted out savagely point-after-point on their dwindling trajectory. Now, as the victims of magic they crawl and subsist in the creepiest corners Beyond Ashop. The Oberst Reduced in a hillock lies bound, his sycophants three – Hipper, Harland and Humberley – run as streams past his mound. And there shall the four play forever. Unless within the dragon's den of Great Worm's Hill they're drawn. For should through boredom dare they trespass, none shall greet the dawn.

But now, from my great cavern's entrance, I recognised the

signs of impending nightfall across my community: the dwindling fires of the cooking ovens all along the valley below, the
returning home of the sacred daughters along the headwaters
of Odin's Sitch, even the bringing in of the royal straw bedding
for my father Old Tüpp. And I noted a chill in the air. Then, I
spied across the floor of my cavern my great fire roaring up from
that deep circular hearth expertly excavated into the basalt floor.
How inviting were its dancing flames, were its crackling logs.
Already lit, already built up large by the dwarf known as Dràwf
– already fearsome. That dwarf must know of his master's pleasure. Jumping down from my raised stone bed, I pulled my finest
robe of sheep's wool and ephedra twine around my shoulders
and walked to my cavern's entrance, screaming out for the dwarf
into the pitch-black night. Quick as a flash he was at my side,
staring nervously.

BJOND: Dràwf, never again construct in my hearth a fire unlike
    this one. For it is as good as any I have *ever* enjoyed. Just as
    you have this time surpassed yourself, next time surpass your-
    self not. Make it not bigger next time. Make it not smaller.
    Indeed, look now upon this fire. Study its form well. Hereafter,
    hold in your head the memory of this fire just as the finest
    dwarf remembers always his own master's fire. Make sure this
    fire is the way of all future fires. Now begone, my fiery one,
    lest you die of respect.

And with that, the horrified dwarf hared off down the hillside
to plan future fires for my enjoyment. Now, over to the great
bath I strode. Here, I tore out three great, damp stringy strips
of shredded ephedra from the thick pasty tidemark that had
gathered upon the bath's sides. Then, hanging them over my left

shoulder, I returned to the heat of the roaring fire, where I rolled up the shortest of the strips – fulsome, soggy and warm, perhaps no longer than my forearm – into a fat, sticky patty which I sank my teeth into, wolfing it down with all the lust of a young child newly encountering blackberries. Slurp, it was gone. Then I walked over to the dish, a large human-worked concavity upon the summit of a waist-high stalagmite, where a delicious paste of honey and ephedra had been prepared for me. I took the two ephedra strips and laid them in the paste, then used my stone grinder to bind it all together. Then I dipped both hands into the paste and tucked in, downing the lot in moments.

Outside, where the flattened outer chamber now roofless leads directly to the sky, I heard at the great entrance beyond my cavern home the ubb-ubb of conversation and walked out to investigate. Aha, these were the winning candidates for my new Select: all had been brought here tonight in preparation for tomorrow's early start. Yes, tomorrow would I strike out for the ephedra fields of N. Abbadon, for the kingdom of Old Ball that lay far, far to our north. My preparations for this new adventure had long danced around dreams of building a fine new Select, each man stronger and younger than my previous band. Not twenty or thirty this time. Perhaps five at most, even four at a push. Drive them hard, keep them few. Pick the smart ones out and make them smarter. My disastrous sea journey to Abbis had brought about the unnecessary early deaths of many great Ashopian heroes. Lost also, therefore, on the high seas of the Vanquash: the dreams of the young heroes still sat at ma's apron strings. Who would their replacements be? Where would I travel to find them? How much I missed all the lost members of my brave Select. None had in Navio served Old Tüpp without first having achieved great fame for heroism in their own district. But as I reminisced about the lost ones, so my heart grew full of faith at the prospect of these new enlisters. And over the weeks, so the tests of strength and feats of endurance had knocked down and down my Select list until at last my preferred number had finally been reached. Four only. Never again shall Ashop deplete its resources just for the sake of grandness and traditions. At last the four winners came before me, but only as performers of excellence and still without names. I asked each one from what source would he draw his new name? Predictably, each winner had chosen to invoke the memory of their district's own lost Select hero, thereby imbuing their own new name with importance and meaning to their own people.

Now the first of my new Select approached my throne and kneeled. Before me was a giant with fists as big as hams and shoulders like an Abbadonian Bull Angus. He said that from his own village came my former warrior: the Select known as Might, whom I had great affection for and whom I had lost upon the Vanquash Sea.

BJOND: Then shall Smite be your name henceforth, for to be 'as Might' is to pay tribute to your blessèd elders. Go now, Smite, and smite our enemies down!

Then the second of my new Select approached my throne and kneeled. Before me now an ash-white, sunbleached, iceberg giant: huge. He said that from his own village hailed my former warrior: the Select known as Quash, whom I'd had great affection for and whom I had watched grow deadly ill and die upon the Vanquash Sea.

BJOND: Then Squash shall be your name henceforth, for to be
'as Quash' is to pay tribute to your blessèd elders. Go now,
Squash, and squash our enemies.

The third of my new Select approached my throne and kneeled.
Before me now a tall rugged birch of a youth whose taut, wiry
frame did carry a long and sharpened wooden spear which, so he
claimed, could not be rammed into the waters of any lake hereabouts without yielding at its tip a fine fish meal. He said that
from his own village hailed my former warrior: the Select known
as Pike, whom all had known as the greatest freshwater fisher-
man in all of Ashop before he was taken by the Vanquash Sea.

BJOND: Then Spike shall be your name henceforth, for to be
'as Pike' is to spike every fish upon whose form your shadow
falls. Go now, Spike, and spike our enemies.

The fourth and final member of my new Select approached my
throne and kneeled. Black bearded was this blue-eyed giant and
broad as any house: a whipmaster was he. In his right hand he
wielded as his whip a nine-foot-long Black Sea snake. He said
that from his own village hailed my own former whipmaster:
the Select known as Lash, whom I had watched drink seawater
and die upon the Vanquash Sea.

BJOND: Then Slash shall be your name henceforth, for to be 'as
Lash' is to pay tribute to your blessèd elders. Go now, Slash,
and slash at our enemies.

And thus without too much ado was my new Select formed.
Ready for travel abroad and each of them capable. That night

before we left for the ephedra fields of N. Abbadon, in praise of the gallant losing contenders, I allowed them to join in the victory party before returning to their own districts of Ashop. My pitchouers of piss of course I denied to them, but now I appreciated our young heroes, and no more would I allow Old Tüpp's kingdom to haemorrhage its homegrown warriors so pointlessly. Knowing now the exhausting perils of travel, I congratulated my new Select once more but reminded them of the importance of sleep tonight. It was already darkfall, so I bade them all good slumber and my dwarves led each new member to their sumptuous cave lodgings nearby.

40. IN THE FIELDS OF N. ABBADON

Sunset, Summertime
A great open cavern, c. 10,000 years ago

Abroad again was I, abroad and refreshed at last from my arduous journey to N. Abbadon and standing now waist-deep in the yellow ephedra fields of Old Ball the Sky-King. What a worthy journey! What an ephedra crop at journey's end! What drinks! What food, what paste, what taste! I speak only in praise and wonder at the Abbadonians' endless uplands of prime ephedra growing space: bountiful harvests, benevolent winds and all running clear to the North Sea coast. How my thoughts grew in these far-reaching and open landscapes! Farmers of Luno)))! Radiant northern-most glories! In truth, the valley fastness of my own land of Ashop had prepared me not for the openness of the Abbadonian horizons, where Old Ball's fields often ran unchecked across several plains and ridges at a time, terminating only at the heads of streams or blocked by the herds of wild Angus longhorns that roamed the river valleys of the Dee, Urie and Don. What creatures! What colours! What size!

Too long is the list of watercraft that bore me to N. Abbadon, and too arduously circuitous the water route. But, despite the current trend for Danish methods of sea travel, under no circumstance could I have engaged my own party in a sea voyage, for trust I had none. Thus were high-ways, hollow-ways and local water-ways my only choice. Nevertheless, still too many were the men who died to bring me here, though mercifully none of my new Select did perish. Surely unnecessary upon those local rivers were the many human sacrifices, most of which obtained due not to ingrown tradition but more often on account of some noble traveller's own jitter: a sop, no more than a reassurance paid for with a life. But considering of the geography and the grand adventure necessary to bring us here, still had we reached our far-flung destination with comparatively few losses. How very contrary are the feelings that rivers inspire in our land bodies. How very slow to return to its calm is the sap of our bodies once flung about upon watercourses. But sitting insensible in riverboats for days on end, high upon ephedra's peak, none can say this river ride was worse than any mild flu. Moreover, when I visited the glowing ephedra fields of N. Abbadon, I was so awestruck by their natural beauty and vast size that I recognised instantly how in need of travel were our highest Ashopians. For surely only by comparison with the achievements of others can we understand what we Ashopians ourselves have truly achieved. Therefore was my own journey to N. Abbadon still worthy of account, if only for other Ashopians.

My account of N. Abbadon must commence, however, with a description of Old Ball himself. For this great Sky-King had knowledge of the planets and their satellites: therefore he knew spheres also. Living in the north where Luno))) flew low, Old Ball had concentrated all of his greatest efforts in understanding precisely the movements of that great orb as he danced and bedazzled his way westwards through the night sky. How sharp were the Sky-King's explanations!

OLD BALL: Luno))) must be nursed across the sky constantly. We watch him from the wooden sanctuaries upon our SW-facing hilltops. Our holy ones approach him only with great courtesy. Wearing tonsured shaven heads, they ascend up cleverly constructed pavements of close-fitting stones, climbing from the NE so that Luno))) – upon glimpsing their moonlit halos – trusts these who dare to approach his sacred hills.

Such knowledge of the planets and the spheres had the Sky-King that he understood even their magical dimensions, their innermost workings. And thus from rough balls of sandstone, whetstone, even basalt did Old Ball construct many perfect spheres, true! Every one made by the hands of Old Ball. Even during our dinner conversations was the Sky-King at his toil, always shaping, scraping, filing, always grinding, moulding, buffing. Until inevitably from his great palms would emerge yet another of those exquisite carved balls! Magic, nothing less! Some of them he rendered with dextrous angled designs inscribed upon their faces; others he decorated with magical divisions upon their faces. Before my journey north, no knowledge had I of Old Ball's extravagant gifts. For nothing of their kind had ever come through Ashop – such curious items being far too rare to have been transported even outside their own local districts. But there upon the conical judgement hill of Inch, all-the-while sat atop his extravagant wooden throne, Old Ball would carve these magical artefacts while holding court, his bubbling mind forever spouting forth new streams of highly stimulating ideas.

In truth, the remote authority that pervaded my father's own methods of rule had prepared me not for this frankness and openness of Old Ball's ways. Moreover, the exploratory methods of Old Ball's kingship inclined him always on an upward trajectory onwards and towards the next stage of humanity's learning. Thus the king wished at all times to surround himself only with the most prime examples of Abbadonian achievements, i.e.: the use of Luno))) in river and sea navigation, the use of Sunno))) in ephedra growing, and the understanding of the sphere itself, the ball, the circle that has no end. To this exploratory end, then, did Old Ball run not with like-kind, run not with others Grand and Ancient, run not with the coronated and the castellated. Instead, Old Ball entangled himself with as rum a bunch of characters as never would have even been permitted to set foot in Old Tüpp's kingdom, let alone been afforded the chance to sully his own pristine dining room! Ah yes, Old Ball's grand dinners wherein I did meet every last one of those most favoured of his court.

And what outrageous nicknames Old Ball did apply to his favourites! Names destined for kings were, in the topsy-turvy world of N. Abbadon, summarily applied to Old Ball's most unregal of associates. His favourite fleetmaster was a drunken brawler nicknamed by the king 'Old Keig'; his favourite sky-watcher was a wall-eyed wanderer named 'Old Reign'; Old Ball's favourite bullfighter was a crippled giant that the king called 'Old Bourtreebush'. It was as though Old Ball was saying by his actions that Abbadon's finest heroes stood outside the rules of life in the wider world, that their experiences and successes placed them outside the laws that elsewhere by tradition placed upon important thrones only hesitant old dodderers. Indeed, it was here at the dinner table of Old Ball that the greatest Abbadonian ideas sprang forth, and here that the latest myths were dispelled. Time-honoured traditions that none other would dare to test? Old Ball brought them all to account with neither fuss nor flourish. Indeed, the Sky-King – at our first dinner together – praised my decision to travel along river routes only. Moreover, Old Ball displayed none of the world's current obsession with Danish sea travel, ascribing its success mainly to the Danes' own hard work, their persistence and more than a modicum of luck.

OLD BALL: I have heard it told that the first sea journey was made by the Danes by mistake. For having learned animal husbandry from Old Dam herself, it's said that the Danes over-farmed and over-plucked their beaver dams, yielding such a plethora of logs that their bridge experiments became unwieldy and easily washed away. One such experimental bridge across the Moray Firth is said, during a storm, to have become disengaged from both riverbanks, causing the bridgers to evacuate each end, despite several local men and cattle having attempted already to make the crossing – unpermitted of course. At storm's end, no sign of the structure whatsoever could be seen. Several days later, however, the 'bridge' was discovered twenty miles out to sea, the men and several cattle still wading in great discomfort upon its stable floor. Of course, the Danmark cleverly claimed this struggler as their first sea-going ship!

Such spirited monologues were never far away during a dinner with Old Ball. Moreover, on that first splendid night of our meeting, the Sky-King's vigour, vim and keen dialogues had extracted from my head more new ideas and possibilities than any sage or teacher that I'd ever before known. How uplifted were my thoughts by Old Ball's methods and ways, by his dynamic progress, his inclined trajectory, his generous quizzing of every mind that passed before him. In this state of eternal curiosity did Old Ball ensure that he would retain always his independence, retain always his reputation for seeking new truths. Oh, and the cauldrons of ephedra mead that flowed! Oh, and the patties of ephedra that we chewed! Bright yellow sheaves abounded throughout N. Abbadon: spectacular achievements!

Now it is my own estimation that the greatest development

of Old Ball's sky worship manifested in the playing of The Ball Game, a spectacular hilltop event that brought together all of Old Ball's sky knowledge. Some early Tale-men have suggested that the fleetmaster Old Keig invented The Ball Game on the beaches of N. Abbadon, a claim never refuted by Old Ball himself. Those early reporters tell of a deadly storm, which had pushed the Abbadonian Fleet a full three days off course – the sailors were desperate. It is said that when the holy river-mouth of the Dee was at last espied with the aid of the rising of Luno))), their fleetmaster Keig – on reaching land first – threw himself down upon the sands of Gask and kissed the ground in gratitude. Then, Keig had his huge low-sailed, two-masted raft of Iberian balsa dragged high upon the dunes of Gask. Next, his men angled his raft just-so, thus enabling Luno))) to appear to dance between its two masts. Finally, Keig took a few good steps back, placed upon this hallowed ground the inflated pig's bladder that every Abbadonian sailor employs for a lifesaver upon the hostile seas, and kicked that Sphere so accurately that it flew – so they say – between the two masts and soared all the way to the Moon. Thereafter, every returning fleet picked up on this Good Luck practice, the accurate kicking of the ball becoming a requirement for all sailors of the Abbadonian Fleet. Old Ball himself encouraged this new tradition of precision kicking by setting atop every southwesterly N. Abbadonian hill a copy of Keig's balsa raft, but affixed into the earth in longer-lasting spruce, that every future sailor of the Fleet might practise at home and in advance what might be expected of him. Thus, through the openness and forward-thinking attitudes of the Sky-King to the ideas of others more humble, did N. Abbadon thrive. Thus, through Old Ball's canny decision to gather around himself always a succession of New Thinkers and Doers have N. Abbadonians continued to sizzle with progress and new ideas.

* * *

And so at last on my final day in Old Ball's splendid company: a treat! Did I know perspective? Did I know judgement of distance? Did I know how time travels? If not, could I be shown it? I did not know any of the aforementioned, or so I thought. But I would very much like to see it all. And thus, armed with two bladders of the finest Abbadonian honeyed ephedra mead, did we upon that final day walk up to meet the Hatton of Ardoyne, a venerable lunar observer whose own hilltop observatory had been set up N. Abbadon-style with the two tall spruce masts. Hatton himself, however, had chosen to enhance his goalposts midway between with a great flat-topped rectangular boulder, which mirrored the mountainous horizon. How curious! How great their motivation! Why, the whole community must have rallied for the moving of such a behemoth!

OLD BALL: Know you of sympathetic magic, Prince of Ashop?
BJOND: Of course, Soeur. A man wishing for a fish dinner carves in wood a small fish and lays it upon the riverbank. He sinks his angled rod into the water, behold his fish dinner!
OLD BALL: (*Triumphant*) Succinctly spoken.

Now did the Sage-King describe to me how time could be conflated by the misuse of horizons and perspective. He said that Hatton's great table stone would outwit Luno))) and entrap the shining one as he travelled along the edge of the horizon. Old Ball explained how expertly placed ball players fabulously clad would, at the rising of Luno))), pitch the Sky-King's geometrically worked stone balls across Hatton's spruce masts, thus causing the shining one through curiosity to follow the same trajectory. I smiled in wonder at this process, but I knew not what either man meant by his words. But then, as time moved on and those specially invited few began to gather around the northern slopes of Hatton's great masts, a veritable new world of experiences opened up to me. Here at the great masts now danced white-painted acrobats making wheel shapes and back flips. Incredible. Now, in preparation for the emergence at the west of the rising of Luno))), were great stone balls being pitched with great accuracy across Hatton's tall masts: sympathetic magic intended to lure Luno))) into the same actions.

OLD BALL: Tonight at the rising of Luno))) will we all of us on this hillside pass temporarily into the future time by so confusing Luno))) that he comes to a standstill right above Hatton's altar stone.

BJOND: The standstill of Luno)))! Then must this Prince of Ashop contribute also to your experiment!

And thus it was that this Prince of Ashop was, at the rising of Luno))), set up as the Principal Observer lying recumbent upon my back across Hatton's great table stone. How divine the night sky! How gentle the wind high atop these slopes of N. Abbadon. But as the balls flew over my head and Luno))) approached nearer and nearer, so I wished that I had better understood Old Ball's instructions. Perspective? What is perspective? And so it was that this Prince of Ashop – being wholly ignorant even of the concept of perspective – misunderstood the accuracy of the stone balls being pitched across his recumbent form, misunderstood the lethal nature of these sacred carved spheres, misunderstood entirely the overall goal of Old Ball and his Lunar party, and – filled to the brim with ephedra's own sweet love – did through sheer childlike excitement now raise up his enthusiastic form better to view this fantastic Abbadonian display. The results? Catastrophic and instant! First one stone ball dealt me a crusher to the temple; next another missed me almost but cracked nevertheless against my forehead. Thus, smiling like a newborn witnessing fireworks and still wishing to witness Time Travel was I snuffed out.

41. SU TALLERI, SLIGHT RETURN

9.30pm, Monday June 12th, 2006
Bidil 'e Pira, Sardinia

Clutching at my head, I got up and tried to walk but kept falling over. I was barely conscious. The sky was tar black. I just couldn't walk. I could hardly breathe. In front of me were gorgeous star beings. Clutching my head, I staggered towards them drunkenly and watched them flee. But try though I might to pursue them, their speed was such that I soon ran out of energy, then huffing and puffing myself to a standstill, I watched as they chased off into the darkness. Then I turned back and returned to my bolthole, I stuck my head back under the great Doorway and lay there miserable, inconsolable. What was life? Where had it gone? And yet, and yet . . . And yet at long last, from outside the very utmost outlands of human experience did I slightly obtain in my nose an espungent and satisfying ripeness quite foreign to my current senses. Gradually came upon me once more the smell of myrthus bushes, the smell of woodsmoke fires, the alien effervescence of patchouli incense, the heady zing of cognac, the rich sweet overkill of marijuana smoke. And with slow inevitability I descended once again into Now. Around my ankles, I felt the firm grip of four big hands dragging me with great care. Then, with equal care was I flipped over on to my back, whereupon my eyes were greeted by a sensational night sky Persian-carpeted with all the stars of the Arabian Nights! And even as I exhaled a great 'Coo!' of astonishment, so did my dark companions announce their presence.

FEATHER: All right, geezer? The perfect encounter!
REVEREND: You had *them* worried!

What encounter? Whom did I have worried? Warming to my compadrés' voices and dumbstruck by the starry night below – or was that above? – I now attempted to raise my head but could not; now opened my mouth and attempted to speak but could not. Nevertheless, my life stirrings had clearly satisfied my companions, who both now made no attempt to lift me further, instead wrapping my body in blankets and feeding me with life-enhancing sips of cognac. Then, as a basic sense of humanity gradually restored itself within me, so I struggled to shake off that ancient world, so I struggled to put back on the mantle of this current one. By-and-by, such basic personal thoughts began to drizzle their way through my un-oiled synapses that they brought about a massive grin to my drooling phizzog. Thus was my first verbal exchange with my two associates more cli-chéd than any hack writer would have dared to feed even to his cheesiest character.

ROCK: (*Weakened*) A toke would be nice.
FEATHER: No problemo, Druid! (*Smiling and shaking a packet of Green Rizla in my face*) You scared those bastards away quick sharp! I felt like running myself!
REVEREND: You returned from your great journey just as the Porcu boys arrived looking for my brother. Luckily, we'd spotted their torches moving along the lanes, so we had plenty of time to hide everything including ourselves in the tomb chamber.
FEATHER: Everything but the yurt! What a fucking giveaway! I was certain we were totally nicked once they'd clocked it! All over it, those Porcus were.

REVEREND: Then came our hero to the rescue!

FEATHER: *You*, Mr Headless! You came tearing out of that tomb with no head on your shoulders and terrorised each Porcu brother individually. I wish I could have enjoyed it more, but I was shitting myself in case you started on us!

Now I understood. Those hot-footing-it star beings I'd tried to pursue had all been Porcus running away from my headless form in terror! How sad to be a Porcu: repulsive in this life but gorgeous in some other unreachable dimension! But as the two brothers' lucky escape had only been facilitated by my utterly impromptu behaviour, my spell in that overlapping, in-between dreamtime was now cut drastically short by the hefty implications of this Porcu invasion of the camp.

* * *

Within the hour, I was back to my old form, now more hugely affronted by the Porcu invasion than ever and determined to seek justice for our noble savage. Both Jim and his brother, however, now appeared to be in no hurry to move on from Bidil 'e Pira, the two of them convinced by my headless display that no return Porcu encounter would be forthcoming. What *had* I done to those scoundrels? But Jim and the Rev, having both experienced first-hand my headless behaviour, now took far more seriously my pre-journey banter. For the brothers saw that it had yielded . . . ahem, results! But what, asked the brothers, were these results all about? And to what great underground network were Sardinia's Doorways connected? Oo-er, what a question! I swayed my head and pursed my lips in prevarication, for each successive Journey Through Time had yielded entirely different results and had even deployed different methods of travel, or certainly arrival. How limited also had been my Doorway experiences! In trying to explain in any depth to the brothers, I was like a nipper on an Early Learning Centre trampoline trying to describe Disneyland to other nippers.

ROCK: I think people were visiting this place for cosmic purposes (*pointing to the whole monument*) thousands of years before they built the mound. Shaman types probably knew of these fissures in the local geology, but kept it to themselves that they were concealed entrances. In recognition of the old people's ways, the new people probably built these tombs for dignitaries looking for a salubrious R.I.P.

Now, I laid my bag upon the ground and sought to retrieve that sheaf of June 14th celebration brochures that Anna and I had nicked from the back of the Opposite club. I was rather hopeful that there might be more clues in its contents that Jim Feather could acquaint me with, so I removed my black shirt and socks, and dug deeper. But when I took out my copy of Hertzog's *Prison Writings* and placed it temporarily on the parched ground, it was not the unsettling X-faced image of the Judge that grabbed Jim Feather, but the unyielding trajectory of the author's blurb, which Jim immediately read aloud to his equally spellbound brother:

Do not live as if God is around you in the trees, in the hills, in the rain and in the snow. He is not nearby but must be looked for, searched for, struggled for. Those that seek their prophet nearby do themselves an injustice, for no prophet of worth ever was worshipped by his own people. Jesus? Rejected by all other Jews. The words of Jesus were

accepted only abroad. Moses? Raised in the Egyptian pharaoh's own palace, his historical place nevertheless would
be as head of a nomad tribe, the Jews. Only the great religions of the world follow prophets from outside their
own lands, for those people sought truths from beyond
their own horizons, yearned for something richer, something apparently outside their present requirements. *Prison
Writings* explores J. M. B. Hertzog's personal obsessions
with what he terms his 'own foreign prophet, Malcolm X'.

The two brothers looked askance at each other, as if diminished
by their sudden encounter with Hertzog's printed words. During
my long months of owning a copy of *Prison Writings* but having
never looked inside it, I'd grown used to this blurb, almost fond
of it. But then, that was before Barry Hertzog had torn a strip
off me at Florinas Penitentiary and showed himself up as the
Munter Cunt from Wankerland. And I tried to imagine how
the two brothers would now be feeling: an imprisoned maniac
with a scary prophetic book already published is the underlying
cause of your life problems. Unlovely. Believe me, I'd had plenty
of time to get used to the idea and it still sat rather harshly in
my gullet. But while Jim seemed floored by Hertzog's blurb, the
Reverend Jim Featherian remained upbeat, even philosophical
about their risky situation.

REVEREND: (*Extending both hands out to Jim*) My brother, I
    don't like the people who follow this fellow, but I can't say
    those words of his are so far off the mark. His belief in the
    'foreign prophet, Malcolm X' is no different to we Gentiles
    worshipping a Jew, or the Aztecs awaiting a white-haired
    blond prophet from far across the sea named Quetzalcoatl.

Hertzog is sharp also to note Moses' lofty beginnings in the Pharaoh's palace. Freud himself explained that fact as possible evidence of Pharaoh Akhenaten's hand in the curious monotheism of the Jews.

FEATHER: (*Not listening*) Yeah, but the way Hertzog's believers go about things, man. They're neo-Nazis, Mormons, Taliban.

Finally, I retrieved the Opposite programmes from deep inside my bag, and the three of us fell upon their contents looking for clues and rum doings. But initially the programme seemed no more than a gargantuan ego trip for Bugs Rabbit, and a funny one at that:

'The Bugs Rabbit Story famously started in Milan, in 1966, with the completion of the *Nice Little Urna* LP by Sardinian soul singer Urna Washington, whose first hit was Bugs' own song "Come Back and Haunt Me". Inspired in 1969 by a London performance of the rock musical *Hair*, Bugs developed an Italian version with new lyrics, but was devastated to learn that the Catholic Church, appalled by the show's nudity, absolutely forbade any performance of this work. Determined to find a home for his songs and new arrangements, Bugs Rabbit next created *Ears*, a homage/parody of *Hair* employing rabbits in place of the hippies. This hugely successful rock musical travelled all over Italian-speaking Europe – Sicily, Albania, parts of Malta – and ran for close to a decade. Contrary to popular rock legend, Bugs Rabbit takes his nickname not from his prominent teeth but from this early Italian theatre success.'

FEATHER: No way, man. Of course it's because of his big teeth! He's got more overbite than a naked mole rat! Even his dear old mother refers to him as *Heterocephalus Glaber*!

But now in the Opposite programme I found the evidence at last, brazenly occupying the glossy pullout Drinks Centrefold, and looking just as I remembered. There in glorious full colour was that same off-kilter South Africanised map of Sardinia. Again, there was that same bizarre re-labelling of Sardinia's most prominent towns and cities with the names of South African cities. And next to the map was the complete price list of Opposite's available drinks, each named just as perversely as before: The Mafeking Make-over, The Bubbling Bloemfontein, The Shady Ladysmith, The Taste of Old Cape Town, The Magisterial Magersfontein, The Durban Shakedown, The Colenso Colonic, The Pretorian Guard and The Kimberley Comeuppance. Brr, I don't like the sound of that last one. I kept on staring at the map, but I was still looking at the outside form of everything, and I was positive there was a whole different truth just waiting to be consciousized. What do you mean there's no such word? Weirder still, emblazoned large across the head of each programme page was a different cryptic fact: *1645 The Battle of Naseby brings victory to the English Parliamentarians; 1667 The Raid of the Medway by Dutch Fleet; 1789 Bourbon invented by Rev. Elijah Craig using maize; 1846 Bear Flag Revolt; 1940 First day of Auschwitz; 1949 Albert II, the rhesus monkey rides a V2 rocket 83 miles into space; 1967 China tests its first hydrogen bomb* – the list went on. But random as the list appeared to me, so did a couple of those facts strike a, well, what did they strike? Wasn't there a king called Albert II? Who'd told me that?

And then I registered at last – and for the first time – the reason for all of this confusing protractedness. Now at last I got it in all of its glorious evil. Wednesday June 14th would be the opening of Opposite precisely because it was the birthday

of our own dear departed Leander Pitt-Rivers Baring-Gould.
It was to be a retribution party! Now I remembered those
final cryptic comments that Breakfast had made to me after
soundly thrashing the Judge in Slag Van Blowdriver's very
public argument. Now, I could hear his voice speaking from
the grave: 'Battle of Naseby, Old Rock. Do drink a bourbon
for me.' I'd been thrown off the scent by Breakfast's comment
about Albert II, mistaking him for some obscure Hapsburg-
type emperor. In reality? Breakfast had merely been compar-
ing Barry Hertzog to the first monkey in space! Wow, these
enemies of ours had been rather too thoroughly evil: What
fucking creepoids!

Convinced that more atrocities would be sure to come to light
in time, I left one of the programmes with the pair of them. For
now had come the time for me to split, time to hightail it north
to Macomér in order to enact the next part of our research. Our
research! Get me! Delighted that my own actions had scared
away the Porcu clan, I could now rely on the two brothers to stay
put for the next couple of days, knowing that both Anna and
myself could find them easily enough should their assistance be
required. Just as I was picking up my bag to hoof it out of there,
Jim told me he'd been thinking about ways in which we could
unite our powers against these evil cunts.

FEATHER: Rock, how much longer you here for?
ROCK: Day after tomorrow I leave. Why?
FEATHER: Have a listen to this. Mull it over and see if it yields
  any bright ideas, right? After Italia '90, the Mackenzie
  Brothers were truly up shit creek, and their island reputation
  and stock fell dramatically. From his work on Spackhouse
  Tottu's homage to the supermodel Annachiara Cani, Bugs

Rabbit was owed a fortune in back royalties. But after seeing the Meatburger desolation at Sant'Elia Stadium, he knew they could never pay. So Bugs took on the brothers' beachfront hotel in Buggeru, took over their Cágliari plumbing business and inherited all of their remaining Meatburger caravans. These he had towed up to Orosei and – after having me repaint their logos – started Circus Meltburger. It's all based on Judge Barry Hertzog's old anti-British installation 'The First Concentration Camps'.

ROCK: (*Clueless*) What? In Sardinia?

FEATHER: Nowadays, it's run by Loon and Walter-Under-The-Bridge out of a two-bedroom cave-house in Gavoi. Cowtown Unslutter is their manager. They hold Bible Class at each town and hold services in the cave-house.

ROCK: (*Head scratching*) What? Who's their audience? Sards?

FEATHER: (*Sardonic smile*) Rock, they don't even need a paying audience. It's the heart of Kidnap Territory. Shepherds get the blame and nobody suspects these able foreign grafters. These mobsters run the circus as a front for attracting unsuspecting tourists, rich British mainly. Who else has heard of the Boer War? It's perfect for spying on unsuspecting tourists, then kidnapping unsuspecting tourists. Plus plenty of scope for other evils along the way.

ROCK: Where on earth do they get up to all this?

FEATHER: Year in, year out, they follow the official D. H. Lawrence *Sea and Sardinia* Heritage Trail up and down between Cágliari and Tavolara.

ROCK: Mándas – Sórgono – Tonara – Gavoi – Nuoro – Orosei. Did I miss any?

FEATHER: (*Smiling broadly*) I'm well impressed.

Startling fucking big result news or what? I now knew the towns where these beasts roamed. Names of towns, oh yes. Go to the towns and just look for the Meltburger sign. The tragic deaths of Brent, Dean and Leander Pitt-Rivers Baring-Gould must in some manner be paid for, that much I knew. In turn, the two brothers now knew that I was off in search both of that magic cloak *and* of its illegal wearers. I bear-hugged Jim and his brother, waved an undefeated right fist in each of their faces, then thanked them both profusely. But – thinking mythologically – I resisted my desire to explain my ease with D. H. Lawrence references. Let these gentlemen think I *was* the new Thomas Chatterton, well, the new *old* one! Let them with all of their current problems be inspired by our mutual aid! I started to walk out into the pitch-black darkness back down the thorny avenues and cattle droves towards the SP 65. And as I pitched forwards into the night sky, some 'little foam upon the deep' inside me was occurring. I felt inside my muddy mind some meagre plan a-stirring.

* * *

One hour into my Macomér walk, with veins elastic and pumping arteries I strode. The newness of this life now upon me in spades, the former life – being not yet receded – did still inform my growling underworld ghoulself as beside me it walked, trudged, trolledged on. Reaching the 131 quickly, I had plugged in my iBeam to 89.9 FM, and was now marching along like Ted Hughes' Iron Man up the well-lit motorway right up to Abbasanta junction. But although I could get only intermittent radio reception, the tar-black sky swallowed every last air football that I punted skywards, dancing like Diego in a new ephedra frenzy, *and* with a new spherical knowledge: with the balls to make it all work. Soon I was cutting around the heritage site entrance of the 3,000-year-old Nuraghe Losa – how the Sards love these cooling towers! – then back up the course of the motorway. Dammit, I felt as though I was walking so fast that I needed a crash helmet. Striding back up on to the unlit section north of Abbasanta, I suddenly saw five stripes on my iBeam, which burst into life. The last classic minutes of 'Can't Cheat Karma' by Zounds was just concluding, then I heard Jesu Crussu announce the 11 o'clock news and traffic report.

CRUSSU: No one was killed today when Fatah terrorists fired upon the Palestinian government building. North Korea will test their Taepodong-2 intercontinental missile. In Sássari City, criminals from the Barbagia Ollolai region have kidnapped a wealthy doctor. The weather tonight is fine and warm. You're just in time for a treat, dear friends. How many remember Gennargentu at fifteen years old? The boy prodigy – some say our own island's Hendrix. Well, here's his first statement from back in 1972, this is all twenty minutes of 'Bruxo' from Atlantis?'s first LP.

In near ecstasy I walked now, hoofing it up the motorway. At my back, a spectral army of Sardu cave anarchists urged me, percussioned me along. In front of the speakers, angelic and alone, one teenage guitarist danced us all Mithraic, light-bringing, flinging us headlong into a new age. And throughout it all I bowled along rampant and roaring with this newfound strength of companionship and indefatigable spirit.

* * *

By 1.30am, I was entering the environs of Birori Valley, Macomér's dark foreboding fortress still menacing as it presided over this most important of ancient junctions. But as I turned left off the 131 and began to hack it up that dead-straight Roman incline into the town, over between the industrial estate and the waterworks did I feel something a-stirring at my presence. Shaking the ground around on account of my presence. Into my head like a telecast I saw myself coronated as Old Tüpp, sat atop my great contraption carried by my stout new Select, one at each corner shouldering my rig onwards. I knew nothing of what this meant. But this was surely the most peculiar vision to which I had ever been privy! Now, I observed my Kingly Self sat atop my great contraption carried out of Ashop forever, carried down the southern waterways of the Vanmark, down through the Danmark into Mediterranean climes. I knew not where they carried me, but I knew that they did right to bring me here. Click! The telecast was over.

I was at the door of Su Talleri barely five minutes later. As planned, Anna had secreted my hotel keys under the flowerpot at the entrance and I ascended the staircase with all the fizzing energy of one preparing to embark on another long journey. As I closed the hotel room door and switched on the kettle, the only discomfort that I experienced was around my jaws and teeth, all of which buzz and rattle incessantly during Inter-Time Travel; knees and elbows also become horribly twisted over and across time. But now I just felt exhilarated at the prospect of kicking some bastard asses, at the righteous prospect of some kind of Cosmic Restitution. Even after having been flung once again across the Universe, I can't pretend that walking the eleven miles back to Macomér was in any way difficult, because I didn't even notice it really. And that fact inspired the hell out of me. While I was in this super space, I could take on all of those immoral fuckers. Hell, I even had Blessèd Anna on my side!

42. THE VALLEY OF THE DOORWAYS

2am, Tuesday morning June 13th, 2006
Room 6, Su Talleri Hotel, Macomér

Cosy in my Su Talleri bed, sheaves of archaeological notes scattered around the floor, I was sitting bolt upright nursing a nice hot cup of some instant hotel-provided sachet froth in one hand, in the other a sweet-as-anything three-skinner courtesy of Jim Feather. Yes, I'd been up all night and no I didn't feel sleepy. Indeed, the residue of my otherworldly travails had this time not entirely left my consciousness, and I lay just slightly in two places at the same time. But now, still raring to go in these midnight hours, I was determined to make good use of this providential return to Macomér and the neighbouring Birori Valley. Nevertheless, however hard I tried to research these places, all I could make out through the language barrier was that the ancient people who'd carved the Doorways had stopped their practice not far south of here. Beyond that point, all the tombs had been accessed through great archways of masonry bricks – and those people didn't even carve stones, just left them rugged and brutalistic. Throughout our troubled descent along the 131 past Macomér a couple of days ago, the Great Being had called out to me from the Altar of Punishment; during the 'events of sixteen years ago', my escape from the Fascist Cheese Factory had led me on a right old Dance of Doorways all across the Birori Valley, but it had – again – all terminated at the Altar of Punishment. Even

Giampaolo's experience had drawn him towards the industrial estate itself, again wherein lies the Altar of Punishment. Aha, then I saw it right there on the map! Of course, the Altar of Punishment was built directly at the confluence of three streams: Macomér's waterworks butts up right next to it, still takes its town water from *those* streams. If our experiences at Bidil 'e Pira had been due to the fissures in the rock strata, then the confluence of three different watercourses was going to act like an Uber-fissure! Score in a big way! I stared outside at the blinking, watery-green hotel light and toked a final one. Then I sunk down into my lazy bed and forgot, at least temporarily, that our place of kidnap and incarceration was now barely 200 metres away. My subconscious mind, however, did not forget this fact. Zzzzzzzzzzzzzzzzzzz . . .

* * *

This horizontal window was so narrow that I tore my cock on the lock as I thrust my naked self out in the half-light, desperate not to lose contact with Brent, whom I'd spied haring off through that very slat I'd next moment had to pass through. But by the time I was out, my eyes could barely grope for his lofty wraithlike ever-diminishing form as it weaved its spectral and sinewy path along the precipice of the gorge 400 yards or so ahead of me. Moreover, attempting to catch him got me so scratched up to fuck that I was raw meat when I reached the place I'd last spotted him. Fuck English nettles, man, the Sards even had some fruit plants that would tear a man's Gore-Tex to pieces, and I was discovering this bollock nekkid. 'Struth! But I couldn't lose Brent. No way. I can't say to Gabriella that I lost Brent; he's fourteen years old and I used to do smack when I baby-sat him. Oh, fuck's sake what am I? Naked, bloody, starving and in Macomér. As the coughing-his-guts-up gimp loved to tell us like we couldn't work it out. Well, one thing I knew? This was Macomér, this gorge was in Macomér, the lights were Macomér, my bleeding cock was in Macomér. I'd seen enough fucking road signs during our police chase north, and that rushing of headlights and roaring of traffic over to my right beyond the gorge? The 131. There's no other road on the island where traffic can go that fast. I never smiled, but I had a plan. Find Brent and follow the 131 south. It's a plan. Find the kid and go home. Rock's progress. It's a fucking plan, man. And as the vicious cuts on my naked legs and feet took my mind off my hunger, I held on to my little comforter itself so lacerated by my overly dépêche defenestration.

But such was the excruciating slowness of my movement as I edged along the steep-sided ravine, shuffled along as though with the bound ankles of some unfortunate Chinese woman, that I did become enveloped in a gelatal mist of my own making, a right old pudding of a fog: and in all of the wide Macomér landscape, this whipped cream haze whirled around my head alone. And now – like some self-pitying Eeyore – I sunk even further into semblance than ever before, even further into progress for the sake of discovery? What? Like Rock's progress? Mmm, I like the sound of that. I like progressive. War Pigs and peace. I love peas. Soaky peas and mushy peas. I'd like mushy peas and fritters, please. With extra salt, Auntie Vera. Thanks so much. Can I put the salt on myself? I'm having a can of something, anything really. Corona. But I'll have two sausages . . . and I'll have the fritters not in newspaper, thanks. It's that *Eastwood Advertiser* newsprint comes off on the chips. I'm drinking at the Man In Space tonight. What time you shutting up? Shall I just pre-order chips with curry now? I'll be supping out in the car park. You can just get your Ian to yell.

Mmm, I wasn't having curry after all. Not in Macomér tonight. I still could not find Brent and I'd been looking since yesterday early morning. Rock's Progress? I was crouching at sundown in that same steep ravine beneath the 131 without a plan. The pain in my side from that kicking the gimp had given me on account of not getting to bum me? Yeah, it fucking killed, man. But the industrial doses of string-out they'd laid on all of us were still comatising me two days later *and* I was seeing spectral Doorways all over the landscape. Yeah man, massive glow-in-the-dark spectral Doorways. How many? All right, all right. Maybe Brent's stashed himself in some great safe house behind a great Doorway and now he's giving out cosmic signals as to his whereabouts. Tell you the truth, when forty-eight hours said No Brent, I was just too thirsty to wait any longer. So I clambered up out of the temporary safety of the ravine to a concealed spot along that great curved, elevated road section of the 131 where it roars like some petrified concrete waterfall out of the great Campedero Mountains, arcing steeply around hilltop Macomér as it rushes towards the valley below. Exhilarating, intoxicating southern views of freedom, it was just incredible to view so clearly my possible escape route and so harsh to accept my excruciating flightlessness when that very route that I so desperately sought was blazing before my own eyes. Now Macomér was Moscow, the winter was coming on and we were Napoleon's stranded soldiers desperate to peg it back to snivilisation.

But although it was sundown, I was still naked and jonesing for drugs and wanted by both cops *and* cunts. However, by now convinced – through hunger, withdrawals and those forcibly administered industrial-sized Largactil doses – that Brent had most assuredly passed through an ancient Doorway into another safer world, my compulsion to hide out – to ferret my naked self away under the 131 – was constantly being undermined by my incontinent fury at the rough justice having been meted out to my accomplices and myself. Still, I danced close to the 131 at all times, itching and teetering along the ravine's steep sides, rubbing my sticky and drugged-out form against the reinforced steel supports – so cavernously cooling; so calming just fifty feet below that seemingly endless Upper World rush of frantic Sardines. And from the pedestrian safety of my Lower World, I hobbled gingerly for close to two downhill miles accompanying this superhighway's vast arc southwards around that dreaded Macomér, always keeping under its massive structures wherever I could.

But right at the point where the road's wide arc begins to hit exactly due south, right there did I spot a great Doorway blazing at me just 400 metres east of the 131's raised concrete stanchions. Convinced that this spectral place must be the escape hatch into which Brent had tumbled, I advanced now with great reckless-ness across the steep sides of the unverdant scrub, hollering for Brent at the top of my voice. But when I was no more than ten feet from the Doorway, I saw that the small standing stone beside the entrance was actually a tiny sentinel, a terrifying fig-ure who screamed at me, and declared that he was Nuscadoré, guardian of the Doorway of Nuscadoré.

NUSCADORÉ: No one named Brent bothered Nuscadoré. Who are you to knock on my door?
ROCK: In my mind's eye, I watched my associate as he entered through a great secret door.
NUSCADORÉ: Aaaaaaagh, fool! Naked fool! (*Waving his right*

arm lavishly across the valley below) This is the Valley of the Doorways! Now begone, naked fool!

And lo, across the valley floor eight great blazing Doorways lit up before my eyes. I thanked the apoplectic midget and set off at once, gingerly picking my way downhill towards the nearest of the eight. Shit, they were all miles apart. I stood silent for a moment trying to deduce a more circuitous and unpopulated route to the nearest of the Doorways, a route that would not compromise my nakedness. But no matter how I read the situation, one way or another I would still have to streak right through the centre of Birori village – and me the very opposite of your typical streaking kid. Fucking hell, off I jolly well trotted with a ger-zillion misgivings. What poor Birori biddie deserved to experience my wretched unfedness? Shit, I was skinny enough at the best of times. But the belting that the gimp had been dealing out had left me permanently blue-black along my whole left rump. No late-night dog walker would wish to chance upon such a morbid sight. Nevertheless, I was nearly caught several times in the matted back passages of Birori before I'd navigated correctly its dizzying maze and tear-arsed out the other side into rural blackness again. Phew, fucking hell. Sweet relief! Out into the darkness I picked my way once more towards the spectral Doorway, now looking quite accessible, no more than 600 metres hence. Nevertheless, my progress was again battered to a halt by tightly constructed drystone walls ensnared with barbed wire, then fastened down with vegetation. How I bled. How I was torn. In the dark. In the arse nakedness of it all. Nevertheless did I – not soon but eventually – arrive at the first Doorway. But no sooner had I approached that handsome shining stone, there he was again,

another Action Man-sized spectral dickhead of the Doorways!
Whoosh!

LASSIA: Begone from here. I am Lassia of the Doorway of
    Lassia. Begone.
ROCK: In my mind's eye, I watched my associate entering
    through a secret door. Do you have dealings with Brent?
LASSIA: I am Pradu Lassia the Holy One.

And with that, the micro-gatekeeper of Pradu Lassia ran about
shouting and summoning up other *pradus*, spectral nosey parkers
who began to pester me and nibble my flesh in, well, in another
dimension. I soon figured Brent would have had no truck with
the place. But now they began to bite harder, to chow down on
my naked arse of all things, probably the only meat left on my
P.O.W. form, to sting and burn me with their suckers of poison-
ous mucus. And all I was doing was looking for Brent. I've been
out for days and I'm on the edge, chaps. Then, freaking out in
agony, I recognised in the corner of the field, well, right where
the field joined some gardens, a tiny shed, probably more of a
sentry box than a shed. And being still plagued, mobbed, bitten
by these spectral *pradus*, I rushed over to seek shelter and with
considerable speed.

Once inside, I slammed the door and felt the hollow thud of
these spectral lava beings pounding against the shed door. But
when one of those rotters crashed at last up against the window-
pane, so sticky was that knobhound that its spectral goo stuck
to the glass and lit my temporary quarters brilliantly, revealing
three pairs of wellington boots and a dirty beach towel. What?
Search me, I just wrapped the towel around my waist, forced the
biggest boots on to my still-too-large tootsies and fucked off

right quick. By now – the spectral rotter having dislodged itself and rejoined its fiendish clan the other side of the shed door – I hatched a wicked plan. I had noticed in the Doorway itself a crack around two-centimetres-deep by three-feet-long. And I now from the corner of the shed grabbed a large old-fashioned hoe, rusty, but hefty and blacksmith-forged. Then I burst out of the shed and rushed full bore over to the great Doorway, where I inserted the end of the hoe into the stone's weakened spot, then went for it like a bastard. Bango, fuck off, bang bang bang! Down went the great stone in six easy pieces, out went the lights all around me. From deep inside the hollow earth, I heard the screams of the gatekeeper of Pradu Lassia. And I felt sick. But I really did think he'd asked for it somewhat.

* * *

Two hours later, I was out of my mind with exhaustion and nature rambling. Personal calls to the great Doorways at Santu Bainzu and Imbertighe had yielded nothing but more insults, whilst at the felled Doorway of Uore the light had actually grown dimmer as I approached, then faded out altogether when I'd yelled Brent's name. The fifth great Doorway lit up the skies all around as I approached, but turned out to be the entrance-way to Bórore Church: a Christian Parody no less – beautiful, but right in the centre of a well-policed village! Thereafter, I had headed up the river to the farm at Puttu Oes, but one even greater attracted me, called to me, beckoned me from the industrial estate across the 131. This was the Altar of Punishment, or S'Altare di Castigadu as the Sards named it. Now, as I approached across the half-lit scrub and burned-out cars of the industrial estate, I saw no micro-sentinel standing with baited breath and disapproving shrieks. Instead, I felt only the rush of the waters, of the three streams where the Altar was erected. Instead, I knew only that in place of those micro-sentinels, here dwelled the Great Being. And here at the waters' confluence I recognised perfection. This was the right Doorway! Down into the waters I stumbled, threw off the wellingtons and the towel, launched myself in. For the rest of the night, I lay with my head facing upstream. Warmed by those cooling black waters for the whole of the night, irrigated by that confluence of energies, that fissure in the Sardu-soil. Came sunrise, came the amphibian crouched within me, warmed by the full Mithraic glow. Then did he finally pounce: The Great Being! Now from under the ground he did grab my arms and legs. Now from under the ground did he bind my head and neck. Lastly, his wishes he announced.

BEING: Remember to bind me correctly, Rock Section. You . . . I . . . we rise at the Madau.

Then, relaxing his grip on my hand, so did he wither back into the land.

And thereafter? Thereafter I waited and waited a full day longer until some waterworks official reported the naked man in the next field. When the police approached me, guns loaded, I was still splashing about at the confluence of the streams. Apparently, Brent had been discovered in a witch's cave and had already been taken back to Cágliari. Somewhere up there on that cliff edge of Macomér buildings, Dean and Mick would remain incarcerated for a full week more.

43. IN A BUICK HEARSE ON THE ROAD TO LANUSEI

11am, Tuesday June 13th, 2006
Sitting in Macomér High Street

I sat on the sundrenched street outside Su Talleri, reading Hertzog's *Prison Writings* and looking for clues whilst I awaited Anna's return. Two local teenage metal heads passed by on foot, throwing an approving 'ciao' in my direction. Stoned and Fernet Branca'd this early in the morning? Sweet! How were they to know I'd just yesterday afternoon enjoyed a full re-fuelling from the delivery depot of the Underworld! Now I was sizzling. No, I was growling, and not a little confused. I'd just spent ten minutes inside the local heritage book shop, followed by a further ten awaiting collection of a salad from the pizzeria around the corner. Food! Both events had involved simple daily interface with three sweet enough, but – alas – fairly nondescript ladies. Nevertheless, I'd felt thereafter as though I'd kicked out accidentally at some old sleeping dog lying slumped across the foot of my bed. What were these feelings that had within me been so suddenly and so rudely restored? Women? I never thought about women. Or rather, I never thought about women until I experienced their absence. And then: what an absence! Having spent so much recent time with Blessèd Anna, my roughhousing with the two brothers had clearly conspired with that long Time Travel into the past to remind me of How Much I Missed Women! Rrrrrrrrrrrrowwwf! Now, I just hoped I hadn't been too, er, slavering around those shop ladies. Eeh! How I hate that sort of male behaviour. Now I made a promise to myself from here on in to compliment Blessèd Anna as often as possible on her effortless femininity. For whilst her wicked combination of smart feisty fucker, edgy politico and gruelling taskmaster had ensured that our Sardu Mission had at all times remained on course, it was Anna's legs, face and hair that had really brightened up these of my last days; it was her smile, her nose and her sometimes prominent bosom, oh yes. Simplistic maybe. True none the less. I hadn't really registered until now – I'd actually needed to exchange words and glances with other everyday women simply in order to make that long-dead sexual connection. Ain't I the sad drugged-out cunt, or what? No matter, now I stared down the Macomér high street looking to distinguish a fearsome locomotive clanking that was suddenly invading my earholes, *everybody's* by the looks of it. But as the clanking only grew louder and louder, so did I lift up my bemused noggin to divine the provenance of said stellar racket. I might have guessed! Approaching Su Talleri at minimal miles per hour was a rather hot be-shaded brunette driving a blue 1948 Buick Hearse – and it was me she was looking for! This beautiful vision parallel parked next to Su Talleri, then climbed across the huge burgundy brown bench seat and jumped down through the passenger side. She wore her long hair up today, with a very cute pale blue dress, above the knee with white low high heels. Anna, you are fucking beautiful. I really missed you. Whoops, I nearly said that. Not.

ANNA: (*Straight in my face, smiling*) I got very good news.
ROCK: (*Not entirely numb below the waist*) I'm so glad. To see you, Anna.
ANNA: (*Serious*) Already it's Tuesday. You are leaving tomorrow, Rock Section. Home to the UK.

I sniffed and hugged her – tightly and fraternally – for we had not seen each other in a long age. Well, technically twenty-two hours. But I had not anticipated any sexual feelings for this woman; indeed, it was only a half-hour ago that I'd first picked up the scent from the women in the shops. What a curious animal I was. But now on the Macomér pavement, Anna was deadly serious.

ANNA: (*Intense staring, smiling*) Rock, we got everything! Everything! Yesterday was so successful! We followed The Reaper to its final destination and we sighed. It was *so* obvious. (*Getting squeaky*) Ciancimino's Highway! They built the white elephant 131 parallel to the real road just so they could demolish it later for the building materials. It's incredible. They are so brazen! They park The Reaper beside the road, then fill and fill and fill it up with massive pipes, also aggregate chips, stones, some rubble, so many bags of cement. Rock, they have the whole road to themselves!

The breathtaking size of this operation now hit me full in the face. For Ciancimino's Highway had been the most infamous civil engineering case in recent Sardu history, in which an entire parallel ghost 131 motorway road had been built three miles west of the present route. The reason? Kickbacks and free access to endless expensive building materials.

ROCK: They're taking it all to build Opposite?
ANNA: They are supplying many different building sites across the island. All obscure locations. (*Holding up a printed A4 sheet*) They are so well organised that I stole a printed schedule from their on-site office on Ciancimino's Highway.

ROCK: Did The Reaper's drivers see you or your dad?

ANNA: No, I think they are blind. Well, almost blind. Did you know the Porcu brothers are quintuplets?

ROCK: What have the Porcu family got to do with it?

ANNA: (*Eyes lowered, grim*) Rock Section, the Porcu family drives The Reaper.

ROCK: (*Horrified*) What? No way!

ANNA: Rock, the quintuplets have an on-site office, and another one at their mother's home in Zinnigas, near Silíqua. She's a famous '60s soul singer – Urna Washington – so no one bothers them.

ROCK: (*Winded, spaced out*) Anna, I had an encounter with the Porcus last night at Bidil 'e Pira!

ANNA: (*Freaked out*) It's the middle of nowhere!

ROCK: And those fuckers are everywhere!

ANNA: They work for everyone! The Porcu family works for Bugs Rabbit and Barry Hertzog.

ROCK: (*Confounded*) Barry Hertzog? I thought they were Hertzog's warders.

ANNA: (*Eyes lowered, voice lowered*) So did I, Rock Section. But not anymore.

ROCK: They work for everybody!

ANNA: Hertzog is no longer in jail at Florinas Penitentiary. He did a deal with the authorities, promised to leave Sardinia forever. But already he's lying. *Prison Writings* did so well that Hertzog has *bought* Florinas Penitentiary. The entire Porcu family works for Bugs Rabbit and Barry Hertzog now. It's a big operation!

Man, was I knocked sideways. I was bowled over. I was fucked up and suddenly feeling foolish in front of this woman whom I'd only just now confessed to myself actually meant something different to me. But I grabbed a hold of myself and reined myself in. Get a grip, Rock Section! Less than three days ago you were living in a perpetual stupor, preying upon any unmunting woman with her own flat and job, and scoring from a cunt who opened his front door with an Uzi. So what if I looked foolish to Anna? Two days ago I was Lord Shittykecks of Shittykecks Manor. You reckon she's already forgotten that lusty imagery just because you now deign to notice that she's properly hot? In the meantime, the ever-compassionate Anna – determined to let me work it all out for myself – simply looked out from under her fringe and smiled at me with extreme prettiness.

ANNA: Today, we have to deliver this hearse to Lanusei, so simple. I'm very excited for Neon Sardinia's Fonni–Mamoiada Re-enactment. Also, we can check in late tonight at the hotel; I booked already. So we'll have plenty of time to explore the wonderful monuments at Madau. They are later than the type you require, no great Doorway. But quite important, I think!

Madau. Whoa, how that name shot through me. Madau? Last night's memory of the Great Being bubbled up once more: his words. What had been his actual words? That's it: 'We rise at the Madau.' Then Anna's phone went. It was her father. The lovely one smiled, nodded her head throughout their brief conversation, then hung up quickly.

ANNA: (*Smiling*) Today my dad is following The Reaper once again and says they are keeping to yesterday's schedule. If everything goes to plan, we will know at all times The Reaper's movements.

I suddenly felt as though I had a whole army of Sardu accomplices at the ready. I wanted to yell, scream, holler with joy. Then, without appearing to notice the international goodvibes that she'd just installed in my heart, the lovely one fired up the radio and set her controls for the heart of 89.9 FM, which burst into life with the extremely strung-out psychedelic thunder of Vesuvio, whose mind-boggling overkill quickly established my hefty need to skin up one of Jim Feather's budding treats. I jumped into the empty backyard of this sumptuous General Motors limousine, furnished only with Giampaolo's latest antique shop bargains. Then I plopped myself down upon his low pine coffee table and put three Green Rizlas together. Then, over the riotous Ur-Klang of Vesuvio, I proceeded to recount to Blessèd Anna my own long-winded account of the previous day.

* * *

Only about two hours into our drive did I realise how slow was our progress today. Boy, are hearses good at going slow! It was not so much the crumbling speed of the vehicle as the killer steering that Anna was forced to manhandle and do battle with every step of the way. I'd come up from the darklands behind to secretly ogle the Blessèd One. But soon I was sitting there unconsciously air-steering out of sympathy, twitching and rocking all over the place. In the end, she sent me in the back again. Fair enough. When a piss stop reared its inevitable head, and we were both returning from our respective ablutions, I fished out the Opposite celebration brochure and directed Anna's eyes to the stills of Jim Feather in *Gelsomania!* She hiccupped with shock and pointed at one stage photo.

ANNA: (*Squeaky*) That's *my* motorbike, Rock! That's my Ural
750 cc they used for Zampano's motorbike-caravan! All the
time I was at Bologna University! Giampaolo worked out the
money deal with them. Your friend was riding my motorbike
all these years and I never knew! So sad!

Sure enough, Blessèd Anna was correct. Remove that gargantuan canvas outer shell from Zampano's extraordinary
mobile home and, underneath, was revealed the same post-war
motorbike-and-sidecar as had been showcased in our mutual
favourite road movie *German Motorcycle Murderer*. I pointed out
Jim Feather astride Anna's motorbike but she shook her head in
unrecognition.

ANNA: I know who he is but I never met him. Never. He was
billed only as The Great Tarzan. We were scared! Zampano
is so evil a character. No one in Cágliari ever saw him in the
streets. We thought The Great Tarzan was a foreign actor
specially brought in for performances only. He seemed so
exotic!

* * *

Weighed down by the locomotive roar of the hearse's V8, I was
dozing in the rear with my feet up on Giampaolo's pine coffee
table, laughing at the idea of this vehicle passing itself off as a
Buick. The divine Anna had hoodwinked me only temporarily.
Now, however, I recognised this hearse for what it really was: a
product of the Flxible Motor Co. F-L-X-I-B-L-E. That's a pre-
literate spelling for you. Tonka consciousness or what? Whatever
you called it, this electric blue mechanical bobsleigh was not

really a 1948 Buick station wagon at all. That was a lovely thing. And this was unlovely – epic but unlovely. Not after everything they'd done to it. Early on in WW2, a Spitfire was fitted out with seaplane floats, thereby reducing its top speed by 70 m.p.h. and forcing it to fly like a stork delivering sextuplets. Surely, it then ceased to be a Spitfire. Same with this auto oxcart. After taking delivery from General Motors, the Flxible Motor Company raised the bonnet up five inches, ignored the inward-facing aptly named 'suicide doors' and added another three feet to the middle of the chassis. So after days of fashionable low riding, we now sat up straight and squarely upon the road like an old-fashioned flat bed truck, a Commer or a Bedford like Grandad had the coal delivered in. For comfort, an old-time '60s Austin Taxi was closer to the Facel Vega than this beast was to the taxi! If anything, this beast reminded me most of those enormous Spanish Civil War armoured cars driven by the Barcelona Anarchists.

ANNA: (*Looking through the mirror, yelling*) Who was very talented on your scene but didn't make it?

ROCK: (*Looking up, yelling back*) Everybody made it, I think. At least to some extent. Perhaps the biggest waste was Cliff Sly, but then even he had his chances. He introduced the Smoke Dopes to Liverpool, but it blew his mind when they got bigger than him. Danial Cupid Jove was just too sly for Cliff! After that, Cliff blew it every time. He mixed his metaphor. Why write a song called 'I Bleed Red' when you support Everton? He had power, but couldn't wield it beyond the village of Liverpool. He could get Sunny Smiles to 'go bad' and change her name to Sunny Periods. But it needed Arthur Tadgell to steal her and mould her first, in order for her to make a classic like 'An Oral History of Blowjobs'.

ANNA: What happened to Gary Have-a-laugh? What happened to Stu?

ROCK: (*Weak smile*) Ooh, two very different answers there, my dear. Gary never got over being left behind sitting on the tractor at Italia '90. He just read that as another of Mick's powerplays. But when the Full English Breakfast hit got the 'Smartprize' at Rapativity's Gift Of Giving '91, the personal tragedies of Mick and Leander obliged Have-a-laugh to pick up the award with Stu.

ANNA: That's when Stu got struck dumb. I heard it even on a record somewhere.

ROCK: Yeah man, legendary in its awfulness. Our old bass player Hippo recorded the whole night on a professional Walkman. But then that Dutch synth nutcase Tiny bootlegged Stu's bit on a 12″ single with some intermittent *Stratosfear*-period T. Dream.

ANNA: So was Stu nervous beforehand?

ROCK: Anna, all Stu could think of was his bum and how much he loved cheese! In private, he'd look at me almost in tears, rubbing his bum, and saying: 'I can't help torment myself. If I hadn't fallen out the cop car, well, I just can't help but dwell.'

ANNA: Were you scared to be in public at this strange time?

ROCK: No, I felt loved really. But that awards night was one of the most surreal events of my mad life. Leander was dead and the award was for *him*! Mick was the writer and he was in hiding. Dean had been raped. And Brent had killed himself. Yeh-Yeh's ancient lawyer parents had guilted him into not going, Stu was happy enough to be there if only for the guaranteed hot dinner, and Have-a-laugh had taken enough speed to fuel the Prussian army.

349

Whoa, how my mind travelled backwards now. All I could feel at the time of the awards ceremony was this great gushing of human sympathy and emotion pouring over us, especially after our weeks of abandonment huddling naked and alone in those white stalls. But now, from the blissful feet-up comfort of the hearse's rear section and the vista of Blessèd Anna's neck, how I drifted back to that peculiar between-time of public demand and sanatorium yearnings.

44. STU AT THE RAP AWARDS

2.30pm, Tuesday June 13th, 2006
Tripping out in the back of the Buick, road to Lanusei

Stu was not a natural rapper, nor would he have been treading the boards at all had it not been for the blessings of the Rave Era. Stu was a scenester primarily; someone who bound projects together and facilitated other people's great ideas. But mostly he was just great to have around, great at hanging out, and had one of those unforgettably malleable Sam Kydd faces that cracked people up. His featured spoken bits in Brits Abroad's videos always got rewound and watched again and again; his role as the feisty ticket collector in the Kit Kats' first single 'Second Class to Dottingham' was even a bit classic. And despite being all-but-ignored for the actual recording of Full English Breakfast's soon to be Mega-hit, Stu had added so much to that video's Mexican Revolution charm with his strutting, autocratic gringo cameo – and on peyote the whole time, I might add – that his presence at the Rapativity Awards was greeted by universal thumbs-ups and hearty slaps upon the back from even the hippest of rapping types. Indeed, that year's compère – the cricket rapper MCC – even pulled one of Stu's Kit Kat Rapper expressions halfway through the ceremony.

But what none of us were to anticipate, as Stu sat tidily through the hot food and schmoozing of the early evening, was that he was in no fit mental state whatsoever to receive some big meaningful MTV-televised award. Therefore, when rapper MCC pronounced 'Her Majesty's Pleasure' the winner of 1991's

Smartprize, the thunderous hoots and hollers, the rapturous applause and standing ovation, the impromptu syn-drum salute from 'Corridor of Uncertainty' rapper Ian Both-of-them . . . well, it all conspired to fill Stu's manic brain not with confidence and the chilled feeling of being surrounded by homeys, no, dear me no. Instead, fresh from the too-quick despatch of a greasy white-hot cheese platter care of the Ritz catering department, Stu was suddenly overwhelmed – or so he told me much later – by the feeling of utter wrongness at his role as award collector. Where was Leander the rapper? Where was M. Goodby the composer? Stu knew that Have-a-laugh considered it politically compromising to make the speech himself, therefore now Stu must be the voice of the Kit Kat Rappers' decimated camp. And thus did Stu ascend the award scaffold, buoyed up only by the snorting, bullish Gary Have-a-laugh and the vicious dairy overload of twenty minutes previously.

STU: Er . . .

HAVE-A-LAUGH: (*Smiling at the audience and at Stu*) Go for it, mate.

STU: Er . . . Erm . . . Erm . . . Er.

HAVE-A-LAUGH: (*So totally not hassling*) No hurry, mate. Take your time.

STU: Erm mmm mmm mmm mmm mmm mmm mmm mmm Ermmm mmm mmm mmm Erm mmm mmm mmm mmm Erm mmmmm mmm mmm Erm mmm mmm mmm mmm Erm mmm mmmmm mmm Erm mmm mmm mmm mmm Erm mmm mmmmmmmm Mmm mmm mmm mmm mmm mmm mmm mmm mmm Ermm mmm mmm mmm Erm mmm mmm mmm mmm Erm mmmmm mmm mmm Erm mmm mmm mmm mmm Erm mmm mmmmm mmm

Erm mmm mmm mmm mmm Erm mmm mmmmmmmm
Mmm mmm mmm mmm mmm mmm mmm mmm mmm
Ermm mmm mmm mmm Erm mmm mmm mmm mmm
Erm mmmmm mmm mmm Erm mmm mmm mmm mmm
Erm mmm mmmmm mmm Erm mmm mmm mmm mmm
Erm mmm mmmmmmmm Erm mmm mmm mmm mmm
mmm mmm mmm mmm Ermmm mmm mmm mmm Erm
mmm mmm mmm mmm Erm mmmmm mmm mmm Erm
mmm mmm mmm mmm Erm mmm mmmmm mmm
Erm mmm mmm mmm mmm Erm mmm mmmmmmmm
Mmm mmm mmm mmm mmm mmm mmm mmm mmm
Ermm mmm mmm mmm Erm mmm mmm mmm mmm
Erm mmmmm mmm mmm Erm mmm mmm mmm mmm
Erm mmm mmmmm mmm Erm mmm mmm mmm mmm
Erm mmm mmmmmmmm Mmm mmm mmm mmm
mmm mmm mmm mmm mmm Ermm mmm mmm mmm
Erm mmm mmm mmm mmm Erm mmmmm mmm mmm
Erm mmm mmm mmm mmm Erm mmm mmmmm mmm
Erm mmm mmm mmm mmm Erm mmm mmmmmmmm
mmm mmm mmm Erm mmm mmm mmm mmm Erm
mmmmm mmm mmm Erm mmm mmm mmm mmm Erm
mmm mmmmm mmm Erm mmm mmm mmm mmm Erm
mmm mmmmmmmm Mmm mmm mmm mmm mmm
mmm mmm mmm mmm Ermm mmm mmm mmm Erm
mmm mmm mmm mmm Erm mmmmm mmm mmm
Erm mmm mmm mmm mmm Erm mmm mmmmm mmm
Erm mmm mmm mmm mmm Erm mmm mmmmmmmm
Mmm mmm mmm mmm mmm mmm mmm mmm mmm
Ermm mmm mmm mmm Erm mmm mmm mmm mmm
Erm mmmmm mmm mmm Erm mmm mmm mmm mmm
Erm mmm mmmmm mmm Erm mmm mmm mmm mmm

Erm mmm mmmmmmmm Erm mmm mmm mmm mmm
mmm mmm mmm mmm Ermmm mmm mmm mmm Erm
mmm mmm mmm mmm Erm mmmmm mmm mmm Erm
mmm mmm mmm mmm Erm mmm mmmmm mmm
Erm mmm mmm mmm mmm Erm mmm mmmmmmmm
Mmm mmm mmm mmm mmm mmm mmm mmm mmm
Ermm mmm mmm mmm Erm mmm mmm mmm mmm
Erm mmmmm mmm mmm Erm mmm mmm mmm mmm
Erm mmm mmmmm mmm Erm mmm mmm mmm mmm
Erm mmm mmmmmmmm Mmm mmm mmm mmm
mmm mmm mmm mmm mmm Ermm mmm mmm mmm
Erm mmm mmm mmm mmm Erm mmmmm mmm mmm
Erm mmm mmm mmm mmm Erm mmm mmmmm mmm
Erm mmm mmm mmm mmm Erm mmm mmmmmmmm
mmm mmm mmm Erm mmm mmm mmm mmm Erm
mmmmm mmm mmm Erm mmm mmm mmm mmm Erm
mmm mmmmm mmm Erm mmm mmm mmm mmm Erm
mmm mmmmmmmm Mmm mmm mmm mmm mmm
mmm mmm mmm mmm Ermm mmm mmm mmm Erm
mmm mmm mmm mmm Erm mmmmm mmm mmm Erm
mmm mmm mmm mmm Erm mmm mmmmm mmm
Erm mmm mmm mmm mmm Erm mmm mmmmmmmm
Mmm mmm mmm mmm mmm mmm mmm mmm mmm
Ermm mmm mmm mmm Erm mmm mmm mmm mmm
Erm mmmmm mmm mmm Erm mmm mmm mmm mmm
Erm mmm mmmmm mmm Erm mmm mmm mmm mmm
Erm mmm mmmmmmmm Erm mmm mmm mmm mmm
mmm mmm mmm mmm Ermmm mmm mmm mmm Erm
mmm mmm mmm mmm Erm mmmmm mmm mmm Erm
mmm mmm mmm mmm Erm mmm mmmmm mmm
Erm mmm mmm mmm mmm Erm mmm mmmmmmmm

Mmm mmm mmm mmm mmm mmm mmm mmm mmm
Ermm mmm mmm mmm Erm mmm mmm mmm mmm
Erm mmmmm mmm mmm Erm mmm mmm mmm mmm
Erm mmm mmmmm mmm Erm mmm mmm mmm mmm
Erm mmm mmmmmmmm Mmm mmm mmm mmm
mmm mmm mmm mmm mmm Ermm mmm mmm mmm
Erm mmm mmm mmm mmm Erm mmmmm mmm mmm
Erm mmm mmm mmm mmm Erm mmm mmmmm mmm
Erm mmm mmm mmm mmm Erm mmm mmmmmmmm
mmm mmm mmm Erm mmm mmm mmm mmm Erm
mmmmm mmm mmm Erm mmm mmm mmm mmm Erm
mmm mmmmm mmm Erm mmm mmm mmm mmm Erm
mmm mmmmmmmm Mmm mmm mmm mmm mmm
mmm mmm mmm mmm Ermm mmm mmm mmm Erm
mmm mmm mmm mmm Erm mmmmm mmm mmm Erm
mmm mmm mmm mmm Erm mmm mmmmm mmm
Erm mmm mmm mmm mmm Erm mmm mmmmmmmm
Mmm mmm mmm mmm mmm mmm mmm mmm mmm
Ermm mmm mmm mmm Erm mmm mmm mmm mmm
Erm mmmmm mmm mmm Erm mmm mmm mmm mmm
Erm mmm mmmmm mmm Erm mmm mmm mmm mmm
Erm mmm mmmmmmmm Erm mmm mmm mmm mmm
mmm mmm mmm mmm Ermmm mmm mmm mmm Erm
mmm mmm mmm mmm Erm mmmmm mmm mmm Erm
mmm mmm mmm mmm Erm mmm mmmmm mmm
Erm mmm mmm mmm mmm Erm mmm mmmmmmmm
Mmm mmm mmm mmm mmm mmm mmm mmm mmm
Ermm mmm mmm mmm Erm mmm mmm mmm mmm
Erm mmmmm mmm mmm Erm mmm mmm mmm mmm
Erm mmm mmmmm mmm Erm mmm mmm mmm mmm
Erm mmm mmmmmmmm Mmm mmm mmm mmm

mmm mmm mmm mmm mmm Ermm mmm mmm mmm
Erm mmm mmm mmm mmm Erm mmmmm mmm mmm
Erm mmm mmm mmm mmm Erm mmm mmmmm mmm
Erm mmm mmm mmm mmm Erm mmm mmmmmmmm
mmm mmm mmm Erm mmm mmm mmm mmm Erm
mmmmm mmm mmm Erm mmm mmm mmm mmm Erm
mmm mmmmm mmm Erm mmm mmm mmm mmm Erm
mmm mmmmmmmm Mmm mmm mmm mmm mmm
mmm mmm mmm mmm Ermm mmm mmm mmm Erm
mmm mmm mmm mmm Erm mmmmm mmm mmm Erm
mmm mmm mmm mmm Erm mmm mmmmm mmm
Erm mmm mmm mmm mmm Erm mmm mmmmmmmm
Mmm mmm mmm mmm mmm mmm mmm mmm mmm
Ermm mmm mmm mmm Erm mmm mmm mmm mmm
Erm mmmmm mmm mmm Erm mmm mmm mmm mmm
Erm mmm mmmmm mmm Erm mmm mmm mmm mmm
Erm mmm mmmmmmmm Erm mmm mmm mmm mmm
mmm mmm mmm mmm Ermmm mmm mmm mmm Erm
mmm mmm mmm mmm Erm mmmmm mmm mmm Erm
mmm mmm mmm mmm Erm mmm mmmmm mmm
Erm mmm mmm mmm mmm Erm mmm mmmmmmmm
Mmm mmm mmm mmm mmm mmm mmm mmm mmm
Ermm mmm mmm mmm Erm mmm mmm mmm mmm
Erm mmmmm mmm mmm Erm mmm mmm mmm mmm
Erm mmm mmmmm mmm Erm mmm mmm mmm mmm
Erm mmm mmmmmmmm Mmm mmm mmm mmm
mmm mmm mmm mmm mmm Ermm mmm mmm mmm
Erm mmm mmm mmm mmm Erm mmmmm mmm mmm
Erm mmm mmm mmm mmm Erm mmm mmmmm mmm
Erm mmm mmm mmm mmm Erm mmm mmmmmmmm
mmm mmm mmm Erm mmm mmm mmm mmm Erm

mmmmm mmm mmm Erm mmm mmm mmm mmm Erm
mmm mmmmm mmm Erm mmm mmm mmm mmm Erm
mmm mmmmmmmm Mmm mmm mmm mmm mmm
mmm mmm mmm mmm Ermm mmm mmm mmm Erm
mmm mmm mmm mmm Erm mmmmm mmm mmm Erm
mmm mmm mmm mmm Erm mmm mmmmm mmm
Erm mmm mmm mmm mmm Erm mmm mmmmmmmm
Mmm mmm mmm mmm mmm mmm mmm mmm mmm
Ermm mmm mmm mmm Erm mmm mmm mmm mmm
Erm mmmmm mmm mmm Erm mmm mmm mmm mmm
Erm mmm mmmmm mmm Erm mmm mmm mmm mmm
Erm mmm mmmmmmmm Erm mmm mmm mmm mmm
mmm mmm mmm mmm Ermmm mmm mmm mmm Erm
mmm mmm mmm mmm Erm mmmmm mmm mmm Erm
mmm mmm mmm mmm Erm mmm mmmmm mmm
Erm mmm mmm mmm mmm Erm mmm mmmmmmmm
Mmm mmm mmm mmm mmm mmm mmm mmm mmm
Ermm mmm mmm mmm Erm mmm mmm mmm mmm.
Sss-sorry . . .

45. THE FONNI–MAMOIADA RE-ENACTMENT

3pm, Tuesday June 13th, 2006
Road to Mamoiada, Central Sardinia

Now, as we headed further down the fast 389 in the Anarchist Armoured Car, rarely hitting 50 m.p.h., for some very stupid reason, the prospect of reaching Fonni was now somewhat overwhelming to me. Who was I to tread where D. H. Lawrence had only yearned to roam? Had I done enough in my own life to deserve this? What pressure I felt to make a good account of myself up there. So when it became clear that we'd got plenty of time today for fun and frolics, I acquiesced immediately when Anna confessed to having wished since childhood to visit the streets of Mamoiada. Aha, the other hilltop Shangri-la! And this one a real centre of kidnapping! I reminded Anna to keep an eye out for Meat-, sorry, for Meltburger stands and caravans. And, thus did we take a brief detour, hanging a sharp left up into the mountain fast lanes of Mamoiada, and taking extra care to avoid the masked *mamuthones* and other festival goers as they bumped and barged their ways through the highly decorated streets. On our first attempt, the Buick hearse glided fairly effortlessly up the long, curling Via Asiago, which snakes right around the village into Via Tagliamento. But the sheer weight of people littering the roads ensured that we soon lost sight of our position and blundered into a tightly drawn net of white churches and domestic roofs. Now, we found ourselves surrounded by bullet-headed football fans dressed all in the blue-and-white of

Folgore Mamoiada, who beat out a death chant to the people of Fonni upon our roof and threw themselves across our bonnet, gurning drunkenly against our windscreen. Now, sliding down the inappropriately named backstreet Via Nuoro, we freed ourselves at last from the grip of F.C. Mamoiada and groaned back up the steep hill into Via Dante.

Onwards through the disobliging crowds we struggled, like driving through an IRA funeral with British numberplates, struggling onwards, ever onwards up to Via Tola. This time Anna navigated the hearse splendidly between two poorly parked estate cars into a tight blacksmith's yard – a dead end. Four *mamuthones* danced wildly in the yard, each clad in their traditional dark wildebeest brown, each laden down their backs with great metal cowbells, each somewhat benevolent in their solemn near-beaked pewter masks. Gingerly, Blessèd Anna reversed 1948's heaviest metal back into the street, where an old boy in a donkey jacket guided her inexpertly into a too-tight corner. Utterly stuffed. He walked away. Catching a gorgeous glimpse of the despondent Anna, I climbed down from the passenger seat and, like Luigi in *Wages of Fear*, rolled my sleeves up and spat on my hands melodramatically. But the lovely one was far too het up by the set up to get my movie fundamentalism. Nevertheless, as this dodgy too-tight new situation would only force us back down the same road that we already knew to be incorrect, Anna and I now took our opportunity to extricate ourselves properly from Mamoiada's myriad ravers, cheekily executing a nine-point-turn amidst *mamuthones* galore. Thereafter did our Anarchist Armoured Bobsleigh scurry and slither back downhill the same way we had arrived. Appropriately, the 'Leaving Mamoiada' metal village sign was riddled with shotgun pellets.

Barely one hour later, we were already parked up and Anna was pulling the keys out of the Buick's ignition once more, as I stared out north-northeast across the Fonni hillside towards Mamoiada's conical hilltop now – by distance – made more inviting. Around us, hurrying festival goers were parking their cars far more shambolically than I'd ever previously witnessed even in the Mediterranean. And right there behind the parked cars, three dingy Meltburger caravans doing a roaring trade. I gave their cashiers all a cursory glance but, recognising none of them, I took Anna's hand and we took off uphill in a state of high excitement: there were barely fifteen minutes left before Neon Sardinia commenced their grand performance. And nobody at the festival wanted to miss Fabrizio Arra's grand entrance. Anna and I headed uphill towards the stage, unencumbered by bags and determined to dance the afternoon away. But staring back at that massive blue hearse parked up beside the stream, I knew I'd be foolish to leave my last remaining worldly possessions to the mercy of randomers and festival goers. So back I ran to retrieve my bag.

The steep, uphill high street into Fonni was rammed with fancy dancers and dozens more spectacular *mamuthones*, who cajoled festival goers and slowed up egression towards the stage. But Blessèd Anna and I soon located a dubious pedestrian rat-run behind and across an undefined garden area, wherein an ancient motor coach was parked up beside a whitewashed meeting hall advertising 'Bible Classes' in hand-painted lettering. Upon its too-large destination board – writ in gold painted letters with black drop shadows – read the ominous declaration: *No stranger uncircumcised in heart, nor uncircumcised in flesh, shall enter my sanctuary* (Ezekiel 44:9). Now, *that* all looks worrying enough to investigate later, Anna. Let's give it a shot.

Thus we found ourselves plonked very nicely directly next to the sound desk opposite the stage, which had itself been built into a natural amphitheatre overlooked by two valleys. And then began the great ritual, the great re-enactment of the shamanic hilltop verbal war between the painted bruxos of Mamoiada and the painted bruxos of Fonni – their *my village is better than your village* battle. First came on to the stage a great warrior *mamuthone*, who whirled around then played a simple, single epiphany on an ancient analogue synthesizer. The sound across the valley was epic and cavernous. Then, he raised his arms to the heavens, screamed thrice into the microphone: 'Fonni! Fonni! Fonni!' and dragged back his great mask, thrusting his smiling blond head out into the sunshine. A great roar went up throughout the crowd: 'Fabrizio! Fabrizio! Fabrizio!' For this was the first time since Fabrizio Arra's infamous kidnapping by F.C. Mamoiada hooligans years previously that the famous Fonni–Mamoiada contest had been allowed to take place. Next on to the stage, amidst more bruxo roars and synthesizer bleeps, walked Neon Sardinia's other favourite Arturo Vaca – son of famed movie director L. A. Vaca – who was today taking the vocal role of Mamoiada's own bruxo. Now, how he roared out his chauvinistic holler: 'Mamoiada! Mamoiada! Mamoiada!' And so, amidst cheering and drinking and whooping and declarations of local allegiances, had the concert began. But as even a cursory glance around the Fonni festival had already revealed to me three of Bugs Rabbit's Meltburger caravans, I knew – what with the added presence of that Bible bus – that poor Jim Feather's antagonists had to be in the vicinity; I would have to act at some point. Nevertheless, such was the atmosphere here and such was my pleasure at Anna's company that I deferred any real action until after catching a goodly portion of Neon Sardinia's ambient panto. Gradually, as the ensemble's bizarre organic epics unfolded across the afternoon, so the bare sprinkles of audience upon the green hillside filled to a throng. But such were the comings-and-goings of Neon Sardinia's mentalizing stereo P.A. system and bowel-crunching sub-bass woofers that Blessèd Anna soon headed off with some Cágliari associates, whilst I tripped out bolt upright on the grass, occasionally leaning against my bulging bag for balance.

And then it happened! My bag took off into the air and rushed uphill towards the village, rocketing off between seated festival goers at a horrendous speed. Indeed, the thing was travelling so fast that most people mistook it for a concert effect, and I was slow as a bastard to come to my senses. Off I chased like a desperate sluggard, but was soon pushed faster and faster with every personal effect that I remembered to be within the bag. Fuck me, my passport, my phone, my stencils, my home! But the bag was entangled now in festival goers still entering the site, and I had caught up to within a few feet when – zoom! – off it jolly well trotted again, apparently still of its own volition. But now a clue! For the flying bag was approaching the self-same meeting room where I had clocked the 'Bible Class' sign. And as I raced around the corner, I saw it flying up the steps of the meeting room into a scattering of old people, most unconvinced that salvation truly lay within. Knowing now that my bag was inside the room, I quickly cut through shrubs and bushes into the backyard where – through a half-open side entrance door – I observed that fucking idiot Loon from Slag Van Blowdriver appear out of thin air, looking much much older now but holding my bag! And wearing Jim Feather's magic cloak all along, I presume!

The Bible Class tableau that greeted me was a perfect picture of early Victorian hierarchy: a prim middle-aged lady this end of the rust-coloured flagstones down on her hands-and-knees scrubbing the waxy flagstones with an old-fashioned tin of kerosene, at the far end of the meeting room up at the bar, well, they looked to me mostly like Scando ferry workers. All of them tall, all biggish louts, several of them smoking and certain protagonists speaking very loudly. Across the far side of the room, trying to keep away from the smoke, was a small wiry weasel-faced guy, Cowtown Unslutter. He still looked like I remembered him aged seventeen back at Slag Van Blowdriver. And from the expression on his face, that fucker still looked about as yes as no. Skinny and mean and sure of his endgame, he clearly ruled this place – and what a place! Loon dropped my bag on to the floor next to the coffee table and took a Dutch Caballeros cigarette from a wide hairy bearded bastard that everybody referred to as Walter-Under-The-Bridge. This was Jim Feather's nemesis – the thief of the magic cloak, no less! In truth, he was a colossal letdown: like Benny From *Crossroads*-meets-Benny From Abba with a secret military fetish, but not enough dosh to explore it far. He had a high voice and wore medals upon his tan tweed jacket. Next to him danced a skinny figure in faded urban blue camo pants, a black-and-white striped Newcastle Utd shirt, hat-on-sideways, toothless almost with a grinning slit for a mouth and fiery red eyes. Why-aye man, it's fucking Pit-Yacker MC AKA Akkrum Sneek himself, Barry Hertzog's old Spion Kop compadré. This was the Northumbrian twat who'd jumped on the Alnwick Pit-Yacker phenomenon back in '87 and eclipsed even its originators. Nevertheless, Akkrum Sneek had – merely by association as Hertzog's erstwhile collaborator – suffered mightily in the press after Italia '90. The Pit-Yacker community had turned against him as one man, the cops had monitored his palatial residential compound far up on the northeast coast, and even his speedway racing circuit up at Hayden Dean had come under scrutiny by the Customs & Excise. Was the Pit-Yacker living down here with this lot? Was Mr Sneek working down here for the Lord? Or was he just over for the party? I soon found out.

PIT-YACKER MC: Why-aye man, I cannot wait to see Barry Hertzog tomorrow!

COWTOWN: You almost cut it too fine, Akkrum! You've had weeks to prepare for your visit.

PIT-YACKER MC: Don't bust my chops, Cowtown! I'm here, am I not? I had to clear a few things up! Besides, after tomorrow the man's free to come and go.

LOON: Free at last! Free at last! I wonder if he'll sign my *Prison Writings*?

COWTOWN: (*Triumphant*) Tomorrow our mission will increase in its power one hundredfold.

LOON: With Barry Hertzog on board, the rich tourist resorts around Ólbia will quake at our operation. Personally, I've got my eye on a couple of mega-rich Italian politicians.

WALTER U.T.B.: (*Smoking and staring straight ahead*) Do we know any sexually abnormal people we could blackmail?

LOON: I knew this young Portuguese woman, Alice, she brought me hot meals and made my room brighter: the woman's touch. But her Sunday dinners were so top notch that I became suspicious of her motives. Then it all came out: she was consorting with heathens that ate no meat – vegans some of them. Alice was putting upon my Sunday roast the Mark of Cain, the cheek! Casting her out was not that easy.

364

She had feelings for me, quite deep. Big breasts. So I had to be kind and considerate. Very long legs. I sat her down and quoted my favourite *Ezekiel 23:30*. I said I've got to kick you into touch 'because thou has gone whoring after the heathen, and because thou art polluted with their idols'.

WALTER U.T.B.: (*Smoking, looking straight ahead*) You know how Barry would respond to that? He'd quote *Ephesians 6*: 'We are up against the unseen power that controls this dark world, and spiritual agents from the very headquarters of evil'.

LOON: *Ezekiel 23:38* was clear enough even for a kind whore like Alice. I told her the vegans and vegetarians in her life had 'profaned my Sabbath'. But right off her own bat, Alice promised that she'd never been menstruating when she'd made my sausages. That's a right taboo in her village.

WALTER U.T.B.: (*No idea whatsoever*) They pretend they're doing you a kindness, these women. But how they love to play the harlot.

COWTOWN: (*To Loon*) Every time I walk into your Bible Class, I hear you quoting *Ezekiel*. You sound like an American. If I find a New Internationalist Bible, I'll know it's yours and I will burn it.

LOON: With all due respect, I believe that those eight years in the fire service prepared me for much that is generally considered to be the sole jurisdiction of the priest. Access to water, access to the sacred flame itself, even commiserating with the loved ones of the incinerated.

PIT-YACKER MC: (*Disgusted*) Why-aye, ya fucker! Fancy yourself as Zarathustra, do ya?

COWTOWN: (*To Loon, with spleen*) We started Bible Class to bring Christianity back to these Catholics! They are only one step away from paganism. Think on this: they worship the saints! Poor things are heathens in all but name! So don't come it with the *Ezekiel*, cut all that Old Timer stuff right out!

LOON: If you think *that*, why waste your time on these heathens? Read your C. S. Lewis: Jesus Christ 'has nothing to say to people who do not *know* they have done anything to repent of'.

PIT-YACKER MC: Why-aye man, take it back to the people. The Pope's aloof.

COWTOWN: Exactly my point, Akkrum. Martin Luther was our prophet, not St. Paul the tax collector who never even met Jesus Christ. Paul led us away from the living Jesus, led us away from the home of Jesus, led us away from the roots of Jesus, led us even to the Romans who crucified Jesus, led Jesus Christ himself into Roman hands – placed us all under the Roman jurisdiction of the Pope. Think on this! The Roman Empire thus did not truly end, but continued as Roman Christianity. Think on this! Our own Martin Luther gave the Lord Jesus back to us, said: Let every man be his own Pope.

LOON: (*Contributing, technically*) I knew this older woman, Joan. She made me hot meals and stuff. Good meals. She told me nothing fires the zeal of a fanatic more than the belief that his government will back him in his exploits.

WALTER U.T.B.: (*Smoking and really considering his answer*) I concur with Joan on that one.

COWTOWN: (*Deflated, grim*) If you lot lived down here without me, you'd all be Catholics within the week and Neo-Pagans within the month.

LOON: Unless we attempt to subvert the minds of Sardinian youth, I foresee only crisis on the horizon. (*Municipal*) Spending these long hours in towns like Mándas, Tonara and

Sórgono ensnaring the minds of the doubtful older generation may add numbers to your statistics, but even full conver-
sion might be brief due to sudden death.

MARIKE: (*At the sink, refilling the bucket*) I still think the cave-
house in Gavoi is our best bet. People loved the Sunday
Services from that hillside. One weekend digging and we'd
have a cave-palace.

WALTER U.T.B.: (*Playing with his Bulgarian Umbrella, to nobody
in particular*) Do we know any vulnerable adults? You know,
anybody local who's fallen behind on their heating bills?

LOON: (*Unrepentant*) Ezekiel *18:6* is one to live by. (*Pointing at
his groin, proudly*) Here's one pecker that's never 'come near to
a menstruous woman'.

COWTOWN: Oh, boogie on, reggae woman. You stupid
Drentheman! Get off your leyline! Go forwards for a change!
You've been hanging around with too many Amsterdam
Trustafarians. All that bloodclat shite; might as well live in
Papua New Guinea.

MARIKE: (*Scrubbing and not looking up*) Cowtown, you're sounding racist and selective in your comments. Not just Papua
New Guinea. Menstruating women had problems all over
Europe with taboos right up to the early 20th century. Loon's
right about Portugal. Spain and Italy, also.

COWTOWN: Er, all Catholic examples, though.

WALTER U.T.B.: (*To nobody in particular*) Maybe we could
co-opt the services of somebody up-to-their-eyebrows in
heavy debt.

PIT-YACKER MC: Walter, Loon's smoking all your tabs!

WALTER U.T.B.: (*Stabbing the air with his Bulgarian Umbrella;
loud, obnoxious*) Oi Loon, don't smoke all my Caballeros, you
knobby.

MARIKE: (*To Cowtown*) Not only Catholic. Germany and the Netherlands, too.

COWTOWN: I don't believe you. (*Walking to the other side of the room*) Marike is wrong.

WALTER U.T.B.: (*Opening book*) I'm not trying to bum the Judge, but have a listen to this from C. S. Lewis. Page 33 of *Mere Christianity*. Sweet music, it is. (*Reading*) 'Dualism means the belief that there are two equal and independent powers at the back of everything, one of them good and the other bad, and that this universe is the battlefield in which they fight out an endless war. I personally think that next to Christianity, Dualism is the manliest and most sensible personal creed on the market'.

LOON: I'm a pacifist.

WALTER U.T.B.: (*Lighting a Caballero*) It's manly, you dipshit.

LOON: Duelling is not manly; it's mad! Especially on life's battlefield of endless war.

WALTER U.T.B.: Are you calling C. S. Lewis mad?

LOON: (*Making a very stupid expression*) Er, in this instance? No!

Temporarily satisfied with the outcome of the joust, the two village genii thrust down their stone tablets and implements and walked upright to the bar, where Marike was now cleaning the tiled floor with kerosene. Theology being hot stuff, Loon now wielded an icy Ichnusa or three, whilst Walter the Beardo picked at his lips and gingerly quaffed a glass of white wine. Outside, meanwhile, I unwatered sweated cobs at the real idea of freedom for the Judge. What would happen to this part of the world?

COWTOWN: Bugs Rabbit is sending one of the Porcus to 'smuggle' the Judge down to the party in the back of his big articulated truck. Once everybody's assembled at Opposite, that's when the Judge will jump out of the back of the truck: Ta-da!

MARIKE: (*Looking up, upset*) I still think I should be at that party, Cowtown. I feel I owe it to Barry Hertzog.

PIT-YACKER MC: (*Pushing it*) Walter, can I ponce a Caballero?

WALTER U.T.B.: (*Looking straight ahead, smoking*) Loon's got some other Dutch baccy. I'm well low.

COWTOWN: (*Back on Loon's case*) All of European history is the story of Protestantism. Before it is nothing. Look to the English Puritan revolutionaries that dared to execute their king.

PIT-YACKER MC: Why-aye man, perhaps our Puritan revolution wasn't a failure after all.

COWTOWN: (*John Knox*) Of course it didn't fail! It taught the French and the Americans and the Russians. And . . . they cut off his head!

WALTER U.T.B.: (*Ciggy in gob, making great sawing motions*) That fucking bighead.

PIT-YACKER MC: (*Reminiscing*) That Egyptian fan had the back of his head cut clean through the spinal cord. No one saw anybody in the vicinity. It was like Jack the Ripper. (*Panto whisper*) Backstreet murder.

COWTOWN: (*Matter-of-fact*) Backstreet euthanasia more like. Put them out of their misery. Even easier than Full English Breakfast. The last doddle! I stuck Walter's Bulgarian Umbrella in the Arab's head. And as he was bleeding and dying, I explained that his murder was not for racist reasons, but on account of superior religious beliefs: mine. I told him how Freud had called Islam 'an abbreviated repetition of the Jewish one'. I explained to the Arab that even though his sacred book may have been spoken by the Lord God himself directly to the Prophet, peace be upon him, nevertheless had its sacredness been thoroughly destroyed by subsequent rummaging.

LOON: (*Not paying attention, reading* Mere Christianity) I'll bet the Egyptian was happy with their 1–1 draw, though. That's the day the Netherlands team looked to me like they *really* represented Holland.

COWTOWN: I explained to the Egyptian how Allah's council workers had sneaked into the Koran equation by re-arranging the sheaves of paper that the prophet's scribes had written all his Visions down on; how the council workers had put the best, fattest stuff at the front of the Koran just to pump people up and kept all the slighter stuff till last.

PIT-YACKER MC: (*Jumping on the bandwagon*) Why-aye man, the hands of Men! Martin Luther wouldn't have let them get away with it! No doubt about it, Mohammed's methods showed poor finishing. What did the bighead have to say about all this?

COWTOWN: (*Not arsed*) He just gurgled and hated my lesson.

WALTER U.T.B.: Why are Muslims so thoroughly opinionated?

PIT-YACKER MC: They can't afford not to be. Rickety Islam. Like a shed put up in an afternoon by cowboys from Hexham. Give it a push, down it all comes.

WALTER U.T.B.: How can Muslim men show their faces when they believe such a load of rot? At least their women know enough to hide their embarrassment by covering their heads!

MARIKE: (*On her knees, scrubbing the floor with kerosene*) Cowtown, I think perhaps Mohammed was the opportunist the Arabs needed. They'd been searching for their own saviour for centuries. Surrounded by Jews and Christians? The Arabs had an inferiority complex three miles high.

LOON: (*Coughing*) Eight Miles High! The Byrds!

COWTOWN: Marike is wrong. Loon, please don't smoke over Marike while she's cleaning with kerosene. One spark.

LOON: I wouldn't worry about kerosene ever catching fire, Cowtown. It's highly inflammable, even says so on the tin. What you need to remember is that flammable stuff will catch fire. Not inflammable.

COWTOWN: (*Looking at a cunt*) You told me you were a fireman.

LOON: (*Perking up*) Eight years in the Brandweer service, sir.

And with that, the surly Cowtown Unslutter led his Bible Class out of the meeting room, leaving Loon to request some black coffee from Marike and me to stalk the fucker. I peeped through the door, only opened a crack, and stared into the main room. Was this my chance? Then this tall, ugly long-haired Jesus Freak of our Nightmares jumped up and immediately started searching about for any remaining Caballero ciggies still hanging about the coffee table. But Loon was out of luck. So, picking up my bag, he thoughtlessly emptied all of its dubious contents right across the most stinky and most recently cleaned part of the floor, scattering my socks, my shirt, my kecks, even my sheaf of graffiti stencils a fair old distance. Shit, Kerosene City, you cunt. Then this lanky knobshine got down on his hands and knees and properly started eyeballing all of my stuff. As he unpacked all of the crappy, ancient paint-caked stencils, Loon began to cough, probably on account of being so near those stinky flagstones. Now looking for ways to grab my stuff back, I stared around the room. But although this was the ground floor, so steep is Fonni that the land dropped away beyond the French windows, which opened out on to a full-sized balcony – quite an extravagant affair overlooked by low trees and south-facing enough to be catching the sun even at this late hour.

Then, through the window came a blast of sunlight and I saw it. I finally clocked it: the magic cloak. Shit, slung right across the balcony was a washing line pegged up with endless men's socks. What? Twenty at least. But there was a big gap in the middle where nothing hung. So what. When the sun's rays blasted the room momentarily, however, my eyes were instantly drawn to the opposite wall, where the shadow of the washing line revealed it to be carrying not just socks but one very magic and very invisible cloak hanging low at the centre. Still utterly oblivious to my presence, Loon stood up and wandered over to the tin bar, where he rummaged and poked about for any last remaining pack of Caballero ciggies. But they were all long gone. So now he took out a plastic yellow wallet of rolling tobacco, put a single skinner together and poured out a can of Ichnusa into a long-stemmed glass. Then he lit the cigarette. It might have been ten seconds, it was probably twenty, but it was true and it hit me like a bolt from the blue! Veritably, the pong from that roll-up cigarette was the self-same pong of Besty the Buggerer, our kidnapper from Macomér! Loon! Suddenly I knew that cough! Loon was our man! Suddenly I knew that yellow tobacco pouch – Van Nelle Zware Shag! I'd not smelled this stink since summer 1990 in the Fascist Cheese Factory. In all that time, I'd just presumed it was some cheap Sardinian stuff. Then I remembered Exterveen. Exterveen! How I remembered Exterveen! And thus, now I remembered Loon *again* . . . this time from Slag Van Blowdriver! Holy Moly, the fucking cook and bottle-washer!

Loon having now returned to my requisitioned stuff, the twat crouched down on his hands and knees rifling once again through everything I still owned. Fearful that Marike would return with the coffee, however, I danced about outside the door desperate to seize Jim Feather's cloak from the washing line. But then I had a sudden and very terrible idea. I can't believe it even entered my mind, but this was after all Loon the Gimp, Loon the Rapist. This was the man who had punished me with fisticuffs and pummellings. This was the man who had beaten and raped Mick and the twins. And now he was kneeling oblivious just fifteen feet away from me, the cloak hanging on the balcony just two feet beyond that. I seized my chance, I took my time, I did my deed. Suddenly, I stepped briskly into the room and walked right up behind Loon, who, presuming that it must be Marike with the coffee, didn't even bother looking up. Then, I breezily removed the magic cloak from its line, stepped up on to the old leather sofa between Loon and the balcony and pulled out from my kecks pocket Giampaolo's box of Coughlan's Waterproof Matches. What they'd been through! Still Loon remained far too engrossed in my stuff, my kerosene-soaked stuff, to have even half a mind on his surroundings. And so with ne'er more ado I lit that match on first strike and . . .

But before I could even enact my murderous plan, so did the Gods take control. For, no more than a microsecond after I had set the match aflame, so did that village idiot thoughtlessly flick not just the ash but the whole tip of his Van Nelle roll-up directly on to Marike's polished floor, which lit up across the room, instantly engulfing all of my worldly possessions *plus* that coughing kneeling asshole who crouched amidst it all. On fire and on his hands-and-knees, Loon – now shrieking in agony – flailed about then flipped over on to his back. But that just made the flaming worse: it basted the fucker. Where's the paraffin, Nero? I leaped upon the balcony from the leather sofa, stuffed the magic cloak into my shirt, then turned around and stood watching that cunt burn. Watched that fireman flame out. Watched that flaming burn-out until the coffee arrived. Indeed, only Marike's horrified return signalled my exit. Whereupon I shinned down the drainpipe, donned the magic cloak myself, then picked my euphoric way through the woods back towards our parked-up hearse, all-the-while enchanted by the synthesizers and wild vocal acrobatics of Neon Sardinia still doing stereophonic battle across the valleys. Score, score, a thousand times score!

46. THE DOOR UNDER THE DOOR

6pm, Tuesday June 13th, 2006
Road to Lanusei, Central Sardinia

The arsonist murderer let off the hook by the stupidity of his victim? I howled for the deaths of Brent and Dean, for the psychic destruction of Mick – and I read Loon's cleansing fire as cosmic justice. I would have done it, your honour, but some great facilitator took the blame instead. Dance by the light of the bridges you burn. That was me. Now was my theme song 'I Who Have Nothing'. Now was my time running out, and tomorrow? My last tomorrow. Looking through things rather than at them, I sat in the front passenger seat with my long legs stretched straight out into the footwells of the hearse – and *still* there was room enough left for the wearing of five-inch Gene Simmons platforms! Everything here was gargantuan, no less. And now I was gargantuan. But what, with the death of Loon, had I become? What stage of humanity had I just entered? This past day had brought together some kind of psychic team: Anna, Giampaolo, Jim and the Reverend . . . When I'd collided with Sardinia two days previously, well, who then could have foreseen my encounters with people ready to rally to my cause! And who could have imagined upon our arrival in Fonni that Loon's nose would have still been so cosmically attuned to me? Ha! I'd plucked that sucker right out of the ether, suckered that clucker and made him Duck. Oh, sweet scent of victory, heaven-sent opportunity invoked through persistence only. Well, that and sheer cosmic luck.

* * *

Still in plenty of time to deliver the hearse to Lanusei, Anna and I reached the great tombs of Madau just as the early evening light was scorching and toasting the distant surrounding hill-tops that ringed the proud agricultural plateau on to which we now climbed. A snaking serpentine portion of the old 389 had been retained as a link road up to the sites: three great southeast-facing tombs overlooking the Madau Valley. These tombs were of the southern stone archway variety, but I didn't care; it was convenient to our journey and a place to celebrate. Once we'd pulled off the road, however, Blessèd Anna decided that the presence of the hearse would attract casual viewers, even ne'er-do-wells. So next she steered the car right up the steep trackway to the summit of the field's edge, whilst I stood on the main road making sure the beast would be entirely out of sight to passing motorists. Then, I raced up the rise and watched Anna open-mouthed from behind the drystone wall, watched as this picture of Sardu beauty stood inhaling the enormous horizons. Wow. Now I hauled open the Buick's colossal rear barn door on its three external barn hinges and climbed up into the beast's dead centre. I pulled out Giampaolo's sofa bed and pine coffee table, and set them up on the ground outside as though for a tailgate picnic. Thus was the vast empty rear of the hearse transformed into a miniature living room with the best view in the world. Herein did I now loll and recline in great spirits. Through the high, rounded, heavily-tinted windows on either side, the deepest purple skies showcased at most three tiny white dollops of cloud each, whilst through the wide open metal barn door ahead I was dazzled by a northwesterly flash of azure skies and pale green pastures uninterrupted all the way to the knobbly black horizons of Mts Arbu, Terralba and Spada. Colossal scenes, mentalising views. Bootless now and stretched right out: recumbent here in the hearse I was – free from the fuckers, at least temporarily. Here I could kickback in anger.

But Blessèd Anna was eager to investigate the three monuments, and quickly disappeared through the stile at the field's edge, skipping down the thirty or so metres to the site entrance. Far far to the north: a change in the sky. Perhaps a storm was brewing. Giampaolo had anticipated as much. But nothing could spoil the loveliness of this day. Sweet relief that I was not on the run for murder. Now I would go to my grave in that same state. Or would I? My current plans for retribution spoke otherwise. Moreoever, the success of today's 'Grand Loonacy' was already fuelling my mind as regards Opposite's Grand Opening tomorrow. Kick-off? 3pm. Those utter fucking bastards. But as I could hardly allow Blessèd Anna to be a party to any of my inner murderous musings, I decided to hang fire regarding any of tomorrow's plans. I decided that my bloodlust must – for the time being at least – remain satisfied with Loon's spectacular exit alone.

Thus, I remained aloof and indisposed in the back of the hearse, not daydreaming of retribution, not bemoaning my loss of all my worldly goods, but instead glorying in all of my current situations: psychic, geographical, even visual. Whoa. For now I clocked Anna's return from her reconnaissance mission at the tombs and how I sighed. Yes, radiating gorgeousness had become something fairly effortless for Ms Sardinia, but now? Now she straddled the wooden stile into our field in a manner so becoming to a woman that I coughed, choked, gagged at her approach. Sweet beautiful life. And in this spectacular fashion, Anna's exhilarating return roused my dormant carcass from the

rear of the hearse, goaded me out of my simple delighted seren-
ity at having witnessed Loon's Extinction, and sent me off to
explore these three great monuments of Madau which presided
like sphinxes over that river valley's spectacular views.

The two largest tombs sat side-by-side, located at the highest
point of a delightful walled enclosure, the third far smaller monument pushed off to one side. But now I had a Madau Vision,
a vast repeat experience of that occurrence near the Altar of
Punishment whilst returning on foot to Su Talleri. Again I saw
myself as Old Tüpp being carried high atop some grand contraption, carried by four tall men up the Madau Valley towards
these three tombs. I stared down into the valley. What meant
these things? But then I became distracted again by the returning loveliness of Blessèd Anna who – not wishing to distract
my solitary musings – sat down quietly, almost primly, knees
together on the raised stone façade of the westernmost tomb.
Distracting? Anna? Why, her face was as radiant as the sun,
her lustrous black hair as smooth as obsidian, her lithe body as
curved as a classical guitar, her legs as long as a LaMonte Young
song. Sweet beautiful life, be my guide, by my side.

Now in meditational mindset, I droned a life-affirming
drone. Auuuummmmmm. Now, without the wherewithal to
photograph Blessèd Anna, I-Who-Have-Nothing stood up
from my squat and walked over to stand precisely where I would
have stood had I still owned a camera phone, which I didn't.
Nevertheless, as I jumped atop the main façade stones in order
to grab a better perspective of the beautiful lady, I was struck
by the sheer size of this so-called later tomb: its twenty-metre
chamber and its great pavement of surrounding precinct stones.
Now I stood upon those entrance stones, aiming dramatically
with both hands directly downwards at the loveliest lady: Primed

and loaded and pointing at you! Zoom! Again a Vision! Now, opening out before me, I saw Sardinia: the Sardinian order of things declaring themselves right below me! See Blessèd Anna, see! Right below her splendid seated posterior did I witness a lost carved Doorway lying recumbent below this present tomb. Why, the ancients had merely constructed it upon one far far earlier! But even as I informed Anna, attempted to inform Anna of the burnished, carved Doorway upon which she rested, even as she traced her fingers around those long-lost carvings, so did the radiance of that shining Doorway engulf me, engulf me, engulf me. Before me enthralling light. Before me this Doorway shining. And then behind me in fearsome contrast a weather cloud of fog did gather. Hunched up round my shoulders, bunched up round my head: woolly and numbing. Blinded to everything was I, save for this lava gateway ahead. Now, into its spiralling tunnel was I drawn, seered then branded my eyeballs with its Sun Radiance. This then was the blinding light symphony into which – like some titanic pylon atop some World Cliff – I was now felled, toppled, tumbled . . .

47. CROSSING THE VANMARK

Last day of Sober,
Isle of Asgard, c. 10,000 years ago

See me now ranging between worlds at last. Gathered me all
up, freshly descended from a top world made without senti-
ment or sense. When what is lost – hurled into dust against the
cyclopean walls of the Universe – is gathered again, gathered
up piece-by-piece until it is re-found, re-furbished and made as
before but for a second time: then – through its creators' careful
reconsideration – is it even improved upon. That was Bjond:
myself through travel much improved upon. Re-made almost.
With the habits and methods of Old Tüpp's rule I would have
remained satisfied had not my adventures abroad brought me
face-to-face with the Great Ab and Old Ball, both of whom
employed systems of government that greatly eclipsed my
father's own ways. Strange how travel had opened into my brain
a number of doors unwanted, unwished for. But was I to be
the inheritor of a fuckle kingdom otherwise? Best to know of
one's own archaic practices; or be like the Arse People who still
through superstition and menstrual fear throw out great quantities of good dinner meat just because Luno)))'s tides did in
their women bring the flow early that month – aye, *and* in front
of guests!

Now abroad had I ventured again this time on a royal progress through the Vanmark. Of its peoples, ways, inventions:
all of these considerations I had made good measure. Now my
searches did terminate here upon Asgard, I was just arrived

with my four stout Select from that dreaded sea crossing from Old Oslow. Here in Asgard walked Ashop's noble ephedra heir. Ephedra Incarnate strides forth upon Asgard. Royal ambassador of Old Tüpp himself am I, invited by Asgard's king to witness the Danish Law Mission as it passed through the northern lands. What changes the Danish Law Missions are bringing! Why, it is said that currents electric pass through the people when the new Danish sea laws are spoken into being. Ah me, the Danmark! Nowadays are those fast-moving Danes at the heart of all things, at the heart of each new experiment. But then, how fine had been that sleek Danish craft which transported us here from the shores of the Vanmark. Who but a churl would curl his lip at such a magical solution to such a dangerous trip? Indeed, without the exotic cargos that travel up-and-down the sea-lanes of the Danes, the lives of all but those in the remotest parts would have been considerably lessened. It is said that long ago we all were navigators of the sea, but that only those who pursued Danish excellence returned from such voyages. Nowadays, Danish Law obtains even at most sea ports on the Vanmark, and I could tell from the great size of these Danish vessels with which we had dealings that my father's new ephedra fields, located as they were in the far-flung Vanmark, would soon oblige Ashopians to rent mast space in the Danes' dry-storage cradles. How do I describe these Danish sea-goers, these vast balsa craft that stay afloat for months at a time? How do I describe these sea carpets, these rolling bridges that navigate the Vanquash, the Anguish, the North Sea and the Ocean? Ah me, that we had instead employed a Danish craft for our fatal journey to Abbis. Truly, I know of none in the Vanmark that loves sea travel, and none in Ashop but myself who has had need to try it.

But now, on this last day of Sober, upon arrival at Asgard did I commence promptly my account of my travels in the Vanmark, all scratched upon slate with a stylus of flint. Such an arduous task, but essential if we are to conserve records of our culture. Thus, through my accounts will future people understand that whereas the people of the Danmark were all of one type – a sea people rushing up whitewater rivers and across shark-infested coastal inlets, their longboats teeming with livestock and fine wares – the people of the Vanmark were, in complete contra-distinction, a heterodox bunch: farmers, cattle breeders, trekkers, fishermen, oyster eaters, flint miners, ditch diggers, wine makers, whose so-called Fedus remained firmly in place only whilst its ephedra crop was guaranteed; but who worked together and struggled through as best they could in these problematic times when inter-communication could not be guaranteed. Indeed, the most inspirational and recurring themes of my entire progress throughout the Vanmark were the ceaseless struggles of the Vanish leaders just to keep their Fedus together. What a thankless task – but what an inspiring idea! For this union has enabled the Vanish populations to share in all the wide varieties of produce offered by the Vanmark's rich geography, to taste the wares of distant lands, to wear threads sewn by others' hands, to be an oyster eater but to know the ways of cattle breeders, to trade your Vanish cutting flints and blades dug up at home for fish and meat and river reeds for twine: all taste the benefits that 'cross the Vanmark dare to roam!

And yet despite these many advantages, what antagonists also live and benefit from their Vanmark locations! When first my Ashopian Delegation arrived in the south of the Fedus, I had furious words with Old Rouge, whose royal self-stylings and utterances plainly aped my father and the Old Ones. Of all the Vanish I did meet, this ignoble wine maker did most disturb me. For he rules his Van Rouge with a shamanic fervour. When the Van Rouge drink their red wine, it is said that Old Rouge paints his own cheeks red, then whips his people up until a red mist comes over them. In this red rage, then does their king set them upon the world. Some say the Van Rouge have killed their old people as they sleep, some say they have torn off the heads of babies. But Old Rouge belongs not to the Old Ones, and those are no traditions of ours! What antagonists lurk herein unchallenged!

Of course there are the Boers whom every ephedra farmer fears, whose dust clouds turned their neighbours' own skies black, whose rustling of each other's cattle through some Vanish farmer's land make flat his fields and soon become their track. Ah me, that the Boers would curtail their reckless ways! When my Ashopian Delegation arrived at Grime's Graves, the people of the Fence had taken up cudgels against the Boerish In-trekkers that hoofed it up-and-down the Linkin Land and reduced to a prairie dust the landscape around. When my Ashopian Delegation arrived to explore the kingdom of the Van Dykes, their entire population was under siege from Boerish In-trekkers, who had taken such liberties across Vanish lands that miles and miles of carefully constructed sea walls had been pounded into destruction through sheer wanton thoughtless-ness. In all of the Vanmark, who but another Boerish leader could be called upon to admonish correctly those erring In-trekkers? Thus, only through this deadly slow political process could the Van Dykes expect to seek restitution. What a thankless task!

Perhaps I am too tired now to make fair account of my travels through the Vanmark? No, not too tired. But too saddened I am to linger long upon any exploit enjoyed therein. For my travel adventures, my walks abroad, have too often revealed those aforementioned flaws in my own father's habits and methods of government. Unlike the Great Ab of Abbis, who rules by the ancient laws and measures, my father Old Tüpp uses his secrets of Longitude *against* his people. Unlike Old Ball of N. Abbadon, who aggrandises his own secrets by co-opting the minds of every great thinker in his kingdom, my father Old Tüpp uses his sacred knowledge to set up intimidating structures, grand feats of civil engineering all across the land.

But by far the worst decision of my father's reign was his obstinate refusal to embrace the horticulture of Old Dam of Ashop. Taking for granted for too long her lodgers, her beavers, her dams, Old Tüpp never reckoned on her higher value. And so through indifference and thoughtless neglect did my father lose for Ashop its finest export. Successfully courted by the Vanmark's most holy ones, thus Old Dam did flee Ashop with her methods and priesthood to set up her temples where she would be appreciated, even worshipped. Now has her horticulture obtained such a hold in the northern lands that the Danish fleets rely on her beaver dams, the fleets of N. Abbadon too! Now has her horticulture obtained such a hold in the northern minds that even sacred caves are becoming vegetable temples. And yet, when I journeyed to the throne of Old Dam, with pride and with longing did she talk of Ashop. Her manner of speaking, her rituals, feasts, even her holies are styled after Ashop! And all of her speeches, her grand declamations, were warmly directed at this Prince of Ashop. Of my father's complacent rejection she would not speak, though plain was it, clear was it that still she burned. On the third night of feasting, however, as though to impress upon me further how great had been Old Dam's loss to Ashop, did the whole Beaver Temple join our royal company for a grand and intoxicating celebration. Then, midway through that great rejoicing started up the ancient chant of Old Dam and her Lodgers, now staged for Ashop's Prince Bjond.

BEAVER: Old Dam of Ashop. What shall ye call her?
LODGER 1: Old Dam is on Abbis called Grand Dam.
LODGER 2: Old Dam is on Iktis called Ma Dam.
LODGER 3: Old Dam is on Paris called Notra Dam.
LODGER 4: Old Dam is on Lindis called Acadame.
LODGER 5: Old Dam is on Lewis called Just Plain Dam.
BEAVER: Here on the sacred coast of Sankey, she is called La Dame.
ALL: Old Dam of Ashop, when shall ye rest?
BEAVER: (*Speaking as Old Dam, magically high, lingering*) When the world is dammed, only then shall I rest!
ALL: Dam the world!

Now, on this last day of Sober, is my account of the Vanmark concluded. Now shall my studies in Asgard commence. Thus will future people understand that Bjond, Prince of Ashop, did – through travels and adventures abroad – make by comparison better judgement of his own lands and people, thereby better to rule that land. More. Let all future kings and scholars and lawmen and holy ones know of these times – the Vanmark, the Danmark, the Kingdoms, the islands – through these careful accounts wrote upon slate, and always reproduced right clear, and in the righteous style of Prince Bjond, heir of Ashop.

48. THE FLAYING AND WEARING OF OLD OSS

First day of Ember,
Isle of Asgard, c. 10,000 years ago

Asgard rises out of the North Sea, a bustling island ten miles by twenty, guarding the Gate of Skaggerak and all of the sea-lanes directly north of the Boers' brutal Kennat Coast. There it was at his hilltop fortress – also named Asgard – that Old Oss ruled for centuries un-numbered. He was perhaps the most successful of all the Old Ones, my father Old Tüpp excepted – and certainly wielded most clout. For Old Oss it was who had in Antiquity named every large four-footed mammal of use to humanity, his mysterious equine understandings brought together by the rituals of the Ostlers – priests of the sacred stables, who practised grooming and who had collected together all of the Sage-King's sayings and doings. Some say it was no more than a dialectal shift that turned the king into Old Ass. Others say it was his foolish decisions. But as providence deemed that I should be there to witness his demise, so now shall I describe to you the final days of one of the Old Ones.

Now, none has suggested that Old Oss had Danu blood, none would dare. But as one of the Old Ones, Old Oss and his island had – like Old Tüpp in Ashop – been permitted to remain unaffiliated and outside the laws both of the Vanmark Fedus *and* of the Sea Empire of the Danmark. So even the least cautious of the Sage-King's High Ostlers were shocked at the cavalier manner in which Old Oss invited the Danish Inter-Mission to tour among his Asgard horse herds that fateful sunny day in late Sober. For, although the novelty of these Danish missions had long been known to entrance more credulous chiefs of those remoter coastal Vanish populations – always impressed by the sheer speed with which the Danes could raise a lawhill – no leader of the stature of Old Oss, High King of Asgard, had ever been so slack as to allow his own judgement to be passed directly into the hands of a Far-Reigner. Yet these were precisely the actions of Old Oss on that fateful Ember day. Had he been entranced by these modernistic supernauts, these wayfarers whose porpoise-straight boats traversed so effortlessly the un-navigable waters of the Skaggerak? Or did Old Oss intend to rescind his power only temporarily in order to a-judge how different were the Odin's decisions from his own? Whichever is the case, Old Oss announced – before his entire Ostler priesthood and elite horse-mounted guard – that the Odin of the Danish Inter-Mission would this day be called upon to make several instant judgements of serious local political importance. Murmurs of disapproval there were none at first, just a collective heaving and a collective sighing and a stellar cast of 2,000 Ostler priests and dignitaries and mounted warriors steadfastly fixing their eyes upon their parade ground. For Old Oss had ruled in Asgard longer even than Old Tüpp in Ashop. A deputation of leaders from every far-flung district of the Island arrived at the throne of Old Oss, but impossible it was for them to petition their holy Sage-King and divine leader who, the Ostlers concluded, was fully intent on directing his own demise.

Next day, with considerable calm and diplomacy, the Odin – speaking on behalf of Old Oss himself – invited this entire elite assembly of Asgard's 2,000 dignitaries, administrators and Holy Ostlers to follow his own party down to the seashores below, where – as a Lawman of the Danish Sea Peoples – the Odin declared that he felt more disposed to dispense good judgement. Without fuss, the great multitude – led by Old Oss himself – descended to the beach, upon whose flat sands a great and handsome lawhill had been thrown up according to the dimensions of the Danmark. Of course, the arriving dignitaries – all utterly ignorant of the size of the Danish fleet – assumed that this great 'hull' as the Danes termed it had been raised entirely of earth in the brief time that the Odin's party had been on the island, little knowing that the Danes had merely inverted one of their empty ships then covered it with soil, sand and stones to a depth of several inches. Indeed, so impressed were Asgard's dignitaries that Old Oss immediately grasped the calamitous nature of his too-generous decision. But he bit his lip and held his peace, for the Sage-King knew what next must happen the following day. Some say that Old Oss sacrificed himself to himself, that he recognised in the new practices of the Odin those truths of which he too should have become a practitioner, and that the forthrighteous Danish had – on that day upon Asgard – forever rendered obsolete all of the old ways. Thereafter, judgement would be for the Danes alone. Some say. But personally, I believe that it was the genius and charms of the Danish Law that scuttled Old Oss – intrigued and charmed him. Perhaps his time might not have come at all, perhaps. But this is what happened next . . .

At daybreak, the Odin stood atop the summit of a real lawhill, one fashioned especially for this occasion upon a natural islet in the middle of a freshwater loch, about three miles inland. It was accessed across a shingle causeway that was said to have been laid down in the time of Giants. But the lawhill itself had only just been thrown up overnight – and with expert precision – by gangers already on the island, mysteriously. Old Oss and his great retinue arrived presently and settled down in preparation for the day's good judgements. But nobody had thus far paid any attention whatsoever to the other two officers of the Inter-Mission, both of whom now leapt into action.

RHOT: I am Rhot.
LIKO: He holds the Law.
RHOT: I am the Lawed Rhot.
LIKO: I am Liko.
RHOT: He holds the Law.
LIKO: I am the Lawed Liko. (*Smiling broadly, raising eyes*) But you may call me Liege. Today has Old Oss chosen not to don the hide of special *privi-liege* but to walk out into the Law.
RHOT: In the name of the Odin and the Inter-Mission, I accuse Old Oss himself of unlawfully practising Danish Law outside the Danmark. How does he plead?
LIKO: In the name of the Odin and the Inter-Mission, I accuse Old Oss himself of tarnishing the name of Danish Law through his gross malpractice in lands ephederated to the Vanmark, ab-using that Law – a Law system that is not his – in order to bring good and fair judgement in cases undeserving of that judgement. How does he plead?

Old Oss plead? Immediately, the retinue of Old Oss prolapsed into a mass of flailing bodies intent upon doing each law officer great harm, but the old Sage-King himself sat firmly in his seat awaiting good judgement, seemingly oblivious to the noisome threats and fusillades of flingable armour, hats and gauntlets that his royal retinue volleyed at Liko and Rhot. But at last, only when the rabble refused to die down, did their remote

Sage-King shush them regally until there was quiet and the two officers of the Inter-Mission could continue.

LIKO: On our journey to Asgard, we passed along the Skaggerak Coast near Oslow. Or that is what they called it.

RHOT: But that surely was not Oslow, Liko Liege. Why, only last year I passed near Oslow as I rode east across Abbadon on my way to do business with The Tenancy.

Now, Old Oss turned whiter than any ghost, for he knew this was his Come-Uppance at last. For not even the sagacious Juddish lawmen of the Ash-Kennat-Tenancy had dared interpolate Danish points-of-law into their own practices for fear of Danish reprisals. And here was an Old One sneaking around the N. coasts with Oslow as his own personal husting! One day here, one day there. Come and go as you please. Now Old Oss stood up full-of-fear but still comprehended not the calamitousness of his own situation. Instead, the Sage-King stood up proudly and turned to his retinue of important personages, whom he now addressed with true gravity.

OLD OSS: Let nobody ever forget this: Old Oss knew Transport and horse breeding before the world began. If today the world turns against the Old Ones, so be it. I now throw myself upon the mercy of Garda Law. May he give a true account of my many splendid judgements and conclusions.

And thus, in defence of their High Liege now laid low, did Old Oss's legendary lawman – Garda Law himself – step forth upon the lawhill. Then he recited the previous one hundred of Old Oss's most important judgements. But knowing nothing of the

Odinist complexities of the Danmark, Garda Law – himself tipsy with the privilege of making account to the Odin – chose not the most appropriate of Oss's judgements to impress the Danish Mission. No. Each new example that he burst forth was more whimsical than the last – 'a thorn just snagged my robe, therefore you must hang'. Until at last the great ruler of Asgard, listening in horror to Garda Law and fearing the worst, himself took on the equine appearance of his own charges. And now he hung his head low.

LIKO: Old Oss, why the long face?

OLD OSS: (*Glum, laid low*) What shall become of me?

LIKO: You shall be cast out of the World. The Fedus shall not dare take you in; the Vanmark would vote against it. So would Old Tüpp. From here only east may your body parts travel. Henceforth, the name of Oss will mean cast out.

RHOT: Ostracised are you.

LIKO: Not to the four corners of Earth shall a quarter-piece of your body be sent.

RHOT: That honour you forfeit.

Then the unhappy throng of Asgard's gathered lawmen and holy ones – the Ostlers, the barristers, the mounted warriors and Liege-men – set up a tragic lowing for their great One now brought to heel. Now the Odin ascended the lawhill from three different directions, each time returning to the level ground of the beach. Then, on his third ascent, did he lead Old Oss and set the guilty one upon his knees atop the summit. Before the Sage-King even could prepare for death, the Odin took a great handled implement and wellied the very life out of the Old One's head. Wump. Then, even as Old Oss writhed in his death throes, the great cutting began. Old Oss felt nothing more, though; such was the Odin's mastery. And within the hour was the body of Old Oss flayed of its skin, and set upon the Odin's shoulders and named 'The Cape of Asgard'.

Across the island the funeral retinue now trudged, at its head the grand en-shrouded figure of the Odin marched alone, behind him the members of the Danish Inter-Mission, behind them the unseated holy ones and dignitaries of the island, behind them the Ostlers and mounted warriors, behind them the orphans. At the tail end of this funeral retinue marched four black stallions, all plumed with feathers of indescribable blue, dragging a great sled: upon it the heaped remains of Old Oss. This heap at first only the scald crows did tear at, but the hours and the march sucked more from the skies, until – upon reaching the sea cliffs of Asgard – so the gulls and seabirds also joined in the feeding frenzy. Upon viewing this cruel scene, so did the Ostlers all marching together at last strike up their lament for their Old One fallen.

OSTLERS: Ostlers gather round,
And sing your song together,
One last time today: Your God is overthrown,
And flayed and worn upon the beach and taken far
away – away.

By dawn of the second day, we had traversed the island twice, and the funeral party had taken on many tribal aspects; here warriors in deep conversation, there holy ones chanting together, the many and various divisions of marchers ranging across several hilltops. Now, from my anonymous position in the procession, I began to question my role, my place, my grand design. What were the Old Ones? Why were we tolerated? Only in the presence of the Odin had Old Oss's judgements seemed worthy of ridicule. Why? How would the judgements of my father Old Tüpp stand up to Danish scrutiny? Brr, I felt my whole body quaver. Try as I might, I could not now return to my former thoughts, and I struck up a conversation with a vishop, one of the fish-headed priests from Vishgard who happened to have been on Asgard during this upheaval.

BJOND: Vishop, tell me why were the Old Ones tolerated? I am Bjond of Ashop, destined also to be an Old One. What say you about our kind?

VISHOP: Truthfully told, Soeur? Since my caste of holy ones were ejected from Vishgard, none of my kind could dare discuss such things with a son and heir of Ashop. In childhood, every one of the Collar learns this alone, and by rote: The Great Ab knows the Cosmic Law and the meaning behind the Star of Vanmark, Old Tüpp knows Longitude, Old Oss knows Transport and horse breeding, Old Bog knows the ways of Sacrifice, Old Ut knows Tracking and the ways of the Boer, and Old Ball knows the way of Spheres, their Shapes and the sky transits of Sunno))) and Luno))). That alone is the extent of our . . . information.

Thus through the harsh actions of the Odin upon the beach at Asgard had I begun my kind's first great leap into uncertainty. No longer truly Bjond was I, where next for me? Now, I walked more briskly than any others in the funeral retinue and soon passed among the mile-long throng between the lawmen, the warriors, the holy ones, the relatives, those marchers all, between Old Oss's remains dragged at the rear upon the sled and – far off at the front – the striding Odin still clad in 'The Cape of Asgard', but now bedecked with garlands of flowers. Behind him strode Liko and Rhot, behind them two more officers of the Danmark, with whom I now struck up a conversation. The Asgard landscape hereabouts was as rough as an old dwarf's neck, and treeless too – nothing could grow in these penetrating winds aswipe the Skaggerak. But as conversations between members of the retinue dwindled along this perishing north coast to a mere Ur-rumble, so did I make now my boldest move, worthy indeed of an Heir to the throne of Ashop: I approached the Odin himself and walked now alongside him at the head of Old Oss's funeral retinue.

49. PETER KROPOTKIN

4th Ember,
Isle of Asgard, c. 10,000 years ago

Behind us trudged the funeral retinue of Old Oss, ahead of us
the untrammelled coasts of N. Asgard. Beside me? The Lawman,
the Coming man: the Odin. Silently now we two walked on
ahead, both of us hided from the explosions of the N. wind that
nevertheless penetrated to my very Ashopian bones. Once I'd
yearned, if only briefly, for a more simple life than that which
this fractured Kingship of Ashop had bequeathed me. But now
in fulfilment I writhed, privy to the new secrets of Asgard that
the Odin was uncovering by the hour. Walked he everywhere
upon the furthest reaches of Asgard's coasts. No stone, no cob-
ble remained unturned as the Odin made his rounds, treading
where none other had yet dared to tread – not Old Oss, nor
even the Sage-King's own Lawmen. At a waterlogged yew forest inundated by the North Sea, we watched dumbfounded as
the Odin – wading waist-high in the brackish brine – made
detailed account of each tree still living, made everywhere fastidious measurings and calculations. Then choosing at last one
yew from among the soggy multitude, he pronounced to our
gathered throng that this tree 'shall now and in future become
the Merchant, that from which all Asgard shall spring forth'.

Everywhere now in living inventory did the Odin walk,
did he beat his bounds. We traipsed across limestone hilltops
of Asgard that never before had felt the weight of horse or
human; on vicious cliff edges we lingered where sea birds made

not their nests; at deep ravines we trudged manfully down into their depths then up the other side, the civil engineers of the Danmark here-and-there being called upon to remove a danger or construct a path. But when we had at long last concluded the Odin's chosen itinerary, none but myself and seven others remained in attendance. All others having long fallen by the wayside – despite this day itself being still only hours old – we nine retainers bedded down in recumbence. And although the vicious winds did tear across our wall of hides, yet did we huddle semi-conscious throughout the rest of the day.

We sunk most of us into sleep, down in that windy combe. But the many experiences of my several journeys outside Ashop confused me, thus I ranged somewhere in-between. Without the differing ways of the Great Ab, Old Ball and Old Oss at play in my head, perhaps I should not have felt so compelled to alter the trajectory of Ashop's kingship. But that was fast becoming my new plan of action. With my own eyes I had observed the fate of Old Oss, and on a sore point I lingered now. When had Old Tüpp done his dealings with the Danmark? How long ago? And why? When had the name of the sacred stream upon Mam Tor's sides been changed to Odin's Sitch? Again: how long ago and why? By what political switch had the Odin slipped quietly into the Land of Ashop? Now I recalled with embarrassment my impolitic question to Old Ball during my stay in N. Abbadon; more I recalled his outburst at my thoughtless mouth.

BJOND: Soeur, to which sacred Abbadon landmark did the Odin first lay claim?
OLD BALL: (*Furious, standing up*) What? When? Never yet has the Odin set one foot upon Abbadon's shores. Never will he. And never would his name obtain in the lands of Old Ball.

(*Staring at me*) We meet but rarely, the Odin and myself. Why?

Embarrassed at being unable to answer this simple question, and me the heir to the throne of Ashop, I had quickly blamed the effects of the ephedra for my mealy-mouthèdness and moved the subject along. But now, in the company of the slumbering Odin, how I worried for the future of my own kingdom. In Abbis, the Great Ab employed unswervingly ancient formulas and traditions for his mode of governing. In N. Abbadon, Old Ball combined his own grand talents with an uncanny ability to marshal the greatest thoughts and ideas of other rich minds in the kingdom. But Old Oss had underestimated fatally the powers of the Danmark, and – in relying solely and for too long on his exalted place as an Old One – I saw in Old Oss too many of those same sluggard ways that proliferated in our Ashopian manner of government. Why, it was even due to my father's own misjudgement that I had suffered garrotting at the hands of the Oberst. Why had Old Tüpp employed such a man to oversee his library? Why had the king a library at all? No books, just the one page. What sophistry! Worse still, whilst nurturing such cultural falsenesses, Old Tüpp had simultaneously ignored the homegrown greatness of Old Dam, had let her magical horticulture slip out of Ashop ignored. Old Dam had made her beginnings not so far from Navio, neither. The locals preserve her name there still, and even claim for themselves Old Tüpp's belovèd Longitude line to the Grand Paradíe – those five triumphant pillars of oke – that he long ago for intimidation's sake set up upon Salisbury Plain. But when Old Tüpp had scorned her horticulture, Old Dam had taken her beaver-priests and, at the canny invitation of the Great Ab, headed northeast to practise her horticulture on the sacred coasts of Sankey, where beaver lodges already proliferated. What a disaster to have befallen Ashop! Nowadays, the holy ones of Old Dam – her beaver-priests, her lodgers, etc. – practise their horticulture solely to maintain the sea fleets of the Danmark and of N. Abbadon. Who but the beaver brings down the great tree? No man never. Who without horticulture sails out to sea? No man never. Without Old Dam and her beavers? No sea travel, no river rides, no Now. And Old Tüpp had given this great Ashopian gift away; let it slip out of the kingdom unappreciated. Oh, how I wrung my hands and gnashed my teeth in frustration and indignation. For how long had my father been depleting needlessly Ashop's homegrown forces, its powers, its riches?

* * *

When at last the nine of us arose from our long rest, I felt refreshed. Again we set off briskly *and* at a pretty pace. My mind at last was polished clear of insignificance and only great horizons of ideas did shape my thoughts. But no matter how I tried to place myself amidst the future plans of Ashop? Came on me like a thunderous bell always the answer: No! Came on me like a thunderous knell, always the answer: Go! In Future Ashop, said the voice, let only greatness rule your famous Navio. Let the ways of the Old Ones fade into the past. Let those autocratic methods wither and implode. Make way for Ashop's Queen of Horticulture – dear Old Dam – and set the Odin at her motherlode. And when at last the nine of us returned to that yew forest? Whilst others rested, I approached the Odin with my plan.

BJOND: As time is time, so now is my time come, Liege.

ODIN: Where next for Ashop?

BJOND: Justice from her son.

ODIN: Where next for Bjond?

BJOND: Death at your hands, I believe. Righteous death.

Righteous death indeed was what my kingdom required. My meditations these long trudgeful hours in company of the Odin, in mute appreciation of his patient observation and diagnoses, had revealed only slackened worn-out ways among my own dynasty. Moreover, was the Odin not surprised at my suggestion; he candidly admitted that indictments were prepared against my father. Thus was I in harmony with the future of my kingdom. Thus was I in harmony with the tenets of the Lawman. Thus could my contraption and my corpse – both brought together – be carried by my stout Select to my eternal tether. Nevertheless did the Odin greatly lament this outcome.

ODIN: (*Sucking air*) The killing of a king is always problematic.

BJOND: Already I've observed the death of Old Oss at your hands.

ODIN: His time was gone. Your time was yet to come, Prince of Ashop.

BJOND: Therefore shall you be killing *not* a king. Not regicide – at most a sacred offering.

ODIN: (*Resigned to it*) Then, Bjond of Ashop, you must hang: I must suspend you. By the neck may none die save for royalty and nobility.

BJOND: Then so be it. You must hang me from the Merchant, from the yew.

ODIN: I must hang you from the Merchant with the river reeds of Asgard. Thus as life expires so seamlessly shall you pass through.

Presently, our nine did return to the Merchant. Rugged, right separate it stood from the rest. Next to it a tree stump they readied as a prince's plinth. Stood upon the tree stump, would I be there wrenched out of life. And whilst the Odin directed, so the seven men with the weight of their bodies did drag down a supple bough from this great yew, a springy limb the men did snare and tie it tight with river reed twine. At the rope's far end did they fashion a noose which the Lawman would slip round my neck. Thus, as the Odin began his great chants, his long incantations, his magical spells, so I stood there in life and I smiled. Then came the Play at life's end: those words we must speak as a Prince of Ashop, those words we must speak as a Lawman of the Danmark.

ODIN: (*As though reading from a script*) Your gallows is ready for you now, Prince of Ashop. And it does not seem too dangerous. Come over here and I'll put the noose around your neck.
BJOND: (*Grim now, determined*) If this device is no more dangerous than it looks, then it cannot do me much harm. But if things turn out otherwise, so then shall I be in the hands of Fate.

And with that, I climbed upon the stump. The Odin put the noose around my neck and climbed down. The seven let loose their grip on the branch and my feet slipped from under me right there on the slippery stump. The branch shot up, wrenching my head into the yew, my neck snapped from ear-to-ear whilst my body and limbs followed only considerably after. And thus, between two worlds did I briefly linger, betaken by justice, betaken by truth. And here I died. And here I hung. No more Bjond. Ashop New Begun.

BETAKES NOW UPON THE WORLD AN EMPTINESS

And as I died and death took hold of me, a sound: a distant sound seven hundred miles hence. From under the ground beneath the stump of Ashop's once-great World Tree came a weeping, came a singing, came a choir of women's voices. The colleges were awakening. Till now mute, rendered so by the tree's infamous toppling infinite years before, so were the singers of Ashop already waking, the singers of Ashop already of their own volition had found their voices. What of the three colleges of the Past, of the Present, of the Becoming Time? All three – so long suppressed – now burst forth into life as never before. Clamorous chants, renegade streams, irrigated dreams. Across the heavens they chimed, across the skies they chimed, across the whole world they chimed.

PAST: Seated and chained: chainèd and bound.
ALL: His life runs out.
PRESENT: Raft ye now across the Asgard Sound.
ALL: His life runs out.
BECOMING: The leaking of life: the taking of Bjond.
ALL: His life runs out.
PAST: Through the Boerlands, down the Anguish pond.
ALL: His life runs out.
PRESENT: Teeth rattle, jaws rattle, elbows, knees.
ALL: His life runs out.

BECOMING: Smartness in sail craft: currents, rigs, seas.
ALL: His life runs out.
PAST: Round the Hondsridge, cross behind Blaar Cop.
ALL: His life runs out.
PRESENT: Down the River Rhine: this Prince of Ashop.
ALL: His life runs out.
BECOMING: Through the southern Vanmark carry ye.
ALL: His life runs out.
PAST: And *then* unto the Sards deliver he.
ALL: His life runs out.
PRESENT: Raft ye now into Ríu Cedrino.
ALL: His life runs out.
BECOMING: Raft ye on into deep Flumineddu.
ALL: His life runs out.
BECOMING: Raft ye now under harsh Su Gorruptu.
ALL: His life runs out.
PAST: Raft ye now along the Ríu Madau.
ALL: His life runs out.
PRESENT: Climb ye at long last up to the plateau.
ALL: His life runs out.
PAST: Bear ye now this weight across the meadow.
ALL: His life runs out.
PRESENT: Waste your time not in bystanders' prattle.
ALL: His life runs out.
BECOMING: Gave this prince his life in love, not battle.

* * *

Here in the sediment of life where I lay, down in the muddiest emulsions of me, still I struggled and twitched in survival. Even at the onset of death, how life is fashioned only to persist. How

I encouraged my marrow, my blood and my vapours! How I encouraged my bones and my flesh to rally once more! Ah me, such is life that, having once obtained, never can it be lightly extinguished. Ask even of the flea so casually ground between forefinger and thumb, still will it confess as it expires: 'How much I did love that life!'

* * *

To be alive in this world and to be dead elsewhere. None should try it, none would bear it lightly as I now discovered. For here in quite another world, a world of light, did I begin to breathe again. Above me, a wash of sluggish shapes and dreary forms and perfunctory patches of warmth rolled by me like sleep matter dragged 'cross the dozing eyes of some reluctant snoozer. And I like a newborn reached out to those shapes, reached up for their meaning, their movement, their life! And as I sunk down and down, so did the face of a human angel stare also down into what people call their 'eyes', what I therefore also called my 'eyes'. For I was human again: some kind of human. Not formed yet, but not dead neither. And in that formation, as low as it yet was, seeped I out of the ground at a trajectory low but yet inclined enough to seek a path downhill, a path of least resistance. This dribbler drizzling lightly upon some not unhealthy upland? Why, this would run and run and soon would I again become: back from Bjond. I was Rock. Or rather I would be soon.

* * *

Crenellated with an unbroken waistband of jagged mountain-tops at its most earthbound edges, the sky above me fried ten million micro pasta star shapes in its vast circular pan. I reached up to each one and blew it a kiss: ten ker-zillions per moment at least. She looked down and told me, no, she was not my mother. But she would stay with me and I would be comfortable. I explained about my descent back from death into human form and she laughed uncomprehendingly. But so beautiful was this woman that I saw only kindness in her eyes when she joked.

ANNA: We have a crazy phrase here in Sardinia to describe you: dragged through a hedge backwards. It's good to know you *also* can look so 'early morning'.

Then I told her of my decision to reject my princely rights, to abandon all notions of kingship, even to overthrow the very idea of there being a king of Ashop. Instead, my kingdom would be restored to a ninefold earthbound collegiate system of horticulture and treelore with the Odin as its armoured facilitator; restored to a Lunar Calendar of 365 days in the year – thirteen months, each of exactly four weeks' duration, with a single holy day at each year's end in celebration of that sacred Doorway through which all must pass. Fuck yeah! I told her that without the self-overthrowing of the hierarchy, that without sacrificing ourselves to ourselves, the sole way forwards into the future would be through Greed, Acquisition and Raw Lust for Power alone.

ANNA: (*Excited, getting squeaky*) You have become beautiful inside! You have surrendered your birthright and restored reason. You have magnified yourself into a white Christ! Rock Section, you sound exactly like Peter Kropotkin!

50. IT'S A FUCKING IN THE WIND

8pm, Tuesday June 13th, 2006
From the Buick Hearse, parked up at Madau

Now, the land hereabouts began to tremble and sweat. One hour had passed since my magnification. One hour in which Blessèd Anna had become overwhelmed with newness at my Sardu story, had herself fallen into a psychic coma of astonished cultural overload. For now had her mind – so recently Sardu-suspicious – become enthralled at long last, become installed at long last with the grandness of our *Missionu*. For now had her island in four short days yielded up to this wasted foreigner more truthful possibilities, more secrets, more fissures, more cultural tweens than all the treasures, tombs and treelore still lying undiscovered across the entire Italian Mainland – or so she would inform me again and again and again. Bubbling, foaming, erupting out of her sleep, she would make stupendous declarations. Then? Again would exhausting sleep betake her, each of these new truths more than enough to overwhelm Blessèd Anna during her long transformation. Steeping herself, basting herself, broiling herself in those fabulous but overwhelming facts, Anna had – upon all these things – meditated, mused and marvelled until and until and until? She had pinged the alarm button in her overdeveloped scholar's brain. Down had come the indoor rains of her cranial smoke alarm. Drizzled down, damped down, clamped down. Until her newly Revolutionary brain capers had – through sheer overwork – been forcibly shut down.

Soon after the first wave of Visions had overwhelmed her, Anna had crept off and slunk into the hearse's rear chamber, where – now properly out for the count – she rested under glass as though lying in state. And while she rested, I watched. And while I watched, I sang. And the songs that Anna did inspire through me did pass so eloquently that not even local troubadours could improve upon the righteousness of my Sardu voice right there overlooking Madau Valley. Spying an obsidian flake upon the ground, I broke into an epic, improvised obsidian ballad, effortlessly extemporising rhymes of obsidian lore – and with considerable expertise. Without effort I sung of the knives, of the mirrors, of the rings; I sung of the lofty obsidian powers possessed by ancient Sardinians. And so beautiful were my tunes inspired by Blessèd Anna that the smallest of animals and all the insects came to marvel, came to hum and sing and whistle every tune that I was offered. Until, until, until no being, no life nor spirit form could extricate themselves from their ringside seats pulled up next to our Illustrious Cabinet of Curiosities right there at the field's edge, our notorious magical kiosk with its Blessèd Anna Window Display.

Surrounded by the watching eyes of Nature and Supernature, shaking and stamping alone how I raged now as the Blessèd One dreamt under glass. Spinning and shimmying, filled with the Dance how I writhed and gyrated unsated around this metallic blue bomb, this inverted bathtub supreme, this armoured Durruti Dream crouched and all ready to spring forth from its summit meeting. And I saw the jagged summit of Mt Arbu to the northwest buckling and twisting like Chesterfield Cathedral. Effortlessly I viewed beneath its outer shell as though staring through glass, the mountain's essence struggling on its axis to break free. At last, this achieved, down towards us it strode now manifested in the form of a great horned warrior, who clasped to his right eye a mighty telescope the size of a nuclear submarine. Striding towards our encampment three fields at a time, this mountain giant crouched down beside me until he was no taller than Big Ben and bellowed as he pointed into the hearse.

MT ARBU: I have seen Giampaolo's daughter as she sleeps under glass. She is as dazzling as the sun. I believe the whole world will be made a wilderness unless I lie with her.

But even as I parried Mt Arbu's advances, there I saw to the southwest the same geological wriggling, pulsing upon Mt Terralba's slopes. And now did the essence of this other mountain sally forth, again petitioning me with its many reasons for choosing Blessèd Anna as its human lover. Persistent too were its entreaties, persistent and even irritated at my apparent procrastination.

MT TERRALBA: Mine is the love that Giampaolo's daughter deserves. Leave us now your song has drawn me to her. Love for her I have when she awakes.

But I would not give up my treasured position – could not. For I knew that these other suitors had been conjured up only through the beauty of my own songs to Anna. Moreover, even my cursory reconnaissance of the mountainous, castellated horizon had revealed in every direction fastidious observers of Blessèd Anna across all 360 degrees of the compass. Should even one suitor be allowed to remain here, so would dozens seek permission to fall upon our encampment. Thus, I explained my personal position to the two mountains then bade them Good Night.

When two hours later Blessèd Anna awoke at last from Lying-In-State, she had ascended to higher places. Her lips pouted as though she'd been cosmically kissed, her lunar breasts were brazen and backlit beneath her brassiere, her Gradisca dress sucked up into her ravenous arse: it was as though she had just got with GOD. I could not take my eyes off her. I tried but I could not. She noticed.

ANNA: (*Radiant*) I'm changed. I'm different. You made me different, Rock Section. Now we must set off for Lanusei. This night has fallen so much darker than anything before I experienced.

Now, Anna fired up the big General Motors V8 – but nothing. Now, she fired it up once again. Zilch. Now, still determined to pursue today's mission to its proper conclusion, she opened the great bonnet and checked out the spark plugs, the electricity circuits, etc. But right there in the darkness the black engine oil soon made such a piece of Pop Art out of her pale blue dress that Blessèd Anna felt obliged to strip down to her white under-slip. I stood open-mouthed in mute appreciation of this unscholarly action, and I now wore a big smile on my face that was not based on reaching Lanusei this evening. Then Anna made her sudden diagnosis. She looked deflated, disgusted with her simple error. For she had, on exiting the car hours before, accidentally engaged the indicator lights thereby running the battery down. She checked her mobile phone, but there was no signal. My big smile increased. For the middle-of-nowhere seemed an ideal place in which to be spending my last hours with this loveliest of ladies – coveted even by the local Gods themselves. And I felt confident that it would be technically possible for us both to sleep comfortably in the hearse so long as we compromised personal space in favour of accepting such concepts as the colleague as counterpane, the associate as duvet. I had me a magic cloak and I was not afraid to use it. Besides, coming so soon after our cosy marathon M. Goodby history lesson, I had been rocked by Anna's sudden absence, rocked by her twenty-two-hour roadtrip with her father. Now, in these my final hours, I wanted to leave this planet super sure of what this beautiful woman had really looked like. Never to forget this time of this life – only to remember.

But none of Anna's demeanour towards me now suggested that we could be lovers. In truth, as spirited friends and associates only had we developed our closeness. Moreover, having caused us now to be stranded in such a remote place, such were Blessèd Anna's current feelings of personal irresponsibility that her newly raised consciousness and psychic trajectory only exacerbated her feelings of stupidity. Thus, looking less like a scholar than ever, and more like some pouting rebel queen from some underground movie, did the gorgeous semi-clad one simply drift barefoot away from our encampment, traipse off into the Moonless night, all the while waving vigorously to me. Then just at the point where darkness engulfed her, Anna turned around, pouted and quoted Kowalski's drowned lover in *Vanishing Point*.

ANNA: (*Dramatic wave, melodramatic voice*) Sayonara! Remember me!

* * *

Now in the pitch-black night I sat and fretted on the ground beside the hearse. Anna had been gone long over an hour, during which time the wind had got up quite severely at the north and I remembered Giampaolo's prediction of a coming storm. Eh, that was no storm, surely nothing but a squall, a hilltop squall hardly even worth a mention? But I knew that the wind had been courting Blessèd Anna since she'd danced atop the Iloi tombstone, danced ecstatically all night and with such high-wire flamboyance! And I knew how the wind at Goronna had befriended her as she'd waited for me in the hilltop darkness, perplexed and too terrified to act. But even after all those events, I'd hardly imagined that I'd now be reduced to squinting through the darkness for evidence of my errant love as she consorted and cavorted with some amorous meteorological phenomenon. Where was she? Was that distant rumble a by-product of games with her ardent lover? Had the flock of birds that now overhead did pass me been disrupted by her cosmic coupling with the wind? Who was I to break up such a wayward partnership? How could I take on the wind? And now out of the darkness I saw Blessèd Anna racing steadily across the distant meadow towards our encampment, and behind her I saw the wind playfully trip her, spin her over and lay her – plop! – spreadeagled on the ground. Dazed, Anna merely rose to her feet and continued rushing towards me. How outraged I was! Had I been the cuckolded lover before even the loving had taken place? How could I even see the wind? And yet an artillery projectile with a painted red tip would not have been clearer to me. At last, Blessèd Anna approached near enough for our gazes to meet. But such was the wind's headlong rush that once again Anna met the prairie flat on her back. There she lay with her legs parted, one knee raised. And with that she was taken by the wind, or rather by the squall, whose essence spiralled upwards into the sky then dived earthwards and disappeared inside her. I heard her moan a low guttural moan. I saw this show, I did not understand. Off into the Madau Valley downhill screeched the little storm and in short everything was quiet again. In blissful peace now, I stared upon Anna fifty metres away on her back: her legs parted and one knee raised. I saw this sight that I did not understand. Came back the storm up the head of the valley at the peak of its anger: broke even the drystone wall to the ground, pitched upside down into a spiral yet again disappeared the storm into Anna, inside her. Thus, my scholar-love rode the currents of the weather, rode the currents of the night. At last all the stars did shine suddenly through the black cloud overhead, fried it up, scorched it into charcoaled fritters and pushed the darkness even further ahead. And my love-scholar rode the currents of the evening rising currents of the night. I heard me moaning, a low guttural moan. Back came the squall headlong up the valley, romping over the stile and wall, bursting down the field, headlong into Anna, right up inside her, fucked Anna as I watched. Down come the walls of civilisation, dams burst and inundation comes rolling in across the white sand beaches. As surely they must – eventually.

* * *

Only after long hours did their meteorological lust die down and the wind disappeared at last, leaving the gorgeous one lying prone just one hundred metres across the meadow. But whenever I attempted to visit Blessèd Anna, to ascertain her physical and mental state, so would the wind return to buffet me away, to bully me off her stricken form. Enduring from that ill-wind more than an hour of these pesterings and exertions, eventually, like an army hospital orderly recovering a wounded soldier from the battlefield, did I race under cover of the magic cloak towards my incorrigible freak-brained lady, my stricken Anna whose wisdom, learning and gorgeousness had each day in my company expanded further and further until even the very elements had claimed her now! Hidden thus, slowly I inched my way towards my desiccated Anna, then dragged and hauled her back to the hearse, wherein I had set up a rudimentary field hospital fashioned from what few clothes Anna possessed and surmounted by the magic cloak, under which we now slipped, under which we now kipped. And I felt confident that both of us would sleep comfortably in the hearse just so long as Blessèd Anna accepted such concepts as the colleague as counterpane, the associate as duvet. *Zzzzzzzzzzzzzzzzzzzzz* . . .

* * *

At 5am, out-of-nowhere – the sunrise not yet even a Mithraic glint – did the ancient kaput General Motors radio roar into life with all the brash fanfare and epic flourish of some glitzy Hollywood movie. It was Jesu Crussu opening his daily show on 89.9 FM.

CRUSSU: For all of you struggling at 5 o'clock to live a new way of life; for all you lovers searching for a new way to love; for all of you just checking to make sure your favourite DJ is doing fine before going back to bed: here's the legendary Hans Vinding with his theme from the movie soundtrack of *German Motorcycle Murderer* – here's Furekaaben.

Loudspeakers built into the floor of the hearse brought forth now my favourite-ever road movie theme. Peace and eternal love be upon you, Jesu Crussu. You've sacralised our entire roadtrip. As the dark acoustic *Paradieswarts Düül*-ian commune emanations of Furekaaben spread thickly through the upper atmosphere of the hearse – bongos, tablas, voices, violins, acoustic guitars – I tasted their fumes and inhaled their sublime music. Next to me, Anna was fast off, snuggled up to me in the sweetest manner, her two praying hands acting as a pillow for her head, both my hands clasped tight upon her large breasts, and her naked butt rammed right into my lap as though we had been fucking just moments before. Waking up in the back of a hearse is not nearly as weird as you'd expect, especially when the broken radio plays all your favourite songs. And even more especially when you find yourself curled up around the warm recumbent figure of smart, scholarly gorgeousness gone up country. Intoxicated by the Scando-Germanic ecstasies of Furekaaben, I was stretching out upon the vast tortoise-shell linoleum floor when Anna awoke. She looked at me astonished, as though it was I who had chosen her favourite music to play on the broken radio. Then, in recognition of Crussu's divine intervention, of General Motors' divine intervention, she hummed and trilled the female vocal line along with the record, stretching out all feline and endlessly curvy.

ANNA: (*Ostentatiously*) Call me Lùviah.

We'd slept at most three hours but what sleep! I looked out through the rear side window of the hearse and noticed the twinkling of a farm on the hill about one mile away. It reminded me of the scene in *German Motorcycle Murderer* when the biker couple in search of petrol blunder into a roadside swamp. In the movie, Lùviah the heroine is forced to escape from an ancient bog full of garrotted sacrifices. In the back of our hearse, Lùviah writhed her naked butt around in my lap, pressed my hands around her swivelling hips, and became my lover.

51. FIAT VET

Last night we made love in a magic cloak – today I die. I felt the throng of unsatisfied mountains hereabouts chuntering a bluff: *Fair enough!* Ah me, that those 'events of sixteen years ago' would be terminating in such ecstasy and human revolution. Knock-kneed nearly, knocked sideways entirely and just awakened from a sexual slumber that only the truly World Doped could hope to imagine, I knew my time was come. I brimmed over with Now. Hell, I was cosmically embattled by actuality. Reality is not a Polaroid, not an instant cellphone moment. The deep consideration? All of *that* must come *before* the action. As a Post-Punk singer, live TV shows had been my abject revelation: I'd watched myself on playback once too often getting it right only at the *end* of the performance. Hmmm. I snorted. Not today. Today – cosmically rewarded, replete – I would perform World Perfectly. For Antonioni's cameras overhead. For Brent and Dean and Breakfast: so long dead.

I stood alone outside the hearse, scouting the horizon for the farmhouse whose light I'd spied a few dark hours previously. If we were going to get back to Santa Cristina for Bugs Rabbit's 3 o'clock kick-off, now was the safest time for us to get our act together. Not much more than fifty kilometres away. What's that? Thirty miles at the most? Why, even D. H. Lawrence's old 1920s motor coach through *Sea and Sardinia* could have made that journey. We were, however, in the middle of nowhere and still in extreme need of a rented/borrowed car. Beyond the abrupt 5am radio magic of 89.9 FM, nothing more had been heard from Old Flxible these past two hours, and I could *not* risk my date with destiny today. Until I had the guarantee of wheels, thirty miles was still an age away. But now, as though to test my resolve, Blessèd Anna stepped down from the rear of the hearse. Wearing only my black jacket and skimpy pink undies, she immediately nestled into me, purring and pawing at my neck. I lost my mind. Right then did we start kissing once more. Right then did we embrace right up against the Buick's bulging front doors. Our feet rubbed together so harshly that my ankles became sore. Kneading and moulding and shaping each other's bodies, we slid and bumped as one entanglement down and down the Buick bodywork until – against the rugged Firestone tyres – at last we shuddered to a halt. And there we remained for a full hour, plans out of the window, our whole world encompassing two square metres at most.

* * *

And when at last we surfaced?

ROCK: You smell exotic.
ANNA: Rock Section! I smell of you.
ROCK: (*Pouts, then gurns noisily*) ?
ANNA: (*Getting closer*) In what way exotic?
ROCK: Mysterious and unknown.
ANNA: If I smell of you, maybe you're the exotic one.
ROCK: D. H. Lawrence said certain Sardinians looked like the Inuit.

ANNA: Eskimos? My Thai friends in Bologna University say I look Eurasian.

ROCK: Yeah man, but you're far too exotic to be Eskimo.

ANNA: (*Coy*) More exotic? Even driving a hearse?

ROCK: (*Right up close, sniffing*) Mmm.

Now I walked in glory, now I walked in splendour – myself eternally transformed. Those who dare to tinker with the Cosmos must know – in precipitating Cosmic change – that reigns shall fall like rains, that thrones shall be o'erthrown, that those who dream of meat may yet remain unmet. But always will the battle for balance *itself* hang in the balance. I wanted to live right inside these last hours, not snuggle up to Anna pitifully, hanged dog with tongue out. Anna currently believed that I would be returning to the UK later today via Fertília Airport, so we had every reason to continue this adventure full bore to its conclusion. And the only way to precipitate such action was to find the location of that farm. Let's properly get on the hunt.

* * *

It seemed fair enough to be knocking on the farmhouse door so early. Don't farmers get up at the crack of dawn? Now it was close to 10 o'clock and we'd been wandering around in the early morning haze for what seemed like hours before we'd located this obscure domicile. At last a puffy-eyed lady came to the door and invited us in. She threw down three tin mugs and drizzled in three weedy dribbles of Fernet Branca. Blessèd Anna passed on this sweet offering, but I gobbled mine down and rubbed my index finger around the rim. Seeing this, the farmer's wife offered Anna's drink to me. When I gratefully accepted, she got started on the coffee. What a dear woman. The farmer was in bed; they'd had a hard night, too much drink, family arguments, she felt perhaps they might still not be talking when he eventually deigned to rise. Wednesday, she said, was his day off. No farming. No mobile vet round. A good day for a hangover. Indeed, such a pall of inactivity hung over this gaffe that it was clear we needed to instil in her the real gravity of our problems. Thus, we guided her still semi-somnambulant form outside to the front of the house, where Anna directed the lady's gaze southeast across the plain below, pointing out the tiny dot of the hearse raised up on the far edge of the vast, lush green field about two miles hence. The dazed woman, deep in sleep until five minutes previously, stared out at the horizons confused and unable to comment. She wanted to go back into the house but Anna pointed to the fine-looking Peugeot 504 Estate and requested that she rent it to us. The lady looked horrified, but Anna was unyielding. She said we had to get to Alghero Airport by mid-afternoon, that I was an international traveller from the UK. Otherwise, argued Anna, it would be imperative that the lady drive us to Nuoro so that we could rent our own vehicle. Cornered thus, the farmer's wife – probably looking for a way to stall our bullying tactics until her husband awoke – now invited us in for breakfast and sat us down nice as pie in front of the fire with bread, tomatoes and some tough-smelling pecorino. The time was moving on, however, and I began to cluck. Now, like a stupid idiot, I briefly considered making Blessèd Anna my accomplice in today's retribution adventure. Letting her in on my real schedule. Perhaps some of the Separatistas would even wish to get involved. And I was already fantasising about rallying the masses to my cause when, er, ye dream did dissolveth. Ptoof! Whoa, whoa! Mercy! Wake up! Back off! Yesterday's fluky Loon result was no reason to become Bonnie & Clyde! Holy kack, Anna would hit the roof if she only knew for one moment that I was planning to be more than an observer at Opposite's grand kick-off – she'd go stratospheric! Judge Barry Hertzog would be there? Her recurring nightmare? How I hated even to imagine that one-sided screaming match: *Rock Section, already I know you too well enough!*

But whilst my own paranoia these past few minutes had merely succeeded in dragging me down several planning cul-de-sacs, Blessèd Anna and the farmer's wife had by now come to an agreement. Having viewed photos of Giampaolo's hearse on Anna's mobile phone, the farmer's wife had chilled out instantly and accepted that, yes, such an American classic would be perfectly fine collateral in exchange for the car that she had in mind for our rental vehicle. Leading us both out to the farm buildings beyond the yard, the farmer's wife took a car key from the row of hooks on the once-whitewashed wall of the open farm office and showed us into a storeroom. She pointed into the hay. That was our vehicle. That was our car. It was filthy – a field car. A farm hack. Worse, it was decorated on its rear with great sunflower motifs advertising the farmer's mobile veterinary service. Worse, much worse than that? It was a Fiat Panda 4×4, a legendary rustic evil. A sit-up-and-beg suicide trap, especially on the raging 131. Anna could not drive it. She said she *could* but she would not. The farmer's wife harrumphed and told us it was the best car that Fiat had ever made. Then she told us to make up our minds on our own and went indoors. Personally, I thought Anna was being rather harsh in our beggars-can't-be-choosers circumstances, so I climbed inside this Farmer Giles' jam car and fired it up. No way! First time, brrrrrrrrrr. Still queasy at the very idea, Blessèd Anna jigged about outside, scratching her nose. Then she got in and looked at me.

ANNA: Fuck it, Rock Section. I don't know the rules. *You* drive today. *You* show me how to be cool in a car like this.

Thus, without a single worldly possession but the clothes on my back, I-Who-Have-Nothing reversed that farm hack gingerly out of its hay-fast locker, slid that mechanical mule into first gear and set off at nobbut a trundle up the undulating kilometre-long farm track. Far across the hillside two miles hence, vast fingers of Blakean sunrays played over the Madau Valley, before us the day bright and getting brighter, bumping along beside me womankind's finest union of grand intellectual, fearless investigator and metaphysical lover. Could somebody, some nobody perhaps, some World Nerd show me how *not* to be cool in this car?

* * *

Already after 11am, it was. And still were we tootling along the fast 389 towards Nuoro at a maximum of 52 m.p.h. Mostly it was much slower progress. Mostly we were stuck in the low gears. Moreover, we were making big enemies of the other farm traffic that jammed up our dusty passing lane – *and* it was all my fault. For despite my unimpressive driving career behind the steering wheels of various rented hatchbacks and borrowed hacks, I'd never been able to shake off the feeling that whatever car was in front of me, surely it could always be overtaken with the right attitude? Thus did I now fail again and again in my attempts to thrust us past that ancient Autocarro bubblecar pick-up, past that grey-rinsed biddy in her slab-sided rust bucket Lawil C2, burn off that melon-laden donkey cart. But as no amount of perspiration and hand gestures could make any difference to our top speed, so I chilled out somewhat, almost content to trundle along in that compassionately placed semi-gutter. So what? We were currently on schedule for a 12.30pm arrival at Santa Cristina: still plenty of time for my planning and checking the lay of the land ahead of Bugs' big kick-off.

And then, at last, rearing up in front of us no more than half-a-mile ahead, we recognised the tall metal stanchions of Nuoro's fast 129 trunk road, the signs for Cágliari, for Sássari City, for Ólbia. Sweet relief! And even as our agricultural golf cart ascended the great arcing slip road, I heard Blessèd Anna's mobile phone surge into life immediately. It was her father Giampaolo. He informed the gorgeous one that The Reaper had this morning left its Zinnigas depot at the same time as on previous weekdays and was now right on schedule for a 3pm return delivery to Opposite from Ciancimino's Highway. Oh, how I wished to trump Blessèd Anna's news by adding that Judge Barry would be arriving hidden in the trailer – The Reaper's celebrity stowaway! The same night I'd been scaring Porcu quins out of Jim Feather's camp at Bidil 'e Pira, Blessèd Anna and Giampaolo had concluded their day of Reaper research by hooking up with Separatista leader Angela Solarussa and hatching a plan: they would follow The Reaper vigilantly over the next few weeks, then present to the authorities all their gathered evidence of Bugs Rabbit's kickbacks, fake civil engineering projects and wholesale purloining of building materials. I was delighted at the very idea that such activism had been stirred up by my own rumblings and stumblings around this island. But my own conclusive plan of action today would surely sideline such worthy endeavours. For, unless those that do battle with evil cleave their enemies with the same thoroughness of mission as the evildoers themselves, always then will the battle for balance *itself* hang in the balance. Those motherfuckers were going down!

Now buzzing along with all the aplomb of an asthmatic bee, the Fiat Panda 4×4 actually made a decent enough steed for one so out of driving practice as myself. Moreover, my battles at the steering wheel were providing me with a much-needed distraction from thoughts of my impending doom. I was delighted to see from the farm hack's speedo that the simple act of driving on a decent surface had upped our occasional top speed to 75 m.p.h.! Well, 73 m.p.h. downhill with the wind behind us! Come on, now! That said, with all the dips and valleys that remained to be conquered between here and Santa Cristina, I still had plenty of time to chunter every time we struggled on the gradients. And, boy, did we struggle. Oh brother! On the incline across the 'e Binzas Valley, where 35 m.p.h. even dwindled to 25 m.p.h., a rage of trucks and farm vehicles slugged it out for the right to overtake us, whilst – from within our tin can – Anna's urging and my knotted back muscles and grim expression seemed to be the only forces that were actively engaged in hauling us along. But now back on the uplands I clocked Anna's mobile phone once again registering full reception – I had to act. I couldn't leave this world without at least attempting to have said farewell to ye Bard. I hadn't yet dared mention my worldly losses to Blessèd Anna in case she had become suspicious at my apparent lack of concern. Back in Fonni, my successful recovery of Jim Feather's magic cloak had allowed me to convince her that my possessions were just hidden underneath it somewhere in the back of the hearse. I knew a lost phone would not faze her unduly, so now I simply asked the gorgeous one to text ye Bard so that he could call me on her mobile. I reeled off Mick's number from memory and waited perhaps three minutes at most.

MICK: Section, can I show you affection?

ROCK: (*Beaming, glancing at Anna*) I'm feeling the affection, youth. I'm feeling it.

MICK: What you doing this afternoon?

ROCK: Oh, today's a breeze, youth. We're just seeing some old friends off.

MICK: Seeing old friends off. (*Big sigh*) When you get back, we should do a sentimental journey. We could drive up to the Peak; have a look at the Dehydrated building. Have-a-laugh's coming up for the funeral. He'll have a hire car.

ROCK: (*Welling up*) Yeah man, we'll get it together.

MICK: I wrote a poem for Dean, well, kind of a poem. I just modified 'Do-Re-Mi'. I used to sing it to him when I dangled him on my knee.

ROCK: Can you do me a bit?

MICK: Better down the phone than face-to-face, youth. I can sing it in the full Brits voice if you want.

ROCK: Oh man, go for it!

MICK: (*Chuntering along rhythmically to get himself into it*)
 Dung-ducker-dung-ducker-dung-ducker-dung.
 Dung-ducker-dung-ducker-dung-ducker-dung.
 Dough is Cash to trade for your stash,
 Ray: a guy whose name is Ray,
 Me: a bloke who looks like Me,
 Far? Anything over a hundred metres away,
 Sew: A needle in me arm,
 La: a scally from the 'Pool,
 Tea tastes better with a spliff,
 That will bring us back to
 Dough, dough, dough, dough . . .

ROCK: You're a class act, Goodby.

MICK: A classified act, youth, that's me. 'Who put the cunt in Country & Western, who put the bullet in J.F.K.?'

The phones always die where the hollow-way cuts between Lake Omodeo and the uplands of the Sédilo-Iloi area. But I was happy enough for our conversation to have ended on such a high point. I didn't want to lambast ye Bard over the phone with tales of the genuine sickos who'd intruded into our every waking moments. The information would reach him soon enough. The real big news was that Mick had written a poem! That had not happened since the one-word 'Kick' had become an accidental semi-hit, what? Four years ago? Just knowing M. Goodby still had some fire in him was enough for me in my present state. Besides, everything Sardu was currently overwhelming me and one glimpse of Lake Omodeo's waters had instantly set my heart-broken psyche moaning and pawing the dashboard in memory of Blessèd Anna's star dancing so recently experienced. Everything was backing up now, memories, the lot. And as we struggled up the steep gradient before the final downhill rush past Sédilo, it was all I could do to keep my eyes on the road rather than giving myself entirely to those vivid pale blue waters. What? I saw something. Behind us still the straining knot of overtakers, before us, a warm inviting lay-by at the top of the incline into which our be-sunflowered mule now slipped gratefully and ground to a halt. We let the honking, rageful hordes surge past us, then Anna, myself and the Fiat Panda let out a collective sigh of relief. This trip, this final trip – I knew what the day would bring, but now I was having to enact it. Now, Anna and I rushed together across the main road towards the observation platform. For I had spotted far below us on the waters of Lake Omodeo the trails of spectral beings: human trails, human beings.

Forty minutes later, we stood together on the shore. I hadn't meant for us both to climb so far down to the lakeside but climb down we had, nevertheless. Well, we had the time. We still had plenty of time. Inside the moment. Let me stay inside these final moments. Anyway, from my first glimpse of the lake whilst still at the wheel of the car, I'd spotted something very curious approaching our side of the shoreline. Thereafter, as we had shimmied and struggled down that treacherous slope, every step had seemed to transport me further and further back into the past – my own past. Now at the lake's edge, I grasped what I was witnessing and I gasped.

ROCK: (*Eyes wide open, staring in wonder*) What do you see?
ANNA: It's the most beautiful mist I ever saw. And it is approaching the shore really fast.
ROCK: (*Staring deeply, mesmerised*) Look further into the mist. What do you see?
ANNA: It's too blurry for me, Rock Section. But it's getting closer to us, soon it will be upon us. Step back a little: it's coming our way.

Now the grand gassy cloud roared past us like some huge spectral hovercraft then set off across the shore and up the steep sheer path down which we'd just scrambled. But whereas the details within the cloud had to Anna been indistinct and blurry, to me their inner structures could not have been crisper: There at speed had passed my contraption and with it my stout Select. Each one of them I recognised, each one of them my own kind. Almost. I wanted to scream, became breathless, became faint,

I clutched at Anna and fell to my knees. On the last leg of their great journey now – Lake Omodeo being on a direct line between Madau and the Altar of Punishment – I had even spied upon the side of Bjond's great contraption these words carved or inscribed in a rudimentary language that I *should* not have been able to read.

None that shall rule shall rule forever. For caution predicts that eternal power would corrupt that ruler with detriment to their people. (BJOND)

Now I walked in glory, now I walked in splendour – myself eternally transformed. Those who dare to tinker with the Cosmos must know – in precipitating Cosmic change – that reigns shall fall like rains, that thrones shall be o'erthrown, that those who dream of meat may yet remain unmet.

* * *

Thus it was not in chaos or with puckered sphincters that we joined the 131 at the Abbasanta junction, but in human righteousness that we headed south on those final few miles to our Santa Cristina destination. This was precisely the same route down which The Reaper would be bringing Hertzog to Opposite, and I kept an eye out to make sure that the hard shoulder was strong and wide along the entire run-up to Santa Cristina. For, if my plan went accordingly, this hard shoulder would soon become my own runway – yup, my own place of take-off. Mamma Mia, the downhill nature of the last few miles pushed our farm hack even slightly beyond its previous 73 m.p.h.! Even faster than a 1914 scout plane! Get the oxygen masks on! And as we descended finally on to the Santa Cristina slip road, I was delighted to hear already the pulsing 20,000-watt brutality of Spackhouse Tottu's DJ-set kicking off proceedings nice and early before guest-of-honour Judge Barry arrived at 3 o'clock. Already, I could see in the well-lit glass-fronted windows of Opposite familiar gaggles of evildoers and international ne'er-do-wells congregating for the big shebang. Bang. The time now was 2.45pm. I needed to get in there and see the lay of the land. So, passing under the 131 and parking up beside the Santa Cristina museum, I walked into the restaurant with Blessèd Anna as we'd planned, knowing that I could duck out as soon as Separatista leader Angela Solarussa had caught the ear of the gorgeous one. There was, however, a super-righteousness about today – one which inflicted poetry on to even the most exasperating of situations. And as I prepared to don the magic cloak and make for Opposite, I was delighted to see the Blessèd One lambasting one of the Hertzog Girls.

ANNA: (*Scornful, almost jeering*) Why are you so determined to attribute to this football maniac all of your own individualistic ideas? Why do you use him to hide behind your own thoughts?
WENDY: The accentuated behaviour of Judge Barry Hertzog has yielded such positive results throughout his life that we feel delighted to follow his way: his is a path. Of that I have no doubt.
ANNA: Put this in your mind: Judge Barry Hertzog is a killer of souls. His Christianity is uncompassionate and unchristian.

52. DAVE DEE, DOZY, BEATY, BIG & BOUNCY

2.50pm, Wednesday June 14th, 2006
Under the magic cloak in Opposite Club, near Paulilátino

As I ducked under the 131 in Jim Feather's magic cloak, I grinned as I visualised Blessèd Anna still tearing a strip off the visibly intimidated Hertzog Girls. Holy shit, now it struck me hard just how Anna would have freaked if I'd let her in on my plans! With the time now approaching ten minutes to blast-off, I piled into Opposite in order to check out this dreadful Bugs Rabbit knees-up. Who would be the first baddie I'd bump into? Oh joy. As I slipped be-cloaked through the big glass entrance door I recognised those ugly tones straight away!

BUGS RABBIT: I had that moron Jim Feather put this place together out of materials trucked in from Ciancimino's Highway. Me and the Mackenzies put a lot of effort into that 131 white elephant. But now, we're really feeling the benefits. The Porcu quins use The Reaper to do the trucking. Bustianu, Efisio and Nani Porcu all have decent temperaments so they do the driving. Zizinu, or Klötz as we call him, is lame in one leg and just gets the clerk jobs. Nàtziu, or Ourgon as we call him, is far too mental to operate machinery, so we employ him for the more heavy jobs: intimidation, wielding tractor tyre irons, biting people and suchlike.

Right next to me – well, miles below me – stood the diminutive

Bugs Rabbit himself, a shot of Fernet Branca in one hand, a copy of Van Der Graaf Generator's epic LP *Pawn Hearts* in the other. Now, he was waxing lyrical about their evil sound.

BUGS RABBIT: I see them many times in the early 1970s. (*Kissing his fingertips*) The best! No question, no doubt in my mind! So very intense that I become violent still whenever I hear. Oh, that saxophone!

LUIS: During Italia '90, we spent the day on Buggeru Beach with Bugs recording the Master Musicians of Buggeru.

JOSÉ: That's just me and Luis on the bongos and vocals in the sand.

BUGS RABBIT: Every time we take the break for coffee, I played *Pawn Hearts* and the Porcu brothers – all five quintuplets – they lose their minds every time! They stand around being Van Der Graaf Generator on their photo inside the sleeve.

Now, in explanation, Bugs Rabbit opened the Van Der Graaf gatefold to reveal a bizarre scene indeed. The striding black-shirted hippie sax player, carrying a football under his left arm and fascist-saluting with his right, advanced at a pace towards a great cast-iron plinth on which stood the other three black-shirted band members, each of whom was fascist-saluting equally vigorously back at him. No wonder they were so big in Italy!

LUIS: So, the Porcu quintuplets run about the beach all day saluting and copying this album photo. Driving beachcombers crazy. Crazy!

BUGS RABBIT: When we return that evening to Cágliari, we stopped off at the nightclub Lord Westminister. Big mistake!

There's three of the Dutch international football squad drinking inside: Ruud Gullit, Danny Blind and Joop Hiele.

JOSÉ: A little bit conspicuous, I thought. Being too famous! Cameras! Women! Rrrr!

BUGS RABBIT: Instant Porcu meltdown! All five Porcu quins went into overdrive copying the Van Der Graaf Generator photo. They walk up to the Dutch football stars in a line-up, extend their arms into fascist salutes, and begin to scream: Hiel Joop! Hiel Joop! Hiel Joop!

JOSÉ: (*Nodding, joining in, looking around*) Hiel Joop! Hiel Joop!

LUIS: (*Grinning at the memory*) Hiel Joop! Hiel Joop! Hiel Joop!

BUGS RABBIT: Ruud Gullit tries to make peace, to calm down the Porcu attack, smooth it over. But the quintuplets just give him the ten million mile stare. *And* still hieling Joop!

LUIS: (*Correcting him*) Ten *millimetre* stare more like. Blind bastards.

BUGS RABBIT: My wife Isuzu is an analyst. She says the Porcu brothers get so angry that they go into a Collective Anger Coma. That's when the milky, greasy stuff starts to collect on their eyeballs. From childhood, allegedly. Urna Washington tells everybody it was in the R.A.F. milk they off-loaded up at Zinnigas after World War Two. All the children were afflicted. Even the village cats suffer.

On the wall behind Akkrum 'Pit-Yacker' Sneek and Cowtown Unslutter was a huge monochrome art poster of Eric Clapton emblazoned with his hateful 1976 stage rant: *Stop Britain from becoming a black colony. Get the foreigners out. Get the wogs out. Get the coons out. Keep Britain white. I used to be into dope. Now I'm into racism. It's much heavier, man.*

COWTOWN: Excuse me, Mr Rabbit! (*Pointing up at Clapton*) Now that's quite a statement!

BUGS RABBIT: (*Bristling with pride*) Ah, my specially commissioned wind-up poster! Clapton at that time covered Bob Marley songs. Quite shameless, I think. Shame also that the poster is only for the party – then into my office it goes. Every passing liberal tourist loves Eric; they don't like to think about the bad times.

COWTOWN: (*Pointing up at the poster*) The liberals love anyone who persists. If we play the same persistence game and play it right, one day, same thing for you and me. Eric Clapton said those things but he's so big that the liberal rags still stoop to interview him. Those *Guardian* whores dare not make judgement against believers!

WALTER U.T.B.: From behind our wall of *Mere Christianity*, we are safe! (*Patting his breast pockets*) Oi, Akkrum, can I borrow Loon's lighter?

PIT-YACKER MC: Why-aye man. (*Handing over lighter*) But now Varg Vikernes has turned Pagan, you lot *really* need a defector from Islam.

COWTOWN: (*To Bugs Rabbit, musing deeply*) Right next to Eric, how about a poster of Queen playing Sun City? (*Pointing*) Then your wall of infamy will lead the liberals directly into the toilet.

Now, Bugs Rabbit walked over to his electric piano and tinkled upon the ivories, as though willing the rest of them over. D major to C major he jammed, over and over and ruddy over again. Like Diana Ross's 'Chain Reaction', like the most redundant garage soul song ever, so compelling I wanted to throw up! Gradually, the Mackenzies wandered over and started to jam, even the Japanese dudes from Nurse With Mound. Until eventually, as the sub-sub-Standells groove of 'Come Back and Haunt Me' hit the twenty-minute permakraut plateau, every one of the invited flotsam and jetsam, the underworld dignitaries, the Axis of Evil that had made our lives so much less: all had accumulated Joe Cocker and Leon Russell's Mad Dogs and Englishman-style around this self-made star of the keyboards. There in the huddle sat Bugs blissed out, shining like that penis that plays for David Letterman. An ugly customer playing free for other ugly customers: World Ugly Customers. Over Bugs' monotonous beatbox-driven soul prowl, Luis Mackenzie was at the Green Matamp DJ booth spinning Fripp & Eno's ambient twenty-minute extravaganza 'Swastika Girls', whilst José at the Orange Matamp DJ booth span a cappella soul from the Expressions, bringing the whole cacophonic jam into Faust territory. How am I forgetting? Down the decades, these cunts had knocked out some of my favourite-ever music! These were the Spackhouse guys who'd nicknamed themselves Wallace & Gromit because of their vast height difference. But then, why should I expect great musicians to have morals? Mick Jagger? Detestable. I'd kill him with my own bare hands. Shaun Ryder's despicable murders? Inexcusable. Had Breakfast lived, he'd have nailed that chav for sure! But to speak of poor poor Leander was to speak of the Devil. For now, over in the corner corridor slightly away from the musicians, I overheard what I could not believe I was hearing.

WALTER U.T.B.: (*Smoking luxuriously*) I even fed that Full English Breakfast bloke two portions of the dodgy gear I made his poison out of.

PIT-YACKER MC: Not castor beans? For fuck's sake! That's not even food! Why-aye, you're fucking still the king of ricin, then! Fuck me, I'd not like to be your attorney come the Day of Judgement. That stuff's fucking well wicked. You'd have been all over mustard gas back in the day.

COWTOWN: (*Shaking his head in disapproval*) Typical Walter-Under-The-Bridge. You stabbed that posh bastard with enough ricin to poison an ox. We were lucky he even made it as far as the stadium. (*To Akkrum Sneek*) Twisted the end of his Bulgarian Umbrella in really far. Must have been agony for His Nibs. Just like Georgi Markov.

WALTER U.T.B.: (*Nonchalant, triumphant*) It's not often you get to stab a pop star!

COWTOWN: I was up on the TV tower in the magic cloak. I told that posh English bastard we'd already nabbed Jim Feather. I told him his time had come right there and then. Cape Town? End of the line! I even had time to forewarn him about the kidnapping. 'Kimberley!' I kept hissing. 'They're gonna get theirs in Kimberley!'

Through a slit in the cloak, I checked the big Opposite map now no more than ten feet away – I felt sick. If Cape Town was Cágliari, Mafeking was Alghero, Pretoria was Sássari City and Ólbia was Durban? Then Kimberley had been Macomér! Breakfast had been trying to warn us. Simple as that. Even as he fell to his death had dear Leander tried in vain. But what had been Boerishly clear to Leander had been opaque and unfathomable to us lot.

Now, under the cloak of magic, I slipped out of this nest of vipers, this armpit of the universe, this rotting cow in the middle of a mountain stream. And as I closed Opposite's big glass front door behind me, I thought of poor Jim Feather putting all of this

together, suffering in the heat and daily fighting off the righteous rage of the Separatistas. I watched those so-called Christian
fuckers boozing it up in their middle-aged *Mere Christianity*
reunion and I reckoned even Jesus Christ would have rained
down heavy blows upon their wretched self-serving butts. Now,
I ran under the 131 back up to the museum, where Anna was
engrossed in a deep head-to-head with Angela Solarussa. She
broke off as soon as I approached, took my arm and held me
tightly, nuzzling up to me as we walked into the museum's quietest corner. Here, Anna explained that she'd screamed so loudly
at the Hertzog Girls that she'd left them both shaking. Oh, and
we must leave for Fertília Airport soon in order to make my
UK flight. I knew I had to act before that tripped-out version
of 'Come Back and Haunt Me' had concluded, and I had to act
now. I acted. I thrust Jim Feather's magic cloak into Blessèd
Anna's dainty mitts and told her I needed to grab something
from the rear of the Panda 4×4. Then, I seized her butt with
both hands and pulled her whole lovely self up to my mouth.
Sparks of electric metallic blue stuttered and shook in metaphysical tune-up. Not like kissing on earth, this was like kissing
once had been. Broken-hearted but undaunted, now – hoodwinking her that it would be just two minutes, four minutes, ten
minutes, no more – I walked Anna back to Angela Solarussa's
table and headed for the exit. For a minnow microsecond, the
world stopped on its axis. We had known each other. She looked
at me across the room one final time. We stared at each other,
smiling. Then we were parted forever.

Now I drove the Fiat Panda back under the 131, past Opposite,
wherein 'Come Back and Haunt Me' was still raging at fullest
stretch. Now, I reversed back up the northern slip road on to
the hard shoulder, and continued thereafter in reverse at around

25 m.p.h. grooving quite nicely alongside the fast-rushing oncoming traffic. To the seasoned driver, this is easy: the hard shoulder is a full carriage wide and I reversed the Panda 4×4 at speed, heading backwards up my narrow allotted strip, keeping an eye out for when I hit a distance of three miles away from the Santa Cristina exit. In this old trundler, I needed three run-up miles in order to build up sufficient speed. Right there I parked. Now I waited. I was positive that providence would today show me a clear path and bid Bad Riddance to the Opposite Club and its entire contents. Still I waited in that tin car, jostled by juggernauts and petrol lorries.

Then I saw The Reaper hurtle out of the horizon: its halogen headlights that burn the eyes even in daylight. Now I started my run. My run! Ha! This farm vehicle's nought-to-sixty should be measured in minutes not seconds. How glad I was that I'd given myself a full three miles to gather my speed. But hunched now over the steering column, my white-knuckled hands hooked around the ripped, worn plastic steering wheel, my back clenched into an artichoke knot, my craned neck shuddering and shaking, how I willed and willed any possible extra m.p.h. out of this dwindler. Now, to my utmost surprise did the Fiat Panda respond at last, until I had built up to a not unhealthy 60 m.p.h. See me now, Blessèd Anna. Now this steed of the hard shoulder grew wings, became a turbo shopping trolley, became a worthy mount and me a worthy charge. One mile from Destiny, now The Reaper's headlights appeared in my mirrors and now I did act. Pulling out without signalling, I overtook a slow-moving tractor then *refused* to re-enter the slow lane. Blue motorway signs for the Santa Cristina exit now loomed. Behind me a barrage of car horns, truck horns, the klaxon chorale of The Reaper itself. I pulled into the slow lane just long enough to release past me the log jam of furious motorists, then pulled out suicidally *again* into the path of The Reaper itself. On came those bright lights now even brighter. Now stood up all of The Reaper's occupants, furious and fist-waving through that vast panoramic windscreen. Not three but five, all five of the Porcu quintuplets there raised their middle fingers at me. And now, even as we approached Santa Cristina's junction – approached at deadly speed – did The Reaper's frustrated Porcu driver even attempt to undertake me in the slow lane.

53. LAST PAGE

2.55pm, Wednesday June 14th, 2006
From the Fiat Panda 4×4, 131 hard shoulder north of S. Cristina

Myself still struggling along head down in the outside lane, I frowned and grimaced as the twenty-two wheels of The Reaper began to strain past me on the inside at 80 m.p.h. The Santa Cristina exit was imminent, but the crazy Reaper driver had long ago forgotten his destination, his entire thoughts crammed now only with *me*, thoughts only of ramming *me*: his dwindling yet unyielding farm hack adversary. And ram me he did at last, or rather clip my skinny rear-end and send me – bim, bam, bom – spinning on to my roof. Thus, only as the Santa Cristina exit was upon The Reaper did its driver strive at last to check himself and – far too late – now steered suicidally off down that right turn, sending his vast land-train and its monumentally overloaded cargo hurtling off along the straight too-short slip road towards the glass façade of Opposite. Meanwhile, myself and my capsized metal ladybird continued inverted at brutal speed along the Santa Cristina bridge, the whole weight of my body pressing down on my crushed neck, until a passing Renault transit van sent me spinning on my roof to the very edge of the parapet, where I teetered and rocked. At the very edge of the abyss, I stared upside down as The Reaper land-train piled at top speed into Opposite's very public plate glass window, instantly obliterating Judge Barry Hertzog, Bugs Rabbit, Cowtown Unslutter, the Mackenzie Brothers, the lot of them. All done in by Urna Washington's offspring. 'Come Back and Haunt Me', motherfuckers! But now I glimpsed for one last moment of this life the white dress of my gorgeous lover running like a woman possessed out from under the 131 towards the impact zone. Hey Blessèd Anna, whoever before died in a Panda 4×4? And as gravity at last washed its hands of my situation, my teetering agricultural ride gave up the ghost and I plummeted off the bridge to my certain death.